Books by Fay Lamb

Amazing Grace Romantic Suspense Series

STALKING WILLOW
BETTER THAN REVENGE
EVERYBODY'S BROKEN
FROZEN NOTES

Ties that Bind Romance Series

CHARISSE
LIBBY
HOPE
DELILAH

Serenity Key Saga

STORMS IN SERENITY

Mullet Harbor Romance Series

CHRISTMAS UNDER WRAPS

Non-Fiction

THE ART OF CHARACTERIZATION: How to Use the
Elements of Storytelling to Connect Readers to an
Unforgettable Cast

Christmas
Under Wraps
A Mullet Harbor Clean Romance
FAY LAMB

F

Write Integrity Press
Christmas Under Wraps
© 2019 Fay Lamb
ISBN: 978-1-944120-89-4

Published by Favored Books: an imprint of

Write Integrity Press
PO Box
Dallas, TX 75370
Find out more about the author: FayLamb.com

Printed in the United States of America.

$\mathcal{D}$edication

This book is lovingly dedicated to the memory of my dear mother-in-law

Saralyn Lamb.

I never saw the magic in Christmas until she shared it with me through her eyes of wonder and love and her gift for giving. During the last couple of years, she was lost in a world where Christmas didn't come. This year, she began her eternity with the Savior whose birth we celebrate.

I miss you—will miss you—until that eternity we will share.

Chapter One

December 14

Pain shot across Christian Abram's empty stomach. He pushed hard against his abdomen to squelch the loud rumble. In the other seat of the pickup, his nephew, Dylan, slept with his head against the window. The boy needed to bathe—they both did.

The kid rubbed the palms of his hands against sleepy eyes. His too-long bangs fell onto his face.

So much time had passed since he'd seen the boy's features without the telltale marks of abuse. Now, he longed to hear the kid's laughter to know he'd survived.

"I'm hungry." Dylan continued to rub the tiredness away.

Christian winced. Nothing short of starvation would make the boy admit the truth. He picked up his wallet from the console. Inside the billfold, the lone five-dollar bill stared back at him. Both Dylan and the truck needed fuel.

Christian had money, but accessing it would alert the FBI, and he hoped that the absence of any clues would cause the authorities to track them in the wrong direction. Kidnapping an eight-year-old and taking him across state lines, no matter the intention, came with a harsh penalty. His capture would condemn Dylan to a harsher prison, although the boy had committed no crime.

A road sign caught Christian's attention. *This Way to Mullet Harbor. In Our Swamp, You'll Always Find a Friend.*

He turned the truck in that direction. The town lay twenty miles west, and he hoped he could find a job that would feed the boy, his truck, and possibly himself.

He'd lost count of the days since he'd eaten—maybe two? The meal had barely filled his empty gut. Dylan hadn't believed Christian's lie and refused to eat unless Christian ate half of his sandwich. Yesterday, Christian easily convinced Dylan he wasn't hungry, maybe because Dylan had been too famished to realize the truth.

"Where are we going?" Dylan asked.

"Mullet Harbor. The name sounds interesting enough, and the sign said we'll meet friends."

"They call Philadelphia the City of Brotherly Love, but that isn't true." Green eyes that could show so much sensitivity for Dylan's age darkened with suppressed anger as he repeated one of Christian's favorite adages.

Christian had to stifle his own rage before it affected Dylan. "We need to stop somewhere." He tossed his wallet to the boy.

Dylan looked inside. "That's why you haven't been eating." He stared out the windshield "Chris, I would of shared my food with you yesterday. I'm sorry."

"I haven't been hungry. And 'would of' is not proper. You meant 'would have.'"

The boy remained silent at both the lie and the correction. He stared out at the passing scenery.

Christian had to remember that proper grammar wasn't important, not now when they were both starving. Proper grammar would put money on the kid's table later in life. But where had it gotten Christian? "Hey, I'm fine."

Dylan didn't turn or speak. He smacked away the tears now falling down his cheeks.

Christian touched the boy's shoulder. "Let's have none of that. We're on a grand adventure, right? This is a minor setback. Tell me. If you could have anything you wished for Christmas, what would you want?"

"I have you." Again, Dylan swiped at the moisture on his face. "You're all I need."

Being with Christian hadn't done him any good.

Dylan turned to him. "I want you to get a job. I—I want friends. I want a home with you."

Finally, Dylan's innocence showed. Christian wouldn't destroy the boy's dreams until he must. They were hedging for time. Christian's sister, Cassie, had to wake up, literally and figuratively. Christian desperately needed her to help her son before they found them and put Christian away and took Dylan back to the life from which Christian was trying to protect him. "Let's have a look at this place. The name sounds hopeful at least. Okay?"

Dylan's growling stomach answered for him.

The fact that Dylan hadn't wished for his mother told Christian all he needed to know about the boy's pain.

Every weekday, rain or shine, Kaylee McFarland walked the few blocks to the little grocery store located at Mullet Harbor's only intersection for a cup of Rose Fish's delicious coffee. At the intersection, if she chose to take a right, she'd end up in the town's business district, a cul-de-sac lined with art studios. Upon leaving the grocer, she'd walk across the street and head straight past the community center and into the neighborhood district nestled along the lagoon and toward the small school where Kaylee taught.

If she chose to play hooky, she could continue walking past the grocery to the harbor where fishing boats, trawlers, and pleasure craft docked. She loved to spend time there watching the boats and the different people on them move in and out via the waterway. Other than that, there wasn't much to do, and she liked it that way. What the town lacked in activities, its residents made up with flavor. She'd not been bored a day since her arrival before the start of the school year.

Thankfully, the rain that deluged the inlet town the night before had moved up Florida's west coast. The ground remained wet, and she had to step around puddles. Still, she enjoyed a rainy, warm winter day in Mullet Harbor much better than the cold, wet snow that probably smothered the ground of her mother's Maryland home and always kept her sick during the long, dreary days.

The skies over the Florida Everglades were supposed to turn sunny today with highs in the mid-seventies. She smiled and said a prayer of thanks to God for allowing her the opportunity to live in what she called a paradise and the locals lovingly called a swamp.

The voices of excited children rang out through the morning air like the jingling of bells, heard but not seen. Today was the last day of school before the Christmas holidays. Kaylee's mood brightened. She'd already informed her mother she preferred to remain in Mullet

Harbor instead of returning to Baltimore. Money was tight, and Kaylee wanted to enjoy her first winter without snow. To say her mother was unhappy was an understatement of extreme proportions, but if Mother wanted a visit, she'd need to fly to Florida.

Kaylee shuddered at the thought. If Mother arrived, she might never leave. Kaylee wanted freedom. She needed to breathe without someone telling her how to do it, and LeAnn McFarland was an expert on everything, including breath.

At the sound of a sputtering engine, Kaylee turned. A man in a newer gray pickup passed her and pulled to the side.

"Chris, everything's okay. We can walk into town," a child said.

Kaylee approached. "Good morning."

The driver leaned his head against the steering wheel. He turned his gaze upon her, and Kaylee stepped forward, touched by the tiredness on his face and the sorrow in his hazel eyes. "Can I help you?" she asked.

He remained silent.

"How far is it to town, ma'am?" The child peered around him.

"It's just a few blocks," she assured, her attention momentarily drawn from the driver to the adorable boy.

"I ran out of gas." The man sat up and brushed his dark

hair from his eyes. "I'm low on funds and ..."

Kaylee started to open her purse, but the man shook his head and opened his door. He stepped out, and Kaylee had to lift her gaze to meet his.

"I'm no beggar." He reached into the cab, pulled out a lightweight jacket, and tossed the boy his. "Do you know whom I might approach about a job? I'd like to barter for food and gas."

The delivery of his English was impeccable. The man before her, a night or two of beard on his face, his hair overgrown, and his old blue jeans and faded shirt, wasn't what he seemed on the outside.

Kaylee looked at her watch. "I'm on my way to class. Why don't you walk into town with me? I'll introduce you to someone who might be able to help."

"I'd appreciate that." The man moved to the bed of the truck and pulled out one duffle bag.

The boy slipped on his jacket then stepped beside him.

"My name's Christian, and this is Dylan."

"Nice to meet you. I'm Kaylee McFarland."

"You said you were on your way to class?" the man asked.

She nodded. "I teach. What grade are you in, Dylan?"

The young boy looked up to Christian. Something unspoken passed between them. Christian resituated the duffle bag.

"Third," Dylan muttered. "I'm homeschooled."

A lazy smile crept across Christian's face. The impact stopped Kaylee in her tracks. Never had she seen a smile so attractive. Suddenly, she didn't need her sweater.

"Is something wrong?" Christian asked.

Kaylee shook her head and forced herself to take one step, then another, squelching the memory of her mother's voice telling her never, but never, speak to a stranger. "I teach first through third grade."

"How can you do that?" Christian asked.

"Mullet Harbor is small, and rather than busing the few kids all the way to the bigger city, this is how they do things. Their system works."

"Shouldn't school be out soon for the holidays?"

"Today's our last day. Are you traveling for Christmas?" Kaylee mussed Dylan's hair, and the boy rewarded her with a smile similar to the one given to her by the grown man.

"We're traveling. What's the town commerce?" Christian asked.

Kaylee kicked a rock out of her path. "Fishing mainly: commercial, deep-sea charters, sailing and airboat tours of the backwaters. We have a small downtown area. It's very quaint with a few specialty shops owned by local artists. Most tourists are fishermen who stay in rental homes owned by people who live out of state. Jobs are a bit scarce here, but I do know some folks who might be able to use your assistance. What type of work do you do?"

"I'm capable of doing or learning anything."

Dylan needed a haircut and a change of clothes. Maybe Christian lost a job and, wanting to keep his son with him, hit the road looking for work. Mullet Harbor was the last place to seek gainful employment, but the town's residents had been good to her.

"You can ask," Christian said.

"I'm sorry?" She blinked.

"You don't have to wonder about us."

"Was I so transparent?" A breeze whipped her blond curls into her face. She pushed them back. A stubborn one sprang onto her forehead.

Another smile crossed his handsome face, and this one reached his eyes. He ran a hand across the growth of beard and remained silent.

"I was wondering how you're going to work when you're obviously very tired, and while you work, what will your son do?"

"I'll be okay. I help." Dylan straightened but soon fell against Christian, who slipped an arm around him as they walked.

They traipsed another block before coming to the business Kaylee hoped would hire the man if only for the day. "Wait right here," she commanded as she entered

Mullet Harbor Grocery. She stepped back outside. "I'll be with you in a minute."

Christian nodded and leaned against the side of the building. He closed his eyes.

Kaylee's heart went out to him. She might have to pick him up off the street when she returned.

Chapter Two

A long time and too many worries had passed since Christian even remotely looked at a woman, but Kaylee McFarland tempted his senses. Of course, he'd be attracted to an educator.

With the wall of the grocery store holding him up and sleep threatening, he recalled everything about her, from the bouncy curl of her short blond hair to the heel of her stylish boots. She wore a nice black skirt with a light sweater that matched the sky blue of her eyes. And every time she looked at Dylan, tenderness engulfed her gaze.

"Pretty nice, ain't she?" Dylan broke into his thoughts.

"Say it correctly." He forced his eyes open and pushed away from the building.

"She's pretty nice, isn't she, Uncle Chris?" Dylan stuck out his tongue.

Christian could have admonished Dylan for his smart mouth, but the mild sass and show of humor offered Christian hope. He shook his head. "Can I get a smile with that show of belligerence?"

The boy pressed a smile in place. Not real, but promising.

Christian winked and slipped the duffle bag from his shoulder, letting it fall to the ground.

"What do you think she's doing?" Dylan stuffed his hands into his pockets and stared at the asphalt parking lot. "Is she telling them we're beggars?"

"No." He wanted to believe Kaylee McFarland was above that. "But it doesn't matter what she tells them so long as I get work." He again leaned against the building and peered across the landscape surrounding this store, which sat at a seeming crossroads to nowhere. Kids, heard but not seen, were apparently beginning to make their way toward school. Christian didn't miss the longing on Dylan's face. He tilted his head back and shut his eyes to close off the painful vision.

"Hello. I hear you're looking for employment."

Christian shook off the sleep and focused. The man who'd addressed him didn't have much hair on top, but what crowned his head was curly and to his shoulders. He was well-tanned, wore shorts, and sported flip-flops. A classic band t-shirt topped off his laid-back ensemble.

"Yes." Christian reached for the man's outstretched hand.

The old guy shook with a strong grip of friendliness and rough callouses that scratched against Christian's too-soft skin. Academia hadn't brought him much physical labor. Christian hoped this stranger would remedy that. He needed some toil to get the fret out of him.

"I have some work at my place. You up for it?"

"Yes, I am." Christian worked to place confidence in his voice.

"And Ms. Fish says she can use a hand here at the store this afternoon. You game?"

"Yes, sir." Christian reached down for the duffle bag.

"How long you planning to stay in Mullet Harbor?" The old man studied Christian then turned his gaze to Dylan.

"I'm not sure." Christian needed to bring the guy's attention back to him.

"I'm Herb Miller." Herb returned his consideration to Christian. "I have some boats at my place that need cleaning and minor maintenance. I also own a photography gallery. I have work for you there tomorrow. Rose owns the grocery. She needs help, but she'd rather you spend some time with me at my place beforehand. I'm sure you know what I mean."

Yes, he did. If Christian hated anything about this

gypsy life, it was the mistrust of others. That's why he refused to lie about their identities though the danger of admitting who they were grew with each passing day. His sister had always been careless with the truth, and lying wasn't something Dylan needed to have reinforced in his life. "Christian Abram. This is Dylan. We appreciate the work."

"Ms. Kaylee has other plans for Dylan," Herb advised.

The teacher backed out of the grocer's door. She juggled a cup of coffee, a glass of orange juice, and a breakfast sandwich. "Help me, Dylan. I got these for you."

At Kaylee's request, Dylan took the orange juice and the sandwich. He licked his lips.

"Follow me," the teacher commanded.

"Where are you taking him?" Christian reached and gripped Dylan's arm. Orange juice spilled over the boy's hand.

"I'm sorry. I thought Herb told you what I planned. We're having a Christmas party today, playing games, crafting—no real school since this is our last day before the break. Would you mind if Dylan joined us as my guest?"

Dylan's face should have glowed with happiness. Instead, stark dread lined his features. "Where will you be?"

"I'll make sure your dad is right here when school lets out," Herb promised. "Ms. Kaylee will walk you back, and

Ms. Fish will put you to work, too."

"Promise?" Dylan stared at him, and his anguished whisper slashed Christian's heart.

For weeks, they'd traveled alone, never separated, not for one moment since he'd taken the boy. Anxiety threatened to undo Christian, too. He swallowed hard, nodded, then let go. "Right here."

Dylan handed the sandwich to the teacher and placed the cup on the ground. He threw his arms around Christian. "Please, don't leave me."

"Right here." Christian tugged the boy away, bent, and pulled him close again. "I hope never to leave you again. Haven't you figured that out yet? Go. Have fun," he whispered.

Dylan released him, and before Christian could stand, the boy returned with the sandwich broken in half. "I can't eat it all," he lied.

Christian waved him off. "I'm fine. Go to school."

"Take it, Chris."

"Hey, boy." Herb winked. "I'll feed your dad."

"We don't have much money," Dylan warned, and Christian laughed.

"That's part of his pay: breakfast and lunch for him and dinner for both of you."

"I like Mullet Harbor." Dylan ran toward Kaylee and picked up his orange juice. He took a swig then bit into his sandwich, looking up at Kaylee with gratefulness—and maybe a little admiration—on his smiling face. "Thank you." He spoke with his mouth full. Then he turned. "Thank you, too, Mr. Miller."

From time to time, Kaylee strolled past Dylan and his crafting partner, Sophie Cooper. Dylan worked diligently on his ornament made from red and green construction paper strips glued at the top. Sophie had many talents, but art was not one of them. As usual, when it came to making things, she was growing frustrated.

"Hang on." Dylan sighed with much put-upon exaggeration. "I'll help you. I need to hold mine for a second or the glue won't stick."

"This is stupid." Sophie ran a hand through her hair. The sticky residue on her fingers stuck in her hair. "Ouch." The paste had pulled out a dark wavy strand.

Dylan shook his head. When he finished his work, he helped his new friend, surprising Kaylee with his patience.

The lunch bell sounded as Dylan presented the finished ornament to Sophie. The class crowded out, but Dylan remained sitting, hands in his lap, eyes focused on the table.

"Aren't you coming?" Sophie tugged on his sleeve.

"No. I'll wait here." Dylan fingered his finished decoration.

The other kids were excited about the holidays. Maybe bringing Dylan to school had been a bad idea. Dylan and his father seemed homeless except that the new pickup seemed to indicate that Christian wasn't a poor man. Yet, they were living hand to mouth. What kind of Christmas could Dylan expect?

"Please come, Dylan," Sophie whined.

"Go on." He shrugged from her.

Tenacity did happen to be the best of Sophie's talents. She stood beside him, hands on her hips.

Kaylee smiled. Determination and loyalty—Sophie had an abundance of both.

"Let's go to lunch, Mr. Dylan." Kaylee waited at the door. "I can't leave anyone alone in the classroom."

"But—"

"No buts." She pointed.

He stood and pushed his chair under the table. Sophie reached for his hand. Instead of shying away, he walked with her down the hall. Sophie chattered as if she had known Dylan all her life.

As the two reached the end of the line, Kaylee addressed the other children in her class before entering the cafeteria. Remaining out of Dylan's sight, she paid for his meal then returned to stand in line beside him.

Dylan peered up at her. "I can't pay." His cheeks reddened.

"You're my guest today. My guests never have to pay. So, how do you like our school?"

"I miss school," he said then pursed his lips.

"How long have you been away?"

"I'm homeschooled."

However he'd received his education, Dylan's level of intelligence and advanced verbal skills did extend beyond his age.

Dylan made his way through the lunch line with the assistance of Sophie, who pointed out every food she liked and advised the ones to avoid. Before he followed Sophie into the lunchroom, Dylan stopped. "Thank you, again, Ms. McFarland."

"For what?"

"I know there's no such thing as a free lunch." He walked to where Sophie stood waving at him.

Kaylee had heard that bit of wisdom often from her mother. Dylan was a very smart little boy, but you didn't learn that type of cynicism inside a school.

Chapter Three

Christian waited on the dock outside of a quaint canal-front restaurant, The Fish Shanty, while Herb paid for lunch. He leaned against the railing and breathed in the humid air filled with the aroma of cooked seafood from the restaurant and salt from the Gulf, which Herb said lay beyond the harbor town.

As they exited, the older man had stopped at almost every table where customers greeted him. Now, he made his way toward Christian.

"Is the canal manmade?" Christian sheltered his eyes from the glaring sun.

"Yep. My granddaddy's daddy brought in workers to dredge it out."

"He was a fisherman?"

Herb laughed. "He probably liked people to think so.

At the time, it was a good place for hiding and transporting contraband. Later, it became the place for plume trade. Once there was a time when the beautiful birds in this area were hunted near to extinction so ladies could put some feathers in their hats and on their clothing. I'd like to say my family wasn't involved in such a travesty, but history is history. You can try to change it, but it doesn't make the truth less true."

"The town's been around for more than a hundred years, then?"

"Yep." Herb pointed to a pleasure boat motoring up the canal. Large birds swooped down upon the boats. Fishermen tossed something in their direction. "Pelicans have always fascinated me. They're beggars just like the seagulls, but for some reason, I despise those rats with wings. The pelicans don't beg or squawk. They expect."

A pelican perched on the boat's port side and waited without a sound. A man reached into a cooler and tossed a fish to the bird. The pelican caught it and lifted from the vessel.

Above the boat, a swarm of seagulls made their wishes and desires known.

"You'd think the man would throw something their way just to shut them up."

"A word from the wise: don't feed those scavengers. They'll swarm you. One single french fry can get you into a world of trouble."

Christian laughed. "Okay. Don't feed the seagulls. Got it."

The Fish Shanty sat on a dock that ran the length of the canal. "So, you're well-known. You must have lived here most, if not all, your life."

Herb motioned to his golf cart. "No. I went off to see the world and married a Yankee with money. We called New York City our home. We had a kid. My life took me around the world. The kid preferred staying in boarding school, and my wife wanted to travel with me. I managed to get a good gig doing what I loved. Thirty-five years in, I wearied of the travel and retired. I brought my wife here for a visit. Never occurred to me to return for good, but the kid had grown and married into money. She never had much use for us anyway. The wife fell in love with the place and the people and didn't want to leave. She'd never made a complaint about the years on the road, so I gave her what she wanted. She enjoyed this life for ten years before the Lord called her home.

"Not a lot of people take to life in Mullet Harbor. When I was younger, I couldn't wait to skedaddle. Now, you couldn't get me to leave." He flipped the key on the motorized vehicle. "Let me show you our downtown." He zipped the cart over the shelled parking lot and out onto the asphalt lane that was the main road. At the crossroads, he passed the market and hung a right. That street took them down an oak-lined lane that stretched out for about three hundred yards. The dangling moss reminded Christian of fingers reaching out to grasp him, yet he found it comforting, as if they were offering him shelter from the life he'd plunged into with Dylan.

They entered a clearing where older homes circled the edge of a cul-de-sac. Four smaller bungalows sat between five two-story Victorians. The most magnificent of the nine homes took center stage—a Queen Anne Victorian restored to what had to be its original glory. Each home, but the first Victorian standing guard on the left and appearing a little more rundown than the rest, had signs outside announcing that they were specialty shops, among them a fudge shop, a souvenir store, an art gallery, and Herb's photography gallery, housed in the Queen Anne.

The cul-de-sac encircled a small green space sprinkled with benches, azaleas, and punctuated by a dramatic fountain with two sculptured mermaid children, water shooting into the air from their heads and falling into the pool surrounding them.

The yard of the last Victorian to the right opened up into a park with a gazebo large enough to house an orchestra. Behind the gazebo, a children's playground caught Christian's gaze. Dylan would love that place.

"That's where we have our big events, like our

upcoming Christmas Eve festival." Herb followed the one-way direction on a wooden sign and parked his cart outside the Queen Anne. "Welcome to my world." He led Christian up the brick sidewalk and onto the porch.

Herb's residence, where Christian had spent the morning working outside, was far from traditional. Christian did his best to reconcile that eclectic abode with this staid traditional historical. Herb smacked his arm. "I grew up in this place. Had to do a lot of work to get it back to good. She was the ugly older sister to the others around here until my wife made sure she took her rightful place."

Christian followed Herb onto the porch and into the gallery, which surprisingly retained the flavor of a home with antique furnishing and heavy draperies. He motioned to ask if he could look around

Herb nodded. "I need to check with Abigail anyway. She filled in for me for a few hours while I worked with you at the house."

Christian meandered into the living room, stopping and taking in the breathtaking work of Herb Miller. He perused the entire house, upstairs and down, forgetting the architecture and fixating on the photography. He'd expected Herb's work to depict local flavor, and most did, but a few prints were obviously taken hundreds, if not thousands, of miles from Mullet Harbor: the Sydney Opera House, the Great Barrier Reef, jungles, crowded third-world streets, and people from every country and lifestyle. Some of the photographs were familiar to Christian. Famous, in fact.

Exiting the upstairs, he looked for any room he hadn't seen and found the library filled with built-in shelves that housed slender magazines with yellow covers. *National Geographic.* The shelves were marked *Not for Sale.* Framed copies of the magazine covers lined the walls between the shelves.

"I loved my job. What can I say?" Herb had slipped into the room.

"You were a photographer for …?"

Herb winked. "Yeah. God truly blessed me with that life so much that when I retired, I was ready. I love the memories, but I don't miss the road. The studio was my wife, Lacey's, idea. I still can't get use to not having a camera in my hand though. Every day I take a boat out or I walk the woods and take my pictures."

"I'm speechless," Christian managed. "To find you here in what appears like the end of the world."

Herb waved him off. "I'd like you to meet Abigail Brewster. She helps me here, and she works with Rose at the grocery store." Herb turned as if expecting to find someone beside him. He shook his head. "Where'd she go now? She's like a hummingbird, flitting everywhere. She's not good with strangers unless she can help them."

Christian followed the man into the foyer, and Herb moved into the kitchen. "Abigail, what are you doing now?"

"I wanted to get these dishes cleaned up while you were here," a woman said, her voice timid.

"Well, I appreciate that. Come meet Christian."

Abigail tiptoed behind Herb as he exited the kitchen. She kept her toes up and her head down.

"Christian, this is Abigail. Everyone who owns a business on this circle finds her invaluable. She's a special blessing to me and Rose—Ms. Fish—and well, the whole town. She's also the town baker. Brings her pastries here each morning, and our customers get to experience a taste sensation like none other."

The woman's forehead reddened.

"It's nice to meet you." Christian held out his hand. "I hope I get to sample your baking."

Without shaking his hand, Abigail hurriedly tiptoed back to the kitchen and returned with a piece of pie on delicate china and graced with a silver fork. She thrust the plate at him.

He had to juggle to keep from losing his grip on it. "Thank you."

She peered up at him. "You're welcome." Her gaze went downward.

Christian shared a smile with Herb and took a bite of

the pumpkin pie topped with whipped cream. He chewed to make the flavor last longer and couldn't bring himself to hurry the experience. The woman might be as shy as a feral cat and as antsy as that hummingbird Herb mentioned, but she could bake.

He savored the last bite before speaking. "This is something else, Abigail. Thank you."

She did an old-fashioned curtsy, yanked the empty plate from his hands, and returned to the kitchen. "I'm going to finish the dishes now, Herb," she called.

Herb winked at Christian. "Fine. I'm going to take Christian outside and sit on the porch for a few minutes before we leave. That should give you time to get it done."

The porch had an inviting swing, and Christian sat on it. He'd spent the morning working on the old man's fleet of boats: an airboat, a good-sized fishing vessel Herb used for charted trips, and a sailboat Herb said he used for an occasional tour but was mainly his pride and joy. The work had been hard, and Christian suspected he'd been put on trial to determine his trustworthiness and determination to get a job done well. Christian might be an academic, but he'd earned his way through college with backbreaking construction work and several other jobs that rounded out his résumé: butcher, baker, candlestick maker. Well, the last was actually soap, and he'd loved that job, working alongside a gorgeous little bohemian who eventually became his bride. "You don't seem in a hurry to get me to the grocery store."

Herb took a wicker rocking chair and sat in silence.

Christian studied the quaint street, the park, and the shops.

"I just wanted to talk with you for a minute," Herb said. "If I don't get you back to Rose's soon, I'm not going to keep my promise to the little guy. You're an excellent worker and a quick study. I could use you around my place and here. Abigail's a baker, not a salesclerk, though she does try to help out because she's good that way. If you stay on, I'd ask you to man this place for a couple of hours. Abigail has a big gig to plan for tomorrow night, so I can't ask her to work, and I have an airboat ride booked in the morning."

"Mr. Miller, again, thank you for your generosity." Christian dreaded telling Herb he couldn't stay. Truth was, he'd like to rest here for a couple of days before moving on, but that wasn't an option.

"Wasn't generosity. I need help, Chris."

Sometime within their working relationship, Herb had slipped in the shortened version of Christian's name that he only allowed Dylan, his sister, and his deceased wife to use. He'd thought about correcting him, but Herb was a benefactor, and Christian wouldn't have to put up with it for long.

"Pray about your desires and God often accommodates," Herb said.

"Then I'm glad I was the answer to your prayer for today."

"I'll be praying for you. Where's your family?" Herb ran a hand over his balding top.

Direct and to the point. Christian liked that about the old guy. "Dylan is all the family I have."

"Well, I can tell Dylan loves you."

"We're very close."

"You have any particular destination in mind?" Herb's gaze bore into him.

Christian shook his head. "We're just seeing the country."

"Taking a road trip without the proper funds isn't very healthy for you or your son," Herb admonished. "Are you running? Is there an ex-wife? A custody issue?"

"I don't have a wife," Christian answered. "I did once, but she wasn't the boy's mother."

"In truth or in theory?"

"Truthfully. She loved Dylan as much as I do, though."

"I'm only asking because you and the boy look worn out, the kind of tired that's born of trouble. I'd like you to remain in Mullet Harbor awhile, but as the mayor, I want to make sure I'm braced for any problems that might come this way."

Mayor? Get out of town. The guy looked like a bum who'd lost his way to the beach.

"We're a small place. We look after our own."

They also did a great job of looking after strangers, but Christian wasn't staying. He needed to move on quickly. Remaining in one place for very long would invite trouble.

"Christmas is around the corner. What are you and the boy planning to do?"

"We'll be on the road." Christian ran his hand along the smooth top of the swing's arm. *Stay.* The word poked at him. *Give Dylan his wish—for Christmas.*

"Don't you think he deserves to rest—that you need a rest—a nice holiday?"

Christian clenched his fist. This Christmas would be a lot nicer than the one Dylan had last year. "I can't give him any more here than I can on the road. Where we spend the day makes no difference."

"Good. Then it's settled. You'll stay with me."

"You? I'm a stranger, Mr. Miller. I appreciate the thought. You're very kind, but Dylan and I need to move on."

"To what? A lonely holiday on the road wondering where you'll eat or sleep? Think about it. Talk it over with the boy. There's a Christmas party tomorrow night. The whole town will show up. Dylan would enjoy it." Herb elbowed him. "You can earn a little extra cash working for me and Rose. What do you say?"

How could he answer this man's kind offer? When it was only him and Dylan, there were no lies.

Still, a rest in Mullet Harbor was inviting. The swamp town seemed a world away from his troubles. If Christian still believed God would listen, he'd pray for peace in this place, but too many tragedies in his life silenced conversations with Him.

"Mullet Harbor has a reputation, and we didn't get it by accident." Herb smiled. "Many road-weary travelers have found rest here. I'm not talking about the tourist. The Good Lord seems to have a way of sending us strays."

God, are You really there? Is this where You've led me despite my anger and self-loathing? Are You doing this for Dylan? Christian received no response.

"The boy isn't your son, is he?" Herb's perception rocked Christian from his reverie.

"In here, Mr. Miller." He pounded his chest. "In my heart, that boy belongs to me."

"But in reality?"

Christian shook his head. "I used to think I knew the answer for the person who asked why God allowed suffering until I had to ask it myself. I'd gladly take my lumps from God, but Dylan is a helpless child. I vowed that if God refused to protect him, I would. The only way I can keep my promise is to run."

"Do you mind telling me who hurt Dylan? Why you've become his self-appointed guardian?"

"I need to meet Dylan" Christian stood. "If you care anything about the boy, please don't turn me in. He's related to me, and I'm all he has right now. That's all I can say."

"An idiot can see your fatherly protection over the boy. You need to work this out, or things are going to come unraveled on you. Stay here. Rest, and I'll keep your secret."

"Thank you, but we'll be leaving as soon as I get the work done for Ms. Fish."

"Chris, you misunderstood." Herb stood and grasped Christian's shoulder. "You stay here through Christmas. You and I will try to figure out what we can do to help your situation. Someone I trust to keep my secrets checked your vehicle identification and tag. Stay and we'll keep your secret. Skedaddle, and we'll send someone after you, and they won't be as understanding. I don't want you or the boy to get hurt."

"You old blackmailer." Christian pulled from his grasp, angry with himself for trusting anyone.

"You call it blackmail. I call it kindness. You're about to come undone, boy. How about it? Two jobs, good food, nice accommodations, memories made, and friendships forged?"

Stay. Give Dylan his Christmas wish.

Christian looked about him at the far outpost's only business district. Why couldn't he just say yes?

Chapter Four

With one hand, Kaylee held to Sophie's and with the other, she gently touched Dylan's shoulder, guiding the two with her to meet Sophie's father.

"I'm sorry I'm late." Pastor Isaac Cooper jogged the last few feet toward them.

"Daddy, meet my new friend, Dylan. He was Ms. McFarland's guest today. He helped me make my ornament and gave me his." Sophie held both of the crafts toward her father. "We ate lunch together. I introduced him to my friends, and he helped me do word puzzles. He's smart. He knew all the answers."

Kaylee winked at Dylan, who fidgeted and looked toward the street. "Nice to meet you, sir."

"Hello, Dylan." Isaac pushed his blond hair from his forehead and smiled, bending to hold out his hand to the boy. "I want to thank you for making Sophie's day such an interesting one. Are you a relative of Ms. McFarland?"

Dylan shook Isaac's hand.

"A new friend," Kaylee assured. "Dylan's father is working today for Mayor Herb and Rose. Dylan graciously agreed to escort me to school."

"Oh, oh … Dylan." Sophie grabbed his arm. "There's a Christmas party tomorrow night. You can come!"

Under Kaylee's touch, Dylan tense. "I can't," he said. "We're leaving tonight."

"Oh." Sophie reached for her father's hand and leaned against him.

"I'm not from here. We just stopped for the day."

Tears sprang into Sophie's eyes and fell down her face.

Dylan looked at Kaylee and back to the distraught girl. "I—I didn't mean to make you cry. I'm sorry."

Kaylee placed her hands on Dylan's shoulders. "It's okay."

"I didn't mean to make you sad," he pleaded. "I just wanted to be your friend for today. Please don't cry."

"Friends are forever," Sophie scolded. "Didn't anyone ever teach you that? You don't throw friends away because they leave. Because you'll be gone doesn't mean I won't think of you."

"Sophie," Isaac intervened. "Dylan didn't mean it that way."

The girl fell against her father, and Isaac picked her up. "You need to say good-bye. Dylan has been very nice to you. This isn't a good way to let him go, is it?"

Sophie wiped her eyes against her father's shirt and turned. "I'm sorry, Dylan. Thank you for helping me and for becoming my friend. I will never forget you. Please don't forget me."

Dylan shook his head and the tears fell. "I promise. I won't." His lips trembled. "I couldn't forget you." He reached out and touched her hand. "Good-bye."

"Good-bye." Again, she buried herself against her father, her sobs deepening.

Isaac placed a tender hand on Dylan's head.

The boy looked up at the preacher.

"You're a special young man to have touched Sophie so deeply. We'll be praying for you and your father." He walked away but turned back to peer at Dylan as Sophie continued to sob.

Kaylee bent down before the crying boy. He leaned his head on her shoulder in the same way Sophie had done with her father. "Why does she care if I leave?" He hiccupped.

"Sophie's a sensitive little girl, and you're a caring young man." Kaylee held him to her. She stared after the preacher, her heart breaking for father and daughter. Dylan had no idea the emotion his actions toward Sophie had probably stirred in their sorrowful hearts.

"I don't want to leave," he cried. "I made a wish for Chris to find a job and for me to have friends. It's not fair." He pulled away from her. "It's not fair."

Kaylee pushed his long bangs from his eyes.

"And don't tell me life's not fair." He wiped his eyes with the back of his hand. "My mom always said that—even when she caused bad things to happen."

Kaylee's heart lurched. Why hadn't she considered that Dylan's mother could be alive, that Chris had a wife? She pushed a smile into place. "Dylan, have you ever prayed?"

Dylan shook his head.

"Well, let's give it a try." She stood and led him to a bench against the wall of the school's office. "God grants our desires if they're what we really, really need. Why don't we ask Him to guide your father's decisions? Then we'll know that whatever happens—whether you stay or leave—God is in control."

Dylan pursed his lips and sat beside her.

"Something you want to say?" she asked.

"God doesn't like liars, does He?" He peered up at her and then stared back at his hands.

Kaylee had to tread carefully, but the truth was the truth. "God loves everyone. But He's very clear about it. He doesn't like lying. Why do you ask?"

Dylan swung his feet out and back. "If God doesn't

like lying, then He won't care to hear your prayers about me and Chris."

"Maybe you should tell God your lie." She took special care to lift his bangs again and push them to the side. "That's the wonderful thing about God. He forgives very easily."

"Chris isn't my dad, Ms. McFarland. He's my uncle."

Kaylee leafed through the pages of memory from earlier that day. "Well, I don't think that either you or Chris said you were father and son." She narrowed her eyes, looked upward, then shook her head. "No, I don't think that either of you mentioned it. I assumed." She smiled at him.

He shook his head. "But even I know that not saying anything is as good as telling a lie. Chris and I talked about it once. He said it's true, but he said that we needed to stay quiet about things because we don't have a choice."

"Well then, let's pray and ask God for that forgiveness He offers to us." She reached for his hand.

Dylan stared down into his lap.

Kaylee bowed her head. "Dear Lord, I pray that You'll forgive Dylan and Chris for what Dylan perceives is a lie, and I'm sure Dylan is asking You to forgive him. Aren't you, Dylan?"

Several seconds passed before Dylan gazed up at her. "Yes." He closed his eyes and bent his head once again.

"See, Lord, he's sorry, and we're here to ask You to

guide Christian in the decisions he needs to make for both Dylan and himself. Remind Dylan, Lord, that his uncle is the one You've placed over him to protect him, and help Dylan to make the decisions easy for his uncle. Lord, show Dylan Your shoulder to cry upon. Come into his life and give him Your peace. He's too young, Lord, to carry such a burden. In Jesus' Name. Amen."

"Amen."

Kaylee pulled the boy into an embrace.

"Ms. McFarland, I want to see Chris." Dylan pushed off the seat. "I miss him."

"Well then, without further delay, let's you and me make our way." She tilted her head to see what he thought of her rhyming abilities.

Dylan laughed.

"Oh, Dylan, what a wonderful sound." She took his hand. "Will you be sure to let me hear a little bit more of that before you have to leave?"

Christian cut the choice piece of meat expertly. The job Rose Fish gave to him came easy. His work as a butcher in the grocer's deli department in University Park, Pennsylvania, prepared him well. If she'd placed him in the bakery, where he learned that only Abigail's baked goods were offered, he'd do just as well.

"The Lord has been good to me today, Mary Alice, sending me someone who doesn't need training." From the front of the store, Rose, a wiry little lady in a dark blue skirt and top addressed an elderly woman waiting on the other side of the counter from Christian.

The front door swung open, and he waited to see Dylan run toward him. Two other school kids meandered through, calling a hello to Rose.

Christian wouldn't feel settled until he had Dylan in his sights.

"I don't want a fatty side," Mary Alice warned.

"No, ma'am," he agreed as he continued to cut the roast she'd requested. Finished, he wiped his gloved hands on the white butcher's apron and picked up the meat to show her the selection. "Now, if this doesn't meet your needs, I'll be glad to cut another."

She studied the meat. "You did a fine job. I hope Rose can keep you, young man."

Christian smiled. "Thank you." He wrapped the meat, handed it to the customer, and hurried back to clean up the area.

The door opened, and he again looked for Dylan.

Mayor Herb entered and held open the door. Another man who appeared to be close to Christian's age thanked Herb as he walked inside. Both men stood to the side of the doorway talking with Rose.

Christian wiped down the counter. Then he straightened the food in the display case, checked the thermometer, and closed the door.

"Chris Abrams." The man who'd entered with Herb stood in front of the meat case. He had hair and eyes as dark as night against an olive complexion. When he spoke Christian's name, it came with a slight accent—watered-down French, maybe.

"Yes, sir, but I prefer Christian," he corrected.

"I'm Sheriff Remy Arneaux."

Christian's heart galloped toward the door, but his feet remained planted. "Yes, sir?" he repeated. The old man had gotten a jump on him, betraying him before Christian could sneak out of town with Dylan.

"Rose said to tell you to take a break. I'd like to speak with you." Remy's accent fell into place. Cajun. "Before the boy gets here," the sheriff stressed.

Christian nodded, slipping the apron off and hanging it on a peg on the wall. He opened the half door to the side of the display case and followed the man through the store to the front of the building.

The bright sun glinted in Christian's tired eyes as they stood on the walkway. The sheriff led him to the side of the building out of the glare. The man's gaze searched the town for a moment. A few children walked the streets. Their laughter and their voices rang out. Was he looking for Dylan? Were they taking him aside so they could get the boy away from him?

Christian fought to release an even breath. "What can I do for you?" he asked.

"The mayor asked me to do him a favor today. I did it. You made it a little easy for us by telling him your name. Not the typical action of a man wanted for kidnapping."

Christian gave a terse nod. This was the part where his academic career would be forever behind him, where everything he'd done to protect Dylan would come to naught. He expected this day to come, but he should have prepared better for it. Still, he'd never give the man an ounce more of information to use against him.

"I trust Herb. He's a good judge of character. He tells me you have a valid reason for taking the boy out of Pennsylvania state custody."

"How am I supposed to answer that?" Christian challenged.

Arneaux's intense stare challenged Christian. The sheriff swallowed hard and again raked a glance over the streets. "Truthfully, Christian, I'm breaking so many laws here, but I had someone else do a little digging. She agrees with me that you probably had a valid reason for doing what you did." He gave back his full attention to Christian. "And I keep my promises. Herb asked me not to take action against you even if I researched more deeply than he wanted. So I need to hear your answer to the same question Herb assured me he asked of you. Is the boy in danger?"

"With me? No, sir. You can ask him yourself. Ask him anything. I'm probably the only male figure in his life that hasn't hurt him, and I plan to never let it happen again."

Arneaux nodded. "I'd like to talk to Dylan. I appreciate your offer. Let me give you a word of advice that may keep us all out of trouble here. I love my job. I want to keep it. You love the boy, and you want to keep him safe."

"I'm listening." Christian stared down the avenue on the other side of the main road. Dylan and Kaylee walked hand in hand toward the store.

Remy nodded in that direction. "That him?"

"Yeah." Christian smiled as Dylan spotted him and waved. He raised his hand.

Dylan broke free of Kaylee's hold, starting across the road.

Christian held up his palm and pointed forcefully at the teacher. Dylan stopped and reached again for Kaylee's hand. They crossed the street together.

"What's your advice, Sheriff?" Christian asked.

"You're blessed that I took patrol in town today. There's an APB on your vehicle. The reports say you're heading toward Texas. Any reason for the authorities to think so?"

That's where he hoped they'd focus the search. "Yeah. My wife was from College Station. Her parents live there."

"Your wife?"

"She's dead. Cancer." Christian stole a second to look away, fighting back the emotion that always formed with those words. "Is there anything else, Sheriff?"

"Call me Remy. That way, when they come to take my job from me, I can at least say we were friends."

"Sure, Remy." He'd be this man's friend if it meant he could hold on to the boy one more day. Again, Christian held up his hand, motioning for Dylan to stand on the sidewalk in front of the store. From Kaylee's wide eyes, he assumed she knew the officer. She led Dylan out of sight.

"Give Herb your truck keys. Let him park the vehicle behind his fenced garage with the back against the door. Keep the vehicle locked. I'm going to be running for sheriff again before too long, and one of my deputies with friends in high places wants my job. I want to keep it, and well, I'm sticking my neck out here—for Herb. The old man means a lot to me."

Christian nodded. "I understand."

"And stay here with the boy. Understand the value of the sanctuary Herb's offering. Let Mullet Harbor show you a little Southern hospitality."

"The boy isn't used to being away from me this long.

I could tell he was worried. Can we step back inside?"

"Once I get your promise." Remy held out his hand. "I'm a man of my word. Are you?"

Christian hesitated.

"He's a tired little boy," Kaylee said.

Christian turned, surprised she stood behind him. She must have used a back door.

"I left Dylan inside with Rose." She touched his arm. "I thought you should know. I didn't do Dylan any favors taking him to school, and I'm sorry for that."

"What do you mean?" Christian's heart ached for the boy.

"He made a friend. The parting was very hard for his tender heart."

Christian applied pressure to his stinging eyes.

"If you'll stay, I'll watch him."

"There you go," Remy urged. "You'll stay?" Again, he held out his hand.

What was he supposed to do with Kaylee's gorgeous sky-blue eyes taking him in, begging him in silence to stay? He gave Remy's hand a firm shake. "We'll stay."

"Sophie invited him to a Christmas party tomorrow night. The whole town attends. He'll be so happy he can go, Chris." Kaylee clasped her hands together.

If he didn't know any better, he'd think the woman was holding back a joyful jump. "Christian," he whispered as Remy turned away from them.

"I'm sorry?" she asked.

"I let Dylan call me Chris. I prefer Christian." He started away to head off the sheriff but turned back.

Kaylee stared at him, her hand touching her cheek as if he'd slapped her.

He squeezed his eyes shut. He had—with his words. He opened his eyes. "I mean, I like the sound of my full name when you say it. Would you mind?"

Her soft lips turned into a smile. "Sure."

"Sheriff—Remy, let me introduce you to Dylan. Otherwise, he'll be a little leery of you." Christian stopped at the corner and waited for Kaylee to catch up with them. "Would you mind staying with Dylan while Sheriff Arneaux talks to him?"

"Sure," she said again.

"See, boy. There he is now," Herb said when Christian opened the door.

"You don't look too happy for a little boy who spent a whole day with Ms. McFarland," Rose teased. "All her students usually come in here with smiles on their faces after a day in school with her."

Dylan wore his distress like a heavy cloak.

Christian stepped toward him. "Dylan, what's wrong?"

"Can we stay, Chris? Please."

"Dylan ..." Christian released his breath. If the boy was hurting, at least there was a remedy—one he didn't think possible five minutes before.

"I'm so tired." Tears poured from the boy's eyes.

Christian fell to his knees in front of his nephew and held him close.

"So tired." Dylan choked on his tears. "Please." The sobs racked his skinny little frame.

"That's what my new friend, Remy, and I discussed outside. I think I'd like to accept Mayor Herb's generous offer to stay with him through the holidays. We'll decide what we're going to do before the New Year. I'll need to work for the mayor and Ms. Rose, so it's not a vacation. I'm sorry, but you'll have to suffer some long days with Ms. McFarland." Christian dug into his pants pocket. He jangled his keys for effect, and Dylan looked up. "Mayor Herb is going to park our truck at his house."

Herb took the keys. "I'll be right back."

Christian smiled at the older man and turned his attention back to Dylan. "We've been invited to a Christmas party tomorrow night."

"The whole town will be there." Dylan's smile was the only gift Christian needed for Christmas.

"Kiddo, this is Sheriff Arneaux. He'd like to talk to you. I trust him. You feel free to answer any questions. He knows the story." Christian stood. "I need to get back to work."

"Chris ..." Dylan reached for his hand.

"Ms. McFarland is staying with you. When you're done talking, come back and let me give you money for a candy bar to spoil your dinner."

"I wanna be with you." Dylan started to follow him.

"Remy, use my office," Rose offered.

Dylan shot Christian a wild glance. "No." He moaned.

"I'll be with you." Kaylee leaned down.

"I want Chris, too. Please, he'll just take a minute, Ms. Rose," Dylan begged.

"Take as long as you need." Rose waved him forward. "I don't see a long line at the meat counter."

"It's fine with me." Remy motioned. "Kaylee, as a child specialist, I'm glad you'll be joining us."

Kaylee nodded and led the way to the office.

Christian grasped Dylan's shoulder and gave it a tender squeeze. "You're fine," he offered.

He only hoped that he told the boy the truth.

Chapter Five

Kaylee sat in the chair beside Dylan. She touched his trembling hand and held it in hers. Remy sat on the edge of Rose's old, worn desk while Christian leaned against the wall to the side of them.

Dylan turned to look at his uncle.

"I'm here." Christian's voice was calm, soothing Kaylee's frazzled nerves.

Dylan sat forward.

"I'm the sheriff, Dylan," Remy began. "I had a talk with Christian outside. Will you tell me a little about you and your uncle?"

Dylan's lips puckered, and Kaylee offered his hand a little squeeze. "I trust Sheriff Arneaux. You can tell him anything."

"What do you want to know, sir?"

"What about your dad? Where he is?"

"I don't have a dad—I mean I don't know who he is. Chris is my dad."

Christian lifted his hand to his eyes and pressed— something Kaylee was beginning to realize he did when his emotions were in play.

"And your mom?"

Christian dropped his hand and stared at a spot on the opposite wall. His cheeks rose as he clenched his teeth.

Kaylee held her breath.

"My mom's in the hospital. She's hooked up to a machine. She's Chris's sister."

"How'd she end up there? Do you know?" Remy asked.

"Jeff—he was her last boyfriend—he smashed her in the head with a lamp, and then he used her head to put a hole in the wall. When he was done with her, he threw me against the wall and hit me in the face with his fist."

Remy cleared his throat and winced.

Kaylee shot a glance at him.

"Where was Christian when this happened?" Remy's accent deepened, a tell that the conversation distressed him.

"He didn't know. We lived a long way away." Dylan bounced in his seat. "Sheriff, Chris didn't know."

Remy looked to Christian with his brows raised.

"I was a professor at Penn State. You probably know

that already, or you wouldn't have told me your name, and I'd be locked up." He cast a glance toward Kaylee and quickly looked away. "I lost touch with my sister before my wife's death. The reason the courts gave for not allowing me custody was my failure to realize Dylan needed me."

"You were gainfully employed, right? I didn't see a record. Did the judge offer a reason for choosing a foster home over family?"

Christian shook his head. "My wife died fifteen months ago. I was consumed with self-pity. Even knowing my sister, Cassie's, drug addiction and her propensity of sharing space with the worse possible human element, I didn't take care of Dylan as I should have." He rubbed at a spot on his hand. "Shook me pretty badly when the authorities called to tell me Dylan and Cassie were hospitalized."

"Uncle Chris tried to keep me with him, but that stupid judge …"

"Dylan, what have I told you about authority?" Christian kept his voice low.

Dylan sat back.

"I need an answer," Christian pressed.

Dylan gripped Kaylee's hand. "We respect authority even if we don't agree with it."

"So, Christian, running from the courts, is that

respecting authority?" Remy asked.

"No, sir." Christian looked him in the eyes. "But my sister and I spent years in the Philadelphia system. There's nothing to respect." He straightened. "And I'm sorry, but I couldn't let that happen to Dylan."

"Dylan, would you like to know about your mom?"

Dylan shook his head. "No. She doesn't care about me."

"Is that you or your uncle talking?"

Dylan blinked. "Uncle Chris loves Mom. He's worried about her, but like I keep telling him, she don't care—"

Christian coughed into his hand.

"No matter how it's said, it's the truth. You know it. She doesn't care about anyone but herself. She always cries about what she doesn't have and what she didn't get, and whenever she did have or did get something, she spent it on her next fix."

Kaylee winced now. Dylan was right. Life wasn't fair.

"One more question, young man, and you're free to go."

"Yes, sir?" Dylan looked to Christian.

His uncle offered him a faint smile.

"Rumor has it that my little niece is sweet on you."

"What?" Dylan's mouth gaped.

Kaylee giggled.

Dylan turned his green gaze upon her.

"I didn't tell him," she said.

"I don't know your niece, sir." Dylan's gaze moved back and forth between Kaylee and the sheriff.

"Is that so? I was leaving her house when she got home from school. She couldn't stop telling me about this boy she met at school. Said his name was Dylan. That's not you?"

"Sophie?" Dylan smiled. "Yeah, that was me. She's a pest."

"Dylan." Christian kicked playfully at the chair. "Apologize."

"I'm sorry, sir, but she really is a pest."

Christian leaned his head back against the wall and rubbed his neck with his hand. Still, a smile lingered on his lips.

Remy laughed. "I supposed she can be."

"Was that your question?" Dylan's words betrayed him. He obviously wanted nothing more than to be rid of the officer.

"No, but I suppose I should ask your permission to ask another since this is actually my second inquiry."

"It's okay."

"If you're going to the Christmas party tomorrow, will you spend some time with Sophie? She's a little sad, and you put the first smile on her face that I've seen in a long time."

Dylan's lips trembled. "But I made her cry, too. I'm sorry."

"I don't think you made her cry." Remy stood. "The thought of your leaving did it. Now that you're staying, I think you'll see her smile again. So, will you do that for me?"

"Yes, sir." Dylan jumped to his feet. "She's a funny pest."

Remy held out his hand. "Dylan, thank you for your honesty."

Dylan's smile widened. "Thank you, sir." He spun toward Christian. "Can I sit with you while you work?"

"I'm sure you could, but I think you meant to ask me if you may, correct?"

Dylan sighed deeply. "May I sit with you while you work?"

"We'll have to ask Ms. Rose." Christian ruffled Dylan's hair.

Remy squeezed out the door.

Kaylee placed a pout on her lips. "I thought you and I would spend the afternoon together. I've wanted to fish since I've moved here, but I haven't had anyone to join me. Christian can meet us after work."

"I don't know." Dylan seemed unsure.

"Oh, go on. I wish I had your luck with pretty women, kiddo. Don't throw the gift away."

Pretty. Kaylee touched her fingers to her curls then dropped her hand. "You can walk to my house with me so I can change, or if Ms. Rose doesn't mind, I'll be back in about thirty minutes."

"I bet Ms. Fish won't mind if you stay here. I haven't seen you all day. I kind of missed you. Funny little pests have a way of doing that, you know. You don't appreciate them too much until they aren't around. Then you can't wait to see them again." Christian bumped him.

"Is it a date, Dylan?" She waited.

"Yes, ma'am," he answered her but threw his arms around his uncle. "I love you, Chris."

"I love you, too, kiddo." Christian hugged the boy with one arm and held out his hand to her. "Thank you," he mouthed.

His warm hand fit hers perfectly. She released his and edged out the door past him before the growing warmth in her cheeks could turn her face red.

Pretty. He said she was pretty. Why did she have this strange desire to thank him?

Kaylee stared at her face in the mirror. She pulled down a loose curl and let it bounce back into place.

Pretty. The word swam in her soul like a buoy. Even

if Christian was simply throwing around compliments, the one word undid all of the unkind comments made by her mother through the years.

She stood sideways in front of her mirror and ran her hand down the front of her shirt. The jeans with the floral top worked.

"Look at you, Kaylee Nicole." She picked up her purse. "Yes, Momma, I'm primping and for a man—a most handsome man—so good on the eyes."

Her mobile phone rang, and she looked at the ID.

"No. No. No." She stomped. "Do you have special radar that tells you when I'm doing something you wouldn't approve?" She spoke to the unanswered phone knowing good and well her mother had a spy in Mullet Harbor. But she hadn't seen Jacob Marin today. She punched the button. "Mother, how are you?" She shut her door to her bayou home and walked the long dock that stretched from her house to the shore. Then she trekked toward the store, hopeful that she could end the conversation before she met up with Dylan and looked into the luscious green eyes of his uncle.

"How was school?" Mother asked.

"Same as every day. The kids were a delight. The day went fast."

"Kaylee, I can get you on a plane tomorrow morning. Why don't you let me buy the ticket? Five months without you is a long time, and without your dad here … What good is all the money he left if I can't spend it on my only daughter?"

Mother used every word to strike the right chord: guilt. She always left it for last, right behind shame and anger.

"I wish I could, but I've promised to help someone during the holidays."

"I thought you were looking forward to the time off?"

As she walked, Kaylee shifted her tennis shoes in the soft, gray Florida sand. They didn't have dirt like this in Baltimore, the kind that moved beneath her feet when she stepped on it. "Mother, a vacation doesn't always have to be about doing nothing. I like to keep busy. Besides, this doesn't interfere with my vacation. There's a new resident. He's asked me to watch his little boy while he works."

"New resident? What do you know about this man? Doesn't he have a wife?"

Kaylee closed her eyes. Why had she started this conversation? Mother would dig so thoroughly that Kaylee couldn't shovel out a foxhole deep enough for her to hide in while her mother fired verbal ammunition over Kaylee's head, hoping to strike a vulnerability. "He doesn't have a wife."

"Still, you don't know him well enough to stay in his home or …"

"He's staying with a friend."

"So, is he staying with a friend, or is he a resident?" Mother hadn't worked as an attorney since the day she'd married Daddy, but she was still as quick as ever with the interrogation. "You know, I wondered if you wouldn't fall for the first man who said a nice word to you."

"Listen, I need to run. I promised to watch the boy while he's working." She didn't have the patience to sit in the foxhole and outwait her enemy. She needed to duck and run.

"Wait, he's staying with a friend, yet he's working. This doesn't make sense. Resident or homeless?" The woman had a knack for making the truth seem malicious.

"Gotta go." Kaylee hung up and changed her phone setting to silent—as if her mother could ever be silenced. Kaylee wished the woman would run for office during the next election, taking Daddy's vacated congressional seat. The campaign would keep Mother busy and out of Kaylee's life. No. She wouldn't do that—Leann's only platform was to stand against anything and everything her only daughter chose to do.

When she arrived at the store, Christian and Dylan were helping Rose stock the shelves. Kaylee smiled at her. Rose was a thin bundle of energy. She was fun and forthright, and Kaylee had come to love the woman—a grandmother Kaylee never had.

Rose patted Christian on the shoulder. "You go on

now. Like I said. Enjoy a nice dinner with Kaylee and Dylan." She turned to Kaylee. "I told him he and the boy could leave, and I'd send you on, but he insisted on waiting."

Beside Christian, Dylan continued to transfer baked beans from a box to the shelf while Christian re-stocked cans of kidney beans, but he stopped. "Are you sure? As I said, I don't mind staying."

"Kaylee, don't keep him out too long." Rose ignored him. "Get some more food in their scrawny bodies and point them back in the direction of Herb's so they can rest."

"I'll be here at seven tomorrow morning." Christian emptied his box. Dylan finished. Then they handed their empty containers to the store's owner.

Christian's warm hand pressed into Kaylee's back as they moved down the aisle. He stopped at the register and leaned over, pulling out a plastic bag containing shampoo, toothpaste, and other like items. "Herb said Dylan could stay with him and sleep in a little bit tomorrow. Do you mind picking him up around nine? I hate to presume upon your time."

Christian held open the door, and Dylan waited for her to walk out first. Together they started toward the dock. "Presume? Oh, no. Here I thought I would have a lonely Christmas vacation, and now I have a buddy. We'll have lots of fun. Maybe we'll catch up with Sophie? And I did volunteer to help decorate the community center for the party."

Dylan rolled his eyes as if the impish pastor's daughter hadn't made an impression upon him, but the sight of Dylan's touch upon Sophie's hand was forever imprinted upon Kaylee's heart.

Christian placed his fisted hand against his mouth and yawned.

She stopped. "I was so caught up fishing with Dylan, when the plans changed, I didn't think about you needing to rest."

He smiled at her, and his green eyes lit with mischief. "Do you know how long it's been since we've had three meals in one day and the company of a beautiful woman to share our time?" He stopped. "Unless we're keeping you from a date or something. It is Friday night."

Beautiful. If *pretty* had overwhelmed her, *beautiful* was her undoing. "No. No. I don't have a date."

Christian reached for Dylan's hand and guided them across the road. Was this the way it felt to have a man care about you?

They crossed a small wooden footbridge to the waterfront buildings on the other side: The Fish Shanty, a bait shop owned by Herb, and a few other businesses frequented by fishermen who tied their boats in the lagoon. "Wow," Dylan looked around him. "This is pretty cool, huh, Chris?"

"Watch." Christian pointed to a pelican that dipped from the sky. He moved the hand he'd pressed against her shoulder to her mid-back as he watched Dylan's face. The pelican swooped down and plopped into the water coming up with a squirming fish.

"Ah, man." Dylan smiled.

The man's eyes softened. Then he yawned.

Kaylee touched Dylan's shoulders. "I'm starving. Are you?"

Dylan nodded. "May we fish tomorrow?" he asked. "I mean instead of tonight." Christian's yawn was contagious, but the boy tried to fight it.

"Tomorrow will be fine. The night air can be a little chilly on the dock this time of year. We can sit inside tonight."

"Is that okay, Chris?" Dylan asked.

Christian nodded and yawned again. They were fading on her.

"Are you sure you're not too tired?" Kaylee asked.

"Go on in, Dylan. Get us a table." Christian motioned.

The boy ran ahead.

"Kaylee, it doesn't matter how exhausted I get. Seeing him this happy is worth it. Thank you for putting the smiles on his face. As you heard, he's had a pretty tough life, and the fact that since my wife passed, I hadn't cared—that eats at me." He looked down the street and back to her. "Is everyone in this town as nice as the ones I've met so far?" He opened the door to the restaurant.

"The ones I've met." Well, there was one guy she wasn't too fond of, but thinking of him might conjure his appearance, and she definitely didn't want anything to ruin this time. She stopped and offered Christian a smile, one she hoped would put him at ease.

"Well, Ms. McFarland, if the rest of them are half as nice as you, Mullet Harbor will definitely live up to its motto."

Chapter Six

December 15

The sun rose in the east, but the start of the day was no less beautiful to the northeast over the bayou surrounding Kaylee's rental. She held the curtain of her french doors with one hand and her coffee cup with her other and blew on the liquid before savoring the dark, rich taste seasoned with sugar and cream.

Since she'd arrived in the harbor, her blessings had been too numerous to count, among them her waterfront home. Herb offered her the opportunity to purchase the place if, after the school year, she wished to remain. He probably feared she might flee the small town separated from the rest of the world by cypress and mangroves. She shared her habitat with storks, pelicans, and other exotic birds. Small lizards abounded as well as one large reptile she'd come to accept, if not give a wide berth. All of it came with the most important factor, something she'd struggled to obtain her entire life: tranquility. Kaylee thought she'd never want to leave.

But she'd wait until her year was up to see if Mullet Harbor wanted her back.

So far, they seemed happy with her teaching. The school was so small she had no trouble relating with the other teachers and the parents and connecting with her students.

Kaylee let the curtain fall back and checked her watch. She couldn't wait to spend a leisurely day with Dylan. She hoped that he and his uncle had rested. Though, who wouldn't sleep well in Herb's funky mansion?

When she'd first seen the mayor's abode, she'd had to keep from laughing if only because the house fit the man everyone saw on the outside. No one would realize what Mother said she'd learned in her research before giving Kaylee her reluctant blessing to leave home. Herb was rich. He'd made big money as a worldwide photographer, and his wife had inherited her parents' valuable estate. To Mother that was more important than character. Though Herb was a character—a live-and-let-live kind of guy.

Herb and Rose had made Kaylee feel completely at home since her arrival in Mullet Harbor, and she had no doubt that they would do the same for the man and child who'd stumbled into town.

The thought of Herb and Rose kept Kaylee's smile in place. A widow and a widower clearly attracted to each other, but each still true to their spouses who'd gone before them.

Now that was love.

She wished her mother loved her father like that. Instead, Mother acted as if Dad's death was no more than his stepping out for another day in the office. Yes, they'd buried him in Baltimore-style, with all the honors bestowed upon a U.S. Congressman, but not a week after the funeral, Mother had again become the star of her party's political fundraising. "Keeping your father's memory alive," she'd proclaimed.

LeAnn McFarland had laughed and joked, sarcastically cruel to some, fantastically polite to others.

On the night Kaylee had asked the limo driver to take her home and return for her mother, the action had not gone over well. The argument that had ensued was the reason Kaylee decided to move as far away as she could from Baltimore.

Kaylee pushed the thoughts of Mother away. Strange. She hadn't called back. Maybe she'd gotten the less-than-subtle hint when Kaylee hung up on her.

Kaylee shook her head. No, it'd take more than that for

her mother to get the picture.

Kaylee's undecorated Christmas tree stood in the corner. She fingered the evergreen needles and bent in to enjoy the scent of pine. Her first tree—all hers, and who cared about its flaws. The tree's imperfections would drive her mother insane, but Kaylee always felt that the season should come with imperfections, and that decorating the tree just right, to cover the imperfections, made it all the more special. Her tree, once decorated, would be beautiful.

But despite all her mother's faults, she had always made Christmas special. And Kaylee missed her mother's ritual for making a tree choice. She pushed that thought aside as well.

Three gifts already rested underneath the unadorned tree, all for others: Herb, Rose, and Jacob Marin, Rose's nephew and the man her mother had reached out to when seeking information before Kaylee moved to Mullet Harbor. Each had been nice to her since her arrival, and she wanted to make sure she showed her appreciation. With Jacob, though, she feared he might mistake her gift for more than she intended. She'd already turned down two offers to dinner and one lunch. Rose said he would tire of the chase, but Jacob didn't seem the dishonest soul Rose portrayed. Kaylee was flattered by his attention, but somehow, she couldn't shake the thought that her mother had something to do with it. Jacob was the state attorney for the circuit. Mother's tentacles had a far reach, and with the connections she'd garnered from Dad's political affiliations, well, anything was possible.

Kaylee went to the kitchen and poured another cup of coffee. She reached into the refrigerator for the creamer. An aluminum foil swan filled with her leftovers sat on the shelf. Christian had made it, declaring that one of his myriad jobs in his past had been a waiter for an upscale restaurant. After fashioning the swan, he'd handed it to her with a shy smile. "Not much, but this is a token of our appreciation." He also refused to allow her to pay for the meal. Instead, he'd paid with the money he'd earned from Herb.

A knock sounded on the door, and she jumped. She made her way quickly there and peeked through the curtain covering the glass beside her entrance. Then she smiled and opened the door. "Mayor Herb, Dylan."

"I'm sorry." Herb looked down at the little one by his side.

Dylan sniffed and wiped the sleeve of his jacket over his nose.

Kaylee knelt in front of the child. He'd obviously been holding back tears.

"He woke after Chris left," Herb explained. "I thought he'd feel much more comfortable with a friend like you than an old man like me. Is that okay, Dylan?"

Dylan nodded. "Yes, sir."

Herb winked at Kaylee. "Well, if it's okay with Ms. Kaylee, I'll head off. I've got some city slickers wanting a morning tour of the swamp, airboat-style. What say we all meet at my place for lunch around noon? I'll fix us up a nice lunch since you didn't feel much like eating this morning."

"Ch—Chris?" Dylan stammered.

"Why don't you and Kaylee stop by the store and bring Chris with you for lunch?" Herb straightened.

"Who's looking after the studio?" Kaylee asked. "Dylan and I could do that."

"Abigail's there," Herb said.

"But she has …"

"She insisted." Herb raised his hands and lowered them. "That girl is as fidgety as they come. I bet she didn't sleep, stayed up all night, and has her project for tonight well in hand."

Kaylee nodded. She should have offered to help Abigail, but no one could keep up with the shy, always-on-the-move enigma in their midst. "We'll see you at noon."

The older man nodded. "Dylan?"

The boy gave the man his attention.

"You're a strong young fellow. I admire you, and I know you love your uncle. Let him work. He's showing you his love that way. You got it?"

Dylan nodded. "Yes, sir."

Kaylee closed the door, and Dylan walked away from her. "You have a neat house. You live on a pier."

She nodded. "Cool, huh? I thought so when I rented it. You're welcome to step out onto the back. Just stay on the dock. A big gator hangs out around here. We have an agreement. I stay out of the water, and he doesn't eat me. I suppose he'll make the same deal with you."

"Really? An alligator? I've never seen one in person."

Kaylee drew back the curtains from her french doors that opened to the backside of her dock.

"Wow!" Dylan pushed open the door. "You live here, and you haven't fished?"

She laughed. "It's not that I hadn't thought of fishing here. I haven't had anyone to teach me."

Dylan stopped, his hand on the railing. "I need someone to teach me, too."

"Well, okay, then. We'll find a local angler to do that, but there's a bit of a problem."

Dylan waited.

"I don't own any fishing equipment, and we need bait. We can rent those on the town dock."

Dylan shook his head. "That's okay, Ms. Kaylee. I don't mind staying here and not fishing."

Something wasn't right, but Kaylee couldn't think of what would change the child's mind. "Let me fix you some breakfast. Do you like french toast?"

Dylan nodded. "I like it where you can taste the egg more than the bread."

"Okay, I think I can manage that. We'll have breakfast and rest here a bit so we can put a lot of energy into helping to decorate for the Christmas party. Right now, enjoy the dock, but I mean it. Don't dangle your feet over the side. I suspect Abercrombie's favorite food might be feet."

"Abercrombie." Dylan rolled his eyes. "Who gave him that name?"

"Ever heard of Izod?" She laughed.

He shook his head.

"It's a shirt, and they always have an alligator as a label. Abercrombie is another clothing brand."

"Huh?" Dylan scrunched up his face.

"Let's just say Abercrombie and I share an inside joke."

Dylan shrugged and closed the door.

Kaylee would fix him a good breakfast, and they could both spend the rest of the morning looking forward to lunchtime.

Maybe it was instinct, but Christian didn't like the man chatting it up with Rose. Probably because his gaze seemed to often travel in Christian's direction where he remained behind the meat counter, preparing for the day and trying to avoid any introduction.

When Rose walked toward him with the man on her heels, Christian read her wary expression. "I'd like you to meet my nephew, Jacob Marin." She waved her hand, the loose bracelets on her arm jangling, and her pink-painted nails flashing. "He so seldom comes by it surprised me, and I forgot to introduce you. Jacob, Christian is helping me during the holidays."

"Nice to meet you, Chris." Jacob reached a hand over the meat counter, lifting it just enough to keep the expensive material from grazing the surface. Like it would matter.

Christian had cleaned that counter the night before, and the hour was early. He'd yet to serve anyone. "Call me Christian."

"Jacob is the state prosecutor for our circuit," Rose added. "He visits us on occasion just to keep in contact with his constituency."

"Aunt Rose," Jacob chided. "I came to say hello. Mom said you begged off of Canasta today. I thought I'd check to make sure you were okay."

"Honey, a phone call would have done just that." She patted him on the shoulder. "Truth is, Christian offered to help, and I thought it'd be rude to leave him to fend for himself. This is a big day for our Abigail."

Christian fought the laugh. Abigail had hurriedly tiptoed into the store early with her stash of goods for the bakery. By the time Herb stopped by, he said she'd swept his gallery porch, steps, and walkway and had placed a bin of plastic covered prints on the porch for customer perusal. The woman was a firecracker when it came to getting things done, but she wasn't much on communication.

"Never seen you around before?" Jacob stepped back and appeared to scrutinize Christian.

"Posh." Rose cut off any explanation Christian could offer with a wave, the bangles on her wrist chiming as if to keep him from saying more. "He's a friend of Herb's. Staying with him, as a matter of fact. Do you think Herb would just let anyone come in here and work?"

"He helped you to hire Abigail, didn't he?" Jacob smirked. "She's been an airhead since we were kids. She has to cost you more money than she makes you."

Christian tensed. He didn't like the man's tone. Yes, Abigail was a bit different, a little flighty, but she was sweet, and no one could say that having her around wasn't a benefit. Christian had only met her a couple of times, and he'd seen the value in her caring nature. This man apparently had known her a lifetime, and he couldn't see it.

Rose stood with her hands on her hips but a sweet smile on her face. "Dear boy, comments like that might just cost you the next election." She turned away. "And I'll make sure of it," she muttered.

Jacob shrugged and looked at Christian. "You can't blame me for looking after the welfare of my aunt. Since Uncle Lester died, she's gotten herself involved in things that he wouldn't recommend."

Rose spun around, hand covering her mouth, her eyes widened in mock horror. "Oh my, like running for the school board and deep-sea fishing with Herb. The scandal I've caused."

"All right, Aunt Rose. I get the sarcasm. I'm being a little overprotective. I'll leave you to your busy, scandalous life if you'll give me a bit of news on my favorite schoolmarm."

"Kaylee is fine." Rose pinched her nephew's cheek. "And let's keep her that way."

Jacob leaned away from her. "What's that supposed to mean?"

"She's not made of the same stock you usually corral."

Christian coughed to cover up a burst of laughter. He suspected Rose wasn't a person to mince words.

"She could do worse, Auntie." Jacob glowered.

"Darling boy." Rose's face softened as she took Jacob's hand. "You wouldn't mean to hurt her, but you're not a one-woman man, not yet anyway. And she's definitely a one-man woman. I doubt she's ever truly been in love. Her life was so wrapped up in being a congressman's daughter, doing the right thing ..." The older woman let her voice fade, and then she shook her head. "You need to let her be."

"We're not talking marriage." Jacob laughed. "I've only asked her to dinner. She would make me look good."

Rose shook her head again. "Life isn't all about impressing the right people or stepping on others to get what you want or withholding secrets from people in order to keep your position. Life is about loving the people you know, sharing your life with others no matter what they can do for you, and giving people the opportunity to grieve and to forgive."

Jacob straightened. "You're talking in riddles. What secret am I supposed to be hiding or who have I grieved. Auntie, it's not like you to spread rumors or outright lies."

Christian ducked into the cooler. He needed to chill. He didn't like this Marin character. Rose could handle him a lot better than Christian could.

And Rose's poignant declaration tore at his heart. The old woman had wisdom. He wished she'd been around when he was grieving and letting his sister and his nephew succumb to danger.

He should have moved in on his sister years before, when his wife, Amy, told him Dylan needed him. But all he'd wanted was Amy and the life they had. Cassie could take care of her own. Christian had carried her for nearly eighteen years, and his sister never seemed to appreciate it, always making one bad decision after another.

He'd wanted more from life, and he'd made the decision to cut her loose. Yeah, he'd been there when Dylan was born. At Amy's insistence, Cassie had moved in with them, but then she'd started using again, met another fly-by-night creep, and she'd taken Dylan and moved out with the guy.

That relationship didn't last long. The next twenty or so relationships had fallen apart as well. Maybe Cassie just wanted to be loved. Christian had been lucky enough to find someone. And Amy had loved him well.

He wiped his hand across his forehead where, despite the cooler, beads of sweat had broken out. He leaned against the wall and swallowed down emotion. He should have asked himself what his wife would have wanted, and he'd have known. She wanted Dylan safe.

She loved her nephew as if Cassie had been her sister and not Christian's.

"Hypothermia can set in pretty quickly." Rose opened the door and smiled at him.

Christian nodded.

"He's gone. We won't see him again for a while."

Christian followed Rose out of the cold.

"Didn't mean to give you a fright about his position. I

just wanted you to know."

Christian nodded again.

Rose made Christian face her. "This isn't about Jacob, is it?"

He half-nodded, half-shook his head, feeling ridiculous. "So, he's got a thing for Kaylee."

"He's got nothing for her," Rose spat. "I love the boy, but he needs a social climber, and even then, I don't think he's ready for marriage. I know Kaylee's glad to be out of that life. It's not like I'm a fortuneteller. She told me as much."

"Her dad is a congressman?"

"She lost her daddy last year. Maryland Senator Robert McFarland."

"Crashed his small plane." Christian recalled the sad blonde on the cover of his local newspaper. She stood beside an attractive older woman who didn't appear to grieve at all. Instead, she'd flashed her own politician-like smile at the camera, and the quote Christian would never forget was plastered underneath the photo. "Life must go on."

That had been before he'd been forced to get on his feet once again. He hadn't understood how anyone could put one foot in front of the other after losing a loved one.

"You're more her type." Rose slapped his back pretty hard for an old gal.

Christian shook his head. "You know nothing about me. I'd expect at first glance, which is mostly all you've gotten, I'm a bum at best. Kaylee deserves more than a hobo."

Rose leaned forward, taking his shoulders in firm hands. "Herb Miller and Remy Arneaux are two of the three men in this town that I place any stock since my Lester died. Both say you're not a bum, and Christian, if you were, you'd make the word a positive one. So, I don't want to hear that from you again."

Christian smiled. "So, who is this third fellow? Certainly not your nephew."

Rose's laughter rang. "Well, I do love the boy. Someday, he'll be a good man if I can just shake that coon-dog daddy out of his blood and get him to confess to a serious wrong we believe he's committed."

When he left here, Christian would miss this woman.

"I have a feeling you'll meet the third fellow soon enough, and when you do, you'll know who he is."

She wasn't going to give him a name. He was sure of that. "What can I do while I wait for your customers to come in looking for meat?"

"I have boxes to break down. Can you make change? Work a cash register?"

"Yes, ma'am."

"Then make yourself at home. If you get too much

traffic, just call out. I'll be in the back. If I get done with the boxes before any rush, I'd like to get to my bookkeeping and place some orders."

Make himself at home? He hadn't felt at home anywhere—ever—except in Amy's arms.

Then why, when Rose mentioned it just now, did he see the blond hair and the bright blue eyes of Kaylee McFarland?

Chapter Seven

Christian came to a halt beside Kaylee and Dylan in front of the mayor's home. He stared at what he'd first thought a monstrosity, but in the last twenty-four hours, after getting to know its owner, he understood why this house suited Herb more than the childhood home that housed his studio.

The place sat on the same canal that ran to the harbor from the open waters. At any given time, sailors, both commercial and pleasure seekers, motored or sailed past. An occasional boat whistle and a wave in Herb's direction announced that many recognized the mayor's residence.

Mangroves lined the opposite shore, and a dock ran the width of the property alongside a seawall. A covered boat lift where Herb kept his pleasure craft sat at the end of the dock. His sailboat was on a trailer parked on the inclined concrete beyond the seawall where Herb could keep the vessel well-maintained when not in use. Herb's airboat was parked on marshy land, and at the very edge of the property was Herb's gated garage area where Christian's truck had been incarcerated.

On the opposite end of the dock from the boat lift, Herb had screened in an outdoor kitchen complete with a commercial grill. The night before, the old guy had burned citronella candles to ward off mosquitoes and had cooked the best steak Christian had ever eaten.

What culinary delight awaited them today?

Kaylee had been silent while he took in the eclectic locale. She giggled. "I think you like this place."

Christian laughed. "Last night, I thought Dylan and I had been bested by a loon, but today, I see the beauty."

Dylan nodded his agreement.

"Why an octagonal mansion on stilts, though?" Christian asked.

"Herb explained that when a hurricane comes through here, it's best to be high and dry, and the home's shape resists the force of the winds. Hurricanes are something I've put off worrying about since we didn't have one visit before the end of the last season."

"How long is hurricane season?"

"June through November, but Herb said the most worrisome time is late August through September."

Four steps led to a grass landing, and there, two sets of circular stairs met above at the home's front porch. The octagon had angles jutting out from it, but a porch railing wrapped around the abode which stood on concrete pillars. Christian led the way up the left set of concrete stairs, which were crayon green to match the door, the trim, the eaves, and the home's metal roof.

Kaylee stepped between two of the five white, square, concrete columns that braced a semi-circular overhang shielding the door from afternoon sun.

Christian wiped his brow. "Do they have winter?"

"Herb says that most years winter arrives on one day, which happens to be his birthday. I'm told that on Christmas Eve, the town gathers in the square, and Herb makes it snow."

The door swung open, and Herb, wearing his flip flops, baggie shorts, and an apron for a shirt, stood before them. "Yammering outside ain't getting the food inside us. We were going to start without you."

"Abigail ran a few minutes late to spell me at the studio. Something about a cake." Christian wiped his feet on the mat that read "Doorbell broken. Yell *ding-dong* really loud."

Rose peeked around Herb. "Then you're forgiven. This is Abigail's night to shine. She was nice to fill in as much as she has today with all she has to do. Come in."

She reached and tugged Christian inside. Then she held her arms out and wiggled her fingers toward Dylan. "And you, come hug this old gal so I can drink in your energy."

Dylan didn't hesitate. He nestled in the older woman's arms like a boy starved for love and devotion.

Christian invited Kaylee to enter first.

"Hey." Remy stood in Herb's focal point—the grand kitchen that took up the center of the first floor—and held up a cup of brown liquid and a bright cocktail umbrella.

"Drinking so early?" Kaylee laughed and nearly skipped to where the man stood as she approached. "Where's mine?"

Rose moved like a dancer around the bar separating the kitchen from the living room. Her bracelets jangled as she lifted the pitcher and poured the drink into three glasses, slipping an umbrella into each.

She handed a glass to Dylan, but Christian held up his hand. "Rose, he's only eight."

"How old do you have to be to drink sweet tea?" Rose teased.

Tea with a drink umbrella? The thought settled over Christian, and he laughed. "In that case, make mine a double."

"Good choice. You might need it. She waved her free hand between Remy and Herb. "These two, they have ulterior motives to your being here, I'm sure."

Christian startled, nearly dropping the glass she'd handed in his direction.

"Herb?" Kaylee questioned.

"Oh, settle down. We just want to work some things out. Remy's risking his neck for us big time, and I heard Christian met Jacob. We need to be one step ahead of that man at all times. The least we can do is hear what Remy has to say." The mayor ushered everyone to the dining room table.

Christian held out a chair for Rose and moved to do the same for Kaylee.

Remy beat him to it.

Christian sat beside Rose and allowed Remy to sit beside the teacher. Christian and Dylan would be gone soon anyway. No need to make her think they could be more than temporary friends.

She studied him with those blue eyes, and he envied the Cajun bruiser sitting to her right.

Herb brought plated roast beef sandwiches with individual bowls of *au jas* sauce, dill pickles, and homemade fries.

Christian's stomach growled. He doubted he'd ever get full again after all the pangs of hunger he'd endured over the long journey.

"You're welcome." Herb laughed. Still standing, he held out his hands, one toward Dylan, and the other toward

Remy.

They each did the same. As the others bowed their heads, Christian held Herb's gaze. The old man winked as if to say, *I've got you covered.* Herb lowered his head and closed his eyes.

Christian did likewise.

"Lord, we thank You for this food. I thank You for these friends, both old and new, and I pray these friendships last. Show us Your will and Your way, and whatever You bring, may it come with Your mercy and Your love. In Jesus' loving name, we pray."

"Amen," the group chorused. Christian suspected they had all looked up, but he remained with his head down. *I've been away too long, Lord. Is this You? God, please let it be You.*"

"Chris," Dylan's worried voice broke into the prayer.

Christian looked up and smiled at his nephew. "We're going to be okay." He patted Dylan's shoulder.

They ate, each chatting about the upcoming evening's festivities and laughing about prior town Christmas parties.

Rose pushed her plate away. "Remy, did you take your momma shopping for this year's ugly sweater?"

"Marielle bought one for her," Remy said. "Isaac has it out and ready for her." He looked to Christian. "My mother is the official winner of every ugly sweater contest. Rose's husband, Lester, won it from her every year, but now that he's passed, Momma gets the prize."

"The dear has dementia." Rose stood and picked up her plate and Herb's. "We wouldn't dream of stealing that award away from her."

"Lacey and I used to always win the annual dance contest." Herb joined Rose in the kitchen. "I taught her to dance on a surfboard in Maui."

"No way!" Dylan wiped his mouth with a napkin.

With the pictures of Herb and his wife on various islands, and with amateur surfing tournament trophies to verify the older man's skills, Christian wouldn't doubt his story.

"Last year's Mullet Harbor Christmas Eve Festival king doesn't have his queen." Rose ran water over the dishes she'd carried.

Kaylee gathered the rest and took them into the kitchen. "Who was the ..." She glanced at Remy. "I'm sorry. I wasn't thinking. Isaac and Sidalee were king and queen, weren't they?"

Remy nodded. "When you think you've gotten past the grief, along comes a holiday, and it pounces on you again. Sophie's hurting." Remy glanced away.

"Is that why she's sad?" Dylan asked. "Is Sidalee her mom?"

"Yes. She died last February."

Christian studied the back of his chair. He could

understand their sorrow. He ushered Dylan into the kitchen to do their part.

Kaylee returned to her seat and reached for Remy's hand.

Christian and Dylan helped finish the cleanup and took their seats.

Herb remained standing, his gaze zeroing in on Christian. "We'd like you to turn yourself in."

Dylan jolted.

Christian held out his hand. His heart hurt from beating against his chest. "Settle down."

Herb remained silent.

"I'm listening," Christian coaxed, but unless this man had a good reason to make the suggestion, Christian and Dylan would be out of Mullet Harbor before the Christmas party began.

"No way, Chris. No way. They'll put you in jail and send me back there." Dylan's voice was one crack away from tears.

Christian looked to the sheriff. "This is your plan? After everything I've done to keep him safe, you want to jeopardize his health and his happiness by returning me to Philadelphia to face a federal crime?"

Rose patted Christian's hand. "Herb likes to startle a person so he's sure they'll listen. Hear Remy out."

Christian turned his gaze to Kaylee.

Her blond curls shook with her head. "No," she barely got the word out. "Remy, no."

Remy took a deep breath and leaned in, elbows on the table, hands clasped in front of him. "Jacob can be zealous. If someone new comes around and Rose shows them kindness, he gets a little ruffled, and he digs. If he stays out of Mullet Harbor, we don't have a problem, but if the man starts coming around too much, we need to make plans."

"Dylan and I need to leave Mullet Harbor before he starts snooping."

"Now. Now." Rose tapped her flattened hand against the table. "There will be none of that. You're dealing with two members of founding families. Mine and Herb's relatives were rascals. We've cleaned up the families' acts, but we've still outfoxed the foxes a number of times. We'll continue to do it. You listen to Remy."

"We're the only residents who know the truth," Remy offered. "I'd like to bring in Isaac. I trust him with my life, and he has wisdom I lack. Isaac has a brother, and I have another sister who can be a big help to us."

"Why would you want to let anyone else know?" Christian demanded.

"Because of Ephraim," Kaylee said as if a lightbulb had brightened her knowledge.

"Who are Isaac and Ephraim?" Christian asked.

Remy directed his attention to Dylan. "Isaac is

Sophie's dad. Dylan met him yesterday. He's a pastor. He's also my brother-in-law. Sidalee's husband."

Dylan nodded. "He's a nice guy."

"And Ephraim?" Christian pressed.

"Ephraim is Isaac's older brother. He's a special agent with the FBI. He should arrive soon for the holidays."

"You've already said that you're sticking your neck out for me. How is this not detrimental to you and to the agent? And how does my turning myself in help Dylan?"

"I'm not asking you to turn yourself in right now, Christian. Herb knows it might have to happen, though, when the time is right."

Dylan left his chair and backed away. "I'm not going back to that place or anywhere like it. I'd rather take a chance with my mom's boyfriends."

Christian held out his arm for the boy, and Dylan walked into it. Christian tucked him into his side. "Let's let him tell us their plan." He mustered bravado into his voice.

"You need to see the full picture here. You're surrounded." Remy drew an imaginary circle on the table. "And we're a force to reckon with."

"You got that right." Herb fisted his right hand and struck the palm of his left. "No one's getting by us." He pointed to his head. "This is what we work with."

Christian wanted to laugh. The man was wearing an apron instead of a shirt. Did he really have a brain in his noggin?

"You have a mayor, a prominent member of the community, and the sheriff already on the perimeter. My baby sister doesn't know why, but she's working for you, too."

"How's that?" Christian asked.

"She works for the *Miami Herald*. Ever heard of it?"

Christian didn't bother to answer the rhetorical question.

Remy didn't wait anyway. "You seem like a well-informed, well-read man. Does the name Marielle Arneaux ring a bell?"

Christian straightened. "She's an investigative reporter."

"That you know her name and her work is a testimony to how good she is. Would you agree?"

Christian nodded, his gaze remaining on Kaylee. Right now, he was drowning, and looking into her beautiful blue eyes was all that kept him buoyant in the depth of his troubles.

"After I contacted her yesterday, Marielle did some quick digging into life inside the State of Pennsylvania's Child Protective Services. She unearthed the real reason why the judge wouldn't let you take custody of Dylan."

"I told you. I let Dylan down. I may have disobeyed the man's order, but I understand fully that I'm the reason he was there."

"It's not like that," Dylan protested.

"The kid's right," Remy said. "Marielle located a reliable source. I'm not going to tell you about it simply because the less you know, the more you have to depend on and trust me. The four of us at this table are your best friends right now. I'd like to bring in the others with your permission. Marielle understands I wouldn't ask her to investigate without reason, and she won't take action until I give her the all-clear. I don't have to ask Isaac if he'll talk to Ephraim or even wonder what Ephraim will do, because we trust one another without need of explanation. The one person who could be a danger to you isn't anyone we have an ounce of trust in. Sorry, Rose."

"No offense taken." Rose waved him off. "Christian, we like to be a blessing where blessings are due, and friends don't let each other down."

A tear slid down Kaylee's face. She looked away and back again. "What she says is true. Herb fought hard to get me to come here and teach. I don't even know how he found me in my desperation to leave Baltimore. He bested the best, and I've found only friends here. Be our friend, Christian. Dylan."

"You're not asking me to turn myself in now?"

"Goodness, no." Rose laughed. "Honey, we keep our word. Herb said we'd help if you stayed. The goal is to keep you from going to prison."

"But you said it might be a possibility."

Dylan buried his face against Christian. "No. Don't listen to them. I don't want to stay here anymore. I'm ready to leave."

"Now, wait a minute." Herb held up his hand. "I don't ever go back on my word without good cause, and I haven't seen anything to make me do it yet. I asked you to stay and enjoy Christmas in Mullet Harbor. That's ten days out. Remy just wanted you to be aware that we're bringing in reinforcements. I'm sorry I scared you with my big mouth."

Remy stood and pushed in his chair. "Give Marielle more time to work her story. She tells me she's got other leads that show the judge hasn't given child custody to any family members in a while, and there's a reason. That should give us a favorable hand to play in case the chips don't fall our way. Unless there's a hitch, we'll meet after the holidays to see where we are. Meanwhile, let me get Isaac involved. Isaac will talk to Ephraim when he gets to town, and I'll talk to Marielle."

Herb took a large swig of his tea and sat down the glass. "It's settled then."

"No." Christian stood, still holding to Dylan. "I don't think it is. By tonight, everyone in town will have seen me and Dylan."

Rose shrugged. "That's the plan."

Christian widened his eyes. "No, the plan is for us to lay low. Working in the grocery store and out here is fine. But with your nephew watching, we don't want to be thrust center stage."

"Yes, you do." Rose didn't blink. "Didn't you listen to a word Remy said? If we're standing in front of you, the rest of the town will have your back. Full circle. You don't have to worry." She stood as if concluding. "I, for one, think Jacob's the one who needs to go to prison."

"Rose!" Herb scolded. "That's not nice."

"As I told Christian, I love the boy. But if he did or has knowledge of what Remy suspects, he's forfeited his right to his elected position, and he deserves to be imprisoned. The hypocrisy of trying others for crimes while he goes free …"

Remy sighed big as if the weight of the world pressed down upon him. "Rose, as I've said many times, I only have a gut hunch. I can't arrest someone for a crime—and one that involves my own family no less—without solid proof, especially when the suspect is the state attorney."

"I understand." Rose turned to Christian. "You aren't going anywhere. Do you understand me? You're safe here. No matter what. Trust us." She slipped her arm in Herb's. "You got time to walk an old gal back to work?"

Herb stared at Christian. "After hearing us out, are you

going to trust us?"

Dylan tilted his head back, staring up at Christian. He had to fish or cut bait here. Dylan needed to feel safe wherever he was even if Christian had a few concerns. "Can I speak with you?" he asked Kaylee.

Chapter Eight

From inside Herb's screened outdoor kitchen, Kaylee stared across the water at the blue heron stalking its prey in the mangroves.

Christian stood beside her. "How well do you know them?"

"I've been here since August. Since my arrival, I've met nearly every resident, even those who don't have a child in the school. They're a strange group of folks, but, Christian, there's not one that I wouldn't trust."

"You understand what's at stake here?" Christian asked. "I'm not worried about what happens to me. If so, I wouldn't have taken off with Dylan. He's never said what happened, but I made my decision when I saw new abrasions on his face—more than his mother's boyfriend caused. They can send me to prison for life so long as

Dylan doesn't have to go back there."

Kaylee sank into one of the cushioned chairs.

"So, tell me I can trust them with Dylan's safety."

Kaylee held out her hand to him.

He reached for her.

She grasped it and folded her other hand over his. "What I do know about this town is that they live by the town's motto. You have friends here, especially if Herb, Rose, Remy, and Isaac believe in you."

Christian closed his eyes looking for the clarity her closeness had pushed away. "Cassie and I grew up hard. I tried to keep her straight, but she never understood I had her best interest in mind. Dylan will live or die by what I say and do. I can't afford to let him down."

"Look at me," Kaylee said.

Christian opened his eyes.

"I'll stand in the middle with you. With the others in front and the town at our backs, I'm sure you'll be fine. But if anyone advances on Dylan, I'll die keeping him safe. But I can't do that if you and Dylan run."

Christian smiled. "Smart and stunning. I'm glad you're in my corner."

Stunning. Wow! The man had a way of making her knees weak even when she wasn't standing.

Herb exited his house, followed by the others, including Dylan. They made their way to the outdoor kitchen. "Well, boy." Herb opened the screen door. "I got things to do before the party. What's your decision?"

"Is Dylan okay with you?" Christian asked Kaylee.

"Oh, definitely. Dylan and I have some holiday decorating to do at the community center. When we're done there, we'll go to my house. Dylan can bring his party clothes and get ready there."

"I'd like you to join Rose and me here before the shindig," Herb said.

Christian touched his nephew's shoulder. "You know those clothes I never let you wear."

Dylan smiled and seemed much more at ease. Kaylee suspected Herb and the others had done a little reassuring.

"Dress up. As I recall, you're going on your first date." Christian laughed.

Dylan's smile faded. "That's not funny. She's a pest."

Christian shooed him toward the door. "Well, she likes you, and you're going to treat her nicely."

Dylan stomped toward the steps leading to the grass landing. He stopped halfway up. "You're going to do the same for Ms. Kaylee, too, right?"

Remy shot Christian a look, and Christian shifted uneasily.

"You listen to that boy. He's pretty smart." Remy laughed as he left them.

Rose and Herb followed the sheriff.

"You and Remy?" Christian stepped toward Kaylee.

"Me and nobody." Kaylee bit her lower lip.

"So, is it a date?"

She clasped her hands behind her back and swayed from side to side like a schoolgirl. "Me and you?"

He closed his eyes and took a deep breath. "Kaylee, tonight, yes. But you know the trouble I'm in, what they want me to do ..."

Kaylee shrugged. "We're not promised the next moment. So, let's take each one the Lord provides. Let's be friends. Friends can date. Look at Sophie and Dylan. They won't get married for, say, fourteen years at least."

"I heard that." Dylan jumped to the landing from the third step up, his clothes in hand. When he opened the screen door again, his eyes shined like Kaylee hadn't seen since his arrival. "This is going to be the best Christmas ever. I know it. I already don't ever want to leave."

The Mullet Harbor Community Center buzzed with activity. In the corner, stood a magnificent tree decorated in a fishermen theme with colorful ornaments resembling fish, coral, and other sea life. Glass fisherman floats, modified with bulbs inside them, hung across old weathered beams inside the center and across the dock.

When turned on, the place would be aglow in aquamarine backlighting.

From the moment Kaylee ushered Dylan inside, they'd been put to work. Tables had been decorated with white tablecloths and garnished with wreaths crafted from bits of driftwood and shells. After placing one in the center of every table, Kaylee was then charged with bringing out a cart with fifty different pairs of novelty salt and pepper shakers depicting Santa, Mrs. Claus, reindeer, and elves as fishermen, and sunbathers. The owner of the collection, Cora Arneaux, hobbled behind, keeping careful watch over Kaylee. Several times Kaylee moved to keep from getting plowed over by the woman's walker.

Kaylee straightened. "Ms. Cora, I'm afraid your feet are going to be too swollen for you to enjoy the party. Why don't you take a chair?"

The older woman looked down at her cardiac-sock clad legs poking out from beneath her Christmas muumuu, which sported dancing reindeer and jolly little elves. Kaylee could imagine the sweater Ms. Cora would wear later.

Cora looked up, her eyes gleaming bright like a child who'd been told a special story. She'd obviously forgotten Kaylee's warning. Too soon, though, Ms. Cora's gaze took on that vacant look that was becoming more and more evident, and her smile faded.

Kaylee forced a smile into place. "You look lovely."

The smile returned, and the woman continued to follow Kaylee from table to table. Thank goodness, they were nearly finished.

Isaac met them at the end of a row of tables. "Momma Cora, you shouldn't be up on your feet. Let me grab Sophie. I think a nap before the party will do us all good."

As the primary caregiver of a woman with Alzheimer's and a rambunctious daughter, not to mention the shepherd to a church full of quirky characters, the man probably didn't get a lot of rest. Remy helped out all he could. The sheriff once told her that he'd offered to put his mother into assisted living, but Isaac had promised Sidalee they'd keep her at home.

Sidalee had been the victim of a hit-and-run accident, the crime still unsolved. With his responsibilities at home, Remy had related that Isaac had no time to come to terms with the loss of his beloved wife, nor had Remy the time to contemplate his great loss. And Sophie still grieved. Her clinging to Dylan was a result of that grief.

Kaylee offered Ms. Cora her biggest smile. "I can't wait to see your Christmas sweater. I've heard a lot about it."

Ms. Cora's winning smile broke through. She giggled and nodded, following after Isaac.

Isaac mouthed his thank you as he moved to where the

children had been put to work preparing the plastic eating utensils and placing them into baskets. Another crew would set up the buffet tables that lined each side of the large center.

He returned a moment later. "Dylan's on his way. He's finishing up the last of the work."

"Bye, Ms. Kaylee." Sophie waved with enthusiasm.

Ms. Cora waved at Kaylee. "You be a good girl, Sidalee."

Kaylee's gaze collided with Isaac. She'd seen pictures of Isaac's wife. Short of dementia, Kaylee would never be mistaken for Isaac's beautiful Cajun bride. Ms. Cora's confusion and languishing in the past had to break the man's heart.

Isaac lowered his head. "Come on, Momma."

"See you soon, Ms. Cora," Kaylee said again.

Isaac stepped beside the woman who shuffled with her walker. Sophie followed after them, patient with her grandmother's slow movement—such a stark contrast from the little one who bounced from one thing to another, almost as if at her age she used the time to keep thoughts of her mother at bay. "See you tonight, Dylan." She waved.

"See ya." Dylan waved and met Kaylee at the last table. "May I take the cart back for you?"

"I'd like that, and then I think we'll follow Sophie's cue and go home. I have something I'd like you to do for me."

Dylan nodded. "Sure. What is it?"

"Oh, you'll see, but if you do it for me, I'll cook your favorite dinner—whatever it is—before we come back here to the party."

"Aren't we eating here?"

"Humor me, okay? I have some insider information. You might be thanking me after the party for the meal I'll prepare. Besides, eating a little earlier will give us more room for Ms. Abigail's wonderful dessert. She's the best baker in Mullet Harbor. For every holiday party, her cake is a secret until the reveal, and she creates magic. You should have seen the ones she made for Labor Day and Thanksgiving."

Dylan didn't seem impressed, but she was sure he would be once Abigail showed off her talents. Baking was one thing Abigail focused on without trouble. Other times, her flightiness could drive one insane.

Dylan wheeled the cart into the kitchen and returned a moment later.

Kaylee waved her good-bye to a few stragglers who were still "making perfect" for their Christmas party volunteer shift.

Stepping out of a large venue decorated for Christmas and into the hot South Florida sun was a rude awakening. Would Christmas be Christmas without cold weather or snow?

Kaylee frowned. Christmas would be perfect because her mother wouldn't be a part of it. Kaylee could breathe. There would be no formal parties to attend, no politicians to schmooze, no pesky lobbyist, no agenda. Her mother did always make Christmas a wonderful time for Kaylee, but while Mother loved the formal parties and the socializing, Kaylee preferred the quiet informal celebrations the family shared at home.

Kaylee laughed at the thought of the dinner she would cook for Dylan and Christian versus the buffet of food that would be served at the party.

Dylan stared up at her as if she'd gone crazy. "Did I do something?"

"What?" She widened her eyes, afraid she'd offended him. "Oh, no."

"Why are you laughing?" His voice fell, and he didn't look her straight in the eyes. This child had deep emotional scars. Kaylee could almost see him bleed the pain.

She stopped and faced him. "Oh, honey, I was thinking about the buffet dinner. I have a very formal mother, and she isn't with me this year. I was imaging the look on her face if she attended this party."

Dylan nodded his understanding.

"You're not off the hook yet, though. I'm going to be laughing at you later, but you'll know why." She tilted her head sideways and put her finger to her chin. "Or maybe you and your uncle might surprise me, and you'll laugh at me."

"You're not making any sense." His clipped words showed his remaining lack of trust.

"I bet I will later."

A sportscar came into view, its driver turning into the center's circular drive. "There you are." Jacob Marin pulled beside her and stepped out.

She shivered despite the heat.

He must be the reason her mother had not called. She'd sent Jacob to find her. Of course, that was only a conspiracy theory.

"Were you looking for me?" Kaylee asked.

Dylan slipped behind her.

Jacob leaned to look. "You must be Christian's son?"

Dylan didn't answer.

"We're on our way to rest and get ready for the party." Kaylee pushed past Jacob. "Did you need to see me?"

"No."

Kaylee turned, and Dylan ran into her.

Jacob smiled. "I wanted to see you. I hoped we could have a late lunch while I'm here."

"I'm sorry." Kaylee moved away from him. "I guess you haven't spoken to your aunt. We had lunch at the mayor's before coming here to decorate."

Jacob lost his smile. "I did see Aunt Rose. She didn't tell me. In fact, she gave another reason entirely for skipping her Canasta date with the gals."

"She's a woman of secrets, that aunt of yours."

Jacob nodded and stood for a long moment as if contemplating his next words.

"I'll see you," Kaylee offered, fending off any illusion that Jacob might have of dating her.

Jacob stared down at the boy at Kaylee's side. "Be careful. You never know who might wander into Mullet Harbor on any given day. This place used to be an outpost for some nefarious folks."

Dylan straightened and stood beside her. She reached down, held to his hand, and squeezed. "Your aunt shared with me that members of your own family were among the nefarious. Good folks live here now."

"Why don't you let me drive you home?" he asked.

No way would she get in his car. Nor would she place Dylan inside. She'd never thought Jacob a danger to her—a nuisance, maybe even a spy for her mother—but now, she sensed something about him she didn't like. Perhaps the lunchtime discussion had amped up her suspicions.

"We're good, but thank you, though."

Jacob turned toward his car. "You know, if you didn't listen to my aunt so much, you might see that you and I could have a good time together."

Now, Kaylee straightened. "I'm not looking for a good time, Mr. Marin."

Jacob nodded, his smile gone, and ducked into his fancy car. He peeled out of the driveway.

"Glad he's gone." Dylan's words mimicked Kaylee's thoughts.

Chapter Nine

Christian walked the sandy path, following the directions Herb had written down for him. Kaylee's place was remote, and he wondered that she didn't fear being out here alone. If he didn't break into civilization soon, he'd get a little nervous.

He turned a corner, and a dock stretched in front of him. Her home sat on a pier twenty yards into the water.

"Ms. Kaylee!" Dylan's voice rang through the darkening surroundings. "The sun makes the trees beyond it look like a painting."

Christian hurried his steps. He didn't see Dylan, but the dock circled the house. He approached the back from the right side. Dylan and Kaylee sat in chairs. They both had their feet propped up on a railing.

"Gosh," Dylan breathed. "I ain't never seen anything

like that."

"Excuse me?" Christian cleared his throat.

Dylan sat straighter. "I mean, I've never seen a sunset like this. Look, Chris."

He pressed a hand down on Dylan's hair as he passed. Then he stood at the railing. He never thought you could actually feel a stare upon you, but Christian sensed Kaylee watching him.

Beyond them, the overly large, orange ball slipped into the Gulf of Mexico. Christian held his breath for a long moment then turned to lean against the railing and peer down at Dylan. "I ain't never seen anything like that either." He winked.

"English major?" Kaylee asked.

He clenched his teeth, took a deep breath, and released it slowly. The admission was bound to hurt, but he owed it to her. She'd been a godsend to him "Once upon a time."

"Once upon a time." Kaylee looked away. "Those words most often come with a wonderful tale of tragedy and triumph."

Only tragedy, but he wouldn't say so. She didn't need to hear his woes. The ending was yet to be written, but time was against him. If his sister couldn't intervene and help him soon—or worse, if she died—he was sure his story would end with the once-English-professor doing time in federal prison for kidnapping a child and taking him over several state lines.

"Once upon a time, there was a little boy who stayed with an evil schoolteacher." Kaylee stood and stretched. "She forced him to do lessons, and he seemed to enjoy them. She suspected that his ploy was to make the teacher believe he liked the work, but everything she gave to the little boy was done quickly and accurately, making her think they bored the little boy. But the evil schoolteacher did grant the little boy whatever he wanted for dinner. In choosing his wish, the little boy showed true valor by stating that he wanted her to serve his uncle's favorite dish." She turned those gorgeous blue eyes in his direction. "You've done so well with him. He's a very smart boy."

"Guess what we're having for dinner." Dylan bounced out of his chair.

He hadn't even noticed, but now the aroma of garlic and oil tickled his nose. "Spaghetti?" Christian raised his brows.

"Spaghetti." Kaylee laughed, and it rang through the air like a tune played against fine crystal. "And salad and garlic bread. The making of the meal has transformed evil schoolteacher into a wicked cook."

Her choice of words brought a laugh out of Christian.

"Good wicked," Dylan announced, his face beaming. "Right, Uncle Chris. That's your favorite meal. Mom used to say you loved it."

Cassie had remembered something about Christian. That was encouraging. His sister usually thought only of herself and her own wants and desires, not that she received very many of them. She always settled for less than her dreams.

He shook the thoughts away. "That's right, and I'm starving, my favorite nephew."

Dylan scrunched his face. "I'm your only nephew. Ms. Kaylee let me choose dessert."

"Let me guess," Christian teased. "Baked Alaska?"

"Huh?" Dylan shook his head as if clearing the cobwebs. "No. I don't know what that is. Brownies ... Ms. Kaylee's special recipe. They didn't come from a box."

"Are you sure about all this?" Christian took in the beautiful blonde. "He's been in your hair all day. You must be tired."

"Have you forgotten?" She turned from him and moved to the french doors that opened into her house from the back dock.

"The party, Chris. We're supposed to go," Dylan said.

"No. I didn't forget." He made a face for his nephew and looked at his wrist to take in the time before he remembered he'd traded it for meals for him and Dylan over a week ago.

"We have time to eat and for Dylan to change before we walk to Herb's."

"Isn't it a buffet?" Christian asked. "Herb did tell me to save room for some local flavor. I don't think I can eat two meals."

"The local flavor is why you'll appreciate this meal." Kaylee winked at Dylan and then moved into her kitchen, plating the spaghetti and topping it with sauce. Then she pulled sliced garlic bread from the oven and placed it onto a plate. Salad bowls with fresh lettuce, onions, carrots, and tomatoes already graced the table.

Christian stared for a moment, swallowed hard, and turned away. He cleared his throat and ran a hand across his eyes before turning back.

Kaylee stared at him.

"It's been a while since I've had a sit-down dinner prepared especially for me by a lovely woman." He stepped around her, lifted two of the plates, and placed them on the table.

When he looked up, Kaylee's gaze still rested upon him. She placed her palm to her cheek as if she'd received a treasured kiss.

Dylan scooted out a chair and sat, breaking the spell the woman cast over Christian.

He cleared his throat and narrowed his eyes at his nephew.

Dylan stood as non-verbally directed.

Kaylee filled three glasses with ice and poured tea over

it. She replaced the pitcher in her refrigerator. "Mullet Harbor etiquette lesson number one: never specify sweet or unsweetened tea. Only diabetics have that privilege. In Mullet, all tea is sweet. I confirmed with Dylan that you're not diabetic."

He didn't like sweet tea, but he'd never tell her, not after her kindnesses. Besides, he'd taken a glass from Rose earlier. He guessed he'd get used to the taste if they stayed much longer. "What do you think Herb's up to asking us to meet him at his house?"

"Herb has a surprise around each corner. If Herb is ever up to anything, I've learned, it's nothing but good." Kaylee lilted her hand on Christian's arm. "Relax," she whispered the words as if she thought the sound would massage his taut nerves. "All Dylan lives for is to see you smile."

He looked away, but his smile came despite his best efforts to hide it.

He pulled out the chair for their hostess and waited for her to sit comfortably before allowing Dylan to sit and then sitting himself.

He guessed they were going to a Christmas party whether he thought it best or not. By the end of the evening, he was sure of two polar opposite thoughts: he'd be known by everyone in town, and he'd be glad he went.

Kaylee sat in Herb's massive living room. Herb had sent Christian and Dylan to their rooms for surprises he had waiting there.

The mayor came from the kitchen and handed her a drink complete with a cocktail umbrella. She sipped the coconut and pineapple concoction and deemed it as delicious as all of Herb's other non-alcoholic smoothies.

"You look beautiful," he said.

"Thank you." She ran her hand over the silken fabric of her red dress. The crinoline made it puffy, but she liked to occasionally dress up. That's why she'd brought such a garment to the backwater swamp. "Where is Ms. Rose?"

"She'll be here in just a bit." He stood at his floor to ceiling window, and for the first time, Kaylee got a full look at the man's attire. She lowered her gaze and bit her lip.

Herb wore a black tuxedo and sported a red bow tie. He looked sharp from head to ankle. But his feet were clad in his signature flip flops. These were not the new fancy type. No. They were the ones she'd seen in magazines from the sixties and seventies. This pair was black-trimmed, but the rubber he stood on was white.

"I see you trying to keep from laughing." Herb caught her attention.

Her cheeks warmed. She stood, leaving her drink on the coaster on the table in front of her, stepped toward him, and planted a kiss on his cheek. "You are a character, and I have grown to love and respect you."

He tilted his head with a smile. "Do you have grandparents?"

Kaylee stepped back almost as if he'd pushed a barrier between them. He hadn't meant to, but the subject was a sore one.

"Did I say something wrong?" he asked.

Kaylee turned her back on him. She lifted her drink from the table, almost wishing it contained alcohol. She sipped the fruity concoction and faced him. "My dad's mother and father died before I was born."

"And your mother's? What do you know about them?"

She focused on her drink. "I've asked. Mother told me they were as unimportant to her as she was to them, and I should thank her for keeping me away from them. I've always wondered if they would love me."

"Honey." Herb lifted her chin. His blue eyes twinkled. "How could they not love you? Even if they couldn't see you, you had to be treasured by them."

She pulled from his touch and nodded. "Thank you for saying that."

He cleared his throat, swallowed down his drink, and turned toward the stairway. "Hey, what's going on up there, boys?"

"We're looking stupid!" Dylan shouted back.

"Dylan!" Christian's warning was almost as loud. "We'll be down in a minute."

"What are you up to?" Kaylee laughed.

"About five-ten. You?" Herb winked.

Dylan ran down the stairs dressed in a nice blue suit, a white shirt, and a white Christmas tie with Santa's reindeer, including Rudolph, prancing on the print, their names on their collars. His feet were clad in shiny beige leather shoes. "I had to get ready twice," he said.

"Oh, Dylan—"

Christian stepped out. As he descended the stairs, he kept his gaze on her. "I was hoping to let you shine tonight against my jeans and scruffy shirt, but Herb had other ideas."

Oh my, did he look good in a gray suit jacket with a white button-down shirt—no tie—and navy pants. He also wore new beige leather shoes, a little darker than the ones Dylan sported. She started to speak but found no voice.

"You three, stand by the stairs," Herb commanded. He went into his den and returned with a camera.

Kaylee stood in the front with Dylan by her side. Christian stood behind, his hands resting on Kaylee and Dylan's shoulders.

"Smile like it's prom night, and you're taking your

kid," Herb teased.

Kaylee giggled and several clicks continued even after she'd turned to look up into Christian's hazel eyes. She got lost in their depths until Dylan, still performing for the camera, stepped on her foot.

"Okay." She held out her hand. "I'd say you've gotten more pics in these few seconds then I've had taken all my life."

A knock sounded on the door behind Herb. He opened it and nodded. "Time to leave."

"Ms. Rose isn't here," Kaylee protested.

Herb swept his hand toward the outside.

Kaylee widened her eyes. "You are so full of surprises."

A black limousine was parked in the sand and shell driveway at the foot of the landing below the curved staircases. Rose sat inside.

Christian leaned over her and laughed. "We've walked or taken a golf cart everywhere in this town. The community center is only three blocks away."

"The Mayor of Mullet Harbor must keep up appearances." Herb stood aside to let Kaylee exit first. "I won this coveted title by appearing to be a loon," he muttered as she passed.

Christian and Dylan followed.

Christian slipped his hand in hers as they made their

way down the steps.

"How'd he manage to know your sizes?" Kaylee whispered.

"He had more than one suit for both of us. Almost every size of everything, including shoes. Move over 'Most Interesting Man in the World.' Herb Miller has claimed your spot," Christian joked.

"Sophie's gonna laugh at me." Dylan trounced to the bottom of the stairs.

Kaylee straightened his tie. "Ms. Sophie is going to be as speechless as I was when I saw Christian. You two clean up right nicely."

The chauffeur opened the door as Herb joined them.

"And you're always stunning, but red is your color," Christian said as he waited for her to duck inside beside Rose.

Stunning. She'd only known the man two days now, and he'd called her *pretty, beautiful, lovely,* and twice in less than a day, he'd called her *stunning.* If he gave her another compliment like that, she wasn't sure she'd be able to tug her heart away from him without causing it to bleed.

Chapter Ten

Christian fidgeted in his suit, and Dylan wasn't fairing much better. That fact brought a smile to Christian's face. The entourage exited the limousine and approached the door of the community center.

The mingling crowd inside the decorated center came to a halt. Applause broke out, and Herb played down the town's affection for him.

Kaylee pulled aside Christian and Dylan, introducing him to as many people as possible before finding a seat.

"No, honey." A woman approached and took Kaylee by the arm. "Come, you three. Herb specifically asked that you sit at the table with him. We reserved a spot."

Christian raised a brow. Herb must want them seen. He pulled out a chair at the table for Kaylee where a place card with her name had been left. His card was beside hers, and Dylan's was across from him. Other than Rose and Herb, they were the only ones at the six-person rectangular table, but the room was large, and tables were arranged in lines to make seven rows with enough room for party guests to loiter in the aisles. Buffet tables filled to overflowing lined the walls on each side of the building.

Christian pointed to the illuminated bluish-green glass, each covered in fishing nets and dangling above them. "That's unique."

"Fisherman's floating glass," Kaylee advised. "A little nautical, a little fishy, but all Christmas." She leaned forward and picked up a saltshaker. Santa wearing a bathing suit. "They're all different. Remy's mother lets us borrow from her collection for every holiday celebrated. Believe me. They celebrate every official holiday as a town."

Rose joined them at the table, taking a seat beside Dylan and across from where the mayor would sit.

Herb climbed the steps to the stage, greeted the citizens of Mullet Harbor, and after asking a blessing for the event and the food, uttered a hearty amen, raised his hands, and declared, "Let's eat and get this party started." He hurried down the stairs, his flip-flops flapping, to applause from his constituents, all who appeared to love him.

Chairs scooted out from under the tables, and people

began to line up. "I'm too full from dinner." He faced Kaylee who'd stood.

"Christian, you have to at least try to pick out something, but only what you'll eat. I've been to several events. The ladies around here get their feelings hurt if you leave anything on the plate. I think they contemplated sending me back to Baltimore after Labor Day."

Rose leaned toward Christian. "Choose wisely," she whispered and shook a finger in their direction. Her ever-present bracelets jingled.

"What does that mean?" Dylan asked.

A little girl ran over from wherever she'd been sitting and grasped Dylan's arm. "Come on. Daddy says we have to wait for the old folks, but if we wait, as soon as the last one gets in line, we can be next."

Dylan shot a look of desperation at Christian.

"Dylan, aren't you going to introduce your friend? Sophie, I presume."

"Uncle Chris, this is Sophie Cooper. She's the one I've been telling you about." Standing behind the little girl, Dylan circled his fingers around his ear.

Christian sobered enough to let the boy know he was being rude and fought to hide his smile. "Miss Cooper, I'm glad to meet you. Thank you for escorting Dylan. If it's okay with your father, we'll make room here for him and your Uncle Remy to join us."

Sophie jumped up and down. "Let's go tell 'em, Dylan. Then we can get in line. Y'all might want to hurry so we can get in behind you, too." Sophie tugged Dylan after her.

Christian bent over in laughter. "Did she just infer that we're 'old folks'?"

"I think she did." Kaylee smirked.

"That little girl is something else."

"Oh, she's on her best behavior." Kaylee laughed with him. "We should get in line." She stepped closer to him. Her soft blond curls touched his chin. "Follow my lead."

"And Dylan?"

"He's on his own. And you are free to sample whatever you'd like. You might surprise me. But save room for Abigail's cake. We're all expected to support her, but if it is anything like her Labor Day, Columbus Day, Veteran's Day, and Thanksgiving masterpieces, that's not a hard thing to do."

"The town celebrates all of those?" Christian moved folding chairs in toward the table to clear a path for Kaylee. They stepped into line, and he spied Abigail who was five 'old folks' ahead of him.

"They're like a large family, and they fold you in and make you feel as if you belong. They live out the town motto, and no one is ever overlooked. It's refreshing, really." She waved and seemed the most assured he'd seen her since they'd met two days before. "I was kidding about my almost deportation."

Abigail left the buffet line and buzzed around the back. She started serving those who needed assistance, checking on the food supply, and keeping the drinks filled so that people could grab one as they moved past. "What's Abigail's story?" Christian asked.

Kaylee stared in the woman's direction.

"She's got a nice smile, and she's always polite," Christian noted. "I get the feeling she's shy if she can't be busy while with you, but Rose's nephew wasn't complimentary of her. Rose used up her Southern charm on her reply. And what's with the tiptoes."

"Abigail apparently took care of her mother and father until they died." Kaylee side-stepped around two women who were deep in conversation. "I don't want to gossip except to say that despite the town's efforts, her parents depended upon her to a great extent. Now, this part she told me, and I think it's safe to pass on because you'll see the proof for yourself. To pass the time, Abigail watched cooking shows, and she began to make cakes and offer it to the families who'd helped her and her parents. She told me once, cake-making became her ministry. She bakes all the wedding cakes in the harbor, cakes for every occasion—and she does it all for free. I've never asked her about the tiptoeing. I don't think she realizes she does it."

"All the baked goods in the businesses and Rose's bakery are made for free."

"No. The businesses pay her, but for events and special occasions for the residents, she won't take a dime."

Rose broke in line in front of Christian with a sweet smile that said she was entitled. "When Abigail's parents passed away, her sister, who, by the way, never bothered to help with their parents' care, came looking for the inheritance, and Herb had to step in. Everything was to be split between the girls. The older sister was always a money-hungry sort." Rose apparently had no problem with gossip, and Christian was all too eager to hear the story. "Herb bought the Brewster home and everything in it, splitting the proceeds between the sisters. Then he turned around and deeded everything back to Abigail. The sister got only half of the money, but Herb made sure Abigail never had to fear losing the only home she's ever known. She tried to pay him back for her half, but he wouldn't take it."

Christian looked around for Herb. The mayor stood at the end of the buffet table talking to folks as they left the line with their food. The old man lived both a pretentious and an enigmatic lifestyle. "He's something else, Kaylee. I've never met anyone like him."

They wound their way to the start of the buffet table where Remy stood with another man, plates in their hands.

Kaylee introduced the stranger as Pastor Isaac Cooper, Remy's brother-in-law and Sophie's father.

"Sophie told us you'd invited us to sit with you," Isaac said. "But we have Momma Cora settled. If you're up for her, Sophie would love to sit with Dylan."

Christian and Kaylee assured they would love to have the child join them.

"But we'll meet up later." Isaac scanned the crowd and waved.

Christian followed his gaze. Sophie and Dylan were in the opposite food line. He'd actually been so at ease with these people that he hadn't worried over Dylan's welfare. The boy was safer than he'd ever been.

"Are they okay by themselves?" Christian asked.

"Sure," Remy said. "Those ladies will make sure they take a kid-size portion, as always." He leaned over. "And they won't give them anything that they think they won't eat."

What was that supposed to mean? Christian shrugged off the man's cryptic comment.

The serving line moved quickly as people scoured the offerings from both sides of the buffet, which started with appetizers, soups, and salads. Christian quirked a brow at Kaylee. Had she been teasing?

Christian's stomach growled. Unbelievable, after all he'd eaten at Kaylee's. Maybe he was fortunate to have two meals. Besides, if the worse they did was serve hard-boiled eggs and not deviled eggs, he could live with that. He always enjoyed them with a little salt. He picked up one with a large scoop spoon, surprised to see the shell was still on it. How hard could it be to peel an egg? The salad offerings looked like everyday vegetables, except for the one that contained only leaf lettuce and green onions.

A man on the other side of the line heaped his plate with the greens. Then he spooned crumbled bacon over it. Christian decided he'd try it. What could go wrong with bacon? Then the man picked up a ladle from a pot on a burner. He poured a clear substance over the mound. Dressing? Christian would have to try it to see.

Beside him, Kaylee picked through a regular salad for a brief second before using the tongs in the bowl to place it on her plate. Then she moved forward, bypassing the soup.

As he looked into the bowls, he found that most of the soup offering was gumbo. Okra wasn't his cup of tea, but the chili looked delicious. He reached for a bowl and filled it full. Then he moved along, picking up chicken tenders and a hamburger patty before choosing corn, green beans, and some mashed potatoes. He was a guest, and he wanted to be sociable. A few of the ladies standing against the back wall smiled as he indulged.

When he happened to stand in front of Abigail, she looked at his plate and widened her eyes, but she said nothing.

Only when they'd gotten back to the table did he realize that Kaylee had only chosen the salad and vegetables, probably full from her great spaghetti dinner. He sat his food onto the table and pulled out the chair, waiting until she was comfortable to sit beside her.

Dylan arrived at the table, Sophie by his side. He started to pounce into his chair, but Christian cleared his throat. The boy moved to do as Christian was suggesting, but Sophie had already pulled out her chair and scooted forward.

Dylan sat. He looked at Christian's plate and then to Kaylee. A twinkle Christian hadn't seen in ages sparkled in his nephew's eyes. Kaylee kept her face turned from them for a long moment.

Sophie's plate had a little smattering of everything, but Dylan's plate was sparse.

Christian started with his salad. One bite in his mouth, he stopped before he chewed. He swallowed without a chomp. "Grease?" he whispered to Kaylee.

Blue eyes danced with glee. "Yes, grease. Melted lard, actually. They call it wilted lettuce."

"Wilted because of the grease, no doubt." He scooted it around. "They really do get upset if you don't eat it?"

"Well, they're polite about it, but you will offend some of these dear cooks."

"They didn't have turkey or ham," Dylan noted what Christian had failed to see.

"I suspect that turkey and ham and dressing are reserved for their family meals. At town functions, the citizens like to share unique family recipes handed down from generations of …"

"Rapscallions …" Christian muttered then forced down the salad. At least the chili would be good. He hoped.

Chapter Eleven

Kaylee hid her grin. Herb had shared with Christian the actual ingredients in the foods that Christian had eaten. The wilted lettuce had been the most benign. The turtle soup and possum burgers might be making a reappearance if the green tint of Christian's face was any indication. Kaylee had stopped him from cracking the egg on his plate, willing to incur the hurt feelings of the person who served the Hot Vit Lon. Christian had balked at her when she offered no reason. Then she explained that what was inside was not a boiled egg but a fertilized duck. Those needed to come with a warning on the buffet table.

Herb slapped Christian on the back as the older man moved onto the stage and took the microphone again. He only had to clear his throat for the clamor of voices to fall silent. "And now, the moment we've all been awaiting," he announced. "Abigail, would you like to do the honors?"

Abigail sat sideways in her chair, her ankles crossed and her hands folded in her lap. She uttered a squeak and gave her head a ferocious shake.

The crowd applauded and encouraged her to step forward.

Abigail continued shaking her head. She'd done the same at each of the events Kaylee had attended. Though the townspeople only meant to encourage, Kaylee could see the fear on Abigail's face.

Kaylee stood and placed her napkin on the table. She'd been a frightened little girl with a spotlight focused on her most of her life. Her high heels tapped on the community center's tile flooring as she made her way to Abigail. She leaned forward. "I'll stay right by your side."

Abigail darted her gaze from the stage and back to Kaylee.

"Let them show you their appreciation," Kaylee whispered. "They don't understand how scary it can be for some of us, but we can conquer this together."

Abigail hesitated only a moment. Then, with trembling hand, she reached out and held to Kaylee's as if clinging to a lifeline.

Kaylee led her up the stairs, pausing while Abigail's legs, supported on tiptoes, seemed to weaken. "They're all your friends. They love you."

Abigail gave a brief nod and stepped forward.

The residents of Mullet Harbor applauded, whistled, and called out niceties. A couple of the men wolf-whistled.

Abigail turned to look at Kaylee. The woman's face reddened.

Kaylee searched the crowd, and her gaze lighted on the sheriff who stared at Abigail as if mesmerized.

"Tell us about tonight's confectionery masterpiece," Herb said and stepped away from the microphone.

Abigail turned to Kaylee and whispered in her ear.

Kaylee smiled and stepped forward. "Abigail says it took the breath out of her to walk up the stairs, so she's asked me to speak for her. Is that okay?"

More words of encouragement rang out.

Abigail whispered to Kaylee again. Behind them, the stage curtain parted enough for two ladies to roll out a cart. A makeshift tarp covered the front of Abigail's cake, but from where Kaylee stood, she could see that Abigail's description wasn't apt for this audience.

Kaylee gasped at the intricacies of the cake. "Our esteemed baker has outdone herself, folks." She motioned for the ladies to remove the tarp. The cake was shaped like a very large wreath. Cookies adorned the green, curved cake bough. Each cookie was shaped to form replicas of Mullet Harbor's most notable locations: a sailboat in the harbor, the Fish Shanty, the community center, Herb's unique home on the lagoon, the mermaid fountain, and Herb's Queen Anne studio. In the center, separate from the wreath, Abigail had fashioned a replica of Mullet Harbor's only church building, which Kaylee never found much to look at, but the plain wooden structure looked perfectly in place.

Again, Abigail whispered to Kaylee.

"The church in the middle of the wreath shows that Christ should be at the center of all of our endeavors, no matter the time of the year."

Loud applause rang out. Abigail had to be overwhelmed by the outpouring of love. Kaylee definitely was.

Abigail gave an abbreviated curtsy to the crowd, embraced Kaylee, and hung on tightly. "No one has ever done what you've done for me. Thank you."

Kaylee shook her head. She'd done nothing but lead the woman on stage.

Now, she trailed behind Abigail as the woman scurried off the stage like a frightened tiptoeing rabbit.

People surrounded the baker while Kaylee made her way back to her seat. She, again, looked to where Remy sat, his gaze zeroed in on the baker.

Kaylee returned to her seat beside Christian. The moment must have erased his stomach's upset. He wore a grin.

Kaylee focused on Abigail, who stared back at Kaylee. Kaylee waved, and Abigail smiled.

She hadn't spent a lot of time with the baker, but Kaylee sensed that tonight would forge an awesome friendship. But why would such a small gesture bring about such a reaction?

The cake was cut, and volunteers rolled plates with portioned slices on a cart similar to the one Kaylee had used to place Ms. Cora's salt and pepper shakers on the table.

A murmur of happy voices filled the air. Kaylee leaned back, closed her eyes, and took it in.

She loved this place, its quirky people, even the heat so close to Christmas.

In the midst of her thoughts, another came unbidden. Her mother had not intruded on her perfect life at all except through Herb's innocent questioning about her grandparents. There'd been no phone call, only Jacob's earlier appearance.

Kaylee opened her eyes. The state attorney's report must have satisfied her mother. LeAnn McFarland could make her holiday rounds to whatever parties were being thrown by wealthy benefactors and know that Kaylee was safe in this little hamlet.

Kaylee was sure her mother was only days away from announcing her intention of running for Daddy's Congressional seat. The time for appearing to mourn had passed. All appearance of impropriety had been avoided. Surely, her mother had no reason to turn up here in Mullet Harbor.

"You okay?" Rose asked.

Kaylee nodded. "Just thinking of Ebenezer Scrooge."

Rose narrowed her eyes. "We don't let him visit here." She patted Kaylee's hand and pointed to the cake that one of the ladies placed in front of her. "Enjoy."

Christian and Dylan stared at their slices.

"Anything I should know about?" Christian asked.

"Just flour, real eggs, sugar, and all the good stuff that goes into baking a cake." Herb rejoined them, taking a large bite of his own piece.

Sophie took a bite of cake and "yummed" as she chewed. "Try it, Dylan."

Dylan did. "This is good."

Christian was a little more hesitant, but when he did, he rolled his eyes toward Heaven. "This woman needs a shop."

"We've tried to tell her that," Rose fussed. "Abigail can't handle the pressure of a business right now."

Kaylee focused on Abigail again. The baker sat straight-backed and staring at the uneaten cake on her platter. No wonder she stayed so wiry thin. She didn't eat her own creations.

Still, someone had to have enforced that lack of

confidence, and the champion in Kaylee wanted to punch that person in the face. Abigail finally lifted her fork and ate her dessert.

Remy approached Abigail, and she looked up, her face so red that Kaylee thought she would combust. The sheriff spoke to her for a moment, apparently complimenting the cake and the cakemaker.

Abigail fidgeted in her seat until Remy moved away.

Without a doubt, the sheriff had no idea how much that woman cared for him, and Abigail was blind to Remy's fascination with her.

Kaylee moved her attention to Christian as he leaned over Dylan and helped Sophie wipe the icing from her face. Such a tender gesture for a child he hardly knew drew Kaylee's heart to him.

Rose patted Kaylee's hand. "He's a good 'un, don't you think?"

The burn started in Kaylee's neck and went to the hairs on her head. She and Abigail had one thing in common. They were both infatuated with a man. Only Abigail's beau returned the feelings.

Christian found himself flanked in the corner of the community center by Remy, Herb, and Isaac Cooper.

"Was Dylan harmed in any way by the people who cared for him?" Surprisingly, the more intense interrogation came from the preacher.

"Pastor, he was harmed by his placement in an overcrowded foster home. Dylan did have some injuries, but he's never told me how he got them. I wish I could tell you the parents in the home were bad people so that it would justify my actions, but I can't."

"Dylan didn't complain?" Isaac Cooper continued his line of questioning.

"He wouldn't. I don't believe my sister ever laid a hand on him, but the last man she allowed in their lives sure did. He almost killed him, and Cassie's in a coma."

"If he wasn't in any real danger, why didn't you work through the system?"

Christian crossed his arms and took a deep breath. "The people running the homes don't have to be cruel. There are forces beyond their control. Kids who have been in the system for years become hardened, cynical. Dylan was only in there a few weeks, and I could see the changes in him."

"You could have trusted the Lord."

Christian bit his lip. Isaac was right, but he hadn't held that kind of faith since before Amy's death.

"Isaac," Remy spoke the pastor's name like a warning. "God has contingency plans for those of us who don't have your faith."

Isaac pushed his bangs from his forehead. The man wore his faith in his actions and his words. If Isaac hadn't been introduced to Christian as a preacher, though, Christian would have pegged him a surfer more at home on a beach than behind a pulpit.

"My sister and I were lost in that system, Pastor. I like to think I came out pretty well. My sister didn't. She never learned to make good decisions. She gravitated toward and eventually became one of those children that steal the light. If she wasn't going to be happy, no one would be happy."

"Perhaps the cynicism you see in your nephew was placed there by his mother. Maybe separation from his mom was for the best."

Herb remained silent. His gaze tripping from speaker to speaker.

"He wasn't taken away from his mother," Christian said through clenched teeth. "The system never saw fit to see his needs before he was attacked by the same man who could have killed her for all I know."

"Not dead. Still in a coma," Remy advised.

Isaac slumped, his resolute demeanor fading. "I'm sorry. I thought maybe the court had reasons before the incident to doubt his safety with family."

"That's just it," Christian said. "He should have been taken from her. I don't blame the system for my lack of interest in his well-being. I blame myself, and I tried to rectify it with the judge."

"A judge who's allegedly haunted by the deaths of three children he'd released to family. He hasn't allowed children out of the system and into the hands of willing relatives in any rulings for two years."

Marielle Arneaux had to be chasing that lead for her investigation.

Isaac shook his head. "Can't you see that the judge is trying to do what he can? He must be shell-shocked by the evil going on around him. How can you make decisions for a child from the bench? You have to know the people who claim to protect them."

"Or you trust a child." Christian looked to Herb as if he were the deciding vote in Dylan's fate. "Dylan begged the judge to allow him to come with me. You're right. He might be shell-shocked, but if so, he should have recused himself from those decisions. Dylan's seen a lot of bad. I only wanted to show him goodness."

"By breaking the law," Isaac challenged.

Herb raised his hand as if to silent that thought. "Boy, if Sophie had been taken away from you while you grieved Sidalee's death, and if a judge placed her into the system, you wouldn't break the law to free her?"

"I'd trust God."

Herb nodded. "No doubt you would."

"What's that supposed to mean?" Isaac countered.

"Only that trusting God in theory is a lot easier than trusting Him in the fire. I'm not saying we shouldn't or that you wouldn't. I'm just saying we don't always. Then there's that contingency plan Remy mentioned. Do you think God was taken off guard by Chris's actions?"

"No. God is always in the details."

"Then He's in the midst of this right now. Chris and the boy are here in Mullet Harbor where we boast that you can always find a Friend. You came up with that slogan, Isaac. The Friend isn't just a resident of this town. He's at the heart of it. I admit we're playing loose with the law, but Chris is under surveillance."

Christian bristled at the thought of being confined, even in such a lovely place as Mullet Harbor.

He looked through the crowd of town residents who mingled in groups, laughing and nodding and hugging each other, all making their way to the woman Kaylee had introduced to him as Cora Arneaux. Remy's mother, as predicted, had won the ugly sweater contest.

"He's living in my home. Remy's keeping an eye out for him and on Dylan. He's agreed to stay. We've promised to help. Things are in motion, and unless something blows our well-laid plans to smithereens, we'll get him through this, get Dylan in his custody, maybe even see Dylan's mom's recovery. We need to be in prayer."

"We've gotten Ephraim involved, too," Remy coaxed. "No one can say we didn't cover our bases."

Isaac narrowed his eyes at his brother-in-law. "You're risking your career and the career of my brother on a stranger."

"Jesus risked much more than that for you and me," Herb stated.

Isaac closed his eyes and seemed to take in the man's statement.

The air in the place grew heavy as Christian waited to see if he needed to duck, run, grab his nephew, and bust through the garage gate with his truck. "Please." The word fell out of his mouth without conscious effort. "All he wants is Christmas."

"His mother ...?" Concern for a woman Isaac had never met flowed through the pastor's words.

"He was allowed to visit her if his foster parents or I took him. He saw her before we left, but the parents in the home had no time. They said so. He's also hard-hearted toward her right now. Time and distance can soften him. Pastor Cooper, I've thought of running, but I couldn't do that to Dylan." He waved to where Dylan and Sophie played with a group of children. "I can't take this away from him. Can you?"

Isaac watched the children for a long moment while anxiety churned in Christian's gut like the homemade ice cream Kaylee assured him had been normal and wild-animal-free.

"Sophie would never forgive me, but I can't help but think that we're missing a variable here that could blow all of this out of the water," Isaac said.

Herb looked to someone in the crowd.

Christian followed the old man's gaze from a nicely dressed woman standing at the entrance then right to Kaylee.

Herb closed his eyes as if trying to clear away an image. He opened them, his gaze once again on the new arrival. "I may have found that variable."

"What?" Remy asked.

Herb rubbed his bearded chin with his thumb and forefinger. "Excuse me." He walked toward Kaylee.

Kaylee turned imploring eyes to him as he spoke. She peered around him to the door and startled.

"What's up with this?" Remy hedged closer to Christian. "Do you know what's going on?"

"No." But he recognized the woman.

"Maybe Herb sees what the rest of us see," Isaac said.

"Yeah, and what's that?" Christian challenged.

"That girl's infatuated with you, and if you scorn her intentions …" Remy had no need to repeat the proverb.

"We're friends, and Kaylee is too mature to think like that. She knows we have no future. We're from two different worlds." He looked back at the woman who still stood near the door. "And I don't know why it bothers Herb that she's here, but that's Kaylee's mother."

Kaylee and Herb moved to the table where they'd sat earlier. She picked up her purse, dug through it, then pulled out her phone. After looking at something on the screen, she paled and showed whatever concerned her to Herb.

Herb cast a wary look in Christian's direction before heading toward Dylan and bringing him back to the corner meeting hub.

Kaylee joined them.

Herb grabbed Christian's elbow. "A bomb of a variable has arrived, and we have to get you out of this party before it explodes."

Christian shook free. "What are you talking about?"

Herb nodded to the front of the community center where LeAnn McFarland stood. She was immaculately dressed in navy slacks and a jacket. Every hair on her head was in place, and she commanded attention.

"Take Dylan and go out the back door." Kaylee gripped his arm. "My mother's here."

"She doesn't know me."

"She doesn't have to know you. You know me, and that's enough for her to cause trouble, especially since you're the reason she is, no doubt, here. Please, leave." Without further explanation, and with stealth, she made her way through the crowd. "Mother," she called as she approached. With her hand behind her back, she motioned for Christian to move.

Christian headed toward the side exit with Dylan but stopped when he realized Herb wasn't behind him.

The mayor stood like a man frozen by fear, his attention riveted on Mrs. McFarland. Finally, he said something to Remy before heading toward Kaylee.

Remy came to them and hedged forward. "Let's get you back to Herb's place."

"I don't understand. How can I be the reason she's here?"

"I don't know, but Herb and Kaylee seem to think you are." Remy pushed open the door.

Christian looked back over his shoulder.

Kaylee's sad gaze was upon him, and Christian got the feeling she felt more trapped than he did at the moment.

Fay Lamb

Chapter Twelve

Christian opened the door to Dylan's room and peeked at the bed where the boy slept. Dylan had been deeply disappointed when he had to leave his new friends.

Christian closed the door and returned downstairs.

Herb made his way inside the house, locking the door behind him. He offered a curt nod to Christian, moved into his kitchen, and began pulling out fresh fruit, yogurt, and a jar of honey. "A smoothie smooths out the wrinkles in our day. Care to imbibe?"

"Sure." Christian pulled out a stool at the kitchen's island as Herb busied himself with the blender and the ingredients. Finished with the concoction, he poured it into two glasses. Tonight, he didn't offer an umbrella. "Here's to those who complicate our lives and make it a challenge." He raised his glass and clinked it against Christian's. "And for the moment, that person happens to be Kaylee's mother."

"You know her?"

"Yes, I do. She's the reason Kaylee's here in Mullet Harbor. I had to get that poor girl some breathing space. LeAnn's a micromanager, only happy when she's in control." Herb moved around the counter and pulled out a stool. "If she even gets a whiff that you're friendly with Kaylee, Jacob will be the least of our concerns."

Christian didn't like the implications. Kaylee McFarland was the best thing about Mullet Harbor, and she was a safe berth for Dylan while Christian worked.

"You need to keep your distance. Dylan can help you at the studio, and he can stay with me while you work for Rose. Kaylee wanted me to pass on to you that her avoiding Dylan is a safeguard for him. I guess that has to do with your earlier conversation with her."

"Wouldn't it be better if Dylan and I leave?"

Herb slapped his hand on the counter. "Bring it up again, and I'll march you right into Remy's custody. I thought better of you."

Christian bristled. "I'm trying to protect Dylan."

"But you gave your word to him. Now the going gets a little rough, and you're ready to break that promise. Isaac was right about one thing. We have to start trusting God because sooner or later, He's going to force our hand—for our own good. Let's make this our stand. Trust Him to protect you, whatever the outcome."

"I trusted Him once. He let me down."

"This about your wife?" Herb gave him a pointed stare.

Christian nodded.

"God doesn't let us down. I lost a wife, too. The love of my life. When she died, I found out how much I'd truly let my family down while chasing my dreams around the world." Herb stood and grabbed a framed photo from a table. He handed it to Christian. "My wife had many folks who loved her and who attended her funeral. The outpouring of compassion for me and grief over her loss was overwhelming. Yet her own child didn't so much as send flowers."

Christian stared at the photograph. He could have sworn he'd met Mrs. Miller somewhere before, but that was impossible. He handed back the picture. "She's gone. So how can you say God didn't let you down?"

"Because he didn't. He can't. He loves me. What we might perceive as failure, God declares is worked to our own good."

"I know that verse," Christian spat. "Some well-meaning person in my church quoted it to me as I stood by my wife's casket."

Herb winced. "Well-meaning and clueless as to the

appropriateness of time, but is God's word any less true when it doesn't make sense to us?"

Christian didn't need to think about that truth. "No."

"Then you need to trust that the reason your wife was taken is beyond your understanding. You have no idea what the future would have brought for her had she lived, but God did. If she was His, the loss was yours, but the gain was hers." He slapped his big hand on Christian's shoulders. "I had to learn to forgive myself for being the survivor. Then I had to forgive Lacey for leaving me. Only then did I look to Heaven and ask God to forgive me for thinking that He would be anything but good to her or for me. Every time I forget, I repeat these words, 'All things work to good for them who love the Lord ...' That's Romans 8:28 if you want to meditate on the principle. Trust God, no matter what."

Christian nodded. He finished his drink, washed his cup in the sink, then took Herb's empty glass from him. "The Lord and I were close once. My wife is the reason for my relationship with Him."

Herb nodded and moved to stand in front of the floor-to-ceiling windows to look out over the darkness.

Christian doubted the man could see anything in the inky blackness because the light shined so brightly inside. He looked at the framed photograph Herb left on the counter, and the truth hit him. "Does Kaylee know?"

Herb turned, his brows raised in question.

"That you're her grandfather?"

Herb laughed. "Where'd you get that idea?"

Christian shook his head. "Silly notion." He climbed the stairs.

"And one you're not going to share with the girl, you hear," Herb warned.

"Why would I share something neither confirmed nor denied?" Christian said before he closed his bedroom door.

If the mosquitoes wouldn't drive her insane, Kaylee would have sought sanctuary on her dock.

Abercrombie would make a better house guest than LeAnn McFarland.

Kaylee opened her refrigerator and looked inside for anything to eat that would quell her stress.

Mother pushed her fingers through the mess that upon arriving had been a stylish haircut. Hair spray, mousse, and whatever else held the woman's coif had been staunchly attacked by the swamp's humidity. Her mother huffed and pushed a wilted strand from her face. "I cannot believe you chose to remain here in this horrid place filled with inbreeds."

Kaylee slammed the refrigerator door shut and spun

toward her mother. "Not one more word about these dear people. I know they aren't your constituents. They don't offer donations to your causes or your candidates, but they are good and decent. If you dare disparage them one more time, you can find your way to the Harbor B & B, which will be more comfortable than where you're going to sleep tonight." She pointed to her sofa bed in the living room. "I would have made you a reservation had you bothered to warn me of your pending arrival." Better yet, she would have talked her mother out of the trip.

"How dare you talk to me in that tone. If I hadn't been worried about you, I wouldn't have jumped on a plane when you didn't answer your phone. I also wouldn't have scoured this swamp to find you at a Christmas party, and I definitely wouldn't have entered said party to be gawked at by those people."

"Jacob Marin didn't report my status?"

"He told you that?"

"So, you admit you talked to him." Kaylee shook her head.

"Yes, I do. Jacob and I have been communicating for some time. I donated to his campaign. He was my logical point of contact. I doubted the mayor would give me any information."

Kaylee should have known. Her mother had allowed her to wander away for a short while. Now, she was here to reclaim her hold. "You set up this job for me via a donation to Jacob Marin who recommended me, didn't you?"

Her mother gawked. "I most certainly did not. I'm surprised at you. The mayor set this up."

Kaylee stepped into the living room. "How did he know about me?"

Her mother shrugged and looked away. She was hiding something. Kaylee had seen her avoidance tactics often when Daddy had confronted her about finances. Dad might have been born into wealth, but he'd compounded it with his frugality. They lived better than ninety-nine percent of his constituents, and that was saying a lot, but he kept a tight hold on funds. Mother had her own money to spend from years behind the scenes in politics, and Kaylee had to admit that since Daddy had died, she had not been so free with her spending, as if afraid the family fortune would dwindle. But Christmas had always been a time when neither of her parents scrimped.

"Herb didn't arrange this with you?" Kaylee pressed.

"I hardly know the man." Mother shrugged.

Her mother didn't lie. That was the one part of her character, besides tenacity, that Kaylee admired.

"Hardly knowing the man means that you do know him."

"Yes, I know him. I don't like him, and I hate that you

hold him in admiration. He's a fake. So was his wife."

Kaylee jerked her gaze to her mother. "You knew Herb's wife."

Mother pressed her lips together. She nodded.

"Then you've known Herb for a while."

"Never said I didn't. Knowing someone long and knowing them well—two different things. Look. Let me shower and get the swamp off me." Her mother tamped down the lid on the conversation.

Kaylee gathered fresh towels and a washcloth.

While Mother showered, Kaylee pulled out the sofa bed and placed linens over it. Then she changed and crawled under the sheets.

Her mother returned, towel on head and wearing her silk pajamas. "I thought I was sleeping there."

Kaylee smiled. "You taught me better than that."

Her mother leaned down and kissed Kaylee's hair. "Thank you for being a gracious host."

Tears welled in Kaylee's eyes. Despite all her thoughts to the contrary, she'd missed her mother. "Thank you for worrying about me and wanting to spend Christmas with me."

Mother smiled. "I met so many of those people tonight. Who was the father of the little boy you're watching over?"

"He left, and you didn't meet him. I did get word to

him that I had a guest and wouldn't be able to babysit."

Mother made it to the hallway without a word. Then she stopped. "Well, if that's true, my arrival did serve a good purpose." She moved to the only bedroom in Kaylee's small, but unique home.

Why did her mother think she could run Kaylee's life? The thought infuriated her.

Once Mother closed the door, Kaylee got out of bed and grabbed her purse. She brought the phone back to the bed. She'd forgotten to take it off silent and thus the reason for the unfortunate turn of events. If Christian had a mobile phone, she could personally text and tell him she was sorry for what happened. Instead she'd had to rely on a third party.

She chose that third-party's number and sent a text: HOW DO YOU KNOW MY MOTHER?

Chapter Thirteen

December 16

A knock on his bedroom door awakened Christian. A creak and feet shuffling on the carpet announced Dylan's arrival.

"Wake up, Uncle Chris!" Dylan bounced on the bed.

Christian turned and wrapped the boy in his arms, playfully tossing him to the other side of the bed. "You dare enter my domain and awaken me from a sound sleep, yon pup."

Dylan giggled. "The king sent his royal page on a journey to wake the sleeping knight ..." He crinkled his nose. "... for church."

Christian looked at the clock on the nightstand: eight o'clock. He sat up and ran a hand through his still too long hair.

Dylan rolled off the bed. "Do we have to go?"

"Yes, we do, and you should think of it as a privilege. Our guest has invited us, and we will go—happily and with smiles on our faces."

"I don't know." Dylan slid from the bed. "Sometimes your manners get annoying."

Christian reached for Dylan before the boy could slip away. "Excuse me?"

"What?" Dylan sassed. "Why do we have to do everything they say? You don't have to work today. We can go fishing or something."

The boy's words sounded all too familiar, and ire long tamped down rose within Christian. "Would you rather I act like your mom who never acknowledged any kindness given to her? They've provided us with so much, and all we have to offer in return is thankfulness and being good guests. If you haven't noticed, your Christmas wish came true because of them. I won't tolerate your ungratefulness."

Dylan's eyes rounded, his lips puckered, and tears spilled.

Christian closed his eyes. "I'm sorry."

Dylan pulled his arm from Christian's grasp and, without a word, left the room.

The morning had started out well, and Christian had allowed the bitterness he had for his sister to overflow. He was angry at Cassie for always giving up, giving in, taking less than she deserved, and never being thankful for anything.

Christian expected his sister to give in now. He wasn't so unaware that Cassie would rather die than come back to them. She hated life, had never seen the good in it because she'd always settled for less rather than working hard to achieve. Drugs were a copout. Every new man she grabbed hold on was just another way of telling herself she wasn't any good.

Maybe it would be better if she never came back to Dylan.

As soon as the thought sprang into his mind, the emotions hit him.

He loved his sister. He didn't want her to die without knowing her worth—at least to him. Forget him. She needed to know her value to God.

The shame at throwing Dylan's mother's failures in his face fell over him. He needed to make things right.

A knock sounded at the door. "You up and decent?"

"Yeah, I am."

Herb stepped inside and hitched his thumb to the wall that abutted Dylan's room. "He okay?"

Christian bit his lip then shook his head. "No, I said something hurtful. I'll talk to him later. How are you with a pair of scissors?"

Herb brushed the long strands of curls that adorned his balding crown. "I cut my own."

Christian pushed from the bed. "Care to let me see how well you do before I let you cut Dylan's? I don't want to go to church looking shabby."

Herb motioned for Christian to follow him. "And both of you will find some church clothes in your dressers."

"You can't keep doing that, Herb."

"Indulge me. It's Christmas." Herb headed downstairs. "Now let me find that bowl I use when I cut my hair."

Christian laughed and followed Herb to the deck where Herb set a chair then grabbed scissors and began to cut Christian's hair without a bowl.

With each snip, Christian winced until Dylan joined them having already showered and dressed for church, his demeanor more pleasant.

"Will you cut mine, Mayor Herb?"

"Sure, kid. I'll do that while Chris dresses. We'll cover your clothes with a towel, though. Looking pretty sharp."

Dylan stared down at his tan dress pants and a light green button-down shirt and then to his brown loafers. Dylan glanced to Christian and then to Herb. "Thank you."

"You're very welcome." Herb patted Christian's shoulder. "All done. Want to go look before I start on him?"

Christian caught his reflection in the window. He

pointed to the glass. "Looks perfect from here. Thank you."

Herb nodded and motioned for Dylan to sit.

Christian went to his room. He opened the drawer to find several pairs of slacks. In the closet, he found three nice dress shirts. He went into the bathroom to shower.

With the warm water running over him, Christian bowed his head. He waited for the right words to come but only two resounded within him. "Help me," he whispered. Then the third fell into place. "Help me ... please."

Christian wiped the moisture from his forehead as Herb swung his fancy golf cart into a spot on the sand and shell parking lot of the Church of Mullet Harbor. The unpretentious building was unadorned by paint, its natural wood fitting well with its scrub pine and palmetto surroundings. Cars and other golf carts filled the parking lot. "Only church in town?" Christian asked.

Herb smiled. "There are other churches. Just not buildings for them."

"All as well-hidden?" There was a story here, and Christian wanted to hear it.

"If you haven't noticed, Mullet Harbor doesn't have a large population. This church building is the oldest and the only one in town. In the early days, Mullet Harbor was a refuge of another kind." He motioned around him. "A fort surrounded this place. Burnt to the ground by marauders who may or may not have had a rightful claim to the land. You'll find everything from arrow points to bullet holes in the wood. It's survived raids and criminal shootouts. It's even harbored slaves. We call it the Church of Mullet Harbor because there are other churches in town who don't have a building proper. Those churches meet in houses, in the park, even at the Fish Shanty. Sometimes, they borrow our building."

"So, do you have a denomination?" Christian asked.

Beside him, Dylan scuffed his new shoes against the shells.

Herb leaned and whispered in Christian's ears.

Christian feigned horror and laughed at the same time. "Oh, no."

"What'd he say?" Dylan stepped back as if he might be afraid to enter the building.

"They're Baptists." Christian gave a fake shudder.

Herb laughed aloud and slapped Christian's shoulder. "Yep. The worst of the worst. But we sure do like to eat. Come on. We're going to be late."

Christian pulled Dylan to him. "They're good people, Dylan." He winked. "Even if they are Baptist."

Herb continued to chuckle, and Christian was happy the old man knew the words were in jest.

"Aren't you a Baptist? Mom said you both were."

Ease wormed its way out of Christian's heart. He and Cassie had been bused to church every Sunday by the system, a deal made. They'd spent summers at a Baptist camp for orphans—perhaps the best times he could remember. As far as he knew, though, neither one of them had garnered anything spiritual from their early Christian interactions.

Herb stood at the church's door without opening it, his ears perked toward Christian.

"Your mom and I attended Baptist services as kids, but your aunt and I attended a non-denominational church, which ministered to the university and its students."

"So are you allowed to go here?" Dylan hesitated.

"God doesn't care what you call yourself so long as you call yourself His." Christian's heart ached. He'd been trying to fill a void for his nephew that could only be filled by Christ. He blinked, hard, against the emotions stirred in him—God was working even before Christian entered the sanctuary.

He shouldn't be angry with his sister. He should be concerned about her. If she did give up and die …

If something happened to Dylan …

"The answers are inside." Herb spoke in a soft voice as if he'd known where Christian's thoughts had skyrocketed.

Dylan scratched his head and gave it a little shake, but when Herb opened the door, the boy stepped inside.

The interior was not what Christian expected. White walls illuminated by bright lights created a comfortable feel. Chairs with red cushions formed rows on each side of a wide aisle. A pulpit set upon a stage two steps higher than the chairs. Behind it was a wall with an opening in the back that housed the baptistery. Men and women stood behind the pulpit, dressed only in their Sunday finery. The choir without choir robes. Christian recognized two members: Rose and Remy. Isaac stood to the side, a guitar in hand. And Abigail Brewster fidgeted as she sat at an upright piano off the raised platform. He chuckled. That shy woman hadn't ceased to surprise him.

"Ms. Kaylee!" Dylan left Christian and ran down the aisle to meet her. The boy's cry echoed Christian's thoughts, and he followed Dylan with his gaze.

Kaylee stood some distance away, her mother beside her.

Herb turned to plaster Christian with a wide-eyed stare. Only then did he remember that they needed to be cautious around Mrs. McFarland.

Christian tried to reach Dylan, but the boy had made it to where the two women stood.

Kaylee bent down and wrapped Dylan in a hug, but the look she sent to Christian had a very clear message: stand back.

Kaylee's mother smiled and spoke to Dylan, who nodded at whatever the woman said. Mrs. McFarland reached into her purse and presented Dylan with what looked like a peppermint.

Dylan's thank you reached Christian's ear before Herb snatched at Christian's arm and moved him around the back of the chairs and to the opposite side of the church.

"She doesn't seem all that bad," Christian said. "She was kind to Dylan."

For a few moments, Christian and Herb shook hands with people who gave them warm salutations for the morning. Dylan managed to find them and plopped into a chair beside Christian.

The boy had already unwrapped the candy and popped it into his mouth. "Ms. Kaylee's mom is nice." His teeth clicked against the candy as he spoke.

Herb offered only a nod before the music started.

Christian tugged Dylan to his feet in front of his chair.

Abigail and Isaac Cooper played well together, and the choir was practiced and ready for worship. Christian enjoyed listening to them, but a sweet soprano standing in the audience, her voice lilting above the others, caught his ear. Kaylee, her eyes closed, her head pointed to the heavens, sang with abandon.

LeAnn touched Kaylee's arm.

Kaylee startled and opened her eyes.

LeAnn shook her head.

Kaylee stopped singing through the chorus. Her lips began to move through the next verse, but Christian could no longer hear her beautiful voice.

He turned to face the choir.

Rose's glare focused on LeAnn, and Christian sent up a silent prayer that the two women would avoid each other through the remainder of the service.

In the middle of the last congregational hymn, the choir stepped down and took their seats throughout. Abigail played a beautiful rendition of a classic hymn during the offering.

Christian had separated his tithe from what he had been paid. He slipped it from his well-worn wallet and dropped the bills inside.

Dylan peered up at him, a question formed in the tilt of his brows.

Christian leaned toward him. "It came to us from Him. We give back a portion of what He's given us."

Dylan remained silent as Pastor Cooper moved to the pulpit. The pastor read out of Numbers about the cities of refuge that Israel was to designate within its lands. At first, Christian expected the message to be directed solely at him. As the preacher continued, though, Christian found that God must have prepared the message for this day, not at

Christian, but for him. No, he hadn't murdered anyone, but he was seeking sanctuary in a city that offered it to him. Unlike the persons who may have killed someone without meaning to take a life, Christian had absconded with Dylan—to save his life. Maybe not physically but definitely mentally and emotionally. And Mullet Harbor had offered sanctuary.

He was ashamed at the thoughts of leaving, of not trusting God.

This message, one Isaac said came in the middle of a twelve-part series, which would be only interrupted by a Christmas message he had planned—"the Lord willing"—for the following Sunday, had to have been prepared far in advance of Christian's stumbling into this harbor of refuge. God had Christian here for a purpose.

And Christian had never felt safer in his life.

The shuffling of chairs and the voices lifted in song clued Christian into the fact that God had so captured his attention through Isaac's sermon that he'd been sitting before the throne, casting prayers, seeking forgiveness for himself and begging God to heal his sister.

Christian chanced to look to where Kaylee stood. Her mother had succeeded in continuing to stifle Kaylee's beautiful voice.

And that made Christian sad.

Kaylee remained by her mother's side, introducing her to the dear people who'd not met her the night before. She sent up a silent prayer that her mother would continue to put on her Congressional-wife's cloak and remain polite to those who wanted to welcome her to the church and to the town.

Mother had muttered against the scrub and pine lined road, against what she called the ghastly appearance of the old building, and against the informality of the chairs versus pews used by the church. The pastor was too young, the choir too underdressed. Nothing suited her.

Her displeasure included Kaylee's joy at lifting her voice in song to the God of Heaven and Earth. Mother always said she had a beautiful voice, but she'd sternly discouraged Kaylee from singing too loudly or performing in any venue, especially church, as if the mere thought of it was beneath the McFarland name.

Rose scooted her way around the people in the aisle. "Kaylee, we missed your beautiful accompaniment from the pew this morning." She grasped Kaylee's hand.

"Pew?" Mother *pffted*.

The squeeze of Rose's hand was the only hint that she had heard. "I do wish you'd reconsider and join the choir."

"Surely not." Mother balked.

"Surely why not?" Rose released Kaylee's hand. She crossed her arms over her chest. "She has a naturally beautiful voice, and if she feels the Lord calling her to use it to worship Him, she should."

Kaylee pressed a smile into place. "I'm still praying about it."

Mother pushed her nose upward. "Get yourself tangled up in church nonsense, and you'll never get free."

Rose clenched her teeth so hard, Kaylee imagined she could hear the grinding of Rose's teeth and the pop of her jaw when she opened her mouth to speak. "Excuse me."

"Ms. Rose." Kaylee reached for her friend, but Rose moved too quickly.

"Hello." Isaac approached. "We met briefly last night, Mrs. McFarland. I'm glad you could join us today."

"Thank you, Reverend." Mother held out her hand. "My pleasure."

Liar. Kaylee bristled. Her mother had wanted to do anything but attend church with her this morning and only gave in when Kaylee assured her that she would do nothing until after church. Her mother could join her or not.

"I'm sure Kaylee's glad you could be with her." Isaac caught Sophie as she ran to him, clasping him around his legs. Well-mannered, the child remained silent as the adults continued to converse.

"Aren't you a cute one?" Mother bestowed a smile.

"Your daughter?" she asked Isaac.

"Yes, ma'am. Sophie say hello to Ms. Kaylee's mother, Mrs. McFarland."

Sophie peered upward. "Hello."

"Hello to you, too." Mother beamed. "I love your dark curls." She brushed Sophie's hair. "You must look like your mommy."

Sophie didn't speak.

Isaac patted her shoulder. "Dylan's here. Did you see him?"

Sophie almost hopped as she looked around.

"Find him. Maybe he'd like to join us for lunch. We can walk him home afterward. You can ask his dad."

"Thank you, Daddy." Sophie skipped away.

"I hope I didn't say anything out of turn." Mother had apparently picked up on the tension.

"No, ma'am. The question is perfectly understandable. Sophie looks exactly like her mother. We lost her not long ago. Sophie can only learn how to handle these situations if she's faced with them. And yours was very kind."

Mother nodded. "All the same, I never want to hurt a child's heart." Her gaze settled across the church. "They don't mend too easily."

Mayor Herb must have felt Mother's attention upon him. He looked up from a conversation with Christian and Remy. Then he began to walk in their direction.

"I think we should go." Mother stepped away, and Isaac nodded as he passed Herb.

Kaylee stood her ground.

Mayor Herb kissed Kaylee's cheek. "It's always good to see you on a Sunday morning. I wasn't sure we would today. Good morning, LeAnn."

Mother stared without speaking.

"Little Sophie asked Dylan to join him for lunch. I think I'll dine out with Rose. Do you have plans?"

"Yes, we do," Mother answered for her. "I'd like to spend precious time with my daughter. I haven't seen her in a long while, as you are aware."

"Yes, I am. And it has been my experience that our children have a mind of their own, and most parents allow their adult children to do as they please, even if what they do doesn't please them."

"Some never spent enough time with their children when they were young to know what pleases them," Mother countered.

Keeping up with the verbal and emotional ping-pong between these two would bring on a migraine if Kaylee wasn't careful. She raised her hand in answer to a covert wave from Christian and wished more than anything that her mother had not arrived in Mullet Harbor. Kaylee wanted to get to know this man, to be of assistance to him, and more than anything, she wished her mother would stop making decisions for her.

She shook herself from her useless desires. "Mayor Herb, did you get my text message?"

He nodded. "I did. We'll talk soon."

Kaylee nodded. "Have a nice lunch." She started away, not caring whether or not her mother followed.

Outside, she scanned the endless blue sky and enjoyed the warmth.

"The nerve of that man," Mother mumbled as she made her way toward her rental car.

Kaylee bit down on her lower lip to hold back harsh words. She sat in the passenger seat and stared out at the scrub and pine her mother abhorred.

Mother started the car and backed out of the parking lot. "That little boy, Dylan, and the girl, they're adorable."

As a politician's wife, her mother had always doted on children, but could that attention have been something less superficial? Kaylee pushed her train of thought on a new track and worked to shift it to the right words. "You're really good with kids."

Mother smiled. "I love them. Always have."

Then why hadn't she, as LeAnn McFarland's only child, been given a hint of the love her Mother had shown for the two children who were strangers to her? Mother's love for her ran hot and cold with Kaylee's fondest memories being those created around Christmastime. But those happy memories had not been enough to make her want to spend the time with her mother this year.

She still needed room to breathe.

Fay Lamb

Chapter Fourteen

December 17

Monday morning, Christian took note of the dark skies that had gathered over the harbor during the night and had failed to move on as a cold front stalled. He'd stepped outside thinking that the temperatures would have dropped significantly. Only a hint of coolness lingered. The weather report he'd watched indicated highs in the upper 70s, but a little cooler weather was expected for the holidays. Christian had almost spewed his coffee when the guy made a big deal about fifty-degree temps. Then Christian had thanked the Lord for his provisions. Fifty degrees could get a little chilly in the cab of a truck sleeping at an overnight rest stop.

Herb had left the home after dishing out a hearty

breakfast. Christian overheard him muttering something about safe distances and a conniving woman as he stomped down the concrete steps, his trademark shoes flapping as he went.

Dylan kicked at a stone as they walked from Herb's home to his studio.

"We need to hurry, or we're going to find ourselves in a downpour." Christian picked up his speed.

Dylan abandoned the rock and hurried to catch up. "I don't understand why I can't hang out with Ms. Kaylee."

Christian bit his tongue. How often had he wished that Dylan would act like a child his age? This was what he'd hoped to see.

"Uncle Chris …" The boy whined and bent forward, walking as if he carried a great burden on his back.

"You like Ms. Kaylee, huh?"

Dylan straightened and rolled his eyes. "Duh. She's nice. We were going to go fishing."

Christian pointed to the dark blue cumulonimbus clouds that threatened to drop rain on them at any second. "Not today even if the clouds do roll by. Dylan, it's simple. Her mother came for an unexpected visit. She needs to spend time with her."

"She could ask her mom to fish with us. I met her yesterday. She's really nice."

"She hasn't seen her mother since before school

started this year."

Dylan stared straight ahead. His silence boomed his answer inside Christian's head. Dylan hadn't seen his mother in that long either. They might never see Cassie alive, and if she were to die, alone in that hospital, Christian had no way short of giving himself up, to assure that his sister received a proper burial. He'd like to think that Cassie would agree with him that keeping Dylan safe was more important. Truth was, Christian doubted that the boy had ever been Cassie's first concern.

Dylan picked up the stone and threw it with all his might. His face hardened as he walked in silence beside Christian.

The apology owed his nephew weighed heavy on Christian's heart where it would have to remain. Now, didn't seem the time.

They rounded the curve and approached the town's only intersection. Rose's market sat directly across from them. They walked past it, down the oak-lined lane, and onto the cul-de-sac.

A narrow road between Herb's studio and one of the bungalows led to the Mullet Harbor Bed and Breakfast. That's what Herb had said. Christian hadn't had time to check it out.

A fat drop of rain fell, and Christian hurried across the empty road, Dylan right behind him.

A car sat in front of Herb's studio.

Christian led Dylan onto the porch with its welcoming swing where Christian had learned customers and locals loved to loiter.

Raindrops on the home's tin roof and the others around it brought music to the morning.

Christian used the key Herb had given him. Then he followed Herb's careful instructions on brewing the coffee in the homey kitchen and placing Abigail's pastries on the table.

Dylan stayed right at his feet like an antsy puppy. He headed around the corner with the pastry box he'd just emptied.

A squeal sent him reeling backward, and he tumbled against Dylan.

Christian grasped the boy to keep him from falling onto anything valuable.

"You frightened me!" Abigail screeched, sounding nothing like the shy creature he'd come to know.

"Likewise." Christian straightened. "Didn't you hear us?"

"I went outside to water the flowerbeds in the back." Abigail kept her hands at her throat. Her stormy gaze softened when she looked upon Dylan.

"I apologize," Christian offered. "I suppose that's your car outside."

Abigail shook her head. "No. I think it's Kaylee's mom. When I walked by, she was sitting inside."

And she'd seen them walk inside. Yet, she hadn't entered. That didn't sit well with Christian.

"What are you doing while your daddy works today?" Abigail bent down to speak to Dylan as if he were four and not eight.

"I was going to spend time with Ms. Kaylee, but Uncle Chris said that she was busy with her mom." The accusation rang in Dylan's words.

Christian placed his hand on top of the kid's head and gave a gentle squeeze of warning.

"I thought he was your son."

"He is." Christian peered down at Dylan with a smile. "In my heart. He's my sister's boy, and his mother's not able to take care of him right now."

Abigail nodded and flitted off on tiptoes toward the kitchen. "Would you like to spend some time with me today?" she called over her shoulder. Then she stepped back, hand over her mouth, eyes wide. "I mean, if it's okay with your—with Chris."

Chris bit his tongue. Abigail was skittish enough without him asking her to refrain from shortening his name. "You aren't needed at the grocery store?"

Abigail shook her head and wrung her hands together. "Rose asked if I'd come here and see if I could help you in any way. Spending time with Dylan is a help, right?"

Christian eyed her for a second. He wasn't sure if her restless energy was generated by her residual fear of finding them in the studio or just a restlessness that seemed to invade her when she wasn't engaged in a task.

She darted her gaze around the room.

"Abigail, what's up?"

Abigail raised up on her toes and lowered again. "Decoy duty." She looked toward the window.

So that was it. The woman was on assignment—a different one than her usual roles, but a job, nonetheless. Christian ran his hand over his mouth as if to wipe away the grin. These people were something else. "Dylan, would you like to spend time with Ms. Abigail?"

"Can we go fishing?" The boy spun toward Abigail. "Ms. Kaylee was going to let me fish."

"I think Ms. Abigail meant for you to help her today. She's a busy lady."

"No. No. I have nothing to do until this evening." She moved to the long dining room table and brushed her hand over the lace tablecloth. "You're helping Herb, and Rose is doing okay. I do my baking in the evening, but I have most of the day free."

"Do you have fishing poles?" Dylan asked.

Abigail's face lit like a girl living in a dream. "My daddy and I loved to fish, and I know the perfect spot."

"Where would that be?" Christian asked. "Nowhere that he could be eaten by an alligator or bitten by a snake, I hope."

Abigail smiled. "There's always a chance of that happening here, but we'll fish off the dock of the community center. Perfectly safe."

"Can I?"

"Well, you are able, but ..."

"May I?" Dylan frowned.

"Yes, you may. Would you and Abigail like to meet me for lunch at the Fish Shanty between my two jobs?" He turned his attention to the woman. "It's the least I can do. He wasn't looking forward to hanging out with me."

Abigail hesitated but then nodded. "That would be nice." She leaned toward him. "If we can. You know what I mean, right?"

Christian wanted to laugh. The woman took her responsibilities seriously, but he doubted that Kaylee's mother had any inkling that they knew one another. Dylan could have been any student greeting her at church the day before. Christian had maintained distance from her.

Probably a good thing. Mayor Herb had been in her company for all of ten minutes, and he'd had trouble hiding his foul mood the rest of the afternoon.

"I'll meet you there around one thirty, if that's okay. And if you need to bring him back for any reason, that's not a problem."

Abigail slipped her arm around Dylan's shoulder. "I don't see that happening. Dylan and I'll go to my house and get the equipment, and then we'll stop by and get some bait."

Christian dug in his pocket for his wallet.

Abigail waved him off. "Herb won't let me pay. We use the bartering system." She smiled, almost serene, none of her jerkiness showing.

"Dylan, you behave." Christian followed them to the door.

Abigail had been correct. Kaylee's mother sat in the car parked outside. Christian remembered the door's sign and turned it to indicate Herb was open for business. He stepped inside and waited.

Mrs. McFarland remained in her car.

Kaylee waited for her mother to return, but the morning had dragged on without sight of her. She closed and locked her door.

Mother would have to wait outside if she returned in Kaylee's absence. The rain had dissipated, so she wouldn't get wet. Herb wasn't answering her text or her phone calls, and Kaylee wanted to explain things to Christian.

She hurried down the puddled drive, her heart pounding. Mother had an uncanny sense of timing, and her return upon Kaylee's decision to leave her without entrance to the house would be par for the staid course of interference Kaylee often endured.

Breakfast had been cordial enough. Kaylee had fixed her mother's usual bland oatmeal and wheat toast, and they'd discussed the town's good qualities. Mother had, to her credit, refrained from any further disparaging remarks. Then she'd helped with the dishes and announced that she had things to do this morning.

Kaylee didn't care to know her mother's plans. What she did want were answers—from Herb Miller.

She picked up her pace, jumping over puddles. A child's laughter rang out from the community center, and Kaylee covered her eyes to peer in that direction. Dylan.

She detoured from her course. If Dylan and Christian were hanging out on the center's dock, she could talk to them there in private.

"That's it," a female said. "You got it, Dylan. The old boy hardly suffered any damage."

Something plopped into the water. "Thank you, Ms. Abigail. I didn't wanna hurt it."

Kaylee stopped.

Abigail.

She continued on cautiously and walked around the

side of the building. "Hey," she greeted.

"Hey, Ms. Kaylee!" Dylan pulled his rod back and released the line. It sailed into the middle of the pond without a problem. "You just missed it. I caught a fish, and Ms. Abigail helped me get it off the hook and put it back in the water."

"Good for you." Kaylee approached. "Hey, Abigail."

Abigail stood from the lawn chair she had parked close to the railing. "Come join us. Dylan told me you planned to fish with him today, but with your mother here …"

Kaylee relaxed. "Are you sure I won't be intruding?"

Abigail smiled. "We'd enjoy your company." She swung a second lawn chair over hers and sat it beside the one she'd just vacated. "The building offers shade, and with the rain gone and the clouds hanging on, it's not too bad."

Kaylee sat. "Thank you for filling in for me."

Abigail's gaze centered on Dylan. "I enjoy spending time with kids. They don't seem so quick to judge." Pain cut through her thoughtful words as she sat.

"Oh, they judge. Mostly, though, it's each other. I had a rough time of it in school. My parents were politicians in an area filled with people who didn't have their viewpoint. Add to it that my dad was in a position to enact policies, and the kids mimicked their parents."

Abigail remained quiet despite Kaylee's opening up to

her.

Kaylee stared out over the water. "All I've heard since I arrived here was how wonderful you are."

Abigail's cheeks pinked. "That's nice of you to say."

"Only repeating what others said." Kaylee shrugged. "I've found those rumors true."

"Not everyone has a small mind, I guess. Just a few."

"I'm sorry you've been hurt." Kaylee touched Abigail's hand.

Abigail's gaze languished there as if she'd been starved for touch. "Thank you, again, for last night. I do let past hurts affect the way I behave. Once I was up there, I still couldn't speak, but I saw that they really do care about me."

"You can't walk up onto the stage, but you can play the piano before the church. I'm the exact opposite. I can stand in front of a crowd, but ask me to sing in the choir, and I go white with terror."

Abigail nearly wrenched her entire body to twist toward Kaylee. "But you have one of the most beautiful voices I've ever heard. The only reason I can play that piano is because I'm not performing for the church. I'm performing for God. He's the only one I have to please."

Kaylee had never thought of it that way, but still, she waved off the notion of standing in the choir loft.

"You do have a pretty voice, Ms. Kaylee," Dylan

hinted that he'd been listening. "You should have seen Uncle Chris watching you when you were singing yesterday."

Now, Kaylee was sure her own cheeks were crimson, molten blood probably seeping from hot flesh. "Thank you." She smiled at the boy.

"You shouldn't hide that voice," Abigail pushed.

"And neither should you." Kaylee waggled her finger at her friend. "I'll tell you what. When you stand on a stage and speak before a crowd, I'll sing a solo."

Abigail hesitated and then smiled. She held up her hand, her pinkie finger crooked. "Deal. And I warn you. Incentives make me work hard."

Kaylee hoped she wouldn't rue this deal. She hooked her finger with Abigail's. "You're on, Ms. Brewster."

Dylan reeled in his line and dangled his bait. "I'm your witness." He pulled the rod back and cast it out very smoothly.

Kaylee joined him at the railing and picked up an unused pole. "May I?" she asked Abigail.

"Sure." Abigail remained in her chair.

"You'll have to show me." She told Dylan. "Then, when we come fishing again, I'll know how."

Dylan smiled big, leaned his pole against the railing with the line still in the water, and took her pole. He walked Kaylee through holding the pole and baiting the line. Then he demonstrated how to cast and how to set the line.

Kaylee's first cast plopped in the water right in front of them. Her second one caught in the air, going nowhere because she'd forgotten to release the line.

With patience, Dylan showed her a third time.

She held the pole in her hand, pulled it back with a side motion, making sure the reel was unlocked, and then she flicked the rod forward. The filament sailed in the air and plopped some distance out into the water. Kaylee released her breath. Nothing had ever felt that freeing to her.

"That was good, Ms. Kaylee," Dylan cheered. "Now, if you feel a tug on the line, yank it, but not too hard. You'll want the hook to catch the fish."

Kaylee didn't want to hurt a creature, but she wouldn't say so. What she did enjoy was reeling in the line a little at a time. Who knew something like that could be so relaxing? "Having fun, Dylan?"

"Yeah! Ms. Abigail said that you and I could borrow her dad's rods and reels once your mom leaves." He turned quickly as the end of his rod dipped.

"Well, I'm glad I ran into you both. I never thought of fishing from here."

"Smaller fish, and we're catch and release." Abigail leaned toward Kaylee. "And if he catches a gator, I can cut the line from the deck."

Kaylee laughed. "Didn't even think of that." She

brought her line in, leaned the rod back against the railing, and sat in the chair, turning her eyes upward as something had moved into sight.

A man leaned over her, staring down at her.

She jumped out of her seat. "Jacob!"

Jacob laughed. Then his gaze fell on Dylan.

"You scared me!" She swung at his shoulder truly intending to hurt him. "How long have you been there?"

Abigail's chair scraped. She scurried to her feet and moved away to the other side of Dylan, engaging the child in quiet conversation.

"I saw the boy, and I wanted to make sure he wasn't alone. This is the harbor's property, and if he got hurt, his father could sue."

Surely, he could lie better than that. If he'd seen Dylan, he had to have spied her as well. She let it slide. "He's in very capable hands with Abigail."

"And with you."

"No. I saw Dylan and wanted to say hello. As you're no doubt aware, my mother's in town."

"Well, in Mullet Harbor word does travel fast. Where is your mom? I'd love to meet her."

"I haven't seen her since this morning. If she hasn't been with you, I suppose she's getting her hair done."

"A lot of good that will do her in the swamp." Jacob winked.

Kaylee couldn't help it. She laughed.

Abigail and Dylan began to gather the equipment and the bait.

"I'm sorry to have broken up the party." Jacob slipped his hands into his pants pockets, raised up on his toes, and settled back. "Abigail," he greeted.

"Jacob." Abigail, her hands filled, curtseyed. "Kaylee, would you like to join Dylan and me."

Her friend didn't specify where, and Kaylee suspected a purposeful omission. "Yes. That would be nice."

Jacob turned. "Have a good day, ladies." He walked away.

"We're going to walk over to my place and put this stuff away," Abigail said after Jacob left. "Then we're meeting Chris at the Fish Shanty."

Christian had invited Abigail to lunch? Why did that hurt her like a punch in the gut?

"I don't want to intrude."

Abigail smirked and then smiled. "You've got to be kidding? Me? And Chris? What kind of a friend would I be if I zeroed in on the man you're already set as your target? As if I'd ever stand a chance against you with any fellow in this town."

"Then you haven't seen the way Remy Arneaux looks at you."

"Gross." Dylan spat into the water. "Can we not talk

about this when I'm around? One of them is my uncle, you know."

Abigail stuck her tongue out at the boy. "She's just trying to make a girl feel better."

Dylan started away but stopped. "Ms. Abigail, you and Ms. Kaylee are the two prettiest girls in town."

The kid had learned a lot from his uncle. "Besides Sophie, you mean," Kaylee teased.

"Well, yeah." Dylan shrugged.

Kaylee hugged the boy to her. "I won't tell her you said so."

"Well, if you do, I'll tell Uncle Chris and Sheriff Remy about the conversation I just overheard."

"You wouldn't dare," Abigail feigned exasperation.

"Oh, wouldn't I?" Dylan laughed.

They rounded the corner of the building.

Jacob had reached his car. He stopped and looked back in their direction before opening his door.

"Watch him, Kaylee. Watch him real close," Abigail warned. "Jacob's name means *liar*, and he can't be trusted."

Kaylee shivered despite the Florida heat.

Chapter Fifteen

Christian shared a smile with Kaylee and Dylan as Abigail continued to study the napkin in her lap. Remy had already been seated inside the Fish Shanty when they'd arrived, and he invited them to join him, obvious in his attempts to sit beside Abigail, who'd not said a word since she sat. Her silence reigned throughout the meal.

"I drove by Herb's place." Remy wiped the napkin over his mouth and dropped it onto his empty plate. "He's not home, but your mother's sitting in front of his house."

Kaylee startled. "You're sure it was her? I thought she'd gone out of town."

"Pretty sure it was her," he said.

"She was sitting in her car outside the studio this morning," Christian advised. "I wondered why she didn't come in."

"Those two are in cahoots about something," Kaylee muttered.

"No. I don't think so." Christian chuckled. "Whatever's going on, I can assure you. She has him rattled."

Dylan bounced in his seat. "Ms. Kaylee, is your mom going home soon?"

Christian knocked the kid with his elbow and frowned down at him.

"I just wanna know when we can spend time together."

Abigail seemed to scrunch up into herself, wrapping her arms around her.

"I mean …" Dylan swallowed hard. "With both you and Ms. Abigail. It was fun. Maybe Sophie can join us."

Kaylee reached across the table. "I'd like nothing better than that, but with my mother here, that wouldn't be prudent."

The waitress came and refilled their glasses with tea. Remy sat back, his attention on Abigail.

Christian kept his eye on Dylan. The boy was pouting.

"Abby, have you gotten your tree?" Remy asked.

Abigail's gaze snapped to the lawman. "I haven't had time."

"Herb has to be putting up a tree," Christian announced. "Maybe we can help him and get Abigail's at the same time. Would you like to join us?" he asked

Kaylee.

She shook her head. "I can't risk my mother asking questions and insisting on meeting you, Christian."

With his gaze still on Abigail, Remy cleared his throat. "If Abby wouldn't mind three helpers, perhaps I can ask Isaac if Sophie could join Dylan and me to help her pick out a tree. I'm off duty around three."

Abigail squirmed a bit in her seat. She looked up. "I just remembered …uh …I need to—"

"What about it, Abby?" Remy asked. "Kaylee's mom's a bit preoccupied at the moment. Maybe Kaylee will join us."

Kaylee smiled, but it faded when she looked to Christian.

"Why don't you all go? It sounds like fun," Christian urged.

Kaylee nodded. "It does. I wish you could join us, though."

"What about your tree?" Dylan pushed.

Christian again elbowed him. "You're being very presumptuous. I told you Kaylee's mother hasn't seen her in a while."

Dylan furrowed his brows. "Wouldn't she want to meet your friends? I think your friends would like her. She's nice. You could have a Christmas party to introduce us."

Christian looked to the ceiling. Dylan was excited about the holidays and spending time with friends. He'd had fun with Sophie and her dad yesterday and while fishing with Abigail and Kaylee today. The kid didn't realize the mess he was causing. "Dylan, we're not going to invite ourselves to Ms. Kaylee's house for a party she never intended to throw."

The waitress dropped the tab on the table and left.

"Dylan, let's get Abby a tree this afternoon when I'm off duty. It's so close to Christmas. I hate that I forgot she needs help getting one from the lot."

"Well, Ms. Kaylee's tree isn't even decorated." Dylan pouted.

"I'll do it tonight." Kaylee clasped her hands together. "You can come by tomorrow while Christian is working to see it."

Dylan slammed back in his chair. "Without Chris, you mean."

The boy was too astute.

"Dylan …" Kaylee pushed air between her lips. "My mother—"

"Ms. Kaylee, why don't you think your mom would like Chris?" Dylan crossed his arms much the way Abigail had earlier.

"Dylan." Christian kept his voice low. "Ms. Kaylee didn't mean it like that. You and I have to stay under the radar. Mrs. McFarland, rightfully so, might be wary of us because we're strangers in town."

Dylan didn't look to Christian. Instead, he kept his narrowed gaze on Kaylee. "Chris is a nice man. He teaches school, just like you, only he teaches grownups. But he gave it all up for me." The boy sniffled and ran his hand under his nose. "If your mom can't like him, I don't want to come to your stupid house to see your stupid tree anyway. If you can't tell her that he's a nice man, I don't want to spend any time with you."

"Dylan." Christian tugged his nephew close. "I appreciate your speaking up for me, but Ms. Kaylee isn't an enemy."

"No, it's my mom and that judge." He took a stuttering breath. "And it's me!" he yelled. "That stupid judge who wouldn't listen to me when I said I wanted to be with you. I'm the reason that people don't trust you! I've made you no better than my mom to people. It's me!" He coughed and buried his face against Christian's side. "It's me. It's all me. Since I was born. It's me." He choked on his cries.

"Dylan." Abigail stood and tugged on the boy's shoulder. "Let's me and you go for a walk. Would you mind, Christian?"

"I don't want to." Dylan cried against Christian's side, each sob tearing at Christian's heart.

"I have a place I want to show you," she coaxed. "I

call it my yelling place. You, and only you, will ever know where it is."

Dylan sniffled and scooted out after her without a glance back or an apology for his outburst, not that Christian expected one. He wished Abigail had invited him to come to this place where he could vent his frustrations and his fears, his anger and his grief.

Instead, he sat rigid, afraid to move because one shift and the walls he'd built to stay strong for the boy would collapse.

Christian's angry words about Dylan's mom weighed heavy in his gut. He still hadn't apologized for them. Dylan needed an outlet for his grief, and Christian's accusations had closed that door. Maybe he'd let loose some of his sadness and fear with Abigail.

Abigail held up one finger and pointed to her watch. "One hour," she mouthed.

Christian nodded.

Kaylee's gaze stayed on her lap. "He doesn't understand all that's going on and why my mom can be a danger to you. I'm so sorry."

"I piled on that pillar of hurt he's been holding up. I've owed him an apology and an explanation for something I said to him yesterday. I should have done it this morning, but ..." He cleared his throat. "I meant what I said to him. I'm struggling with forgiving my sister." Christian reached for her hand. "This isn't your fault." He had to make her smile before she left him, despite the crush of his heart. "You've gotten caught up in this because I ran out of gas and got blackmailed by an old dude."

Kaylee peered up at him. A smile played on her lips, but it didn't quite get there.

"By an old dude and a cop," Christian continued.

Remy laughed aloud.

Kaylee giggled. "I don't think badly of you. I think— I think you're incredible."

Christian pushed her blond curls from her face and tucked them behind her ears. "And I think you're awesome and incredibly breathtaking."

As she'd done when he last complimented her, she pressed her hand against her face.

"Dylan was hurt by careless words I tossed out yesterday. I suspect he's angry at me for saying it, and he's angry because what I said makes him stand up for his mom. He's learning that when you're angry with someone, you can still love them. Despite anything that either of us say, we love Cassie very much." Christian fought to control his voice. "So, like I did to something he said, the boy took your words, made them a mountain, and stood on it to vent his frustration."

Remy tapped his hand on the table. "I've become the third-wheel, and I think I should be getting on patrol. I'll drive by Abby's yelling place and make sure they're okay." He stood and pushed his chair under the table.

"She said no one knows about it. You do? Where'd she take him?" Christian asked. "Is he safe?"

"He's safe with her anywhere he goes. I don't want to tell you where it is because Dylan must be special for her to share it. She's never taken anyone there that I'm aware."

Kaylee turned to look up at him. "Then how do you know about it?"

Remy's attention went to the shanty's screen door. "Let's just say I've known about it since we were little. She doesn't so much yell. She cries … and I've always wished I could dry her tears." He moved to stand behind Kaylee. "Christian, you need to walk out with me."

Christian leaned around him. Through the screen, he caught a glimpse of Herb and Mrs. McFarland in what appeared to be heated debate. "Kaylee, your mom found the mayor."

Kaylee startled. "You do need to go with Remy."

Christian fished in his wallet.

"I got it." Remy handed the tab and some money to Kaylee. "The tip's included."

Christian followed the sheriff out of the restaurant, pausing in the door when Herb glanced his way.

"I don't care what you want." LeAnn McFarland snarled. "She's mine. She has no reason to be here in this swamp. She's the daughter of a senator, for ..."

"Don't take the Lord's name in vain in front of me, young lady," Herb countered. "She's not a child. She has a Ph.D. in education. The town needed her, and she chose to come here."

"Because you baited a trap. She's gullible and easily led. There is nothing here that will see her promoted beyond an elementary school level. If she wanted a small-town, no-account job, why'd her father and I have to pay the tuition for a worthless higher degree." Mrs. McFarland folded her arms across her chest.

"Some things aren't about promotion or prestige." Herb nearly growled the words.

"Well, they definitely aren't about throwing away your life." Mrs. McFarland stormed toward her car. "She'll be out of here before school starts again. You mark my words, old man." She opened her door and glared at Remy and Christian. "What are you looking at?"

Remy straightened. "I'm looking at a woman yelling at one of the best men I've ever known, and she's very close to an arrest for disorderly conduct."

"I'm not drinking," she challenged.

"Doesn't matter to me. You're causing a scene in an otherwise tranquil locale."

"Oh, go blow your whistle up some other woman's skirt." She got inside the car and slammed the door, backed up, and headed off.

Remy turned to Christian, mock surprise on his face. "Did she really say that to an officer in uniform?"

Christian laughed. "Yes, she did."

Kaylee exited the restaurant cautiously. "Is she gone?" Behind her, the restaurant's customers and staff had gathered.

"She's gone." Herb smiled. "And now, I suppose you want to talk to me."

Kaylee touched his shoulder.

Herb stared into her eyes.

"I'll wait. I know that arguing with my mother can take a lot out of you. I'll trust you to confide in me when you feel the time is right."

Herb placed his hand over hers. He didn't lose his smile. "You are most gracious and merciful." He winked. "You must have gotten that from your father."

"Well, it certainly didn't come from my mother." She nodded. "Oh, and she's wrong. I won't be leaving my position before the Christmas break is over. I'll be here until I'm ready to leave."

"I appreciate that," Herb said.

"And ..." Kaylee turned toward Christian. "I don't think I can get my tree decorated as quickly as Dylan would like in order to have that Christmas party because I haven't bought decorations yet, but I'll be extending invitations for said festivity in a couple of days. I'll expect you to be there." She walked away from them.

"Hey," Herb called after her. "Don't rush out and buy anything. I have some, and I'll get them to you."

"Okay." Kaylee swung around and back.

Christian kept his gaze on her as she walked down the street.

"I think," Remy said, "that if Kaylee knew where Abby's yelling place was, she'd love to join them. But if I took her there, Abby would know that I know, and I couldn't stand to see her embarrassed by my knowledge." He scuffed his shoe on the ground. Then he looked to Herb. "Kaylee's party puts a crimp in our plans. We need to have all contingencies in place, don't you think?"

"That girl's taking the right tact." Herb's gazed stayed on Kaylee as she walked the main road toward her home. "Hiding Chris will make LeAnn just as curious as if we parade him out before her." He gave his attention to Christian. "But if you make that woman feel as if you have an interest in her daughter, Remy's right. We'll have to pull out our contingency plans before we intend to do so. I want Dylan to have his Christmas wish." He moved away, but not before placing a hand on Remy's shoulder. "Even if it means arresting LeAnn McFarland."

Remy laughed. "A woman that mouthy might just give me the opportunity."

Fay Lamb

Chapter Sixteen

Kaylee expected to see her mother's car parked in the sandy lane in front of house alongside the vehicle Kaylee so seldom used, but the spot was empty. She shrugged and made her way onto the wooden pier. Some pine needles had fallen from the trees towering above. She sat her purse inside and with an energy similar to that of Abigail's, grabbed a broom and swept away the debris.

Finished with that chore, she tugged out her vacuum and cleaned up any stray dirt on her floors and carpets. Her last chore was to place water in the tree's stand. She'd been so preoccupied with Christian's arrival and then with the unwanted visit of her mother, that she'd forgotten the poor unadorned thing. The sweet smell of the tree filled her home, and she sank onto the corner of the couch.

Distress sent her in search of the good Christmas

memories she held close. Both of her parents doted extra attention on her in different ways. She and mother baked cookies and decorated the home. Daddy had taken her shopping, buying lavish gifts for her mother. Kaylee had eventually realized that while her father was shopping with her, Mother was buying lavish gifts for their only child.

They attended church on Christmas Day. Other than Easter, though, her parents indicated that their busy lives kept them from worship. In her teens, Kaylee had attended church with a friend. There, she'd gained an intimate relationship with her Savior. Daddy had listened to her joyous declarations of Christ's love, and he'd attended church with her on occasion.

Mother's view of God was that of a father who lived apart from His children. The children were only there for His pleasure. While that description was correct if you understood that God's pleasure was always good toward His children, Mother's depiction was skewed and ugly, representing a mostly absent parent. But when Kaylee had discussed it with her father, telling him that in many ways, she'd been drawn to Christ because of the way her father had loved her, Daddy's heart had been touched, and he had asked her how he could know such love. Together, they'd bowed in prayer.

Kaylee took a shuddering breath. Though she would see him again, she missed him terribly. Tears filled her eyes. "I need you, Daddy."

She missed his ready smile, the kind that Mayor Herb always had for her. She longed to joke with him once again—the way Mayor Herb teased her. And she longed to feel her father's arms around her, telling her that everything would be okay. She had no doubt that if she ran to Mayor Herb for comfort, he would embrace her and tell her that all would be fine. But Mayor Herb was not her dad.

She lowered her head and cried into her hands. "Daddy." The word wailed from her as it had so many times in her youth when her mother's cutting words had dimmed her spirit, like the statement she'd made to Herb about Kaylee being gullible and easily led. Those words sunk into her gut, making it ache. "Daddy, I need you."

Your Abba loves you.

The soothing words slipped into her soul, and her tears ebbed.

Your Abba is here.

She took a stuttering breath and looked to the heavens. "Abba, Father." Her lips trembled with the words, but with them came an overwhelming sense of peace and belonging. "I need You."

And with that came God's strong embrace, as tangible as any of Robert McFarland's fatherly hugs.

Kaylee stood. "Abba, Father," she repeated. "Thank You."

A knock sounded at the door, and she swiped her tear-moistened face. "Great," she muttered as she paused in the kitchen to tear a paper towel from the roll to get rid of any sign that would announce her decline into self-pity.

Her mother would allow none of it, and until now, Kaylee had kept her grief at bay. Funny, it seemed to have arrived with her mother's critical demeanor.

She peeked through the window and opened the door. "What a surprise," she greeted Abigail and Dylan.

"Are you okay, Ms. Kaylee? I'm sorry if I made you cry. Ms. Abigail told me I needed to apologize. I didn't mean what I said."

Kaylee tilted her head and scrutinized him. "Are you saying that your uncle isn't a nice man, and he doesn't deserve to meet my mother?"

Dylan pinched his lips together and shook his head.

"Well, I'm glad for that. Because you are correct. Perhaps the apology is for ..." She allowed her words to linger in the air between them.

"Because I wasn't nice to you. Ms. Abigail told me what's going on. I didn't understand." He scuffed his shoe against the wooden dock. "Uncle Chris tried to tell me, and I didn't listen."

"Apology accepted." Kaylee bent down in front of him.

He nodded.

She stood. "Where are my manners? Come in."

"Are you sure?" Abigail peered inside the home.

"Mother isn't here, and if she were, I'd still love to have you visit."

Abigail moved inside with Dylan behind her. "This house looks great. This place used to be an old shack until Herb learned you were coming to town. Then he set to work getting it ready, especially for you. I haven't been inside to see how you've decorated."

Kaylee thought it had always been one of Herb's rentals. "When you say shack, you mean a dilapidated home where no one lived?"

Abigail walked around the kitchen and into the living room. "I mean a shed. The place was only the size of your kitchen. It had all kinds of junk inside." She shuddered. "Not to mention snakes and spiders. The whole town couldn't believe he'd do anything but tear it down and use it as a fishing hole, except there's old Hilditch." She fingered the limbs on the spruce in Kaylee's corner.

"Hilditch?"

"Surely, you've met him by now. He's the old scaly, gray guy who lives in the waters outside."

Kaylee laughed aloud. "Who named Abercrombie Hilditch?"

"Mayor Herb did years ago when he first met him. What a monumental meeting that was." Abigail melted into a fit of giggles. "Rose still laughs when she tells the story of Herb walking on water and his wife, Lacey, screaming so loud that Hilditch fled back into the bayou after chasing Herb onto solid ground."

"Well, Herb and I must think a lot alike. May I get either of you something to drink?"

Abigail raised her hand to tell her no, and Dylan shook his head. "Your tree sure is pretty," he complimented. "Do you have the ornaments and lights?"

Kaylee shook her head. "Mayor Herb said he had some for me, but I'll probably go shopping with my mother tomorrow to buy a few things." She'd take her mother with her and get the woman out of everyone's way.

Abigail studied Kaylee with intense scrutiny. "So ... why'd you say that Herb and you think alike? Something about Hilditch."

"I named the gator Abercrombie."

Abigail squinted her eyes and gave a quick shake of her head.

"It's something about a shirt." Dylan sighed. "I don't get it either."

"A shirt?" Abigail shrugged, her face a blank. "I don't get it."

"Izod. A play on names. Izod ... Abercrombie."

The blank slate filled with knowledge, and Abigail smiled. "Got it." Then she scrunched her nose again. "But what does Hilditch have to do with shirts?"

Kaylee retrieved her phone from her back pocket and searched the Internet. She held up the screen so that both Dylan and Abigail could see the high-fashioned, tailored shirt.

"I get it." Abigail's smile faded as soon as it lifted her lips. "Herb must be pretty rich to know that brand."

"I suspect he is." Kaylee used her finger to scroll through the website. "My father preferred to wear those shirts. I bought him one every year for Christmas. It's a wonder I didn't give Abercrombie that name."

Dylan fidgeted in his seat.

"Would you like to go outside and say hello to Abercrombie Hilditch?" Kaylee teased.

"I—I'd like to go see Chris now," he mumbled.

Kaylee glanced at her watch. "Is he getting off early today?"

"No, but I can help him at the store. Ms. Rose said I could." Dylan bounded to his feet.

Kaylee's front door swung open and her mother glided in. "I'm home." She stopped and took a step backward. "I'm sorry. I didn't know we had company."

Home? We? Kaylee bristled. This was not her mother's home, but she would usurp Kaylee's authority no matter where they were.

Abigail stood. "That's okay. We were just leaving."

"No," Kaylee said, probably a little too loudly. "Won't you stay a little longer? Mother, this is my friend, Abigail Brewster, and you met this young man yesterday at church. His name is Dylan."

Dylan stepped forward with his hand held outward to Kaylee's mother. "Nice to see you again. I'm Dylan Abrams."

Mother smiled and held out her hand. "Well, it certainly is, Dylan."

Dylan nodded.

Abigail joined him, holding out her hand. "Nice to meet you." She curtsied and, walking on tiptoes, scooted out past Dylan. "Bye."

Mother turned and watched them leave. "She's an odd duck, isn't she? Nice little boy, though. One of your students?"

Where was the foxhole when you needed one? "I hope you've had a better day than you were having outside of the restaurant yelling at the mayor."

"Don't take that tone with me, Kaylee McFarland. What would your father say if he heard you speak to me like that?"

Kaylee closed the door and leaned against it. "You and I both know that he would never have heard me talk to you like that."

"Well, then, we agree."

"Because he always stood between us. You would never speak to me the way you do now that he's not around, and while he was alive, I never would have hurt him by standing up for myself."

"I was going to ask you to dinner. I found a little bit of civility in this forsaken outpost. It's that bed and breakfast you told me about. They offer fine dining, and I made us a reservation." Mother stepped into the living room. "And just when are you thinking of decorating that tree?"

"Tomorrow." Kaylee hid her smirk behind an emotionless smile.

"Well, when you bought that thing, did you buy it correctly?"

Mother was teasing her. The stress in Kaylee's shoulders released. "I walked around it five times. I pushed down on the limbs, and I had the man shake it all around." Christmas tree shopping with her mother was a box full of treasured memories.

Mother beamed. "Did you ask him to do the hokey pokey?"

"Actually, I did not. No one does that questions justice like you do, but I bet you can guess from the looks of it, I did what I always wanted you to do."

Mother examined the tree. "I don't think so. This one looks very nice and not at all like those bare ones with the twisted trunks you always felt such sorrow over remaining in the lot without anyone to love."

She'd never explained why she'd begged for the ugly trees, the ones no one would want, but Mother had known.

That was at least something.

Her mother's face softened. "Oh, honey. I don't want to fight with you. I love this time of year so much."

Kaylee pushed back her emotions, not wanting her mother's reprimand to spoil yet another time she could treasure and keep stored for all the times her mother wasn't like this. "I would love to have dinner with you. What time?"

Mother looked at her watch. "We have an hour. Would you mind if I showered and changed? Then I'll wait for you."

Kaylee nodded and paused until her mother ensconced herself in the bathroom. Then Kaylee opened the french doors and stepped onto the dock.

Abercrombie was just beyond the edge of the wooden structure, his body still. "I got the lowdown on you," Kaylee whispered. "Abercrombie Hilditch, what in the world were you thinking chasing Mayor Herb out of the water and scaring his wife to death?"

As if the gator recognized the reprimand, his entire body moved with the swish of his tail. He drew closer to her as if he were about to explain his side of the episode.

She pointed at him. "Bad boy. Very bad boy."

He paused.

Kaylee could almost see Herb in the water and Abercrombie emerging from the deep in his slow methodical way. She clasped her hand over her mouth to still the humor that bubbled up inside her. She imagined she'd walk on water, too, if that happened.

Herb's wife must have pealed out a scream louder than a storm siren to scare the old boy.

And that thought made Kaylee's laugh bubble over. She closed her door so that her mother wouldn't hear. No good would come of LeAnn McFarland learning that a gator in Kaylee's backyard had almost eaten the town's mayor.

Then, again, Abercrombie might just earn Mother's undying devotion.

Chapter Seventeen

Winter had night descending early on Mullet Harbor, but Christian sat in Mayor Herb's old pickup with Dylan in the middle. The mayor was on a mission. Tucked into the back of his truck were boxes of lights and decorations. Herb had asked Christian to sort, unwind, and box the lights a certain way and add a ladder to the back of the vehicle. Herb had taken care of the decorations, and from what Christian could tell, some of the ornaments were family treasures. One box had been filled with bubble-wrapped items.

Now, the old man traveled slowly down the dirt lane toward Kaylee's little swamp cottage. He carefully traversed each bump until he came to a stop beside the dock. "Let's get the ornaments to the door. We'll leave them there. Then we can put these lights up lickety-split."

The inside of the house was dark, the only light shining in the back.

Mosquitoes buzzed Christian's ears.

Dylan swatted at a few.

"Here." Herb tossed a spray can in Dylan's direction. "Put that on ya, and don't step off that dock. Either of you. There's a gator out here, and he's a real opportunist."

Dylan's giggle split the air. "Abigail told me and Ms. Kaylee about you and the gator."

Herb chuckled.

Christian put a light hold on Dylan's shoulder. "Ms. Kaylee and me … and what did she tell you?" He picked up the box of ornaments, looked around for any gator eye-shine, and quickly led Dylan to the dock.

"I hope she told you I confronted that gator with dignity and extraordinary bravery."

Dylan gave an exaggerated shake of his head. "Nope."

Herb passed them with one of the boxes containing lights. "Then she told you the truth."

Christian placed the box on the dock at Kaylee's front door and moved back to the truck for another box of lights.

Herb met him there.

"Why don't you have the gator removed?" Christian asked.

"I spent too much money protecting him. That's why. I built the pier, and I put the house on the pier. He doesn't bother anyone. We don't feed him. He helps himself to the smorgasbord of wildlife and keeps a safe distance. The day he nearly nabbed me I was right smack in the middle of his watery turf. Granted, I was taking out some metal garbage left by the previous owner years before, but he didn't know that. He was doing what comes natural to him."

"How do you know the gator's a male?" Christian hefted the lights, and Herb grabbed a tool belt.

He walked with Herb to where Dylan remained on the dock.

"I've heard him in mating season. He's a bull gator. Loud and boisterous, like his namesakes at that university north of here."

"So you're a Gator fan, too?" Christian teased.

"You bet I am. Not popular around here for it, either. Most of the town prefers the Ibis. What kind of a mascot is that?"

"Well, that natural disaster they named their team after is pretty strong."

"Ain't one of them felled me yet, but that gator came mighty close." Herb placed the box on the ground. "Now, if you'll get that ladder, we'll start stringing these."

"Are we sure she's not home?"

"I'm sure. I saw LeAnn leaving the B&B. I paid the place a visit. She made reservations. It's a nice leisurely meal, and I made sure to ask them to slow it down even more. We need to hustle, though."

"This is a nice thing you're doing," Christian called as he trudged back to the truck. He returned with the ladder and opened it at the edge of the house. Herb had Dylan helped him unwind the lights and lay them across the dock. "I think they should stretch all around. I have exterior outlets on both sides of the house, so we just need to make sure we have them up correctly so that they plug in where they're supposed to. Hand Chris that tool belt, boy." He motioned for Dylan. "That's got the clips inside."

Christian climbed the ladder and strung the lights that were fed to him by Dylan while Herb assured the extension cords would do the trick. Finished, Christian folded the ladder and stood back with Herb and Dylan to take in the effect of the larger, old-fashioned bulbs. They illuminated the dock with orange and blue and green, and they reflected in the water.

"If I didn't know better, I'd think you'd done this before." Christian handed Dylan the one box that had housed the outdoor lights, folded and carried the ladder, and followed behind Herb to the truck, Dylan ducked inside.

"He didn't do this here." Dylan leaned out of the cab. "This house wasn't built, was it, Mayor Herb?"

Herb stopped before getting in the truck. "Abigail may be shy, but that gal has a big mouth. I had it built for the pretty little schoolteacher." He jumped inside and waited for Christian to do the same. "And the answer is yes. God has been good to me, and I tend to respond with goodness to others. I have a few families on my list, and over the next few days, we'll be doing the same for other people and their homes."

Christian shook his head, overwhelmed at the man's giving nature. "But this was special." He waved toward the house.

"Yes, it was," Herb agreed too readily.

Christian smirked. He knew it.

"Because this town loves that little gal. She's made a difference here. All the teachers have, but her especially. I don't intend to lose her to that woman."

Christian's smirk vanished. He didn't want to lose Kaylee either.

A soft glow filled the skies beyond the trees in the area of her house. Kaylee held her breath and said nothing to her mother as she drove the rental car forward. Mother tapped her hands on the steering wheel in time with the Christmas music, apparently not seeing anything amiss.

To Kaylee's surprise, her mother hadn't been rankled at all when she'd learned Mayor Herb had paid for their dinner.

They entered the clearing, and her mother hit the brakes. "What in the world, Kaylee?"

Kaylee folded her hands in front of her, holding them to her chin. "Oh, he's so wonderful. This has to be Mayor Herb's work. It's beautiful."

Mother pulled forward. "He's really outdoing himself, trying to make you believe he cares about anything other than himself."

"Mother!" Kaylee scolded as she stepped from the car and slammed the door. "Mayor Herb has been nothing but nice to me, and he paid for our dinner."

"Dinner was reparations for the way he treated me, and apparently, he wants something from you," Mother stewed.

Together, they walked toward the dock. The scrub near the dock moved, the rustling loud.

Mother sidestepped into Kaylee and drew her close, her arms shielding her.

Kaylee hugged her mother. "I'm sure it's just a raccoon or a possum."

"It's larger than that," Mother whispered.

Kaylee slipped from the embrace and drew Mother to the dock. She halted and stared back in the direction of the noise.

A doe stepped into the clearing. Her nose and her tail twitched. She startled when she noticed they were close, but she didn't flee. A buck stepped out and nuzzled the doe. They strode across the dirt to the bushes on the other side.

"I stand corrected. They were much larger than a possum or a raccoon." Kaylee laughed.

Her mother swatted at her. "You!"

Kaylee allowed the moment to sink into her treasury of memories. The unexpected visitors had quelled their discussion of Mayor Herb's intentions.

Two cardboard boxes sat by her door. In the glow of the Christmas bulbs, Kaylee could see tree lights filled one. The other housed ornaments. Her heart soared. "We don't have to go shopping." She unlocked the door and tugged the boxes inside, leaving them along the entrance wall.

Mother remained silent. She slipped down the hall and returned in her nightgown to sit on the couch.

"Is something wrong?" Kaylee joined her.

"I thought you were looking forward to shopping with me. I suppose you have other things you'd rather be doing."

Of course. Mother loved Christmas shopping.

"That's not what I meant. I'm sorry. I meant we wouldn't have to spend time buying ornaments and lights. Even when Mayor Herb said he had some I could use, I didn't realize he meant this many. Of course, I want to test the lights. We might need to get some new ones if the bulbs are burned out."

"I'm sure he checked them before he brought them. He

wouldn't do otherwise."

Kaylee sat on the couch. Her mother was much more familiar with Herb than she'd let on. "How do you know him?" she asked.

Mother waved her hand in the air as if dismissing the discussion. "I know him as well as you do." She stood and kissed Kaylee's cheek. "We did enjoy the dinner. You'll have to write the old man a thank you note."

"I'll pick up one tomorrow." Kaylee yawned. "But, Mother, I enjoyed it because it was time spent with you, no matter who paid for it."

Her mother smiled. "Then pick up a card to send from me, too."

Kaylee turned her mother toward her room. "Good night."

Mother made her way down the hall, and Kaylee turned off the lights and returned to the couch, not bothering to unfold it to make her bed. The glow of the outside lights came through the thinly dressed windows around the home. She should make sure they were turned off before she went to sleep, but the illumination comforted her. Leaning back, she closed her eyes.

Did Herb want something from her? Was she being gullible in accepting his gifts? She hoped not. More than anything in life, Kaylee hated for her mother to be right.

Chapter Eighteen

December 18

If Kaylee could shop with the stamina of her mother some twenty years from today, she'd consider herself blessed. The woman floated from aisle to aisle in one store after the other. Kaylee had lagged behind because the life she had chosen required a budget. Her mother, while very generous when Kaylee lived under her thumb, was not about to make life easier for her until she returned with her mother's thumb completely holding her down.

Little did her mother know, Kaylee wouldn't trade her freedom for money. She loved her new life on Mullet Harbor. Nothing would take her back to Maryland except for a short visit … or an emergency.

Kaylee looked through some young boy's clothing on

a rack while her mother was preoccupied and on the phone. She picked out a nice pair of jeans and a pullover shirt that seemed to be Dylan's style. She'd have to pick out a toy for him as well. Dylan's uncle would be harder to gift, and she'd definitely have to come back by herself to do the shopping or purchase it online. While her mother might not question buying a gift for a child, she'd be all over Kaylee, lobbing questions at her to determine who the man could be.

Yet the gift for Jacob sat under her undecorated tree. If Mother had snooped, she hadn't let on, or she'd let her guard down. Worse, she might think Kaylee and Jacob were involved.

Mother came to stand beside Kaylee in the checkout line. "Yes, good. See you then." She hung up from the call. "How about lunch? I hear the restaurant near the mall's entrance has good food."

"And how did you hear that?" Kaylee's suspicion rose.

"I asked." Her mother swayed her head from side to side. She might as well have sung out "La-tee-da," which was the name of the spa where her mother had made reservations for haircuts, facials, and manicures after lunch.

That revelation had caused Kaylee a change in plans. She'd wanted to decorate the tree and call and invite others for an impromptu party either tomorrow or the next day.

Already, energy drained out of Kaylee like the water in the locks of the Panama Canal.

She paid for the clothing and walked with Mother toward the mall entrance and the restaurant there. She stutter-stepped when they reached the door being held open by Jacob Marin.

"Kaylee McFarland." His smile dripped honey. "And this must be your mother. Mrs. McFarland." He held out his hand. "Such a pleasure to meet you."

Kaylee took a deep breath. "'See you then'?" she whispered the repeated words from her mom's call. "You planned this."

Mother never lost her smile as she held out her hand to Jacob. "Mr. Marin, nice to meet you—finally. Will you join us?"

"Wasn't that the plan?" Kaylee asked.

"Young lady, what gave you that impression?" Mother narrowed her gaze in Kaylee's direction.

"The fact that you didn't have to ask his name when you are otherwise very suspicious if a man pays attention to me."

Jacob had the decency to appear embarrassed. His cheeks even reddened, but Kaylee supposed his embarrassment came from getting caught in subterfuge. "Now, Kaylee," he said, "I thought we'd already established that I'd spoken with your mother. She donated to my campaign."

Well, he had her there. Kaylee let her shoulders slump in recognized defeat.

Jacob gave his name at the register, and they were shown to a nice table by the window looking out at the mall's parking lot. Not her mother's typical choice for dining.

As they walked, Kaylee picked at a seam in her defeat that unraveled his victory. "Counselor," she said as she sat, "the question still remains as to how you happened to show up here and seemingly with a reservation for three."

Jacob cast a wary glance to his not-so-abashed accomplice.

"Kaylee, I called Jacob while we were in the store. He said that he'd set up the reservations and would like to join us if he was welcome. Of course, I told him I'd love to meet with him to find out about his office and his campaign."

Kaylee accepted a menu from the hostess and leaned back in her chair, ready to concede. But she couldn't. She had to make her mother understand that she would no longer be treated like a child. "That is all well and good, but you failed to be forthcoming with me. Jacob would have been welcomed to join us, but you, for some reason— guilt perhaps—chose not to tell me that he'd been invited."

"Kaylee," Mother warned. "We can discuss this later."

"Listen." Jacob stood. "I see I'm causing problems.

I'm sorry if my intrusion has come between the two of you."

Kaylee stood as well. She might have gained a slight edge by being so far away from home, but Mother had aligned herself with a local ally, and she'd won this battle. "Jacob, I'm sorry I made you feel unwelcome. That isn't what I intended. I'm very glad that you could join us." The last sentence was a lie, a polite one, but nevertheless, Dylan had reminded her that God didn't like liars. *Sorry, Lord.* She sat back down.

Jacob hesitated, but then he smiled and rejoined them. "Thank you, and I apologize for any misunderstanding."

She nodded and perused the menu while her mother and Jacob delved into a conversation about his job, his district, his campaign, and about … Kaylee blinked from her thoughts long into the lunch when Jacob mentioned familiar names.

"I don't like seeing Herb and Aunt Rose together." He pushed his empty plate away. "They're too old to marry, and my aunt would lose benefits if they did. I suppose they work around their relationship in other ways."

Kaylee bristled at the implication. "Their relationship is exactly what you see. They're friends."

"Well, good to have you join us." Mother chuckled. "You were so quiet I could see you were far away, wherever that imagination of yours takes you."

"Obviously, it takes me in a lot better direction than either of yours." She leaned forward. "Shame on you, Jacob, for even insinuating that about Rose."

Jacob held up his hands. "Okay. I give. Just don't tell her I said so." He winked. "She'll write me out of that will of hers. I'm sure that grocery store will bring my net worth up a few thousand dollars."

Mother had the good sense to look down into her lap. She ran her hand across her napkin and subtly touched Kaylee's leg. The brief shake of her head indicated she would accept no further attack upon Jacob.

But she had to find Jacob's comments distasteful. Kaylee drank her tea, using it as a snap on her lips to keep her mouth from protesting.

"Maybe you'd like to join us tonight." Mother gave her full attention to Jacob. "Kaylee and I were going to have a quiet dinner at home alone."

Kaylee swallowed wrong and coughed.

Mother kept her gaze on Jacob.

Kaylee clenched her teeth.

"We could use the help decorating the Christmas tree."

Kaylee breathed deeply, almost expecting fire to flow through her nostrils. She needed to turn the small dinner party her mother was negotiating into something bigger—and quick.

"What? You didn't invite the town's newest resident?"

Jacob raised his brows.

Kaylee swallowed. Then she smiled. Jacob had just solved all her problems. "He's Mayor Herb's house guest, so yes, if I decide to invite others, I would naturally invite him. Abigail would be among the invited as well."

"And her adorable little boy," Mother announced.

Jacob laughed. "Abigail doesn't have a son. Thank goodness."

Mother turned to Kaylee. "That little boy with her yesterday wasn't her son? I caught that they had different last names, but you never know. She could have a dozen kids by different husbands."

"Mother!" Kaylee slapped down her napkin. She forced herself to calm. "Dylan and his uncle are staying with Mayor Herb. Abigail was watching him yesterday."

Her mother actually moved in her seat to stare at Kaylee. "He's the little boy you were watching for the man. The reason you couldn't be bothered with coming home for Christmas and the reason you wouldn't answer your phone when I called, which prompted me to have to come to this horrid swampland." She peered back at Jacob. "No insult intended."

"None taken." The lines around Jacob's eyes crinkled with mischief.

"Mother, I wasn't coming home before Dylan and his father arrived. They aren't the reason I wanted to stay here."

"Then why on earth would you want to remain here?"

"You." The atom bomb with the power to nuke the already tenuous relationship torpedoed from Kaylee's mouth with a whisper. She couldn't have stopped it if she tried.

Kaylee's unintended target straightened and raised her shoulders, a sign that Kaylee's truth had wounded her mother, but the woman would limp on like a true soldier toward another battle line. "Ha-ha." She forced the sound. "Please join us tonight, Jacob."

Jacob nodded. "Sounds like fun. I wouldn't miss it. Kaylee, is there anything I can bring?" The waiter returned with the bill, and Jacob waved off Mother, who graciously allowed him to pick up the tab. After all, Mother never threw her money at campaigns in a small way.

"Just yourself," Kaylee managed. "Thank you for lunch. If you'll excuse me." She stood and made her way to the restroom where she remained until her mother stepped inside as well and clearly pretended not to notice that Kaylee had intentionally made herself scarce until Jacob's departure.

Kaylee walked to the car with her mother, and neither spoke at the spa or while shopping for the now more impromptu party for which only one guest had received an invite. When they arrived home, Mother allowed Kaylee to exit the car with the gifts and the small bit of food she'd bought for the party. Then, without another word, she drove back down the sandy lane.

Kaylee unlocked the door to her house and stepped inside. She closed the door and leaned against it.

She would not cry. That's what her mother wanted her to do. That's what her mother's silence always made her do, but Kaylee was an adult now, not that her actions in front of Jacob had shown that.

She breathed deeply and pushed away from the door. Actually, Mother had left her no time for crying. She had a party to plan, people to invite, a tree to decorate, presents to wrap, and food to prepare. Mother had abandoned her to the work.

"Touché," Kaylee shouted the words to the ceiling. How much more childish would she become before she got a handle on herself, acted like an adult, and showed her mother why she adored Mullet Harbor.

She called her secret weapon—one she'd never had before in these battles of will—a best friend. Abigail promised to get right on things and told Kaylee to worry only about decorating the house. She'd take care of everything else.

Kaylee rushed to the boxes Herb had left. At least the outside was adorned. She could decorate her small tree and the inside in no time at all.

The lights for the tree were wound perfectly, and she had them quickly in place on her Charlie Brown special. Then she pulled out a ribbon of fabric, studying it for a long moment to determine how it had been used in the past. Beautiful red cardinals sitting on snowy evergreen branches peppered the thin swath, which was sewn together at several points. "Garland ..." Kaylee let the word escape with wonder. "What a wonderful idea." She threaded the fabric in a circle, weaving it in and out and under the tree's branches from the top to the bottom. When handfuls remained—obviously meant for a much larger tree—she started close to the tree's stand and wove an impromptu tree skirt.

Standing back, she marveled at the uniqueness the garland provided, but she didn't have much time. She delved into the boxes and began to separate the ornaments from small to large and then by color. These were special, a collector's dream of glass and wood, of snowy scenes and churches. Many different countries were represented in the collection. They had to be from Herb's travels.

She held close a heavy oval ornament depicting Moscow's St. Basil's Cathedral. How could Herb have allowed her to borrow these treasured memories? She had to be careful. If she broke one, she'd never be able to replace it. What memories they must hold for him—obviously handpicked by his wife, Lacey.

She placed the St. Basil ornament in a prominent spot on the tree where it could also hide a defect in the evergreen she'd purposely chosen. A good-size wooden box lay in the bottom of the cardboard container. After unearthing irreplaceable items, she couldn't imagine what it contained. The lid opened with a creak, and Kaylee peered inside. Bubble wrap covered whatever he'd left for her. She lifted the first and lay it on the floor. Then she did it with the others, deciding it best to open them carefully one at a time.

Kaylee peeled back the bubble wrap on the first one and stared. Then she opened the second, and the third, on to the last one. Thirty beautifully crafted, dated personalized ornaments lay in front of her. Each told the story of a family.

A story, a life, and loved ones her mother never shared.

She reached for one with trembling fingers.

Her phone rang, and she pulled back as if caught peering into a life that someone truly special had once hoped for her to take part.

She stood and moved to where she'd left her phone after calling Abigail. She answered and heard the familiar noise that indicated that the caller was a telemarketer. She hung up the phone and stood staring down at the ornaments that told her all she needed to know from Mayor Herb and about the depth of her mother's selfishness.

Since his arrival, Christian had never seen the doors of Rose's store open and close so much. Women and men, even a child or two, came in with a sense of purpose. They ordered deli food from him and scanned the aisles for baking ingredients and spices. One couple purchased a pre-cooked ham and muttered a complaint about a hasty invitation. At the cashier, Rose leaned close and spoke to them. Their frowns turned upward. "Ah, well, this will do, won't it?" the man exclaimed. "Add some brown sugar and a little pineapple and no one will know better."

"Just none of our usual fare." Rose waggled her finger. "This one is put on for a stranger."

Something was going on in Mullet Harbor, and Christian's curiosity was piqued.

Abigail swung into the store with Dylan on her heels.

"Abigail," Rose called, "so glad you're here. Can you make the fruit tray? I've been so busy I haven't had a chance to leave the register."

"Dylan and I are on it." Abigail waved to Christian as they passed. "We'll grab some fruit and take it back to my place."

Dylan ran over to the meat counter. "Did you hear?" He jumped up and down like the eight-year-old boy he always should have been allowed to be. "Ms. Kaylee's having a Christmas party, and we're invited."

Christian shot a look at the store's owner. "She said she planned to have a party in a couple of days."

"Well, she changed her mind." Rose stomped toward him. "You have someplace better to be?"

Christian laughed. "Wouldn't matter if I did, would it? What can I do to help?"

"You and me can do the most good staying right where we are. The call's gone out, and people are gonna need us."

Dylan smiled up at Christian. "This is the best Christmas I've ever had."

Christian moved through the half door separating the meat counter from the rest of the store and bent down in front of his nephew. "Listen, what I said to you Sunday about your mom, I didn't mean it. Not one word of it."

Dylan blinked. "Yes, you did."

"No. I love her. We were very close growing up. I don't want you to think that I don't care about her. I'm worried about her every day just like I know you are."

Dylan looked down. A tear fell and weaved through some dirt on the toe of the shoe. "She's gonna be okay," he muttered. "It's just that while she's in the hospital, she can't—" He looked up with tear-filled eyes. The tears flowed over, and he swatted at them in an angry motion. "She can't drink or take stuff. When she gets better, they'll all be out of her system, and she can be my mom."

The one thing Dylan had never had. Cassie had to have stayed clean while she carried him. He'd give her that. Dylan was born without addiction, a perfect baby boy with lungs so strong, Christian and Amy had heard his wails long before they made it to Cassie's room shortly after his birth.

Dylan stared at him as if needing assurance.

Christian had none, but he forced a smile. "Miracles happen, don't they? You made a wish, and it seems to me it's all coming true."

Dylan shook his head. "I don't think it was my wish that came true."

"You don't?" Christian stood. "What do you call all this? We're not only staying in this town, we're a guest of the mayor. We drove to a Christmas party in his limo. We're going to a party at Ms. Kaylee's house. We've been fed and well-taken care of. I don't just have one job. I have two."

"I think that it's a Christmas miracle because Ms. Kaylee prayed, and I've been praying ever since. I prayed for you to decide to stay. I prayed for us to have fun and for you to find a job. I prayed for Ms. Kaylee to have a party so you could meet her mom. She's a really nice lady. And … and I've been praying for Mom. She's going to be okay. I know it. God won't let anything happen to her. He won't let anything happen to us either."

Christian wished that he had a minute particle of Dylan's newfound faith.

"I've prayed, too." Abigail joined them, her cart laden with seasonal fruits. "You ready, Dylan. I need your help. We'll have this done shortly, and I'll walk Dylan back here so that you can get ready for the party. Then I'll go help Kaylee finish up."

"Time?" Christian asked.

"Seven o'clock." Abigail bounced on her toes and saluted him.

If it had been anyone else, the action might have seemed strange, but now that he was getting to know the quirky girl, he'd expect nothing less. Christian shook his head. "How is she pulling this all together?"

Abigail beamed. "In Mullet Harbor, your friends help. You'll see."

Rose waved her hand, the bangles on her wrist clinking. "You're gonna see, all right." She turned to greet Isaac Cooper and his daughter. "So, what are you two in charge of?"

"Cookies!" Sophie squealed. "Dylan, we're going to have another party."

Dylan nodded. "And there's Mayor Herb's Christmas Eve party, too."

The door opened again. A younger woman beelined

toward the meat counter. "I'm in charge of the beef tray," she announced as she breezed past Rose.

Christian shook his head. Just how many people were going to show up at Kaylee McFarland's little house on the bayou?

Chapter Nineteen

Kaylee had long since allowed the grief to run its course. Her emotions had gone from surprise, to anger, to hatred, to remorse for that hatred, and then settled on utter sadness at all she'd lost through no fault of her own. She'd debated hanging the ornaments, but when the grief returned, so did truth.

Kaylee had been caught up in trying to recapture her Christmas memories because those times wrapped her mother's hugs around her and made her feel loved. Yet, during the rest of the year, she'd felt used by her mother, a prop for her life. Never had her father made her feel that way. He had protected Kaylee from Mother in the same way his presence made Kaylee perform as her mother's dutiful daughter. After his death while in Baltimore, she'd continue to wear that duty.

In Mullet Harbor, she had been free of it until her mother descended upon her, trying to regain possession.

Breaking free of her mother's psychological hold, she'd taken her time placing each ornament on the tree, the older ones first. At the top of her tree, hung an exquisite glass ornament in the shape of a church with the names Herb and Lacey and the year Kaylee assumed had been their first Christmas. Six years were missing, maybe broken or lost, but each was unique in shape and style and year, but all read, Herb, Lacey, and LeAnn, with the year of the family's Christmas. The last year recorded was the year of Mother's eighteenth birthday.

That made sense to Kaylee. Her mother often said that when she turned eighteen, she left home and never returned. She'd seen her parents at her wedding, and she put them far behind her after she returned from her honeymoon. "They never cared about me. Why should I care about them?" her mother would say. But the tree's decorations told Kaylee that Herb and Lacey Miller had cared deeply for their daughter—and their granddaughter.

Eighteen pristine ornaments from "Baby's First," through Kaylee's eighteenth Christmas, were personalized for her. Clearly, they'd been saved to give to her. Interests that she had during childhood and events in her life were chronicled, including her graduation from high school. When she'd found that her graduation was the last one collected, Kaylee had searched online. Lacey Miller had died before Christmas that year.

Kaylee had held the ornament and wept for a grandmother who'd never gotten to hold Kaylee in her arms and for the void she felt as a daughter to a woman who could be so cruel.

"Kaylee!" someone called from the other side of the front door. "I can't knock."

Kaylee rushed to the door and opened it to find a stack of filled food containers staring at her. The legs, feet on tiptoes, announced that the person was Abigail.

"Here. Let me take some of those."

"Please." Abigail waited until Kaylee took half the load. Then she entered. "I have fruit trays and some sandwiches. Isaac and Sophie are bringing cookies. The Purdues insisted upon a ham, but other than that, it's going to be finger foods and dessert."

Abigail looked around the house at the lights Kaylee had strung and the wonderful crafts that had turned her home into a picture that could be placed on a Christmas magazine cover. "It's beautiful, and look at the tree." As if drawn, she tiptoed to the corner.

Her eyes widened. "Isn't your mother's name …?"

Kaylee nodded and forced herself not to show one more bit of emotion.

"I don't understand. These are dated long—" Abigail

covered her mouth with her hand. Then she straightened. "Your mother is—you're their—"

Kaylee nodded, and the choking tears fell. "She kept me from them. All these years, I had a grandfather and a grandmother who loved me."

Abigail wrapped Kaylee in a comforting embrace. She held Kaylee until Kaylee had no tears left. Then she used her thumbs to wipe away Kaylee's tears. "I'm sorry. I really am, but those ornaments on that tree tell you the most important thing you need to know. Herb and Lacey loved you. They could have easily forgotten you, but those beautiful keepsakes tell you that you were never absent in their hearts. And Herb made a way for you to come and spend time with him." She fell back, her hands clasped against her heart. "What love is that?"

"But Mother …"

Abigail placed her hands on Kaylee's shoulders. "I'm sure you've heard I have a sister. We were close until my parents both got ill. Momma had a stroke and struggled with speech and movement for the rest of her life. I tried to help Daddy because he had to work, but my sister was only interested in her social life and what Momma's illness did to it. The stress made Daddy sick. He had heart issues. We struggled financially. Someone needed to take care of them, and I needed desperately for my sister to find a job. She never would. I'm sure you've heard what happened after my parents both passed. I can't explain how ugly that all got. But I still love my sister."

"How?" Kaylee begged to know of a way she could hold to a yawning relationship with her mother.

"I have one memory that I hold close. When we were small, my sister got stuck up in a very high tree, and she was afraid to come down. I climbed that tree, and though it only took a few minutes, it felt like hours as I guided her down from branch to branch. When we had our feet on the ground, my sister hugged me and told me she'd have never gotten out alive if not for me. An over-exaggeration, but I remember that day and how proud I was to be her big sister. And I remember something else. My sister is climbing so recklessly in life, and one day, she's going to need me to guide her down. Your mother's going to need you too, and you want to show her love like your grandparents had for you."

Kaylee nodded. "Thank you for sharing your wisdom."

Abigail slapped at the air as if what she'd shared was of no consequence when it had been a lifeline for Kaylee.

"Speaking of Mother ..." Kaylee moved the curtain on her kitchen window and looked outside. Mother had not returned.

A bit of unease crept into Kaylee's soul. She'd hurt her mother after she'd gotten on a plane and had flown to a place Kaylee knew she most definitely wouldn't choose if it were the only place on earth to spend Christmas. She'd faced a very looming ghost of her past, and she'd done so because she'd been worried about Kaylee.

"Call her," Abigail urged. "Tell her you're sorry. I can see the apology written all over your face. You might as well humble yourself now."

Kaylee nodded and picked up her phone. She dialed, and her call went to voice mail. "Mother, it's Kaylee. I'm sorry for what I said in the restaurant." She paused, almost ready to lie and say she didn't really mean it. She closed her eyes. "I was upset. I felt trapped with Jacob. We are having a party. People will be arriving at seven. It's six-fifteen now. I hope you'll be here to greet everyone." She held to the phone a bit longer as if it were a landline and her mother might pick up after hearing Kaylee spill her guts on the answering machine. "I love you, and I'm really sorry." She hung up.

Abigail began to fuss with the food on the table, placing it around.

"I don't know what I'd do without you," Kaylee said.

Abigail giggled. "You'd do just fine. All I did was make a few calls, bake a cake, put together a fruit tray, and make a few sandwiches."

"And kept me afloat on a very stormy sea." Kaylee laughed. "Are we ready to party or what?"

"We're ready to par-tay." Abigail twirled on her tiptoes as if she'd been born to be a ballerina.

There would be no limo ride to Kaylee's party, not that Christian had expected one, but he sure never imagined that Herb wouldn't have been home getting ready for an impromptu party thrown by his favorite schoolteacher.

Unease worked its way into Christian's thoughts. He and Dylan had detoured to Herb's studio only to find it closed. Maybe the mayor had been helping Kaylee all afternoon. He picked up his pace until he realized Dylan couldn't keep up despite the new hiking boots left in his room by Herb. The kid had been overjoyed with them.

The night air held a heavier chill. Maybe the weather reports had been right, and they'd get a cold snap before the holidays.

They reached the turnoff to Kaylee's road. A car slowed and pulled beside them.

"Running late?" Rose leaned over. "Climb in, boys, and I'll take you the rest of the way. Herb ain't with you?"

Christian opened the back door and allowed Dylan to climb in first. Then he entered and shut the door. "I was hoping you'd seen him or that he'd been helping Kaylee with the party preparations."

Christian lurched as Rose hit the gas on her sedan. She peered at him in the rearview mirror. Her stare held a world of concern. "Abigail's been helping. Neither of us has seen Herb." She took a deep breath as if to calm her emotions. "He may have had an early evening or night tour on one of his boats."

"Then he doesn't know about the party."

"Not unless someone else got word to him." She pulled the car along the side of the lane about ten in line from the front. "Going to be interesting to see how that place holds the entire town, ain't it?"

Christian smiled despite his worry. "I wondered about that as I watched all the residents come into the store today." He stepped out of the car and held the door open for Dylan. Then he opened Rose's door for her. "Look, if he isn't here, and we don't see him in the first half-hour, I'm going to go looking for him. I didn't think about checking to see if he'd taken one of the boats."

"If he's not there and a boat is gone, don't you do something foolish like try to find him in the mangroves. You come back and get Remy and Isaac. They know this place."

The old gal was rattled. And so was Christian. "I wouldn't worry you by doing something like that," he assured.

"And if he shows, you let me be the one to fuss at him.

He'll take it from me." She linked her arm with his. "The old goat."

Dylan ran onto the pier and waited for Christian and Rose to follow him to the front door. The boy knocked.

Kaylee swung open the door and smiled. "Dylan Abrams, come in, kind sir. Sophie's here, and she's holding court with a lot of young suitors. None of them have her favor, though, because she's looking for you."

"Ah, Ms. Kaylee, that's embarrassing." Dylan slunk by her. "Look." He showed his shoes to the pretty teacher. "Herb got them for me."

Christian would have to remember that shoes made the kid happy.

"Where is the pest?" Dylan searched the house. Then, without waiting for an answer, he ran off.

"Dylan!" Christian warned. "Good evening, Ms. McFarland."

"Come in, you two," she invited. "I wondered if you got word, Christian."

"How could he not?" Rose kissed Kaylee's cheek as she passed. "This party was a boon for business. We kept busy all afternoon."

Kaylee pointed to her table and two or three other folding tables set up around the kitchen and dining area. "I would think so." She leaned close. "Thank you so much for helping to make this special."

"We're always up for a good party in Mullet Harbor," Rose advised. "I'm going to find a seat." She walked into the mingling crowds, and Christian doubted she'd ever make her way to a chair as she greeted one after the other.

Christmas music played in the background, and the home was aglow in Christmas lights and decorations—the ones that Mayor Herb had donated. "The place looks nice," Christian told her. "But it sure doesn't shine as awesomely as you. Red is your color." And that was an understatement.

Kaylee put her hand to her curls as if taken back by his words. "You say the nicest things, Mr. Abrams. They take my breath away."

He tilted his head. "No one's ever told you how breathtaking you are? I find that hard to believe."

"No, and if no one else does, your compliments will hold me all of my days." The tears in her eyes told him that her words were truth. If she were his, he'd never let a day go by without letting her know how special she was.

A woman approached the open door, and Kaylee greeted her.

Christian stepped aside to allow Kaylee the opportunity to give her new guest attention. When the woman waved and moved further inside, Christian closed the door. "Herb isn't here, is he?"

"No." She straightened. "I actually thought he'd have arrived already."

"We haven't seen him." The worry on her face told him he needed to change the subject. "Is your mother enjoying the party?"

She shook her head absently. "She's not here either." She bit the red-polished nail on her index finger and lifted her gaze to him. "You don't think she killed him, do you?"

Christian laughed aloud, and Kaylee joined him. "All the same, if they don't show up soon, we probably should go looking for one or the other. Mother is absent because of my actions."

"Oh?"

"Yeah, I kind of said something ... probably like what you may have said to Dylan. She didn't take it well and stormed off."

A knock on the door followed its opening. Remy and another woman stepped inside. "Hey, there. Kaylee, I don't think you've met my sister. "Marielle, I'd like you to meet Kaylee McFarland, our newest schoolteacher here in Mullet Harbor, and this is the gentleman that gave you such a good lead on that story you're running down. Christian Abrams, Marielle Arneaux."

Marielle wore her jet-black hair in a ponytail, no-nonsense style. Dressed in tan slacks and a crisp white button-down blouse, she made a stunning picture. Her strong cheekbones added poise to her power. Christian had seen her picture on the *Miami Herald*'s website, but it hadn't done her justice. She was as petite as a gymnast, but she held herself like a Green Beret. "Ms. Arneaux, it's my pleasure. I'm a huge fan."

She shook his hand with one pump and narrowed her obsidian eyes. "Really? You know of me from Pennsylvania?" Yep. No nonsense. No trust, either, it seemed.

"Associated Press reports, yes. I've followed several of your investigations. The reporting into the conservation efforts of the sugar industry ran against the normal reporting of how they're destroying the ecological balance, and I found it fair and accurate without opinion. You hung some companies out to dry, and you cleared up the reputation of others."

She gave a curt nod. "And thanks to you, I'm on the trail of another investigation. Remy tells me that we'll be talking either later tonight or tomorrow."

"I look forward to it," he said.

She didn't wait but headed into the house as others called out her name.

"She's a bit on the terse side," Remy winked, "but like you said, she's fair and accurate. If you have anything to hide, you might want to tell her upfront. She'll ferret it out, and she doesn't like to dig if she doesn't have to dig."

"Open book." Christian raised his hands.

"Ephraim here?" Remy's gaze turned to Kaylee.

"Yes," Kaylee said. "I haven't had a chance to introduce Christian yet, but he arrived with Isaac, Sophie, and your mother. We have another worry on our hands."

"Can I help?" Remy offered.

"Maybe," Christian said. "Herb and Kaylee's mother haven't shown up yet."

Remy leaned back on his heels and came forward again. "I know right where they are."

Kaylee startled. "They're okay?"

"Depends on who's telling the story."

"Remy ..." Kaylee punched his arm. "What happened?"

"They got in a heated discussion outside the studio. Mrs. Purdue called the station, said this woman was causing a scene, and Herb didn't look like he could handle it. I arrived, and your mother wouldn't back down."

Kaylee covered her mouth with her hand, but the edge of her smile curved over its hiding place. "You didn't."

"Second warning in two days, and I gave her three chances."

"What did Herb do?"

"He tried to talk me out of it. I told him I'd charge him with obstruction and put him in the same cell with her. He claimed that to be cruel and unusual punishment and backed off. Then he followed me to the station and offered to post her bail. She wouldn't accept. She wanted her lawyer. I gave her a phone call …"

"Her lawyer in Baltimore isn't going to help her here."

"She didn't call him. She wanted Jacob's number. I tried to explain to her that he was the state attorney, and he couldn't help her, but she insisted. I left her in the station awaiting his arrival."

Christian couldn't imagine Herb lingering anywhere in LeAnn McFarland's presence, let alone the sheriff's satellite station. He hadn't seen the inside, hoped he wouldn't have cause, but the outside didn't look like much. Surely, the old guy had headed home. Maybe he could ask Rose to call him and tell him about Kaylee's party.

"And Herb …?"

"He wouldn't leave her in there alone. He was waiting outside the holding cell. Said to tell you he knows about the party, and he and your mother will be along soon."

Well, he didn't know the mayor as well as he thought.

Another knock sounded, and Kaylee opened the door. "Mr. and Mrs. Purdue, so nice to see you. Come in."

The couple who'd bought the ready-made ham entered. Mr. Purdue carried a pan, placed it on the table, and removed the tin foil. The titillating aroma announced the arrival of a maple-glazed delight. At least this was a dish he didn't have to be afraid of. And if this Mrs. Purdue was the one mentioned earlier, she'd been a pretty busy lady this afternoon, cooking a ham, and calling the sheriff on Kaylee's mom. Quite the multitasker, that one.

Kaylee thanked them and ushered them into her overcrowded living room.

Guests had begun to spill out onto the back pier, and some had worked their way back around to the front. Still, the room was crowded.

Kaylee took a deep breath and fanned her face with her hands.

"Are you okay?" Christian asked.

She smiled. "I'm perfect." She turned toward the sheriff. "Remy, you're brilliant. Mother's arrest was the diversion we needed. Mrs. Purdue won't be able to resist sharing the gossip. If she didn't know who Mother was before, she'll certainly know once she arrives, and Mother will be too busy trying to squelch the rumors to be interested in anything else."

Christian straightened. He didn't know whether to be impressed or distressed at Kaylee's devious ease.

Fay Lamb

Chapter Twenty

Kaylee chatted to her guests as they approached the food and drink table. Many complimented her on her party. How gracious and humble were these people that they would provide everything and give her the credit? She'd tried to give them their due, but after three dear ladies had shushed her and advised that she would do the same for them, she began to accept what they said with a "thank you very much." The fact that they'd provided normal fare for the festivities hadn't escaped her either.

Laughter rang through her tiny house and out onto the bayou. Couples even danced on her pier to the Christmas music that played from speakers through her windows. Abercrombie was probably grousing about his noisy neighbor.

Rose drew close. "I just got a text from Herb. He's on

his way. He said to warn you that your mother's ahead of him, and she has company."

Kaylee nodded. "Jacob."

Rose leaned back. "What's going on that I don't know?" She brushed her gray hair from her eyes.

"Remy arrested Mother this afternoon for causing a scene outside Mayor Herb's studio. Herb tried to bond her out, but she wouldn't let him. He stayed until Jacob answered Mother's summons."

Rose tilted her head. "Young lady, what else is going on here?"

Kaylee bit her lip.

"Herb isn't going to follow some strange woman to the jail and try to bond her out if she caused him trouble even if she is your mom," Rose pressed.

Kaylee grimaced. "I'm not one-hundred percent sure why they dislike each other so much. The only thing I know is that Mother's starting the arguments. He's never said anything to you about her?"

"Nope even when I asked him how he so readily recognized her when she entered the community center the other night. He alerted you quick enough. So, why don't you tell me what's going on?"

Kaylee couldn't explain everything to Rose. She hadn't lied when she told Rose she didn't have all the information she needed, and though the woman was close to Herb, he obviously had kept some truths from her as well. Kaylee wanted to spare the woman her half-truths and save Herb from the explanation until he was ready. Herb would talk to Rose in his time. "Rose, you'll have to ask the mayor."

LeAnn McFarland's ability to hold a grudge had never been something her mother would try to hide. She reveled in vicious attacks, and on occasion, Kaylee had found the issues non-existent or petty. She long since tired of Mother's drama. Her father had dismissed the incidents as her mother's escape from boredom, but Kaylee had never known how deep her mother's bitterness flowed or why. Now, she knew the source and the depth, but she didn't know the real reason.

"Kaylee, what's going on around here?" Rose insisted.

The opening door saved Kaylee from explanation.

Mother waltzed in and did a turn, a true overreaction.

Jacob was close on her heels.

"Kaylee, how magnificent that all of your friends could join us tonight." Mother pulled Kaylee close for a hug and released her just as quickly. "Look, Jacob. And we thought it would be a small, comfortable crowd."

"For Mullet Harbor, this is small." An elderly woman stepped forward and greeted Mother.

The socialite in LeAnn McFarland would not allow her to show her rudeness. Not yet anyway. Mother made her way through the crowd as if she were the hostess.

"You heard?" Jacob stood beside Kaylee.

"I heard." Kaylee kept her gaze on her mother. "You couldn't post bond, could you? Wouldn't it be a conflict of interest for the state attorney?"

Jacob, a head taller than her, peered downward. "Herb asked me to pretend like I'd taken care of it. He'd called the local bondsman and had it arranged before I arrived."

Kaylee took a deep breath. "But you were happy to take the credit." She rounded on him. Then bit her lip, a reprimand to herself for allowing her emotions to fuel her ire at Jacob. "No. I'm sorry. My mother's a lawyer. She knew it was a conflict of interest for you. She put you in that position. I apologize on her behalf."

Jacob grasped her arm and pulled her toward the door and to a quieter side of her dock. "I didn't do it for your mother. I did it for you. And because Herb asked me to appease her. I'm sorry that my aunt has painted a picture of me as someone who likes to have his palm greased or would hurt innocent parties. I play into the role they placed me in because even if I were a choirboy, they wouldn't let me into their inner circle. I'm sorry that you and I have never hit it off, but you know, that's fine with me. This place—this forsaken outpost—you can have it, and every opinionated and prejudiced person in it." His stare cut through her. Pain reflected there, taking her breath. He stomped away from her.

"Hey." Christian was by her side. "You okay."

She nodded. "I have to talk to him." She touched Christian's hand. "Please, excuse me." She ran, careful that her heels didn't stick in the slats of the dock. "Jacob!"

He stopped, his car door open. "I've got to go. A mid-week party is too much for a dishonest, illicit working man like me."

"Please. Stay for a while. Mother will be disappointed."

He shook his head and started to sit inside his car.

"I'll be disappointed." She turned and spread her arms wide. "After all, this was meant to impress both you and Mother."

"I don't think I'm much welcome here."

"You are. By me. Besides, I have a gift I need to give you so you can put it under your tree."

He hesitated another moment but then stood. "I'll stay for a half-hour."

"Good to hear it," Herb said and stepped from the dark. "I appreciate what you did, son."

Jacob and Herb remained silent as they walked with Kaylee back toward her house.

Christian had remained outside where she'd left him.

"Excuse me, gentlemen," Kaylee said. "I'll be right with you." She waited for Herb and Jacob to enter the house before going to Christian. "Sorry. Jacob went out of his way to help Mother. I wanted to make things right."

Christian sipped from a small plastic cup. "No umbrella. A sure sign that Herb was late for the party."

Kaylee smiled. This man was so good at putting people at ease. "Are you having a good time?"

"Absolutely," he assured. "I watched the kids while they played on the back dock, and I met Isaac's brother."

"I didn't get to talk much with him before everyone began arriving. Getting Ms. Cora settled took a while."

"He's a bit like his brother, but a lot different than I expected for an FBI agent."

Kaylee agreed. Ephraim Cooper had arrived wearing a floral shirt, shorts, and a pink lei around his neck. The attire, he said, was picked out by his favorite—"and thank goodness"—only niece.

"I don't want to be too far away from Dylan," Christian said. "Want to join me for a walk around back?"

"I'd like that." She slipped her arm in the crook of his. "Christian, you do understand why I was leery at first of holding the party and inviting you and Dylan?"

"Completely."

They came to a dark corner where no one loitered. She tugged his arm to stop him and leaned close. The aftershave he wore wasn't an expensive brand, but the hint of spice warmed her. "Jacob isn't to be trusted," she whispered, closing her eyes against the emotions welling in her.

"Uh-huh," he said so softly she almost hadn't heard.

She opened her eyes and turned.

Christian had tilted his head so that they were closer. He stared at her lips.

"It's getting complicated." She breathed in the scent of him.

"More complicated than you could ever imagine." His breath fanned her already warm face.

"Oh ..." She let the word linger as he closed the remaining space between them.

His lips brushed hers ever so slightly before he pulled away. He searched her face.

Almost on its own accord, her head tilted with the acquiescence of desire.

He kissed her again. This time his lips lingered on hers before he turned his head and kissed her hair. "Kaylee." The intimacy that came with her name on his lips warmed her even more deeply.

"Kaylee!" Her mother's whispered ire drew Kaylee away from Christian.

Mother's nostril's flared, and her eyes bulged. "What are you doing?" Her voice remained low.

"Well, woman, don't you know?" The cackle came from Ms. Cora who stood behind Mother. "I'm a little addled in the brain, and even I know those two are in love."

"Momma Cora." Isaac stepped over and tugged his mother-in-law away. "I don't think that question was meant to be answered."

"Well?" Mother's insistence proved that theory false.

"Mother, others will overhear. Can we talk about this later?" She turned to Christian. "Please, don't leave. Enjoy the rest of the party."

Mother stepped closer. "Where's your son, Mr. Abrams?"

"LeAnn." Herb joined the intimate argument. "Get away from the two of them and get back to the party or you're going to embarrass yourself and your daughter."

"I think he's already done enough of that," Mother spat.

"We'll go," Christian offered.

Kaylee reached for his hand. "I'll never forgive you if you do." Her hand trembled as she held his. "Please, don't."

He smiled. "How can I deny someone as lovely as you?" He rubbed his thumb over the back of her hand before he released her and moved beyond her mother's reach.

Kaylee didn't miss the scowl that Herb gave to Christian under Mother's watched. When her mother turned away from him, he offered Kaylee a playful wink, and she had to stare down at the plank beneath her feet.

"That a daughter of mine would behave so brazenly with a grifter," Mother chastised. "I don't know why I'm so surprised. It's in your blood, I presume. Go back inside and tend to your guests."

Kaylee thought about standing firm, about championing Christian and refusing to do as ordered, but that was silly. This was her party, and these people had shown up to support her. If Ms. Cora could remember what happened less than five minutes ago, and if Isaac couldn't keep his mother-in-law quiet, the truth would soon be known to everyone.

But what truth would that be? Mother's truth: that her daughter was a brazen hussy who kissed men in the shadows of a party. She'd been brazen, but she'd never been kissed in the way Christian had kissed her. That was for sure.

Could it be Herb's truth: one couldn't fully appreciate life unless they chanced to live it, accepting what was to come, and reaching beyond their wildest dreams? She touched her fingers to her lips and fought against closing her eyes to relive the moment that Christian had given to her, the one that could never be taken back so long as she lived. That kiss had been one that she couldn't have dreamed about because she'd never been kissed in that way. One touch of his lips to hers and Kaylee's wildest dreams had been fulfilled. But she wasn't one to chance love. The emotions had to be real. Her father had taught her that love was a verb and not a noun. A kiss on her dock fueled emotions and flamed desires. Real love was put into action, standing beside the person, overcoming obstacles, doing whatever it took to keep each other in love.

Right now, there were huge obstacles to overcome, and whether Christian Abrams knew it or not, Kaylee had made a decision. She'd not allow his kiss to rule her actions, but she would stand by him, and if these feelings were any indication that she could be in love, she'd test the waters with actions that showed she cared for him and for his nephew ... and for anyone else he considered important in his life.

That was Kaylee's truth, and no one would take it away from her. She didn't have a clue how tomorrow would turn out, but she was willing to take it a moment at a time on the chance that one day she might realize that she could love this man.

"Young lady," Mother demanded.

Kaylee smiled. "Yes, ma'am. You're right. All of these lovely people have shown up to support me and love me, and I've been rude to them." She pushed past her mother, accepted a high-five from Herb, and decided that for the first time in her existence, she'd be the life of a party.

She'd handle her mother tomorrow.

Chapter Twenty-one

December 19

The sun filtering through the french door's glass warmed Kaylee's face. She turned and snuggled against the back of the couch. She'd fallen asleep here almost as soon as the last guests—Mayor Herb and Rose—had departed. Christian left around midnight with a too-tired Dylan, who'd played with Sophie until her uncle Ephraim had taken her home a few minutes earlier. Isaac, Remy, and Marielle had left together to take Ms. Cora home and get her comfortably to bed. Jacob had stayed longer than his pre-determined half-hour, and she'd bid him good-bye by handing him his gift from under her tree.

She didn't miss the lingering of his gaze upon the ornaments and the telltale jerk that told him he'd seen the same truths that Kaylee had. No one else had taken much notice of the decorations, including her mother. And, to his credit, Jacob said nothing.

Others stayed laughing, dancing, and talking, and Kaylee had played the perfect hostess.

When everyone had departed, leaving them alone, Kaylee had expected a long lecture, which could have covered everything from the birds and the bees to how Kaylee's reputation was important, not only for herself but for Mother's political ambitions and Daddy's good name.

Instead, Mother had said a terse *good night* and sauntered to her room.

Kaylee dozed for a moment, a fleeting dream of Christian causing her desire to linger in sleep a bit longer. Movement in the room, though, pulled her head from dreamy Christian and back to reality. Though she turned away from the back of the couch, she kept her eyes closed for a long second, relishing the memory of the too-brief brush of Christian's lips against hers.

Finally, when no other movement sounded, Kaylee opened her eyes.

Mother stood by the tree. She touched one of Herb's precious ornaments with one hand. With the other, she covered her mouth. Her shoulders shook in what appeared to be silent grief.

Kaylee remained still, not wanting to intrude on her

mother's thoughts.

"You would have loved your grandmother," Mother said without turning.

Kaylee sat up and wiped the sleep from her eyes. "Then why did you not let me visit them?"

The strangled sound that came from her mother was both a laugh and a cry. "What makes you think they wanted you to visit?"

The barb slung Kaylee's way hurt deeply. "Oh, I don't know. Perhaps it's the ornaments collected for every year of your life and mine. Or maybe the way Herb worked to get me to Mullet Harbor and the care he's given to me since I arrived. Perhaps, it's the gifting of those ornaments he so obviously treasures."

"Kaylee …" Mother swung around, her shoulders slumped as if carrying a great burden. "He gave you these because he doesn't want them any longer."

Kaylee jumped to her feet. "How can you say that? Everyone here talks about how much he loved his wife. If you hear people talk, you'd think their love was magical."

"But she's gone. He's not going to linger on thoughts of her any longer. Hasn't he already found someone to replace her—that Rose woman?"

"Rose hasn't replaced anyone. Even if Herb married her, I don't think he'd forget the woman he loved for all those years. Did you go inside his studio?"

Mother shook her head, and for the first time, Kaylee realized that her usually put-together mom had not gotten out of her gown and robe. Her hair was a mess. If Kaylee had to wager, Mother hadn't slept at all.

"I couldn't go inside that place. What's there is too painful for me."

Kaylee moved to her mother's side and slipped her arm around her shoulder. "I need to understand. I'm angry at you for keeping me from them. If I could only understand why."

Mother seemed to fall into her, wrapping her arms around Kaylee's side and laying her head on Kaylee's shoulder.

"Your mother was the instigator behind renovating your father's childhood home—the home of your ancestors. She made it a perfect place for him to showcase his art. Why would it be too painful for you?"

Mother sniffled. "It's not important."

Kaylee turned, pulled her mother away from her, but held to her shoulders. "It's very important for me to know. I think your telling me would help me to understand you a bit more. I don't know why you treat me the way you do, and it hurts sometimes. I think your relationship with my grandparents is the key. If you share, maybe we can work through it together."

"You couldn't understand." Mother brushed Kaylee's

hair with her hand. "I never left you. I would never think of leaving you in prep schools or keeping you out of the life your father and I lived."

"Is that what you feel my grandparents did to you?" Kaylee couldn't see it. Not Herb. He was too involved with so many people. His actions were inclusive, not exclusive.

Mother waved her hand as if the matter were closed.

Kaylee stepped back. "If you're not going to tell me, I'll ask him. It's only fair. I've given you the chance to tell me your side of the story. He should have the same opportunity."

"You can ask him. Go right ahead, but you need to examine his answers—see if I've ever made you feel the way my parents made me feel."

"Unnecessary except when necessary." The words slipped from Kaylee's lips. Feelings that had long been held in her heart had found their way to the surface again.

Mother widened her eyes and stepped back. "Is that the way you've felt? Your father and I—"

"Father never made me feel that way." Why couldn't she shut her mouth the way she'd always done?

Mother backed away from her, reaching behind her as if seeking support. She brushed a chair arm and moved around it, her pained gaze never leaving Kaylee's face. "I'm sorry you feel that way. I never meant for you to feel anything but an asset to me."

Kaylee sighed. "I don't want to be an asset. I want to be someone you treasure no matter what."

"No matter your kissing that man in the dark. Don't think I didn't see all of it. He would have had you pinned against the wall if I hadn't interrupted."

Kaylee's face burned with the embarrassment of such an implication. Her mother saw things through a skewed prism. "He wouldn't. He isn't like that. You don't know him."

"And you don't either. Jacob told me that Daddy's still drawn to the loose types. He and Momma congregated with them: surf bums, writers without any real trade, adventurers who didn't care that they could die at any second because of their foolishness."

"You won't even give me credit for having a modicum of your intelligence, will you?"

"I'd like to think you'd inherited some brains from either me or your father, but you can rest assured that I'd never take a chance on my future being ruined by a man I didn't know anything about. I dated your father through college. I didn't let him kiss me until our graduation day. That's the way to keep a man. You don't just dole yourself out there."

"Dole myself? Mother!" Kaylee nearly hissed. "It was a kiss. Yes, a tender kiss, but I won't let you sully it with your innuendo. You need to count the years and be reminded that I'm almost thirty." She paced away. Then the truth hit her. "Fear." She spun around. "You didn't let Daddy kiss you because you were afraid that if he got what he really wanted from you, he'd leave you. Not allowing him to kiss you dangled the carrot in front of him until you were sure the relationship had gone on long enough that he couldn't leave you."

Mother remained silent.

"What's your side of the story, Mother? Were you left in prep schools?"

"I wanted to be in prep schools," Mother raised her voice. "Because the life they lived scared me to death. I needed to be in one place. I didn't want to fly across the oceans or live in huts in the middle of Africa so that Daddy could do his job. I didn't want to be inoculated against every disease known to man because they wanted to cart me off to the far reaches of nowhere."

"So, they let you do what you wanted." Kaylee sank to the sofa. "And you're mad at them because they did?"

"I expected them to stay at home where I could visit on the weekends. Instead, I had two weeks at Christmas with them."

"What about summers?"

"They wanted me to go with them to see the world. They never got it. I couldn't."

"But you flew here. You've flown with Daddy ..."

"And I'm scared to death of flying, but I had to do it ..."

"To keep Daddy ..." Kaylee let the words fill the space between them. "Didn't you know that he loved you more than life? Everything he did was for you and for me."

"I wanted to believe that, but I couldn't. And now you've done what I've always feared you would do."

"You believe that by living my life that I've abandoned you, but I haven't."

"You said it yesterday. You didn't want to be with me at Christmas." Mother's words flowed like a river of insecurities and pain, one she must have worked a lifetime to keep from flowing over the banks of her soul.

"I'm sorry that I said it that way. The truth is, I feel confined by your need to keep me close to your wings, but I don't know if you shelter me because you're afraid I'll bring shame to you and to Daddy's name or whether you really cared so much for me that you didn't want to let me go."

Mother slumped once again. She covered her eyes with her hand. "If you didn't know, then I guess I have failed to show you." Her lips trembled when she lowered her hand, and tears filled her eyes. "I have loved you since the moment I learned that you were inside of me. And when the doctor told me that I had to be extremely careful because of the high risk and to never plan on giving your father another child, I loved you all the more."

Kaylee stood, "You've never—" but Mother stepped away and held up her hand as if to erect a wall between them.

"I suppose you'll think that drove me to fear that your father would leave me if I couldn't provide him a son."

Kaylee sighed. "That would never occur to me because I know how much Daddy loved you. Your fear keeps you from seeing what's in front of you. No matter where I go in life, I will always love you."

"I have a migraine." She turned and left the room.

Kaylee stood in stunned silence. Neither her father nor her mother had ever mentioned the reason she was an only child. She had assumed that they both wanted it that way, that they couldn't be bothered with another child like Kaylee. She turned and moved to the tree, lifting from its limb the ornament Mother had been touching. She carried it outside with her onto the deck where chairs—including her dining room chairs—littered the space.

Abercrombie was in the water at the edge of the deck. Hopefully, the children had not tossed food to him the night before. She'd forgotten to give them a warning. If they had, it could make him a lot more dangerous than he already was.

She'd forgotten a lot of things since that party started: how to be extremely chaste, how to be extremely dutiful, and how to respect her Mother's feelings beyond her own.

Abercrombie closed his eyes slowly and opened them again. "Go," she whispered. "You might think you're the top dog in these waters, and you might be when LeAnn McFarland isn't around, but she's here. She'll have you hunted down and wear your skin as a purse or shoes."

Abercrombie didn't budge.

Kaylee lifted the ornament and stared at the picture imprinted on the expensive glass. Herb and Lacey Miller stood with a little girl against a backdrop of Rockefeller Center at Christmastime. Even if the family names and the date had not been painted onto the glass, her mother's secret had been given away. Kaylee could almost believe that she, herself, had been in that picture in another lifetime. She favored the childhood image of her mother so much. The unruly blond curls that Kaylee never had straightened were mirrored in the photo. Now, her mother no longer allowed her hair freedom to hang naturally. She shifted her gaze to the older woman and touched her face. "I wish I'd been able to meet you, Grandmother."

Grandma. The word seemed to sweep by her in the breeze. Lacey Miller didn't look like someone who would insist on formality.

"Grandma," Kaylee whispered. "I miss getting the chance to know you."

But she had Herb, and she wouldn't waste time any

longer pretending that he was the mayor who brought her to town to teach school. He was her … what would he want her to call him?

Her phone dinged a text message, and she rushed inside to retrieve it. Her grandfather was calling a meeting at the high school in thirty minutes.

Kaylee needed to take a shower. First, though, she needed to interrupt her mother's solitude to get a change of clothes. She knocked on her bedroom door.

Mother didn't respond.

She knocked again, and when she didn't get a reply, she opened the door. Her mother was not inside. The bed was made, and her mother's luggage was gone.

Chapter Twenty-two

Christian wandered around the schoolroom. He picked up the marker for the large dry erase board and looked back to where a diverse group of people sat around a table. They were staring at him: Remy and Marielle Arneaux, Isaac and Ephraim Cooper, Herb, and Rose.

He put down the marker. "Sorry. I miss teaching." He continued to pace while they awaited Kaylee's arrival. From the posters of Jane Austen, Mark Twain, and several other American authors, the actual diagram of a sentence on another poster, and some papers sharing Haiku, no doubt, they were sitting in an English classroom. He'd love to teach the class one day, just to get some of what was inside of him out. He'd always loved to teach, and Language Arts was his passion.

The door opened, and Kaylee slipped in, her gaze

colliding with his for a long second before she advanced.

"I figured it'd take you longer to lose that momma of yours," Herb teased.

Kaylee pulled out a chair, sitting between Remy and Ephraim. "She's gone for all I know. Her room is empty. Her car isn't there."

Herb moved and patted her shoulder. "I never meant for it to come to that."

"She's got a court appearance," Remy muttered. "She needs to hire a better lawyer than Jacob Marin."

"Remy!" Marielle narrowed her eyes. "Be nice. You two have never gotten along. Time to grow up and grow out of it."

Christian returned to the table and took a seat beside Rose on his right and Isaac on his left.

Herb remained standing. "LeAnn does complicate matters, but more so in light of what she saw last night." He drilled Christian with the same look he'd given him this morning before launching into a sermon on why kissing Kaylee had been the stupidest thing he could have done. "She's got her dander up when she saw these two in a compromising position …"

"Ah hem." Kaylee cleared her throat. "There was nothing compromising about it." She looked to the other members of what seemed to be a jury of their peers. "Christian kissed me. A kiss …"

"To be honest ..." Isaac gave her a patient look. "Two kisses, and the second one was ..."

"Not compromising," Kaylee insisted.

"I was going to say passionate." The preacher looked in her direction, cocked an eyebrow, and smiled. "But I stand with Momma Cora. She saw what she saw, and your mother saw it, too."

Christian set his gaze on Kaylee. "My intent was never to compromise Kaylee in any way."

"We understand that. But still, it brought on complications." Herb drilled him with that same glare.

"The problem we have here isn't Christian or Kaylee or whatever might be going on between them. That's their business." Rose slapped her hand on the table. "The problem is that dame has somehow gotten to know my nephew, and if she so much as asked him to look into Christian's background, you can expect those sorry feds to descend on us at any moment. Don't take offense, Eph."

"I'll take offense if I want." Ephraim leaned back, a lazy smile on his face.

"Where's Dylan?" Kaylee asked.

"He's with Abigail," Christian answered.

"Out of sight?"

"You don't think ...?" Christian moved to stand.

Herb motioned him to sit down. "I have friends minding our businesses. Abigail and Dylan are with Sophie and Ms. Cora at Isaac's place."

"Yeah, where I'm staying. Herb would rather my job be compromised than Remy run a chance of losing the next election," Ephraim teased. "But we need to be pro-active here and track down your mother, Kaylee."

She stood and paced. "We had an argument. She said she had a migraine. I stepped outside on the back deck, and when I returned, she'd packed up and gone."

Herb rubbed his temples. "Sounds about right. Never could settle if she couldn't have her way. If the fit she pitched wasn't loud enough to get her what she wanted, she'd cut and run."

He had the attention of everyone at the table. Christian's suspicions had been answered by the ornaments on Kaylee's tree.

"What's going on, Herb?" Rose asked.

"I'll talk about it when it's time, but now, the focus is keeping Mr. Kissy Lips safe."

Kaylee smirked.

"Why isn't bringing Jacob in an option?" Marielle asked. "If he knows what we're doing, he can set a roadblock."

Rose pushed out her chair and went to stand in front of Marielle. "Trust me. Bringing him in is not an option. Girl, have you been gone from here so long that you've forgotten that the boy was born with two liabilities: his mother and his father? His daddy would chase anything in a skirt, and my dear sister would tell lies that would make you think Mother Teresa was a villain if she thought it would give her leverage."

Ephraim and Remy laughed, but their siblings scowled at them.

"But that's not the worst of it," Rose continued. "We're sitting ducks. That boy has enough on us to bring down the mayor, a federal agent, and our sheriff."

"He wouldn't, Rose," Marielle disagreed. "You said we should trust you, but I think you're clouded by ancient history. Jacob isn't what you say he is. Sure, his dad has a reputation, and his mother has been known to lie to make herself more important, but you have him wrong."

"Marielle," Isaac kept his tone low. "I won't trust him until he tells the truth."

When pleading on Marin's behalf, the petite gymnast in her seemed to have taken over. Now, she soldiered up, straightened, and turned her dark eyes upon her brother-in-law. "About what, Isaac, his spiritual condition? We don't all have to wear God on our sleeve like you and Sidalee."

Isaac stared at his hand. "He either ran over your sister and left her on the side of the road to die, or he knows who did."

Marielle opened her mouth to speak but slammed it shut. Her gaze cut to her brother who only gave a slight nod.

Kaylee placed her hand to her chest. "He wouldn't be that cruel."

"To hide his guilt or his involvement and to keep his coveted position, yes, he would," Rose asserted.

The room fell silent. Then only the scratching of Marielle's pen against paper was heard. She zigzagged a line and punctuated it with the slam of the pen head against what she'd written. She'd probably had an all-to-personal inspiration for her next story.

Christian produced a small amount of pity in his soul for Jacob Marin.

Ephraim leaned forward. "Jacob doesn't have a clue that we suspect him, not unless anyone here has mentioned it to him. We want it that way."

"You've been investigating?" Marielle demanded.

"When I can," Ephraim admitted. "It's an unofficial collaborated effort."

"And you didn't think to cue me?" She crossed her arms, probably to keep from wrapping her hands around someone's neck.

"Knowing how you feel about him, we didn't dare," Rose said.

Marielle shot the older woman a look. "I don't feel one way or another about Jacob. Like you said, he chases everything in a skirt."

Rose apparently had the wisdom not to push Marielle's buttons. After all, the dead woman in question was Marielle's sister.

"You continue to feel for him." Isaac reached for her hand, and Marielle placed hers in his. "We don't have proof, and until we do, I wouldn't make an accusation outside of this room." He pinned Christian with a look. "Understood. No matter what, I'd never use that against him. Even if he killed my wife. All I want from him is to give Sidalee the justice she deserves even if it costs him. I've forgiven him. I don't have to trust him." That kind of faith wasn't built quickly. Isaac Cooper must have surrendered to God daily to be able to voice such forgiveness.

"Understood." Christian nodded. "What have you learned, Marielle?" He hoped to draw the conversation in another direction.

"Plenty. I have a few sources to verify before I can move it to print."

"When will you present it to your editor?"

"Oh, I've already told them what I've dug up, but I've asked them to hold off. They're only willing to do so because I hinted that something may be coming soon that will make it look like we're the ones who broke everything first. They're ready to put it on the front page at any time."

"Christian," Remy said. "I have word on your sister."

Christian steeled himself against the news.

"The hospital is anxious for a family member to step forward. They'd like to talk about end-of-life preparations."

Like pulling the plug, no doubt. Christian closed his eyes and said a silent prayer that his sister would defy medical expectations and that her life would be saved. If Dylan were by Cassie's side, would it make a difference, give her a reason to live?

He couldn't take that chance. Dylan would end up in the child welfare system and he'd, no doubt, go to prison. Though Christian expected that outcome no matter how things played out, he'd like to delay it as long as possible. If he had to choose between Cassie or his nephew, Dylan had not thrown his young life away, and if Christian could, he'd fight the demons of Earth to make sure Dylan never ended up like his mother.

"Christian?" Kaylee touched his arm. "I'm so sorry."

"Someone needs to be with her," Isaac said. "She shouldn't be alone. Perhaps I could fly there. Sophie could stay with Ephraim or with Marielle and Remy."

"No, Pastor." Christian held up his hand. "It's wonderful that you would do that for her …" Surprising, in fact. The offer overwhelmed Christian. "But your family is here for Christmas, and Sophie needs you."

"I'd do it for you," Isaac offered. "You need the

comfort of knowing someone's with her."

Marielle pushed her chair out and stood. "You know, those sources I need to confirm are all in Philadelphia. What say, weather cooperating, I go there and chase them down. If the hospital will let me, I'll work in her room, stay with her, report back, and I'll set my return flight so that I can be back here before Christmas. Isaac, you have to keep Sophie with you. She's hurting too badly."

"Will they let you in Cassie's room?" Kaylee asked.

"Oh, they'll let her." Remy smirked. "By hook or crook. We won't ask, and she won't tell."

Marielle kissed his cheek. "I'll check for flights." She pulled out her phone. "Christian, what's your number, so I can report back."

"I don't have a phone."

"And we don't want him to have one," Ephraim said. "If they suspect you know him, they'll get it from you and trace him back here too quickly."

Marielle remained still for a moment, the wheels apparently turning. "Okay. I'll report to my assistant. He'll call you if I have any news."

Christian stood and moved around the table. "Thank you." He'd have engulfed Marielle in a hug if she didn't scare him so badly.

She punched his arm. "I owe you. You've practically handed me a Pulitzer."

"All the same, I appreciate it."

Marielle sprang out the door.

Kaylee came to Christian's side. "I love these people," she whispered.

He nodded. At least when he was doing prison time, he'd have a nice memory to look back on, punctuated by a kiss in the dark with the woman who stood beside him now.

"So, we're laying low," Herb announced. "We'll watch for LeAnn, keep an eye on Jacob, and wait for Marielle to gather stronger ammunition to help when things come unraveled."

When, not if. Fear shot through Christian like an arrow. Even the mayor was worried.

Isaac bowed his head. "Lord, let Your hand be in all that we do. Keep Marielle from trouble and help her to use truth and not lies as her weapon. Help us each to know what You would have us do. We put our trust in You."

"Amen, and amen," Herb said.

Chapter Twenty-three

Kaylee walked out of the classroom with Christian. The small, one-story school was built on raised concrete to sustain hurricane-force winds and prevent significant storm surge damage, but Kaylee suspected that if the big one ever hit, the waters of the Gulf would be pushed inward over the swampland. Yet, the U-shaped building had stood for fifty years. Four steps lined the entire U, and they stood together in a courtyard filled with concrete tables and benches where the few high school students in Mullet Key brought their lunches.

Christian remained silent as they turned and faced each other.

The sun beat down upon her, and she raised her hand to shield her eyes when she sought his face. "I'm not sorry for the kiss." The words in her head had not been those, but they spilled out just the same.

"Neither am I, but it came at the wrong place and the wrong time."

Kaylee winced. "Those words usually precede a brushoff."

Christian stared beyond her out to the parking lot and the scrub on the other side of it. "We live a thousand miles apart in more ways than one. I'm a fugitive. Reality doesn't seem to often reach Mullet Harbor, but I took a child out of state custody and carried him across state lines. Several, in fact. If all I had were literal miles between us, nothing about how I feel for you would be wrong. But right now, we barely have time to explore our feelings. If Dylan and I make it unhindered through the holidays, we have to leave."

Kaylee laughed. "You think so, do you?" She lowered her hand. "Christian, you're being offered a hedge of protection that defies logic. You have an FBI agent who knows who you are and what you've done. You have the county sheriff and the town mayor fully aware of the situation they've placed themselves in to protect you, and you have an old woman who is willing to fend off the state attorney, and a pastor who will petition Heaven to protect you and Dylan."

"And you?"

She took several steps away from him. "Me? This

defies logic, but I feel that my place is beside you and Dylan."

"I'd kiss you for your faith, but there's a cranky man in that classroom who said if I tried it again, he'd put me in the airboat fan cage and be done with me."

Kaylee laughed aloud. "He didn't?"

"He did. And he's serious."

Kaylee brushed her tennis shoe over the courtyard grass. "Well, I need to speak to that cantankerous fellow. What are you doing later?"

Christian shrugged. "I'm heading out to take over at the studio, and I'll probably help Rose close. Afterward, Herb asked me to join him to help on some Christmas projects and to start the prep for the Christmas Eve festivities."

"Give Dylan a hug for me, and I'll be praying for Cassie."

Christian nodded and walked away. Kaylee followed him with her gaze until he moved out of sight. Perhaps she should have been the one to volunteer to visit his sister. The distance would separate her from her mother and offer an excuse to get LeAnn McFarland out of town and away from Jacob Marin.

"You know ..." Rose stepped out of the classroom and down the steps. "If you told your mother how you feel about that young man, perhaps she'd lighten up."

Kaylee offered a smile. "She'd hurry right into a background search. No one must taint the McFarland name." Even as she said the words, her heart lingered on the hurt on her mother's face when she confessed her love for Kaylee. "I did Christian no favor by kissing him where she could see us."

Rose patted her arm. "Honey, half the time when we think we have all our bases covered, God's pushing the dirt off of 'em and making things work His way. Don't kick yourself too much."

Kaylee let the woman leave and said good-bye to the three men who exited after her. Isaac, Remy, and Ephraim made their way to the one car left in the parking lot after Rose left. Christian had walked away, but he must have been in Herb's golf cart when he arrived.

Herb exited, locked the classroom door, and joined her in the courtyard. "Where do you suppose your mother went?"

Kaylee moved to the steps and sat. "In all my life, I've never seen her show as much emotion as I saw in five minutes in my living room this morning."

Herb joined her. "I saw you hung the ornaments, and I supposed you put the pieces together." He patted her knee. "I can't say I haven't wanted to tell you, but your mother has the way of twisting truths in her mind. I promised I wouldn't say a word if she allowed you to come here and teach for a year, let me get to know my only grandchild. When she arrived like she did, she broke her end of the bargain. I was free to let you know, and I had hoped that seeing her mother's treasures might soften her heart."

Kaylee placed her hand over his. "She didn't allow me to come here."

Herb studied her.

"She fought me until I got in my car and drove away from home." She breathed deeply of the freedom that had caused. "I allowed her to keep me chained to her far too long. Daddy always expected me to show her respect, but what I'd learned is respect isn't always equal to obedience, especially when a child is grown and well past the time when she should be out of the house."

"LeAnn always liked being in control. She got that from me."

Kaylee laughed. "You? Controlling? I don't see it."

"Being in control and controlling are two different things. If those who like to take control of situations aren't careful, they tend to micromanage everything and everyone around them. I discovered that early on when I met your grandmother. She was the true free spirit. I would have been content with studio photography and magazine layouts, but she encouraged me to take my talents out and show people the world through my camera lens. When I signed on with *National Geographic* ..." He lowered his head then looked to her. "Lacey was so proud. She purposed that no one would stop us from seeing the world as a family."

"But Mother wouldn't leave with you." Kaylee repeated what she'd learned.

"LeAnn was nearly a teenager. Of course, we wanted her to go. We'd have seen to her education, and seeing the world and learning about it at the same time is better than anything a classroom can offer. But your mother, she wanted to control us and everything around her. She was a frightened soul."

So, he had known what drove his daughter to do what she did.

"I don't know what made her that way. Lacey and I talked about it for years. She didn't want to see the world. She wanted to stay in New York and attend school. I wanted to resign the job before I started, but Lacey determined that our child was not going to have the rule of our family. If LeAnn didn't want to travel with us, she could stay wrapped in a cocoon at the boarding school."

Kaylee had enough education in child behaviorism to understand that Lacey's free-spirited personality had probably taken away the control her mother needed to keep her fears at bay.

"I know what you're thinking. If she was frightened, how could we leave her behind?"

Kaylee remained silent.

"Your mother was a willful child. She sought to have her way at every turn. From an early age, your grandmother tried hard to teach her how to play well with others, but LeAnn had to be the boss. If you tried to take that authority away from her, she could be difficult. Her personality only strengthened over the years, but she learned how to use it in a way that wasn't off-putting. I credit your father with that. He was a fine man."

"Yes, he was," Kaylee agreed. "Mother did tell me once that you attended her wedding."

Herb snickered. "The only reason your grandmother and I were invited was because she needed for us to pay for it, to keep up appearances with Robert's family. And what an affair that was. I worked an extra year or two to pay off the creditors."

"Did you wear your flip-flops?" Kaylee teased.

"I donned the flip-flops only after your grandmother decided we were going to live here when I retired." He situated himself and gave her his full attention. "This thing with Chris …"

"We discussed it."

"And you decided what?"

"Well, at the risk of sounding like my in-control mother, I decided that when this is all over, I'm going to make the first move. You know, to save him from the airboat fan cage."

Herb laughed. "He told you about that, huh?"

"Only because he believed you." She leaned her shoulder against him.

"And well he should. I don't think I could have chosen a nicer man for you, but honey, he's in a world of trouble. I understand he's trying to do the right thing by that boy, and any man who'd give up what he's left behind, is a good one, but it's a little too dangerous for you to give your heart to him right now."

She shrugged. "I've got to have faith that the Lord is going to hear the prayers I'm planning on asking and that I know other people are asking." Kaylee stood and offered Herb her hand.

He got to his feet.

"So, one question remains." She again shielded her eyes with her hand.

"What question is that?" He ran a hand over his bald head and the curls that fell around the crown. Curls just like hers … at least where he had hair.

"What am I supposed to call you?"

Herb started to walk.

She stepped beside him.

"Herb is fine with me," he said.

Disappointment filled her. Did he not want anyone to know the truth? Maybe her mother hadn't seen him through a view skewed by her wants.

"But Lacey, she dreamed of you calling us Grandma and Grandpa ... I'd like that if you think you're not too old."

Kaylee threw her arms around his neck. "I always dreamed of having grandparents." She kissed his cheek. "And I'll treasure the sound of that name for as long as I live."

Herb sniffled and wiped under his nose. "I've prayed for this moment for a long, long time. So did your grandma."

Kaylee walked with him, their arms linked until they reached his golf cart. "Then I'd like to share our first secret with you, Grandpa."

"Ain't no secret, girl. You love that boy. Everyone can see it."

Kaylee laughed. "My heart decided upon Christian Abrams from the first time he told me I was beautiful."

Fay Lamb

Chapter Twenty-four

December 20

Early the next afternoon, Kaylee stared out the french doors to the back deck beyond. Hours had dragged by without her mother answering her phone. Knowing how much she hated the use of text messages, calling them impersonal, Kaylee had even tried to earn her ire by sending a text every hour.

Still, she'd received no reply.

She placed the phone to her ear. The call again went to voice mail. "Mother, I'm worried about you. Please call me … or reply to my messages. Let me know you're okay."

Though worried about her mother's safety, a second sense of sorts told her that someone was watching. Walking home from the school yesterday, she'd spied a black sedan parked just beyond the turn to her lane. She'd also seen it when she'd walked to the community center to help organize some of the games for the town's Christmas Eve festival where she'd clued Isaac into what she thought was happening. He'd called Ephraim who said he'd heard nothing. Even on leave, if he was the agent in close proximity, they'd call him in, and that was to their advantage.

Her phone rang. She answered it quickly. "Hello."

"Kaylee, it's Jacob Marin."

Kaylee's heart sank, but she mustered up the courage to talk with him. "How are you?"

"I was going to ask you the same. Thank you for the mug, by the way."

"You opened it," she balked. "Shame on you. That was a Christmas gift."

"Couldn't wait. I've always been that way. So, how are you?"

"Jacob, where's my mother?" Kaylee cut to the chase. "Is she still around here?"

Jacob went silent.

She walked to the tree and touched the ornament that had become her favorite, the one with the picture of her mother and grandparents. She closed her eyes. As Abigail had advised, Kaylee found a memory to help her with the difficult relationship. Mother had insisted that the family travel to Rockefeller Center during the holidays when Kaylee was close to the same age her mother had been in the picture on the ornament. She'd asked a stranger to take a picture of them in the same poise. Perhaps her mother's memories of Christmas had been a comfort in the same way Kaylee's memories warmed her like a toasty blanket— even if she didn't need a blanket in Mullet Harbor. "I only want to know that she's okay."

"Oh, it was the perfect gift. I keep it here at work. It's on my desk now."

"Okay ..." Kaylee blinked. The conversation had taken a strange turn. Then she blinked again. Jacob was giving her a hint. "She's with you now?"

"Yeah. I love the colors."

"Jacob, is she trying to stir up trouble."

"Of course. I'll be there on Christmas Eve. I wouldn't miss Herb's big birthday bash for the world. Things happen there that you will not believe."

"Christian's in trouble, isn't he?"

"Yeah, I'd say. Wait until you see the ice slide Herb adapted, and the snow job he'll have for the kids. It'll captivate you."

Captivate. What a strange word to use. *Captivate. Take captive. Christian. Take Christian captive.* "Please," she begged. "Don't let her do this. The situation is not what you think it is. She has it all wrong."

"Kaylee, I understand. You don't see me as anything but a friend. And the situation with me is the same."

"Are the authorities already in town?"

"No."

"Someone's here." She sank back onto her couch. "Could they know?"

"No, that's from me. A special gift to you, but unlike me, don't open it. I have to go now. Give my regards to Aunt Rose. She'll love to know that I'm coming to town for the festivities. See you on Christmas Eve."

Kaylee clicked off the call. She stood and paced for long moments, digesting the strange conversation. Mother was with Jacob. He'd either helped her dig up the truth about Christian, which wouldn't be difficult, or her mother had presented the facts to the state attorney and obligated him into action.

Either way, for whatever reason, Jacob had warned her. But what had he meant about the men in the black sedan being from him? Had he placed them in town? Who were they? What purpose did they have? Whatever happened, Dylan couldn't be seen by them, if he hadn't already been on their radar."

Kaylee mulled it over for a moment before grabbing her bag and rushing out the door. She usually walked everywhere in town, but today, she used her car, parking in the harbor parking lot.

The Fish Shanty was bustling, but Kaylee found one friendly face. "May I join you?"

Abigail smiled. "That would be nice. I've already given them my name."

"My treat, for all your help." Kaylee stared out at the parking lot. She caught sight of the black sedan and the two men inside. They'd parked off the road. She'd hoped that everything had been her imagination, but Jacob's confirmation and seeing them again put her on full alert.

"Ladies ..." A hostess approached. "There are two gentlemen inside who asked if you'd like to join them. There's room at their table."

Kaylee spied the obvious invitee. He'd stepped outside and waved.

"I—I don't think so." Abigail hadn't seen him. "I don't want to eat with strangers."

"Live a little," Kaylee prodded.

Abigail blew out a breath that clearly held frustration and followed Kaylee.

Their benefactor had stepped inside. They walked behind the hostess, through the restaurant, and to a table near the window facing the harbor. Remy had to have seen them outside. He and Ephraim stood and held out the chairs beside them.

Kaylee sat by the federal agent, and Abigail did her nervous curtsy and plopped into the chair beside Remy.

"Glad you joined us," Remy said.

"Thank you for inviting us." Kaylee took the menu Ephraim offered her. "Have you ordered?"

"No, we'd just been seated when I saw you." Remy perused his menu, apparently made a decision, and passed it to Abigail. "Did you close the grocery store so you could have a break?"

Abigail nodded and buried her face in the menu.

Remy turned his smile to Kaylee and gave a slight shake of his head.

Kaylee made her choice and placed her menu on the table. An awkward silence continued until the waitress came and took their drink and meal orders at the same time.

"Where's Isaac?" Kaylee turned to Ephraim. "He must be refusing to cook you dinner."

"Ha-ha." Ephraim folded his hands and atop the table. "Christian, Dylan, and I convinced him that one day out of the Christmas holiday and away from the church wouldn't crimp his Christmas sermon preparation. He's on the Gulf with them."

"Sophie took an immediate shine to Dylan," she told him. "It's nice that you're here and able to watch Sophie while Isaac works."

"We've always been a tight family group. This Christmas, though, we needed to be together. Turned out to be fortuitous this year in light of Christian's stumbling into Mullet Harbor."

Remy's phone rang, and he excused himself, mostly to Abigail, before he stepped through the restaurant.

"Jacob called me this afternoon." Kaylee tapped her fingers against the table. "My mother was in his office. He didn't say much, but he did hint that things might unravel on Christmas Eve."

Abigail started, and Ephraim nearly jumped to turn in his seat to face Kaylee. "What'd he say?"

"The conversation was strange, but I know that's what he was hinting about. Isaac told you about the black sedan? Two men inside."

"He did. They're not ours. A black car would be too cliché." He winked over the glass of tea he lifted to his lips.

"I think they're from Jacob's office or someone he's sent to keep a lookout, but I don't know why. He's seen Christian and Dylan. Why surveil any of us?"

"And why tell you?" Ephraim questioned. "If he's working with your mother, you'd be the last to know."

Kaylee raised her brows. "Exactly what I was thinking, so the natural conclusion is that he isn't working for her."

Remy returned. He wore a frown. "That was Marielle."

Kaylee leaned forward. "Is she in Philadelphia? Has she seen Christian's sister?"

"Yes, and yes, and the answer to the next question is that when she first got there, things didn't look well. As only Marielle could do, she's inserted herself into the situation. Cassie is now receiving more attention. Probably wishful thinking, but *Mare-ree* says Cassie's improved since her arrival."

"Mare-ree?" Kaylee repeated. "That's a beautiful nickname for her."

Abigail giggled. "You should have seen the black eye she gave him when he used it in front of us when we were kids."

Remy smiled and bumped Abigail. "I walked into her fist by accident."

Ephraim laughed. "After the first time, I'd think you'd be able to watch for that fist."

"Anyway …" Remy narrowed his eyes at Abigail and then Ephraim. "That'll be good news for Christian and Dylan."

Remy shook his head. "The doctors are telling Marielle not to get her hopes up. Sometimes patients rally only to fail more rapidly soon after."

Kaylee lowered her head and said a prayer for this woman she didn't know.

"According to the nurses, Cassie wasn't in the best condition when she arrived," Remy said. "That boy must be a survivor because his mother apparently was a serious addict."

"I'm sorry." Abigail stood. "I seemed to have fallen into a conversation not meant for me."

Remy grasped her hand. "Sorry, Abby. Keeping you out of the loop wasn't intentional. You've been helping us in other ways. If you'll stay, we'll clue you in."

Abigail hesitated.

"Please?" Kaylee asked.

Abigail sat.

Kaylee explained the full situation to her friend, and Abigail seemed to relax.

"Christian ever say how he allowed his sister to get like that?" Ephraim asked.

Remy straightened. "No more than I'd ask your brother why my sister was out walking on that road so late at night by herself."

Ephraim's jaw raised as he clenched his teeth. He took a deep breath. "Fair enough. We can't always make the right choices for the people we love. They have to want to make them."

"Fair enough," Remy repeated. Then he gave his attention to Abigail. "We didn't mean to keep you out of things. You've been a big help, especially with Mrs. McFarland's arrival."

"Seems I didn't do enough." Abigail shrugged. "From what little I've learned from Christian and from Herb's and

Rose's directives I realized he might be in serious trouble. If I'd known the full story ..."

"You've done well," Ephraim told Abigail and then turned to Remy. "Kaylee shared some things with me. I'd like her to tell you."

Kaylee hurried through the information about Jacob and the men following her.

Dinner arrived, and they kept the talk to unrelated topics like what to expect during the Christmas Eve festivities and how everyone would spend Christmas Day.

When the meal ended, Remy offered to walk Kaylee to her car and Abigail back to the store. Ephraim wanted to call his office to see if they planned anything on Christmas Eve in Mullet Harbor.

When Kaylee, Remy, and Abigail reached her car, he opened the door for her. "Stay close to your phone. We may need to have another meeting, and this time, I want Abigail there."

"I can drive you home," Kaylee offered to Abigail.

"No," Remy said. "I want her with me."

Kaylee didn't argue. She got in her car. As she turned onto the lane toward her house, she spied the black sedan in her rearview mirror. They slowed then moved on.

Christian had relaxed once Herb turned the boat toward Mullet Key. Dylan had a panic attack when he noted that he couldn't see the shore from the boat. Sophie, in her sweet, little-girl way had tried to calm Dylan, but the boy hadn't been able to get his breath.

Herb asked if Dylan thought he'd be okay if they moved more inland so that Dylan could see the shoreline. The boy had nodded, and the green on his face had faded.

Once Herb assured Dylan that they were close enough to land that if he had to send a distress signal they would be rescued in minutes, Isaac set about helping them to prepare the larger deep-sea reels. Line in the water, Dylan calmed. They'd been fishing for hours without a single bite.

Christian sat and watched his nephew, the preacher, and the preacher's daughter. All seemed endlessly intent on their endeavors. Christian couldn't see why anyone liked the act of throwing a line into the water and hoping to catch a fish.

"Don't let the fact that they haven't gotten a nibble fool you. Isaac knows what he's doing." Rose sat in the crew chair. "He was Herb's boat captain for years before he went to seminary."

"Through high school." Isaac looked over his shoulder. "I got my captain's license and my fishing know-how by learning from the best."

Christian leaned back in his seat and let the sun warm his face. If life had not abruptly changed for him, he'd be in Pittsburg right now, probably sitting in his apartment, heat cranked up and reading a book. Or he'd brave the elements, don his winter coat and scarf, and sludge toward his favorite diner for a very lonely meal.

Strange. He didn't miss it.

But he suspected Dylan missed his mother.

He and Herb had been awakened by his nightmarish cries during the night. That's why Herb suggested the sea air and the adventure. That was also the reason the fading shoreline may have induced the anxiety. Christian rubbed his eyes.

"He'll be okay." Herb kept his voice low.

Christian shook his head. Since Marielle had left to take the place of Cassie's son and brother and to stay by her helpless side, Christian couldn't shake the fact that Philadelphia would play a key role in what would happen to him. Did it mean that Cassie would die, leaving her son without a hope of avoiding the system and her brother to a lengthy prison stay? Whether Cassie lived or died, Christian was bound for incarceration.

"Whoa!" Dylan called out.

Christian startled.

Dylan's rod was bent in a full arch.

"Hold on to your pole, Sophie," Isaac warned before

reaching over Dylan and grasping the rod above Dylan's hands. "Don't let go, Dylan. I'm just making sure you don't get pulled overboard. This is your fish to catch."

Dylan struggled with turning the reel. "It's big!" His excitement rang in the air.

Christian stood and took Isaac's place by Sophie. If something as large as whatever Dylan had on his line decided to bite and run, Sophie could go overboard.

Sophie stared with wide eyes as her father and Dylan struggled with the fish.

Herb and Rose remained seated, but their encouragement was more in line with Dylan breaking free of a tackle and running eighty yards for a touchdown.

After five minutes, sweat rolled off Dylan's forehead and beaded around his lips. "I can't do it."

"Yes, you can. Look. There it is. Herb, get me a gig."

"What's that?" Sophie asked.

"It's a spear. He's close enough to bring in." Isaac smiled.

"Noooo." Dylan let loose of the reel. Christian reached out to keep Isaac from going overboard.

Herb withdrew his offer of the gig to Isaac and grabbed the rod that Dylan had relinquished.

"Don't kill it." Dylan cried. "I don't want to kill it. Ms. Abigail does catch and release. Please don't kill it."

"Daddy, don't." Sophie joined in with Dylan's cries.

Still holding to the rod, Isaac managed to look back at Dylan. "It's your catch. You can do whatever you want."

"Let it go. Please, let it go."

Herb took Christian's place beside the pastor and nodded toward Dylan. Christian moved to Dylan's side and bent beside him. "Catch and release it is," he assured.

Dylan turned away, staring out over the opposite side of the vessel toward shore.

Sophie dropped her pole and moved to console her friend, and Rose made quick action to reel in the line.

"He's gone, boy," Herb told Dylan. "Free as if you'd never caught him."

Dylan nodded. "I don't want to fish anymore. Can we just …?"

"You want to go home already?" Rose asked. "I brought us a feast."

"No. I just don't want to fish. We can stay on the boat if that's okay." He swiped his arm over his sweaty forehead.

Sophie plopped down on the deck. "Let's play I Spy." She tugged on Dylan's pant leg. "I spy something blue."

"The sky." Isaac secured the poles and returned.

"No, Daddy. That's too easy."

Herb made a great pretense of looking around the boat and into the horizon. "Are you colorblind, youngun?"

"Huh?" Sophie asked.

"I don't see anything blue. I see green water and a white boat. None of us are wearing blue."

Sophie pointed to Dylan. "He's blue."

Dylan scratched his head. "I ain't."

The boy had been spending too much time with Herb. "Dylan ..."

"I'm not," the boy corrected.

"Daddy says when people are sad, they turn blue. I've never seen the blue, but Daddy says it's there."

Christian held back the laughter.

Herb wasn't above showing his amusement. He cackled. "That little gal never ceases to amaze me. Just like her momma. Never could get past the literal meaning of anything."

Isaac ran his fingers over the light shadow of beard on his face. "Remember that photography class you held at the studio when we were in high school. She wanted to do something with her pictures, and you told her she needed to learn the basics first or she'd be putting the cart before the horse?"

Herb roared. "I didn't understand that look she gave me until she came up to me after class. She said, 'Mr. Herb, it isn't possible to put the cart before the horse. The horse would have to shove it and not pull it."

Sophie jumped up. "Momma was right, Daddy. The horse wouldn't want to push the cart. It should be behind the horse so he could pull it."

Herb roared even louder now, but his laughter turned to silent tears. The old man wiped them from his face, and he pulled Sophie to him. "Your momma, she was a smart girl, just like you." His lips trembled. "Always had a smile and a wave for me when she passed, and she loved to take pictures as much as she loved to sculpt." He shook his head. "I wish—I wish—" He gave up speaking and shook his head. "Don't matter what I wish."

"I wish, too." Isaac put a hand on Herb's shoulder.

Herb's phone dinged, and he retrieved it from the pocket of his cargo shorts. He read a message, placed his phone back, and turned to Rose. "Let's have that feast you've prepared. Then we need to get back to land. Eph wants us to meet at my place in a few hours. Kaylee located her mother, and something's up."

Christian stared back toward shore. He had a wish, too, and it seemed as impossible as bringing Sidalee back to her husband and child.

Chapter Twenty-five

Christian checked on Dylan one last time. His nephew wasn't asleep, but he was pretending to be. "Remind me to pay for some acting lessons." He spoke to the silent figure beneath the sheet.

Dylan remained perfectly still except for the slight curve of his lip he clearly tried to suppress.

Christian bent down to tickle him. "We had a good day, didn't we?"

Dylan flopped over onto his back. "I'm sorry I got scared."

Christian pursed his lips for a second then smiled. "I was scared. You just chickened out before me. I'm glad you did. Seeing the shore was pretty important for me, too."

Dylan stared at Christian without a word.

"You okay?"

"I'm still afraid." The boy's lips trembled.

"I am too," Christian admitted. "But we're in this together."

"Why'd you do it, Uncle Chris?"

Christian sat on the bed. "Do what?"

"Why'd you take me out of that place and not leave me there until the next hearing?"

Christian took a second before he touched Dylan's cheek just beneath his eye. "When I took you for visitation, you had a light bruise right there and ..." He touched Dylan's nose. "A small cut was here." He continued to touch Dylan's face where every injury he'd sustained in that home was ingrained in his memory.

"But I didn't tell you what happened."

"You didn't have to tell me." Christian ran his hand along the sheet. "I had a few of those bruises and cuts in my lifetime. So did your mom. I stood up to the bullies when your mom and I were younger. I kept us together, and I promised her that I'd never let anyone hurt her again." He rubbed his hand over his eyes. Emotions clogged his throat, emotions he wouldn't let rise again. He swallowed ... hard. "I let her down, Dylan, and I let you down by not being there."

"It's not your fault," Dylan whispered the words. "Mom let the guy hurt her and hurt me."

"Don't you see?" Christian brushed his hand over

Dylan's forehead, pushing his bangs from his head and bending closer to peer into his nephew's eyes.

"See what?" Dylan asked.

"That my promise made so many years ago should have always included you. Dylan, your mom has done a lot of things, but the one thing I know about her, the one thing that makes me love her the most is you."

"That doesn't make sense."

"I know she loves you more than anything in the world."

"No, she doesn't." He shook his head loose from Christian's hold. "She loves her drugs and her boyfriends. If she loved me ..."

"You were born without an ounce of drugs in your veins. You were a healthy little boy with rosy red skin and lungs so loud I heard you crying before I ever met you. When I peered in the hospital bassinet at you, I found hope that your mother could be someone else. And she had been while she carried you. And she was for some time after you were born. She loves you, Dylan, more than life itself. She told me that the last time I took her to a treatment center. Remember, you stayed with Aunt Amy and me?"

Then why doesn't she stop doing what she's doing?" Dylan begged. "Why doesn't she take care of me?"

Christian stood and went to the window in Dylan's room, which looked out over the lagoon. A boat passed.

Christmas lights hanging on its cabin illuminated the darkness. He closed his eyes and leaned against the glass for a long second. "Someone once explained to me that drugs are like a long dark tunnel in a scary ride. You crave the thrill and the feel of them, and you're willing to risk your life to take that ride. When you get off, you miss the thrill. No matter if the ride makes you sick, you want to get back on it."

Dylan was silent again.

Christian made his way back to him. "I'm done with promises, Dylan. All I can do is my best for you and your mother. If I can prevent you from that life your mother craves, that's all I'll ever need. I pray you learn from her mistakes. And though I'm not perfect, I'm trying to set an example for you. It's why I'm after you all the time about the way you speak. You're a smart boy, but sometimes the smartest of us fall into trouble. I bet you didn't know that your mother has a higher IQ than me."

Dylan smiled. "Yep. She said she did."

"But I got all the commonsense." He sat beside Dylan again. "About that fear we both have, you know there's Someone who can help us with it."

"Ms. Kaylee?"

Christian shook his head.

"Mayor Herb?"

Christian pointed upward. "God. I'd forgotten that He

wants me to cast all my cares on Him and not to worry about tomorrow. How about we pray and ask God to take care of us, to show us what we should do?"

"How will He show us? Will He send an angel?"

Christian shrugged. "I suppose He could send an angel, but He's more likely to either make things go a certain way or send someone to us to tell us where to go next and what to do. And sometimes when God does that or He sends someone to give us directions, they might not always make sense. We just have to stay still and ask if it's Him, and peace in our hearts will show us what's right." He was talking over the kid's head, but the words calmed Christian's fears.

He closed his eyes. "Dear Lord, Dylan and I are afraid. Help us to give that fear over to You and to listen for Your direction. Help us to be strong when things don't make sense to us. Protect us and those who're trying to help us, and Lord, I pray for my sister. Don't let her leave us." He paused to keep the trembling out of his voice. "Let us see her again. Help Dylan to have a relationship with his mother that is free of drugs and alcohol and the other things she seeks to shut out the hurt in her life. And, Lord, thank You for Dylan. Because he's with me today, because he needs me, and that's why I'm alive in so many ways where I was dead to life before."

"Amen." Dylan's warm hand lay atop of his. "Good

night, Uncle Chris. I love you."

Christian kissed the boy's forehead. "I love you, too." He stood and moved to the door. "Get some sleep."

He closed the door behind him and almost collided with Ephraim.

"I was coming for you," he said and pointed toward the stairs. "We need to get started."

Christian followed him downstairs.

Kaylee smiled at him from her stool and raised a glass of something pink and capped by an umbrella. "Grapefruit smoothie."

When had it happened? She was reading his thoughts, and he could read hers. She was afraid, just as he had been moments earlier. "Yum." He intentionally placed sarcasm in the single syllable.

"Try something before you bash it." Herb smirked.

Abigail rushed to pour Christian his own. She sat it in front of him.

"Thank you, Abigail."

She backed away, giving her signature curtsy in response, then went about busying herself in one area of the kitchen and the next as the others who gathered continued with their conversations.

Christian smiled and took a sip. "Not bad. Ever think of opening a smoothie place?" he asked Herb.

"A time or two. Wanted to work out a deal with the gal

there, but she won't open a shop—not yet anyway. Besides, I'm too busy keeping folks out of trouble." The old man winked. "So what's brought us together, Eph, and why have you brought Abigail into our troubles?"

Abigail stilled for the first time. "I can leave. I don't mean to intrude."

Remy offered Abigail a smile. "Abby's here because I want her to be here, Herb. Besides, all of us may need her as a character witness so that we get less jail time."

Not funny. Christian choked on his next drink of the smoothie.

"Isaac's not here purposefully," Remy said. "He already knows your story. Abigail knows a little, but I wanted her to know what we're doing and why we're doing it."

"Also," Rose interjected, "the last person that Jacob is going to believe would be in cahoots with us is Abigail. I'm sorry, honey." She turned to look at the woman still hanging back in the kitchen. "But that boy has underestimated and undervalued you all your life."

Abigail bit her lip but said nothing.

"Jacob is the reason we're here," Kaylee announced. "He called me. Mother was in his office. He hinted that they're thinking of moving in on Christian on Christmas Eve."

Ephraim's phone dinged, and he turned it over and

looked at it. "Excuse me." He stepped into the living room.

"What's Jacob doing?" Rose mused. "He's not going to put his job on the line for someone he doesn't know." She stopped and then cackled. "He's not going to put his job on the line for anyone. Not even you, Kaylee." She pointed. "If your mother was in that office, you can bet it's a setup."

Christian straightened. "Meant to get us together at one time."

Kaylee's eyes widened. "And I helped them do it."

Remy raised his hand. "He's got to assume that I know the truth. Herb and I are too close on this one. If Kaylee's mother got him involved and he dug up the dirt, it wouldn't take an investigator in his office too long to look here for evidence."

"I ain't seen anyone around," Herb said.

"Two men in a black sedan. Ephraim said that it was too cliché for his office. Maybe that's it. Jacob wanted them to be obvious, to put us on the defensive, which, along with his cryptic call, worked."

Christian looked around for the FBI agent. He was no longer in sight. A second later, he came through the front door, but Christian had never seen him leave. "Sorry. Did I hear my name?"

"The black sedan I told you about. You said it wasn't the FBI," Kaylee said.

Ephraim shook his head. "No, it wasn't. I saw them after we left the Fish Shanty as well. They had a bead on Kaylee."

"Did they follow you here?" Herb asked.

Kaylee shook her head and pointed to the boots she wore over her jeans. "I trampled through the brush to the road by Rose's grocery so they wouldn't see me when I left. Then I stayed off the road on my way here. My hope was that if they were watching me, they'd stay put. I'm not as convinced that they aren't federal agents."

"Those men in that car are not agents. End of discussion." Ephraim retook his seat.

Rose stood and pushed her chair under the counter. "Are we going to sit here and wait for them to come for us, whoever they are, or are we going to disperse and make it harder for them to find us?"

"Rose," Ephraim calmed, "there is no *them* as it pertains to the FBI. At least not right now. There will be, though, and I have a plan. I've talked with Marielle. She knows her part to play. There are critical actions that each of you ladies need to take no matter how small they seem. Remy, Herb, and Christian, your parts aren't going to be easy, but you have to listen to me."

Remy ran his hand through his dark hair. "When you said that to me as a kid, I always came out on the losing end."

"Well, you have to admit whenever I made those plans, you were the losing end of a winning cause." Ephraim smiled. "As a left tackle, you took one for the quarterback so he could make that winning throw to the receiver, and we won the state championship our senior year."

"Me, left tackle, on the ground with my spleen in my throat. You quarterback, on the shoulders of all of the other team members who could stand after that play. You on the sidelines being interviewed by the reporters. Me, on a stretcher."

Christian hadn't realized how close these men were to one another. For some reason, their banter calmed his fraying nerves and reminded him that God had placed him and his nephew in the hands of an FBI agent, a sheriff … and a mayor.

"What do we have to do, Eph?" Remy pressed.

"You, Christian, and Herb are going to be taken into custody." Ephraim scrunched his face and ducked away from the sheriff.

Abigail squealed

"What?" Kaylee cried out.

Rose wrapped her arms around Abigail. "Give him a chance."

Christian dared to peer at the stairs. What about Dylan?

The security he'd felt only a second ago evaporated.

Ephraim held up his hands. "Remy, even after all the losing ends I placed you on, do you trust me to make this one a winning cause as well?"

Remy didn't hesitate. "Yeah, I do."

"Then Christian Abrams, you're under arrest for the kidnapping and taking of Dylan Abrams, a minor, across state lines." Ephraim pinned Christian against the counter and had his hands in cuffs behind his back with a deftness Christian didn't see coming. "And Sheriff Remy Arneaux and Mayor Herbert Miller, I suggest that you come quietly with me to the station where you will be held on the suspicion of aiding and abetting a fugitive. I'll read you your rights on the way, but I seriously advise you to keep your mouths shut at all times."

"Dylan?" Christian tried to pull away. "I can't leave him alone like that."

Ephraim eased up on his hold of Christian. "Kaylee, I think you know what to do. Then go home. Abigail, you need to drive Rose home, give Kaylee thirty minutes, and then drive to her house to see if she's okay. From there, you need to think quick with what you have and with what you'll discover?"

"What? Eph, that doesn't make sense." Abigail nearly screeched. "What will I find that will help us out of this situation?"

Kaylee didn't move her gaze from Christian. "I'm so sorry. This is all my fault. I'll keep Dylan safe."

"None of this makes sense," Abigail protested. "I can drive Kaylee and Dylan to her house after I drop off Rose. Why are we doing this? Why would you …?"

Remy stopped in front of her. "Do exactly as he said. Don't do anything else. Understand?"

"But …?" Abigail cried.

"Do exactly as he said." Remy leaned his head against Abigail's forehead. "There are two things I'm going to do if I get out of this mess without going to prison."

"What?" Abigail squeaked.

"I'm going to show you how valuable you are to everyone, and I'm going to murder Eph."

"Careful now. I'll add threatening a federal agent to your list of crimes."

Remy winked at Abigail, pressed a comforting hand into Christian's shoulder, then smacked Ephraim upside the head.

Christian walked, hands cuffed behind his back, to the future he had known would eventually come. He turned toward the stairs and the room where his nephew slept.

Dylan would blame himself for everything.

Christian hung his head. He sure hadn't meant for that to happen. He'd failed the boy again.

Kaylee sprang up the stairs as soon as the door to Christian's freedom closed. While Herb had shown her his unique home the first time she had visited, she didn't know which room belonged to Dylan. But that didn't matter. The boy was in none of them. She knocked on what she knew to be the closed bathroom. When Dylan didn't answer, she stepped inside.

Empty.

"Where is he?" Abigail joined them.

Had he heard the adults? Did he know that Christian had been arrested?

"Dylan, please come out. We need to go." She went through each room again, looking in the closets and under the beds. She even searched Herb's bathroom. Rose did the same, as if the boy could be conjured at will.

Rose passed her at the upstairs landing. She pressed a finger against her lips as if trying to think.

Kaylee wrapped her arms around her waist. Christian hadn't acted as if he—or any of them—had hidden Dylan. If they had, they should have said so. "I don't know."

"What do we do?" Abigail couldn't stand still. She paced and moved erratically up and down the landing.

Kaylee stood in silence for a long moment. "Ephraim told me to go home and do what I need to do. What'd he mean by that? What would I do except to sit and wring my hands until I can wring my mother's neck?"

Abigail grasped Kaylee's hand. "Remy told me to do exactly as Eph said."

Rose clasped her hands together. "Then we do that."

"But that leaves me walking home and Abigail driving you to your place before she goes to her house. Where does it leave Dylan?"

Rose raised her brows but said nothing.

Abigail marched through the entire house. She opened doors and moved clothing and other items.

Kaylee went behind her. Dylan was not there.

"We need to do exactly as Eph said." Abigail gave a curt nod as if her statement was the end of an argument. "You need to keep your eyes and ears open as you walk home. Maybe Dylan ran away. He might call out to you. I'll drive home and do the same. Rose will wait at home."

"No," Rose said. "I'll wait at the store."

"But Ephraim …"

"Dylan has no idea where I live, and as smart as Eph can be, he doesn't know that the boy's cut and run. We need to be where Dylan can find us whether that's Kaylee's place, your house, or the store."

"Stop by the community center, Abigail. He might be hiding on the backside." Kaylee fought to hold her fears inside. "The poor baby. The mosquitoes will eat him alive."

"Kaylee." Abigail grasped her arm. "I don't know why, but I think the plan is for you to be seen walking back to your house. Please be careful. Rose and I'll lock up things here, look for Dylan on the way, and I'll be by your house in a bit. Maybe by then, we can figure out what it is Eph wants us to do."

The winter sky had darkened early. Of course, it would. Tomorrow would be the shortest day of the year. Kaylee walked slowly, hoping that if Dylan had run out of the house after hearing what they were talking about, that he'd meet up with her.

No such luck. She tensed as car headlights drew near behind her when she turned left onto the main road leading to her house. With deliberate measure, she kept her pace calm and collective. No one could know that the world was quaking beneath her feet.

As she walked, thoughts of her mother's actions sent ire running through her veins. How could she do something without at least asking her daughter to explain? Why couldn't she trust Herb? Or were her actions meant as vengeance against Herb for bringing Kaylee to the harbor? Would her mother be so petty?

Yes, she would.

And Kaylee was partly to blame. Her belligerence had driven her mother to this.

Kaylee swiped at a warm tear that tracked down her

cheek. This certainly wasn't the way to win back a daughter's affection. Mother would no longer have the control over Kaylee's life that she desired. Time to break that unhealthy bond.

And Mother would have to work hard to repair the damage between them.

The black sedan was parked on the main road. The men obviously had assumed she'd remained home. Kaylee stomped her way toward the car. Part of her hoped they'd back up and run. The other half of her, the half that wanted to have words with her mother, to tell her what she really thought of her actions, begged them to remain where they were.

The angry side of Kaylee got her wish. She pounded her fist on the hood of the sedan as she approached.

The two men inside stared. "Why don't you get out and tell me who you are?"

The men made no move to acquiesce.

"I have a message you can give to LeAnn McFarland." She hit the car window with her fist.

The man in the passenger seat flinched.

"You can tell her we're done. She needs to go back to Baltimore and stay there unless she wants to come back and apologize to her father, to me, to everyone she's wronged here. She's fabricated an evil to keep me away from someone I care about, and I don't want to see her again."

She started away but stopped. She moved back. "And you can tell Jacob Marin ... you can tell him that ..." She choked on her angry sobs. "You can tell him that the people in this town have treated him far better than he's treated them." She ran toward her lane and all the way to her house. On the deck, she dug in her pocket for her housekey.

"Dylan," she whispered as she fumbled with the lock. "If you're here, I'll meet you around back."

No answer came.

She opened the door, hurried inside, and locked herself in. In the darkness, she moved to the french doors and swung them open.

After several minutes, she knew. Dylan wasn't here waiting for her as she'd hoped.

A splash drew her to the water. The inky blackness around her revealed nothing. She hurried back inside and turned on the dock lights and crept to the railing.

Abercrombie peered up at her with his beady eyes. Something shadowy floated in the water beside him, and Kaylee leaned for a closer look.

Abercrombie turned his massive head and bit down on his catch. He tossed it like meat.

Kaylee caught sight of something like strings on either side of the object.

A shoe. A black shoe. She'd seen it before.

She closed her eyes and pictured the moment.

Dylan had stopped at her door when he arrived for the party. He'd told her Herb had bought them for him.

She fought down the scream that threatened to erupt. The massive creature no longer looked benign to her. He was evil.

The gator released the shoe, and with another giant splash, went beneath the surface.

"No!" Kaylee barely got the word from her heart into her throat. "No!" Could the gator have pulled Dylan beneath the surface? Was he returning to finish him or to drag him further into his murky home?

She searched the black water for any sign that Dylan could have come to harm. Why would he have gotten in the water?

She gasped. Abigail said that the massive gator had chased Herb on to land. If Dylan had walked to her house and hadn't seen the creature near the dock, if the kids had fed him during her party, the gator could have sprung on him.

There was no keeping the scream within her. The force of it tore at her throat.

Then her breaths kept coming, too fast, her chest heaving uncontrollably. The world around her grew dark, and she reached for the railing to hold herself up. She slipped onto the wood and darkness enveloped her.

Chapter Twenty-six

Someone called to Kaylee, but the tunnel she found herself in offered no light. Again, the voice called. She couldn't raise her arms.

No, it wasn't that. Someone held to her arms.

They shook her.

"Kaylee," Abigail cried.

Where was she? Who'd brought her here?

"Ms. Kaylee, please be okay?"

Dylan. His shoe in Abercrombie's mouth.

"Ms. Kaylee, please."

Had he been here in the dark waiting for her, afraid to go on to the comfort that she had long believed Heaven would have waiting for her? But why the darkness?

"Did someone hurt her?" Abigail asked.

But Abigail wouldn't be in Heaven.

"Is she dead?" Dylan raised voice screamed his alarm.

"She's breathing," Abigail answered.

The tunnel faded away. Kaylee opened her eyes only to stare into Dylan's green-eyed gaze filled with fear. She sat up and drew her to him. "I thought … I thought … your shoe. Abercrombie had your shoe."

Fear turned to confusion on the boy's face.

"Dylan, how did the alligator get your shoe?"

Dylan shook his head. "I—I don't know."

Abigail stayed on her knees beside Kaylee. "Are you hurt?"

Kaylee shook off the residual fear. "No. I think I fainted when I saw Abercrombie with Dylan's shoe." She touched Dylan's face. "I thought he'd somehow taken you. Why did you leave that house, young man?"

Dylan shrugged. "I had to. They're coming for Uncle Chris. If they find me, they'll know for sure he took me. If they don't find me, they can't prove anything. All Uncle Chris has to do is keep quiet."

His reasoning was a little too much for his age, despite his intellect.

"Where were you?" Her anxiety raised her voice a notch.

"He was hiding in the backseat of my car." Abigail stood and offered Kaylee her hand. "Let's go inside." She slapped at a mosquito. "I think I know what Eph wants us to do."

"Why didn't he tell us the whole plan?" Kaylee stood on unsteady feet. She bent forward and grasped Dylan's cheeks between her palms. "Young man, if you ever do anything like that again, I'll feed you to Abercrombie."

Dylan mustered a smile. "Yes, ma'am."

They stepped inside, and Abigail rushed to the kitchen and returned with a glass of water for Kaylee. "Here's what I'm thinking. Ephraim must have seen Dylan leave the house when he was on that phone call. Remember? With Dylan out of the house, he could take Christian, Herb, and Remy into custody. He probably thought Dylan would run to one of us."

"But why?"

"To hold off a raid. To keep us from being hurt if things went wrong. To give you time to get Dylan out of town."

"They're watching me. I can't get in my car and drive away."

"You can get in my car while I stay here. You can drive to my house with Dylan hiding in the backseat. You can wait a while and then leave, take him somewhere safe."

"My hair is much different from yours."

"It's dark. We're the same build. You're getting in and out of my car. I don't think they'll follow."

"A hat …"

"A hat will make it more obvious that we're pulling a switch." Abigail paced. "You're going to have to pack. Dylan has a duffle bag full of his things in my car."

"Where am I supposed to go?"

"To Philadelphia," Dylan said.

Kaylee rounded on him. "What? Dylan, that's crazy."

"No. No, it's not. They aren't looking for me there. They think Uncle Chris has me here." Tears filled his eyes. "I gotta get away from him so they can't charge him with kidnapping. If Uncle Chris isn't a kidnapper, then Mayor Herb and Sheriff Remy can't be charged."

Kaylee narrowed her eyes. More suspicion entered her mixed-up emotions. Dylan was a smart boy, but he wasn't that smart. Had Christian talked to him about this possibility, put these foolhardy notions in the boy's head. "That plan has a large flaw in it," she said. "Practically everyone in town has seen you with your uncle."

Abigail smiled—big. "Kaylee, you haven't been here long enough to know us that well, but this town has a secret motto, never spoken. "We don't tell each other's important secrets unless there's a very good reason to tell. Herb's not stupid. I figured it out. Part of his plan was for Christian and Dylan to ingratiate themselves here. Christian proved himself to the town, and when word got around about that kiss he planted on you, that just added cement to their resolve. Mullet Harbor will do what it needs to do to protect us all."

Kaylee guessed a passionate kiss wasn't an important secret, and she did imagine that the entire town had heard and whispered about a possible budding romance. She started to bite on that little bit of manna thrown her way, but she shook her head. "Isaac Cooper isn't going to lie for anyone."

"He doesn't have to lie if he's not asked."

"Abigail, you know that isn't how Isaac operates."

Abigail placed her hands on her hips. "Isaac Cooper doesn't do a thing unless he's sure that God's in it. You leave Isaac's intentions to God."

"Ms. Kaylee, please." The tears fell down Dylan's face now. "I wanna see my mom. I know she's dying. If she wasn't, she'd be awake by now. Uncle Chris told me when we left that time would heal her or take her away. She's not coming back. I just wanna see her again. One more time."

Abigail was crying, too. "Take him there, Kaylee. Marielle's up there. She'll find a way to get you in."

"She won't know we're coming, and it's too dangerous for anyone to notify her. I can't take my phone. That's why Christian doesn't have one. They can be tracked."

"We can find a way in," Dylan urged.

"He's right." Abigail paced. "They aren't looking for him in Philadelphia. He hasn't been there in a long time, and Dylan is the only evidence they have to link Chris to kidnapping. You have to get him out of here."

"Then I'm the kidnapper." Kaylee backed away. "And there's other evidence. Herb bought him clothes." Even as she said the words, she thought of the empty closet in one of the guest rooms. "Did you pack everything?" she asked Dylan.

"Uh-huh."

"But the shoe? How did it get in Abercrombie's possession?"

Guilt fell upon Dylan's face like a raging waterfall after the rain.

"Did you throw it in the water to mislead someone?"

"No. No. I promise. I—I didn't take those shoes."

Kaylee narrowed her eyes at the boy. "Dylan, I won't be lied to. There's no other way that shoe got into that water unless you threw it in there. Where's the other one?"

Dylan swiped at the tears drying on his face. "I don't lie, Ms. Kaylee. You know I don't lie. We prayed about it with God. I want Him to hear my prayers. I want Him to get Uncle Chris out of this and to let my mom live. I wouldn't lie to you or to Him. I didn't have those shoes when I packed."

Kaylee paced and looked at the clock. She stopped in front of the child. "I trust you, but here's the thing. I have to get that shoe out of the water."

"Why?" Dylan widened his eyes.

"Because if they find it, however, it got there, they're going to think the worst about that alligator. They'll kill him, and they'll open him up to see if you're inside. I wouldn't blame them, because I wanted to do the same thing when I thought he'd taken you." She went to her pantry and pulled out a flashlight. "Stay inside. Both of you."

Kaylee stepped back onto the dock. She shined her light into the water. The shoe still floated nearby. She hurried into the kitchen and pulled a broom from the pantry. "I may need your help." She grasped Abigail's arm and pulled her along. Outside, she reached out the broomstick with one hand and held to the flashlight with the other.

The tip missed it by mere centimeters.

"Can you hold on to me and hold the flashlight at the same time?" She handed it to Abigail and climbed onto the railing.

With one arm, Abigail held Kaylee around the waist. With the other, she put the beam on the shoe.

Kaylee reached and caught the far side of the hiking boot. She began to tug it toward her.

When she got it close to the dock, she slipped the handle inside the shoe and lifted it from the water.

A dark silhouette rose from the depths and crashed

back down.

Kaylee reeled back, and the shoe flew off the broomstick and over her head. It flopped onto the deck along with her, Abigail, and the flashlight, which rolled into a far corner.

Kaylee climbed to her feet, helped up Abigail, and retrieved the flashlight. Peering over the railing, she narrowed her eyes at the gator who'd given her the fright. "Bad boy. Bad, bad boy!" she admonished. Then she stopped.

Abercrombie was guarding another treasure: the shoe's mate. If Dylan wasn't lying, someone else either had it in for the gator or didn't think that it would cause him any danger.

Abercrombie closed his eyes and opened them. Was the gator toying with her or giving her a gift. She had to assume the former because gators weren't known for attachments. Given the chance, Abercrombie would eat her in the same way she'd thought he'd eaten Dylan.

Yet the eyes shining back at her in the beam of her flashlight seemed no longer evil but mischievous.

Abercrombie blinked again and swished about, almost like a puppy daring her to play with him.

"Boy," she said, "you have to give me that shoe, or you're going to be in a lot of trouble. You know it doesn't taste good, but some people think you do, so you better return it before you end up on the New Year's Eve party menu." Kaylee slowly eased the broom over the railing and dipped it downward. Her hand trembled the closer it came to Abercrombie's new toy and to Abercrombie.

He blinked.

Kaylee jumped then stilled all motion.

The gator didn't move.

She poked the handle into the shoe, which was considerably closer than the other one had been.

The gator nudged the handle and the shoe.

"Bad boy," Kaylee said.

The gator swished again.

Kaylee jerked up the handle. The shoe flew into the air, coming toward her.

She reached out her free hand over the railing.

"Kaylee!" Abigail's scream pierced the air.

Abercrombie's massive, dark body sprang upward. His mouth open.

Kaylee plucked the shoe out of the air.

The force of Abercrombie swirled the air around her. Water spotted her face.

She drew back, shoe in hand, and her hand whole.

Abigail had not yet stopped her screams.

Dylan ran outside.

"I'm okay. I'm okay. He missed," Kaylee assured. She peered over the railing again.

Abercrombie wasn't there.

"Poor sport!" She cast the words at the ripples that proved he'd made a big commotion in the waters around him before he went under. She picked up the other shoe and marched inside. Tossing them into a plastic garbage bag, she handed them to Dylan. "They have to come with us, but somehow, you know that, don't you?"

Dylan gulped and nodded. "Abercrombie's safe."

Abigail braced herself against the couch. "At least until he kills someone."

They paused and stared at each other. Kaylee was first to let loose her nervous laughter. Then the other two did the same.

Once they again sobered to the conversation, Kaylee went into her room. She picked out a few things and tossed them into a small overnight bag. When she stepped out, Dylan wasn't in the living room.

"He's out by the car. We turned out the lights, and he went out the back door and around. I told him to wait because opening the door will trigger the interior lights of my car. He can crawl in when you open the door and sit on the front floorboard." Abigail held up her car keys and showed Kaylee which key opened her house. "Stay there for a bit. Then you can go."

Kaylee stopped. "Abigail, that won't work. They're sitting on the main road. It's bound to look suspicious for you to leave town in the middle of the night."

Abigail put a finger to her lips and tapped. Then she smiled. "Give me your car keys, your house keys, and your phone."

"Why?"

"I'm not going to steal them."

"I know that!" Kaylee spat. "But what are you going to do?"

"It would be natural for me, after I leave you, to head straight home. And it would make sense to whoever those guys are sitting out there on the main road to think you were still here. And they'll think if I—pretending to be you—leave and head in the direction of Herb's house that you're meeting up with Herb or Christian. They don't have to imagine why. They'll buy it, and I'll be suspicious enough to draw their attention. They'll have to follow. I'll ring my phone with your phone when they leave the main road. You leave my phone at my house, and I'll leave yours here. GPS can work for us just as well as it works for them. Oh, and please take my car key off the chain and leave the other keys at my house. They're to the businesses in town. I'll need those."

Kaylee stared at her unusually calm friend. Abigail hid a great deal of genius behind her anxiety-prone antics. Kaylee hugged her, and they exchanged phones.

A ding caught them both off guard.

"Yours," Abigail announced. She showed Kaylee the text message.

GET YOURSELF AND THE BOY OUT OF TOWN AS SOON AS YOU CAN.

The text message came from Number Unknown.

"Don't text them back. Delete it. That could be a trick to get us to admit Dylan's with us."

Abigail nodded her understanding.

Kaylee paused before opening the door and lifted her bag sideways as if carrying out a heavy box. If anyone was watching, no use handling a suitcase like a suitcase.

"Smart," Abigail whispered. "Be safe. I'm praying."

"If I don't see you, have a Merry Christmas, Abigail."

"I'll get a message to Christian." Abigail assured.

Kaylee nodded and swallowed down a lump of emotion.

As Rose had indicated, Jacob Marin, and probably everyone who hadn't gotten to know Abigail Brewster, underestimated her, and that was to all their disadvantage. Somehow, this unassuming bundle of energy had become one of the most important people in an impossible plight.

And Remy's involvement of her made absolute sense.

Chapter Twenty-seven

December 21

The lightening sky seen through the frosted and barred windows of the sheriff's interrogation room was the only way Christian knew morning had dawned.

He stared at the FBI agent pacing the floor on the other side of the table. The man had drooping jowls, and a beer belly flowed over his belt. He'd cursed often when he had Christian alone, but his crass demeanor changed when Ephraim stepped inside the room. Ephraim either had seniority or a testimony that didn't allow that type of behavior in his presence.

Ephraim sat across from Christian, rubbing tired eyes. "Again, Mr. Abrams, do you know the whereabouts of your nephew?"

Christian had stayed silent during the interrogation by the foul-mouthed man. Ephraim's earlier questioning had been well-worded and truthfully answerable, giving Christian the appearance of cooperation. "No, Agent Cooper, I do not." An absurd thought went through Christian's mind. The moniker *Agent Cooper* had seemed so familiar to him, lingering on the edge of his memory. An old television show. The obscure reminiscence hit him, and he tried hard to keep from smiling. The only reason he would feel this way is that he knew none of these people would allow harm to come to Dylan. They'd kept his whereabouts from him so that he could answer with truth the carefully crafted questions asked by *Coop*.

"Any reason you're smiling," Foul-mouth asked.

Christian shook his head.

"Care to share," Ephraim pushed.

What could it hurt? Maybe it would show a false bravado as if Christian didn't need to worry about Dylan. "Ever visited a scary little lumbering town in the northwest where they serve really good cherry pie and coffee?"

Ephraim bit his lip, looked down, and kicked Christian under the table—and none too lightly.

"What does that mean?" Foul-mouth leaned over the table. "Where's the kid, Mr. Abrams?"

Ephraim recovered. "Jenkins, do you think the man's going to tell you something different? They've scoured the mayor's house without the need for a search warrant. There's no indication that the boy was ever there or has ever been with Mr. Abrams since he arrived."

"Then we need to go to the schoolteacher's house. Tear it apart."

Ephraim stood, pushed in his chair, and faced the other agent. "Last time I checked, we need probable cause. The two men we brought in—investigators for the state attorney—say they kept a watch on her, and she's done nothing to give a judge reason to provide us with a search warrant."

"The schoolteacher went back to the mayor's house." Jenkins' face reddened, and Christian could almost hear the verbal assault on his senses being poured out.

Ephraim raised his hands, apparently to thwart any cursing. "Those two men said Ms. McFarland drove to the mayor's house, found it dark, and returned home where she went back inside. When we pulled them off their surveillance, they indicated she had not left the home since she re-entered the place. That's not suspicious behavior. The worst she did, they said, was to confront them and implicate her mother and the state attorney in some kind of plot against Mr. Abrams. Mr. Marin has been known to seek opportunity to spend time with the younger Ms. McFarland. That gives us more probable cause to search his office, not her home."

"LeAnn McFarland, who is well-respected, I might add, assured us that the boy has been in this … this …"

"Watch your language, Agent Jenkins. This is my hometown."

"This swamp hole," Jenkins finished his thought.

"And Jacob Marin has not corroborated her story."

Christian jerked his gaze to Ephraim. Then he studied his hands and prayed that they wouldn't ask him any follow-up questions.

"And there's that woman no one can find," Jenkins sputtered in an entirely different direction.

"We've been over this. Ms. Brewster's whereabouts aren't exactly unknown," Ephraim said. "The mayor, the sheriff, and even Rose Fish—the three of them also very well respected—indicate that Ms. Brewster sometimes takes Saturday morning trips to shop for her baking supplies after she drops off pastries at the local businesses. She's trusted enough to have a key to every business where she provides the food. I've asked the deputies to check. The food has been delivered to each business she serves. The owners tell us it's not unusual for her to slip in and out without being seen. So, the assumption is that she went out of town to shop for her supplies. When she returns, we can question her."

"She could have the boy!" Jenkins raised his tone.

"Abigail Brewster take off with a child?" Ephraim

laughed. "You see, the advantage I have is that I know most everyone in this town. That girl is timid and fearful. She'd never do anything like that."

"But ..."

"Has anyone else besides Mrs. McFarland indicated they've seen the boy?"

The agent clamped his mouth shut and shook his head.

The good people of Mullet Harbor had to be working in tandem. *God, please forgive them for their lies.*

"Again, Mr. Abrams, do you know where Dylan Abrams is? Did you give him to anyone to hide or to flee from Mullet Harbor?"

Christian didn't have to lie. "I don't know where the boy is, and I did not give him to anyone." Christian stared at the table. "I wish I did know where he was." That was the absolute truth.

"All the same," Ephraim said and moved toward the door, "we're going to hold you."

"I have rights," Christian balked.

Ephraim folded his arms across his chest. "I'd like to hold you for your safety. The good people of this town might think you've done harm to the boy they've been questioned about. I'd rather not have the sheriff officially charge you, but I can."

"Does that mean the sheriff isn't being detained?"

Ephraim shrugged. "I'm quite sure if the state attorney

had the slightest reason to cast disparagement upon Sheriff Arneaux and Mayor Miller, he'd have done so. He wants his guy to win the next election. If he had proof they were involved in anything untoward, he'd have called the governor to put in a word for the deputy he's backing to have him appointed in the interim. If Marin has nothing. I got nothing either." He opened the door and paused. He turned back toward Christian, eyes narrowed. "Unless we find the kid in Mullet Harbor, harmed or unharmed. In that case, there will be considerably more people charged, and you would have brought this down upon all of them."

Christian opened his mouth to speak.

"Do you understand?" Ephraim moved back and got into Christian's face. "You better hope that the boy is found in the custody of someone you trust with his life, because these people are my friends. I can imagine their good hearts getting them into trouble. They're good at finding it all on their own, and they don't need help from you." He leaned closer. "Stay mum!" The man barely moved his lips to speak the last two words, and they were spoken in a tone that did not match the anger on his face.

Christian lowered his head. Ephraim was risking his career for him. He'd do exactly as the man said.

And he'd just told Christian who had his nephew, and he did trust her with Dylan's life.

Chapter Twenty-eight

December 22

Another night in jail, and Christian had gotten neither sleep nor word about Dylan's whereabouts. The sun began to peek through another of the jail's frosted windows and the bars that held it in place. He rolled over on the uncomfortable cot and raised himself up to a sitting position. Not one person had come to see him since they'd led him to the station's single cell.

His body ached, but his heart hurt worse. He missed Dylan.

He rubbed a hand over his whiskered face. Ephraim, along with the entire town, seemed determined to cast doubt on LeAnn's assertions that Dylan was in Mullet Harbor. They had him almost believing he'd dreamed up the entire adventure—if not for the fact he was in jail because Dylan was missing, and Dylan would not have left Philadelphia with anyone but him.

One weak link could threaten the carefully crafted misguidance of the town's favorite FBI agent. That link happened to be Ephraim's brother. Christian wouldn't expect Isaac to lie, even if his brother made it possible to twist the truth in Christian's favor. The man had stood firm on his conviction to trust God. In fact, Christian would think less of the preacher if he didn't tell the truth. Christian had placed Isaac Cooper in a bad situation, and he prayed that Ephraim was as crafty at steering his fellow agents away from Isaac as he had been at misdirecting the interrogation Christian had endured.

He shouldn't have come to this town and placed anyone in the positions they faced. If he'd wanted Dylan to have a Christmas, they should be somewhere snowy and cold with a continental divide separating them from the authorities.

He laid back and covered his eyes and envisioned Dylan laughing and pounding Christian with snowballs.

Then he thought of the little dark-haired girl who'd sat at the table at the community center and who'd fished beside Dylan on Herb's boat. Sophie Cooper had no way of knowing how much her friendship would mean to a friend-starved boy. He would have had that nowhere other than Mullet Key.

Christian took a deep breath. All he wanted for Dylan was to have the small bit of happiness that Christian had enjoyed with Amy and with his job at Penn State. But he should have had the boy with him in his happiness. He could have made an effort to prove Cassie as an unfit mother, but he hadn't. And look what it had caused.

Christian huffed out a breath.

The clink of the heavy gray door that opened into the short corridor housing the cell brought Christian to a sitting position again.

Abigail entered, a tray of food in her hand. An officer motioned her in front of the door and told her to stand back as he unlocked it. She apparently had gone supply shopping. "Is he under arrest, Cody? Remy said he was being held for his safety."

"He's being held. That's all you need to know. Marin's going to get to the bottom of this, and then he'll be charged."

"But until he is, he's here because he didn't fight to be released." Abigail tensed. "So, let me in to visit my friend, and kindly leave us alone."

Deputy Cody, whoever he was, must be the one planning to run against Remy in the election. He opened the door and allowed Abigail to enter with her tray. When she did, he closed and locked her in. "I guess you can just wait until I get back to let you out."

Abigail smirked. "Sounds fine to me so long as you're not too long. False arrest is pretty serious."

Christian laughed.

The deputy glared in his direction.

"I have my cell phone," Abigail said. "When I'm ready to leave, I'll ask Sheriff Arneaux to let me out. Have a nice day."

The deputy hesitated for a brief moment, apparently decided to keep his misplaced pride, and stormed out, leaving Abigail locked inside the cell with Christian.

"I brought you breakfast." She held out the tray. "Remy suggested it."

"Can you tell me anything about Dylan?" He took the tray.

"Dylan who?" She winked and patted his hand. "If I had any bad news, you can be assured that I'd tell you."

"So, the news is good."

"No bad news," she repeated. "Christian, you need to eat. Keep up your strength."

Christian looked down at the pancakes and bacon. His stomach growled. "No utensils."

"Even Remy said no."

"Probably thought I'd want to get out of here badly enough to threaten you."

"I don't think that's true. The people here have been

only kind toward you." She sat on the cot and picked at a knit on her sweater. "Another cold front came through," she announced. "It arrived this morning. Did you hear the rain?"

"I heard the rain. I did get a bit colder in here."

"It's down to sixty-five degrees." She stilled.

He looked at her, and she offered a mischievous smile. "That's downright winter for us. The weatherman said it might even stick around through Christmas. Could even get a bit colder."

"What? Sixty-four?"

"The fifties." She continued to pick at the knit.

Christian decided not to use the syrup. He'd enjoy the pancakes and keep his hands from getting sticky. He took a bite and swallowed. "Might even snow on Christmas Eve." He allowed the sarcasm to drip from him. "I can just see it now. I'm let out of jail, Kaylee's by my side. Dylan might be with her—even my sister, smiling, clean and sober. We'll look up into the night sky. The stars will twinkle above us, and one shooting star will stream across the sky."

"Watch romantic holiday movies much?" Abigail quipped.

"My wife did. She loved them. I loved her, so at night during the holidays, we'd snuggle on the couch and watch them."

"Never liked them much." Abigail stood and paced. "Too unrealistic for me until …" She allowed the last word to trail off.

Christian took a bite of bacon and chewed.

She still hadn't continued even after he'd wolfed down the food.

In his opinion, Abigail's thoughts on matters went far too unasked. "Until what?"

"Until I saw the love Kaylee has for you and for, you know …" She left Dylan's name off. She sat again and held to his hands. "Everything's going to be okay."

"Like the end of one of those romance movies, huh?"

Abigail rolled her eyes. "I wouldn't go that far, but I'm certain the outcome of all of this will be a good one."

A commotion arose on the other side of the heavy door leading to the holding cell. "Where is my daughter!" LeAnn McFarland's panicked voice rang shrill—and terrified. "What has he done with Kaylee!"

Abigail jumped to her feet and began to pace, one step, two steps, and back the other way, short distances. She wrung her hands. "Oh, no. Oh, no. Oh, no," she muttered over and over again.

"Call Remy," Christian told her.

"No. No. No." She continued to pace.

The door opened, and Remy rushed inside closing the door behind him. He pulled on the iron gate, but it didn't budge. A frown fell across his face but evaporated quickly as he pulled out his key and unlocked the cell. "Abby, you go out at the same time. Just keep going." He pulled out handcuffs. "Turn around, Christian. You tell that woman and the press with her everything you know."

"I don't know anything."

Remy smiled. "Exactly."

"Will they let me by?" Abigail's breath came in short spurts.

"They won't even notice you, especially if you carry out the tray. You go first, head toward the break room with the tray, and use the door the deputies use to enter and exit. Why was the cell locked?"

"Cody decided that I needed to be locked in," Abigail advised as Remy led them forward.

"Cody's going to walk his way right out of a job if I win the election instead of him." Remy opened the door, and Abigail skirted by with the tray, disappearing in the crowd of reporters before they got one click of their cameras set on Christian.

"You murderer! Murderer!" Kaylee's mother flew at him. "What happened to my daughter? Did you kill her the same way you did that boy?"

Christian stumbled, visions of Dylan and Kaylee, their lifeless bodies found somewhere in the wooded area of the swamp filling his imagination. "Remy?" He attempted to turn to look at the sheriff.

Remy pushed him into the interrogation room. He shoved Christian and turned back to an advancing LeAnn McFarland. "As far as I know, ma'am, Kaylee is at home where she's been since Marin's men followed and watched her enter the house. Her car is there."

"But she's not answering the door. I can hear her phone ring inside the house. She wouldn't leave without her phone."

Remy shut the door, leaving Christian inside. "I'll send a deputy to do a wellness check. You can go along."

"Fine!" LeAnn huffed.

"But, Mrs. McFarland, your having these reporters here makes me believe this is a publicity stunt."

"These aren't my reporters!" LeAnn screamed. "I don't know why they're here."

Christian tensed. Something must have happened to Cassie. Marielle probably published her investigative piece to draw light to the situation that caused Christian to have to do what he'd done. Marielle's report would add more confusion to Ephraim's contrived mess.

If Cassie had died …

He'd hidden away memories of Cassie as a playful child for so long. Now, they were all he had to keep him from attempting to break his bonds and tear the room apart.

Chapter Twenty-nine

Kaylee dreamed of a nice bed, like the one she hadn't seen since leaving her home in Mullet Harbor nearly twenty-four hours before. The cheap hotel they'd found in some town whose name she'd already forgotten, hadn't afforded her much sleep. The temperature dropped the further north they'd traveled, and she suspected that the change had brought on a cold for Dylan. She'd tried to sleep, but the place hadn't been the best, and Dylan had awakened her with a slight cough throughout the night.

She'd allowed Dylan to sleep for about five hours, and she'd dosed off and on. The little bit of rest and the meal they'd eaten rejuvenated her enough to allow her to limp into Philadelphia. Dylan's cough persisted, on respite now only because she'd stopped at a drug store and purchased children's cough medicine. If teaching school had taught her anything, it was that you didn't give any medication to a child without a parent's permission. But she didn't have that luxury.

Now, she stood with Dylan in the short line of people awaiting clearance to visit patients at Pennsylvania Hospital. She'd always been awed by early American architecture, but she'd had no time to gawk at the beauty of the building. Blood pumped so rapidly in her beating heart that it swooshed in her eardrums. Dylan needed to see his mother, and the only way was through this checkpoint. She sent a silent prayer that she was not yet being sought in connection with Dylan and stepped up to the desk with her driver's license in hand.

The attendant took the license, looked at her, then at Dylan, and asked each to stand to have their picture taken for the visitor's pass. She'd apparently assumed that Dylan was Kaylee's son.

Once finished, Kaylee took back her license and held fast to Dylan's hand. They moved to the information table, and Kaylee asked for Cassie Abrams' room.

The young girl behind the desk smiled. "Room 342. You must be Marielle's friend. She said you might be in today."

"Yes—yes, I am. Is she here now?"

"She just stopped by. Such a nice woman."

Kaylee nodded and led Dylan away. "How did

Marielle know?"

Dylan remained silent, too silent. Kaylee hadn't thought about much since receiving the text message from the unknown number. She first imagined it a ploy to get her to declare that she was planning to leave with Dylan, but what if the person sending the text was a friend who already knew that she had Dylan with her? Might they know because they'd helped the boy get away? She and Dylan needed to have a heart-to-heart.

They waited at the elevator. "You were told by someone to tell me you wanted to come here, am I right?"

He nodded, covered his mouth, and coughed.

She touched his forehead and felt a slight warmth but nothing alarming. "I'm going to ask you once again: did you throw your shoes in the water?"

"No. I—Sophie's uncle wouldn't let me pack them. He woke me up and helped me gather everything I had, but he kept the shoes. He brought them outside and put them in his car. He told me to get in Ms. Abigail's car and hide in the floor of the backseat and not to get up even when Ms. Rose and Ms. Abigail got inside. I just needed to tell them I was there. Uncle Chris said that God sends people and that they might ask us to do things that don't make sense. That's what Sophie's uncle did."

She'd have laughed if she weren't seething at being used by Ephraim as a pawn or for the danger in which he had placed Abercrombie. What must the man have done to get the shoes there without the men in the sedan seeing him and before Kaylee could make it home? "Dylan, why didn't you tell me this before?"

"Sophie's uncle said if I did anything but beg you to bring me here, you might not do it. He said that it was very important that you bring me to see my mother."

"Why couldn't he tell me?"

Dylan shrugged. "He said that Sheriff Remy's sister knew we were coming, and she'd look out for us."

"I don't understand," Kaylee spoke more to herself. "None of this makes sense." They stepped onto the elevator and rode it to the third floor. When the doors opened, she paused inside and peered down the corridor. Nurses entered different rooms or stood at the floor's station. A security officer leaned against the counter and laughed at something one of the female nurses must have said.

Dylan clung to Kaylee's shirt. He'd said he'd only been allowed to be with his mother the night they'd arrived by ambulance. Would anyone remember Dylan, or would he be just another face in the crowd?

"Why don't we go?" Dylan asked.

Kaylee slipped an arm around his shoulder and led him to the waiting room for that floor. "Let's stop for a moment and say a prayer."

Dylan plopped into a chair, and Kaylee sat beside him.

She bowed her head. "Lord, we thank You for Dylan's health and that his mother is still alive. We're going to see her, Lord, and we're asking You to heal her soon. In Jesus' name."

She looked up. Dylan still lowered his head.

The security guard entered the room.

Kaylee tensed but offered him a smile.

The man nodded and returned the smile before leaving them alone.

Dylan looked up. "I wanted God to know Uncle Chris and I both need Him."

Kaylee messed his hair. "I bet He was very happy to hear that you know your need for Him." She took his hand and followed the markers that pointed the way to Cassie's room.

Outside Room 342, she took a deep breath. "Are you ready?"

The warmth of Dylan's hand left her, and he started into the room without answering.

Kaylee followed.

A nurse who'd been studying the machines beside the comatose patient looked up. She startled a bit when she spied Dylan. "Hello," she said.

Dylan took a faltering step backward into Kaylee.

"There you are!" Marielle bounded from a chair that had been hidden by the wall. "Cassie will be so glad that you came. So few of her classmates know what happened."

Kaylee didn't like to lie or to play games. She'd never been good at it, and Marielle wasn't setting a good example for Dylan. She sidestepped Marielle's lie. "How is she today?" she asked the nurse. "We just got to town, and I had to come for a visit."

"Are you family?" The nurse's gaze was on Dylan and not on Kaylee.

Kaylee grasped Dylan's shoulder to keep him silent. "I'm a friend of her family."

"I'm sorry then. I can't give out any information, but her cousin might be able to fill you in on what she's learned." She motioned toward Marielle.

Kaylee nodded her understanding as Dylan moved to the bed. His emotions were beginning to show.

The nurse stepped by Kaylee. "But she's improving each day," she whispered. "She hasn't awoken, but she's been crying out her son's name. That's been a great sign that she might wake soon."

Kaylee stood in stunned silence. "Thank you for telling me."

"I'm telling her son. You just happen to be in the room," the nurse continued. "Someone else who was in the ER that night might recognize him, too."

Kaylee reached for the woman's arm. "You won't tell. Please. He's safe."

"He looks much better than the night I first saw him, but I'd hurry if I were you."

Marielle stood.

"Is something wrong?" Kaylee asked.

The nurse eyed Marielle. "I thought you'd already know, being her cousin and all."

Marielle apparently had the smarts to know her gig was up.

"They've taken a guy into custody. They found him in some small town in Florida," the nurse continued.

Kaylee swallowed hard. Her mother's arrival in Mullet Harbor had brought this all down. "Thank you. We'll stay a few minutes and slip out. This little boy's been through so much. Please let me keep him out of the system."

"Like I said, I saw him and his mother when they first arrived. I saw the guy whose picture's on the news. They say he's his uncle. That guy was shook up but good when he was here. I saw how much he cared for them. I thought he'd done good if he'd been the one to take the kid, but I guess it was you and not him." She winked. I suppose the little guy's improvement is due to your care."

Kaylee wanted to refute her and tell her that Christian had taken very good care of his nephew, but if she said a word, everything could come unraveled.

"Now, listen." The nurse went to the door, looked both ways down the hall, and walked back. "Opinions are split here. I recognized him. Someone else might, and they might turn you in. You need to hurry." She left, closing the door behind her.

"Uncle Chris was arrested?" Dylan slapped at his tears. "Did you know he was arrested? Mr. Ephraim said they'd come out and get in his car, but to stay still. He didn't say he was arresting Chris. He lied to me."

Kaylee bent down to his level. "Whatever Ephraim did, he did to help Christian. I've asked if I can trust you. Maybe you should ask yourself if you trust me. Would I lie to you?"

Dylan smacked his tears again. He shook his head, and a long bout of coughing ensued.

Kaylee looked toward the door. If a doctor or nurse heard them, they'd be asked to leave immediately. Dylan's cold could put his mother in danger. "Dylan, we shouldn't be here in your mother's room if you're sick, but I'll give you a few minutes. We have to leave. I know where we can go, but if they hear you or see you …"

"Mom." Dylan turned his attention to the woman in the bed.

Marielle stepped close to Kaylee and slipped her arms around her. "I like these Philly people. New Yorkers have nothing on them. They say what they think. They don't hold any punches. That nurse has our back for a few."

"But she didn't hear him cough. I think he's running a

temp." Bone weariness filled every pore in Kaylee's body. She joined Dylan by his mother's side. "She's beautiful," she whispered to him.

Marielle leaned toward Kaylee. "They told me she had a tough go at it with all the drugs in her system," she whispered. "Her body had to be weaned from the drugs. She's been months without them. If she ever makes it out of this, her body will probably not accept the abuse it hasn't had to endure since her hospitalization. I did an investigative piece on the opiate crisis. A doctor told me that the body is miraculous. It can heal to a certain extent from abuse, but if you allow it to heal and then abuse it again, it may just turn on you. It'll be important to keep her clean. Christian needs to find a very good rehabilitation center."

"Mom." Dylan shook his mother. "Uncle Chris needs you. I need you. Please wake up. Please." He sobbed against her shoulder. "Mom, please. I came back to wake you up. Uncle Chris kept me safe, but they're going to keep him in jail unless you tell them it was okay to take me. You always told Uncle Chris he was the only one you trusted to keep me. If you die, Uncle Chris might die, too."

Kaylee held to Dylan's quivering shoulders.

"For once in your life, please be here when Uncle Chris needs you. He's always been there for us." Dylan touched his mother's face.

Footsteps in the hallway sent Kaylee's nerves on high alert. Had someone heard the boy's pleas? "Dylan, we need to leave."

"Please …" Dylan coughed the plea. "I want to stay with Uncle Chris. Don't let them send him to prison and put me back in that home. They hurt me there."

"Honey, you need to get out of here, and causing a scene isn't the way to do it," Marielle urged. "I'll be with your mom. I'm pretty tight with the staff now that I'm in."

"You'll make sure they don't kill her."

Kaylee jerked her gaze to Dylan. This little boy was too wise for his age. He picked up on things too easily.

Marielle bent down. "She's more responsive, Dylan. I'm not going to lie to you. She's not out of trouble yet. If they continue to think I'm who they think I am, they can't do anything to her. But she might pass on her own."

Dylan cried without sound, his shoulders heaving. Marielle had been too brutally honest with him. He was only a child.

"All I'm saying is, I can't make promises. But the nurses even said they think her vitals are steadier now," Marielle backtracked.

Dylan reached out to touch his mother without making contact, almost as if he feared the bond between them would be broken by his touch. "I love you, Mom."

Kaylee could barely see through her own tears.

Dylan's hard shell had cracked, and he'd let his vulnerability show. He fell against Kaylee. "Make her come back. Please make her come back. I don't want her to die. I thought I did once, but I don't. Please, God, don't listen to my other prayers. Please let her come back."

Kaylee squeezed her eyes shut and allowed the tears to fall. "God knows when we say things we don't mean, and He knows what's best for us," she whispered. "Whether you prayed for her to die or to live, God's plans will not change. But we have to leave."

Dylan turned back toward the bed. "Mommy, please."

Marielle stepped to the chair where she'd been sitting. She pushed a newspaper into Kaylee's hand along with something else. "Here's my room key. I'm at the downtown Marriott. I'll meet you there later."

Kaylee shook her head and pushed the key away, but she kept the paper. "We're not staying here. He can't come back to the hospital. The authorities have probably determined by now that he's with me. And you heard the nurse. It's not safe."

"I thought if Cassie heard Dylan ..." Marielle began.

Kaylee narrowed her eyes at the investigative reporter. "You were behind this with Ephraim. Marielle, you can't lie and cheat your way through things. You and Ephraim can't abuse a little boy's heart like this. I appreciate all you've done, but you could have called me and told me your plans. We could have talked them out …"

"And you'd have gone right to Herb, and he would have included Christian in the plans. After I left, Ephraim received an anonymous warning. We knew that you had to look as innocent as you are, or Dylan would be taken into custody. Ephraim and I decided that to sacrifice Christian's freedom over his was the right thing to do. We put everything in place that we could to get everyone out of this predicament that Herb got us into by helping Christian."

"Did Ephraim find out who warned him?" she demanded.

Marielle smirked. "The last person on this earth you would expect to warn us."

"Jacob? But …"

"But nothing." Marielle straightened, appearing for all the world like a female drill sergeant. "I liked you from the start. A little too cutesy maybe, but Remy said you were good people, that you were there for our Abigail. Don't make me change my mind. Where are you taking the kid?"

Dylan had returned to his mother's side. "Mommy, wake up. Please wake up. I need you."

"Come on, Dylan." Kaylee took his hand. She faced Marielle. "I'm taking him to the last place LeAnn McFarland would think to look for him." She walked out the door with Dylan tucked into her side.

If she got him out of this hospital, and if they all got out of this without going to prison, one day she might thank Marielle Arneaux for all that she'd done.

Right now, she was so mad at her that she could throw her out that hospital window and not think twice about it. All she could think about now was the little boy beside her who'd stopped crying and was working hard at hiding his emotions.

She walked past a trashcan and started to toss the paper Marielle gave her. Then she caught the headline. "Judge's Fear Keeps Children from Their Families and in the Philadelphia Child Welfare System."

No wonder Marielle loved Philadelphians. The woman hadn't held back her own punches—at least not in her headline, and Kaylee didn't have time to read the rest of the article. She had to keep one of those children as safe as his uncle had tried to do.

They rode the elevator down. The door opened, and Kaylee, her attention on the article, moved out without looking up.

"Sophie!" The little girl's name rang from Dylan with a cough. "What are you doing here?"

Kaylee looked into the compassionate face of Pastor Isaac Cooper.

"We're here to pray for your mommy," Sophie said with all the seriousness of the situation. "We didn't have a chance to pray for my mommy because we didn't know she was hurt. But Daddy said we should come here and pray with your mommy."

Dylan raised tired, rheumy eyes to Isaac. "Thank you." He turned his head and coughed away from their direction.

"Yes, thank you." Kaylee swallowed her surprise. "But what about services at the church tomorrow?"

Isaac smiled. "I always say I'll deliver the next message if the Lord is willing. Even though God knows that Christmastime sermons are my favorite, He wasn't willing for me to preach one this year. Perhaps, he wants me to listen to one. I asked a retired pastor friend of mine to stand in for me at church. Sophie and I will attend one here."

"Christian will be overwhelmed with gladness that you came to pray with Cassie."

"He doesn't know. Ephraim and Remy probably won't miss us until church tomorrow. They're all busy not trusting God. Even Ms. Rose, who's staying at my place with Momma Cora. And if I'd stayed and someone came seeking answers from me, I'd have put my trust in God."

"So you're running from the truth." Kaylee cocked her eyebrow at him.

"Actually, I'm not." Isaac kept his eyes on Dylan. "I prayed, and the only peace I had since Marielle shot down my offer to come here was the decision I made for Sophie and me to join her."

Kaylee touched Isaac's arm. "Marielle's ingratiated herself here by claiming to be Cassie's cousin."

"Marielle has never trusted God," Isaac said. "Sophie and I don't have to lie, though. We're here for one reason." Kaylee kissed the pastor's cheek. "We have to go. A nurse recognized Dylan."

Isaac nodded. "You okay, Dylan?" he asked.

Dylan shook his head. "I don't feel so good. I want to lay down."

Isaac cast a worried glance to Kaylee. "Don't let your fear put him in danger," he warned.

Kaylee nodded and led Dylan out of the hospital and to Abigail's car. His cough medicine was wearing off. "Let's take another dose of the med, and you can sleep while I drive, okay?"

Dylan nodded and coughed.

"You'll be able to recuperate where we're going."

As Kaylee pulled onto the road, she cast a prayer upward for God to heal not only the sick little boy's cold but his family as well.

Fay Lamb

Chapter Thirty

December 23

Sunday afternoon, Christian was led once again into the interrogation room. The handcuffs were removed, and he waited.

He'd grown tired of the questions, weary of Ephraim's deftness in steering the line of interrogation to suit Christian's answers, and sick of LeAnn McFarland's continued accusations that he'd murdered Kaylee and Dylan.

Jacob Marin walked into the room. He took off his suit coat and placed it on the back of the chair that faced away from the one-way mirror. Then he sat and took a deep breath before clasping his hands in front of him and exhaling deeply. He released the breath slowly and looked down, almost as if he wanted to draw attention to his index finger, which he lifted up and down. "I'm about to request a warrant for your arrest. It's a little strange that I have to do that since you're sitting in the jail right now."

"Arrest me," Christian challenged. "What's the difference if you do it formally or hold me here against my will?"

Jacob gave an almost imperceptible backward nod and moved his index finger again.

What was the guy doing?

"You might ask yourself if you can remember if I've seen you with Dylan." Jacob spoke softly and moved his index finger left than right. "Or you might ask yourself if you were alone when I saw you." He moved the finger up and down. "Yes or no?" The man raised his voice as if what he'd said had been threatening to Christian.

Why was the man doing this? Was it a trap?

"I met you at Rose's store. We were introduced by your aunt. Did I have Dylan with me then?" Christian challenged.

"So the answer is no?" Jacob moved his finger sideways. "The answer is no. You did not have Dylan with you when we were introduced. We also met again. Do you remember when?" Jacob again moved his finger up then down.

The man was definitely leading him where he didn't

want to go, but Christian couldn't lie. Even if he wanted to, they'd both been at the same location with the woman that Christian was sure watched through the glass. "You were at Kaylee McFarland's Christmas party. We both attended. You and Kaylee argued, you left, she ran after you, and you came back."

"Did I see you with Dylan during that party?" He moved his finger right then left.

Any hesitation on Christian's part could be thought to be evasion if Agent Foul-Mouth stood outside.

Jacob motioned his fingers again—right then left.

"No," Christian offered and prayed that he wouldn't remember he had been in the presence of Marin with Dylan in tow.

"Can you describe your nephew for me?"

"He's eight, blondish hair. His eyes are the same color as mine. He's about four feet, maybe a couple of inches high and growing, last time I saw him."

Jacob turned to look at the glass and turned back. He stood and pushed in his chair.

Christian gripped the underside of the table to keep from panicking. Had Jacob tricked him?

Jacob leaned down and grabbed Christian by his shirt. He pulled him upward.

Christian struggled to get away, but the man was stronger than Christian had imagined. Jacob turned him to face the mirror and kept his back to it. "You may think you know who I am because everyone around here thinks they do!" Jacob shouted. "But they don't know me at all. Justice!" He shouted. "I live for justice." With each word he lowered his voice, "And," he whispered, the tone menacing. "It will pay you to remember that I push my friends away from me when there's danger, and I pull my enemies close." He released Christian.

Christian flailed as the door opened. He nearly fell over the chair but managed to right it and to sit.

His breath came in heaves.

"Marin!" Ephraim got in the state attorney's face. "What do you think you're up to?"

"I'm trying to get to the truth, Ephraim. Kaylee's mother said she's seen Christian with the boy. I haven't met the kid, but Abrams' description matches hers. She saw the kid or one of Kaylee's students that look just like him."

"I didn't just see him." Mrs. McFarland screeched from outside the room. "He was introduced to me as his son. He was with that Abigail girl."

"Well, there you go, LeAnn. That might be our problem altogether. Abigail Brewster isn't a reliable witness. If you've met her, you'd understand. She's not all there."

Christian wanted to pound the man. Abigail wasn't like that at all. If she heard him say that, she'd be crushed.

Remy entered. "Talk that way about her again, and I'll—"

"You'll what, Sheriff Arneaux? Go ahead and try. One call to the governor, and I'll have Cody Withers appointed in your stead. Now, get out of my face, step aside, and let the FBI do its job."

Things quietened down for a moment, and the door was closed, leaving Christian alone and no closer to finding out if something had happened to Dylan or Kaylee.

The door opened again, and Remy walked in. "I don't know what he's up to," he growled each word.

Christian stood and held out his hands for the cuffs.

Remy didn't bring them out.

"I think he's on our side," Christian whispered and lowered his arms.

Remy laughed under this breath. "Not on your life."

"I thought he was trying to lead me into something, but he prompted me. He's not as smooth as Ephraim, but he was feeding me the answers."

Remy leaned against the table. "And he lied." He scratched his head. "He met the boy," he continued to whisper. "Dylan wasn't with you at the grocery store, but Abby told me that he knew who Dylan was when he ran into him at the community center. She got the impression that he'd already met Dylan—maybe when he was with Kaylee."

"He disparaged Abigail for two reasons: to eliminate her as a viable witness for Kaylee's mother and to intentionally provoke you so that it would look like he's doing you no favors."

Remy let loose another growl. "I like it better when I think I have him figured out."

"Back to the cell?" Christian asked.

"Only if you want. Herb says he'll have a T-Bone ready to cook as soon as you get home, get showered, and are ready to relax. He's waiting in his golf cart outside."

Christian followed Remy from the room. The small lobby was crowded with Ephraim, Agent Foul-Mouth Jenkins, Mrs. McFarland, Marin, and—he blinked—Rose and Ms. Cora.

"Momma, you need to sit down." Remy moved beside his mother who smiled wide and big. "Remy, dear, I'm so glad to be here with you at school. Which one is your teacher?"

Remy led his mother to a seat. "I'm sorry," he apologized to the others. "Momma's staying with me for a few days. Ms. Rose tried to keep her at home, but she was too agitated with Isaac out of town, and I couldn't leave her alone."

Jacob whispered something to Mrs. McFarland.

"Why would I want to go home!" She raised her hands like claws, her exasperation with Jacob Marin showing in her tense state. "You know that boy was here. You were at Kaylee's party. He was with that woman—Kaylee's weird friend."

"Watch it, missy." Rose stepped forward.

Jacob stepped in front of his aunt. "I said I don't recall meeting him. Aunt Rose, sit down, please. And Abigail is prone to flights of fancy. She could have been babysitting any one of Kaylee's students."

"But Kaylee confirmed ..."

"And Kaylee isn't here to back up your story, LeAnn."

Ms. Cora stood and waddled toward them, her shoes scuffing against the floor. "I saw him. Cute little guy. He helped my Sidalee at the ..." She wavered, apparently trying to recall where she'd seen her granddaughter she'd mistaken for her daughter playing with Dylan.

Christian held his breath and stared wide-eyed at Remy.

Rose, though, raised her brows and smiled as if they'd been given a gift.

"I can't remember ..." Ms. Cora waved both hands, her agitation showing, "But I've seen them together a few times."

"See ..." Mrs. McFarland grasped Marin's hand. "This lady's seen him, too." The woman was about to come undone.

Rose winked at Christian.

Remy stepped close. "I'm sure Mr. Marin will agree that my mother isn't a reliable witness, Mrs. McFarland. Not that she isn't being truthful in what she believes she saw. She has Alzheimer's."

LeAnn covered her face with her hands. "Where is my daughter? I can't help but be worried about that little boy."

Mrs. McFarland wasn't only worried about Kaylee. She feared for Dylan as well. Christian's heart softened for her. Dylan's heart had seen what the adults had not.

Jacob turned to look at Christian and Remy. Then he pulled Mrs. McFarland aside and lowered his voice. "What I do remember is a conversation we had at the restaurant when we met for lunch with Kaylee."

Color drained from Mrs. McFarland's face. "She wouldn't just leave."

"LeAnn, I'm sorry, but what I do remember is the frustration your daughter had with you. She clearly didn't like you being here. She's on vacation from school. You told me that you'd since argued over a family secret. In fact, you said you were letting her simmer down, that when she came to her senses, she'd want to go back with you after what she'd learned about this secret you're trying to keep from everyone."

"She doesn't need to be here. Not with him …" She turned and motioned toward Christian. "Or with my father." She sobbed.

Remy, Ephraim, and Rose came to attention.

"I'm sorry. What did you say?" Remy questioned while leading his mother back to her seat.

Mrs. McFarland looked up as if she hadn't realized she'd said anything they couldn't understand. "What?"

"Your father, LeAnn. They're asking you who he is," Jacob prompted.

Ms. Cora cackled. "Why everyone knows it. All they have to do is look at her. She's Herb's daughter."

Everyone turned to look at the older woman who beamed with pride at her knowledge.

Remy's mouth hung open. "Momma, that's not true."

Christian started forward. He grasped LeAnn's hand, surprised when she didn't pull away. "Kaylee is priceless to me. I'm sorry you're so worried."

"Who. Is. Your. Father?" Remy moved in, apparently not believing his mother.

LeAnn blinked as if waking from a fog. "She just stopped … She doesn't love me any longer."

Christian placed his arm around Mrs. McFarland's shoulders. He drew her to a nearby bench and sat with her. "The sheriff wants you to tell him the name of your father."

"He hasn't been a father to me since I was a young teenager."

"You need to tell them, LeAnn," Marin said. "I think he's at the center of all of this, at least for you emotionally."

He looked around him. "She's distraught. I don't think she knows what she's seen. Kaylee was harsh with her when we had lunch. I can imagine what must have been said in private."

"That's not it at all." LeAnn clenched her fist. "My daughter and Dylan are missing, and I want to find them."

"Who is your father?" Ephraim asked this time.

LeAnn stared up at him, her eyes narrowed. "The woman's right. He's your illustrious mayor."

"You knew this?" Remy questioned Christian even as he was heading toward the door.

Christian patted the woman's shoulder. "You're wrong about Kaylee's love for you. She's a strong woman. And if she was harsh, I suspect she feels a little under your thumb, but she'd never do anything to hurt you purposely."

"Then if you didn't harm them, where are they?" LeAnn cried.

"Perhaps she found someone that needed her more than she thought you did." Christian pulled away and took her hand in his. "Because she's good like that."

Remy returned with Herb.

"She's going to get hurt. Terribly hurt by that old man. He doesn't care about anyone but himself." She sobbed into her hands like a small girl needing comfort. "He never has."

"Again." Rose's dander was raised. "Watch your

mouth, missy."

Herb kissed Rose's cheek. "She has her reasons, Rose, and we can hash them out later."

Christian stood to let Herb take his seat.

The old man wrapped his daughter in his arms and pulled her close to him. "I have always loved and cared about you, but your mother and I thought we were giving you what you wanted—the structure of school that didn't go along with my job."

"I wanted you to stay close by."

"That's called having your cake and eating it, too." He pulled away from her. "How do you think I paid for that school, darlin. That place wasn't cheap. You didn't want to stay with us when we were home. The only reason you wanted us nearby was because of your fears." Herb rocked her. "Darlin', you were always afraid when something didn't fit in your bubble, and you only came out of that bubble when you wanted your way. You only allowed us in when you needed something. Kaylee loves you. When she first got here, she was homesick as all get-out. I thought she'd leave after the first week, but she stuck it out, and she loved being her own person. She may not have been happy when you arrived, but like you always do when things aren't exactly as you want them, you shut her out, left her. Same as you did with your mother and me, you punished her for daring to want things you never wanted." Herb continued to rock. "Her leaving you to come here doesn't mean she hates you any more than your mother and I choosing to travel the world while you were in very capable hands—and believe me, we checked on you daily. We let you spread your wings very early on, hoping that being without us would push out that fear in you. When I met Robert, I knew you'd overcome most of it. His career wasn't easy for someone like you, but you embraced it."

LeAnn sniffled.

Marin handed her a handkerchief.

"Kaylee never liked the life we gave her, but I tried to keep her safe, and I wanted her close to me. I wanted her to have what I didn't have." She pulled away from Herb. "You and Momma."

Herb's face hardened. "And keeping her from us was your way of paying us back for what you felt we'd done to you."

"I didn't think you wanted to be bothered."

Herb shook his head. "That's not true. Your mother would have packed up everything to be with you when Kaylee was born. You never asked. When your momma was sick, you never came. When I needed you to be there for me, I was left all alone to grieve." Herb stood. "When you did that, I began to make sure that Kaylee got away from you and saw life differently from what you must have painted it for her. What I learned when she got here is that she was nothing like you, and I was glad." He walked to the door, the only sound in the room was the *flip-flop* of his shoes. He turned. "Now, I've had my say, young lady. I'm sorry if you felt unloved. You were not. Your mother never said an unkind word against you. You don't have to forgive me, but I forgive you."

LeAnn stood. "Daddy, where is Kaylee?"

Herb stared at her for a long moment. "I honestly don't know, but I do know that wherever she is, there's a good reason for it."

"What should I do? I'm afraid."

Herb lifted his gaze to Jacob. "Marin, you know you're the last person on earth I'd ask to call in a favor, let alone two, but LeAnn and I need to get out of town."

"Wait!" Remy held up his hand. "I have a woman and a little boy missing and a town getting ready to put on a small circus, buddy. Where are you going?"

Herb's cheeks raised, and he looked to Christian almost like a rosy-faced Santa Claus. "Leave the missing people to me. I have an idea. But I need more than one favor." He eyed Marin as if his refusal wasn't an option.

"I guess that means I won't get my T-Bone." Christian smiled.

"To the contrary, son. It'll take the state attorney a bit of time to get his rich donator pal to ready his plane. My daughter and I might need a referee in the meanwhile."

"I will not stay around this man one more second!" Mrs. McFarland stomped her foot like an angry child. "He knows where Kaylee is. Whether she's dead or alive, she's with that boy."

"I know nothing about my nephew. The last time—" Christian clamped his mouth shut.

"The last time what? The last time you saw him …" she baited.

"The last time I saw Kaylee, she was in Mayor Herb's house. Dylan was not with her. I think you should trust your father and go wherever he plans to take you."

"Is that so!"

"Yes, Mrs. McFarland, it is so. Kaylee trusts him for a reason. Maybe you should learn to do the same."

Chapter Thirty-one

Kaylee sat on her childhood bed beside Dylan who slept. He'd been so sick when they arrived at her home in Baltimore the evening before that he hadn't balked about sleeping in a pink room under a canopy bed. She'd never thought of changing it after high school or while she was away at college.

She understood now that she'd kept it that way because it meant she was home and safe.

Dylan had been listless most of the day. Night had fallen, and she'd just gotten him out of a tub of lukewarm water, which had worked to lower his temperature, but if it climbed again, she'd need to get him to the hospital.

That would be tricky because she wasn't his mother, and well, his name had increasingly been the topic of every news channel, local and cable. They'd made it their mission to find this child before Christmas and reunite him with his comatose mother. Dylan and his uncle were known worldwide, and the court of public opinion was split on whether Christian was guilty or innocent and what should be done to him.

She'd taken comfort that Ephraim's ploy had worked. No one interviewed in Mullet Harbor could recall meeting the boy. To her surprise, Jacob also said that although he'd met Christian, he was unsure if he'd met his nephew.

A bald-faced lie and one Kaylee couldn't understand. Jacob was up to something, and whatever it was, it was bigger than the problem her mother presented.

Dylan coughed and shivered, pulling up the covers around him.

What the reporters didn't say was where Christian was or if he'd been charged with kidnapping. Was he still being held?

Christian's whereabouts were a lot less interesting than the news that paralleled it. Marielle had filed a full investigative report into why Dylan had been placed in state custody by a judge who should have recused himself from the placement of any children. The man had never gotten over the three children that had ended up dead within a year when the judge had allowed them to return to family.

Marielle's investigative reporting revealed the judge

had indicated he would no longer take that chance, no matter what the circumstances. Her no-nonsense interviews she'd given, all taken from several Philadelphia news affiliate sets and broadcast on cable news, showed her to be a strong woman of conviction. "I understand the judge's concern, but if someone on the bench cannot be impartial when it comes to the lives of children, to take each circumstance on its own merits, then perhaps Dylan Abrams was in danger from the beginning of his placement." Marielle never mentioned her relationship with the town of Mullet Harbor, where Dylan's uncle was detained, nor did she mention if she personally knew Dylan. Her only response was that she'd been informed of an issue involving child welfare in the Philadelphia system, and she'd followed a lead to learn the information about the judge and about the missing child. This led her to an investigation of the home in which Dylan Abrams had been placed. What she'd learned and what she'd shared with authorities had caused the removal of the six foster children in the home and authorities were looking into the removal of two of the natural children as well.

Kaylee heaved a heavy sigh and pushed Dylan's bangs away from his forehead. She was tired.

Dylan's forehead was beginning to feel feverish again. He kicked at his covers and turned in the bed. "Mommy," he muttered. "Help me."

Kaylee leaned down and kissed his forehead. "Shh. Shh. It's okay."

A rattle downstairs brought her to her feet. Had she locked the doors last night? Dylan had been so sick, and she'd been worried about him. She may have forgotten. She definitely hadn't bothered to reset the alarm.

Chatter fell on her ears, an argument.

She slipped to the door and listened.

Someone moved into the entryway. The estate was big enough that not too many people would have noticed her driving up to the house, and she'd used her garage door opener to put her car inside.

"LeAnn, let's not fight any more about it. I don't know where she is. I'm as worried as you."

"You expect me to believe that none of those people have a clue as to where my daughter could have gone. Jacob Marin lied to the authorities. He knows that boy was in that town. If Christian Abrams …"

"The man who comforted you in my absence."

"What are you talking about?"

Herb and her mother were here? How in the world had that happened?

"When I stepped into that police station, the man you were so recklessly accusing of the unthinkable was the one who cared the most about you. If you'd open your eyes, you might see what's really been going on while you've been so busy trying to wreck a man's life."

A scream pealed from her mother. "He's not innocent. He stole that child from a foster home. Jacob said he's wanted in connection to the child's disappearance. I know Jacob saw Dylan, but for some reason, he turned the tables on me, made me look like a fool."

"I think you did that all on your own, darlin'."

"That boy was safe in a home where a judge saw fit to place him." Mother continued to raise her voice. "How can you not think that his uncle could have sensed trouble coming and killed the boy to hide his guilt. Kaylee may have been at the wrong place, and he had to kill her, too."

Herb grunted. "That man didn't kill Kaylee. They were meant for each other, even if neither of them realizes it yet."

Kaylee stepped down the stairs.

Herb caught sight of her. He reached out his hand and touched Mother.

Mother pulled from him, caught sight of Kaylee, gasped, and ran up the stairs. Her features seemed to relax, and the relief swept the hard lines from her face. "Kaylee, I was so worried." The lines returned to her face. She narrowed her eyes. "How dare you worry me like this!"

Kaylee hugged her mother. "I love you, too."

"Mommy!" the little boy upstairs called. "Mommy! Uncle Chris."

Mother held Kaylee at arm's length, her eyebrows furrowed.

Dylan coughed.

Mother pushed past Kaylee and up the stairs.

Herb grasped Kaylee's hand and followed after Mother.

"Kaylee!" Mother snapped. "He's burning up."

"I've given him a decongestant and alternated it with a child's fever reducer."

Mother rushed past her and dug into the hall closet. She returned with two medicine boxes and the humidifier Kaylee hadn't seen since she'd had a severe cold as a teenager.

Dylan opened tired, feverish eyes. "My uncle saved my life," he said.

"Your uncle is fine, Dylan," Mother soothed, pushing back his moist hair from his forehead. She tugged Dylan's shirt up and rubbed smelly cream on his chest. The scent brought back Kaylee's memories of her mother sitting by her side when she was a sick child. Mother hurried into Kaylee's bathroom with the humidifier.

Kaylee started to sit by Dylan, but Herb held her back and shook his head.

The water in Kaylee's faucet ran for a moment, and Mother returned with the machine, sitting it on top of Kaylee's nightstand. She turned it on and only then seemed to breathe a sigh of relief. With a careful movement, she sat on the bed beside Dylan, who'd drifted to sleep. Mother didn't look away from the boy for a long while. When she did, she appeared to have aged ten years. "You both need to rest, Kaylee-po."

Kaylee's eyes filled with tears at the use of the nickname her father had given her long ago, a name never used by her mother, and one she'd missed hearing.

"I'll sleep beside Dylan."

"Your mother's right." Herb touched her arm. "You're in danger of getting sick yourself. You look like the devil drug you down to his abode."

Kaylee leaned her head against his shoulder. "Can I trust you to call a truce and to let me know if he doesn't get better?"

Mother nodded.

Herb kissed her forehead.

Kaylee started out of her room. "I'll take the guest room if that's okay?"

Mother stood and held her by the shoulders. "A guest room is only a guest room if the house doesn't belong to you."

Kaylee's lips trembled. "I can't come home. Not to stay."

Mother's face softened. "I'm an old nag, Kaylee, but you can lead me to water. Eventually."

Kaylee laughed at the thought. "Even the water in Mullet Harbor."

Mother leaned her head against Kaylee's forehead. "We shall see, and only if you really want me there."

Kaylee wrapped her mother in a tight embrace. "I want you, and I need you. I just think I've moved on from the little girl who used to lay in that bed and have the best care in the world—the care you're giving to the child that I so dearly love. Mother, please, please, don't do anything that will harm him or Christian."

Mother nodded. "Go." She gave Kaylee a playful swat on her behind. "Get some rest. Seems I have a lot to do if we're going to get this boy back to his uncle in Mullet Harbor by tomorrow afternoon."

"But we can't."

"Kaylee Nicole McFarland, what did your dad always tell you?"

"'Can't never did anything.'" Kaylee smiled. "Yes, Mother." She brushed a kiss on her mother's cheek and one on Herb's. "Wait!" She stopped and then ran down the stairs. She picked up the paper she'd left on the kitchen counter and returned. "This might help you to know that the good people of Mullet Harbor do have a bit of scoundrel in them, but their hearts are in a very good place. And Grandpa, he's the head rapscallion." She turned on her heels but not before she heard her mother do something she'd never heard before.

LeAnn McFarland actually snorted when she laughed.

Fay Lamb

Chapter Thirty-two

December 24

Kaylee woke to the whirl of a blender and the clinking of pots and pans. She opened her eyes and sat up. Sun poured through the large windows of the guest room.

She rubbed tired eyes.

"Think I should wake her up?" Dylan spoke, his voice a bit croupy.

Dylan! She sprang out of bed. She trotted down the steps and into the kitchen.

Herb stood at the kitchen counter. He poured a concoction into a glass and reached to hand it to Dylan. "Well, there she is now."

Kaylee lifted the glass that housed the orange smoothie. "That looks good," she said.

"Good because you're drinking one, too," Herb told her. "Orange juice, coconut, papaya, mango, and ginger root. He ran the blender, stopping all discussion. Then he stopped and poured her a drink.

"Mother doesn't have that stuff here, I'm sure." Kaylee eyed her grandfather.

"After the boy woke, I left him to babysit you, stole your car, and found a fresh market. Granted, I had to cheat with a few frozen fruits, but it's just as potent. It'll soothe his throat and boost you both with Vitamin C."

"Is Mother sleeping?"

Herb shook his head. "Don't let that woman ever tell you that the apple doesn't fall far from the tree. She left out of here about 4:00 a.m. Haven't seen her since."

"While Mother rises early, she's never up at that time unless she's causing trouble." Kaylee spun to search for the clock. "Nine. She's been gone five hours? That can't be good. She didn't say where she was going?"

Herb shook his head. "She didn't know I saw her leave. Actually, I don't believe she slept. When I got up to check on Dylan a couple of times in the night, she was sitting by his side."

"When I woke up, she sang Christmas songs to me." Dylan smiled. "She told me I needed to get better because this was going to be a good Christmas for me."

"It's Christmas Eve," Kaylee said. "Oh, Herb. It's

your birthday."

"I thought you were going to call me something else besides my given name." He pointed to her. "Would be the best gift ever."

Kaylee moved around the counter and wrapped him in an embrace. "Happy birthday, Grandpa."

"What?" Dylan coughed, reminding Kaylee that he wasn't completely well.

"Kaylee here is my granddaughter, Dylan." Herb winked.

"And today's your big party!" Dylan clapped then stopped. His face fell. "We aren't going to be at the festival."

"We can still have fun," Herb told him.

Yes, they could, but Kaylee needed to resolve things with her mother, whom she hoped wasn't digging an even bigger hole for Christian.

Herb's phone rang. "You'd think I'd left a bunch of idiots in charge and not men with brains and muscles." He acted like a grump, but his smile told her he was anything but grumpy. "Yeah," he answered. He listened and spun back to her. "Get to the television. Your mother's stirred up a can of worms now."

Kaylee took a deep breath. They went into the family room, and she turned on the television.

"Where?" Herb asked. Then he hung up. "Rose says

the coverage is everywhere."

"She betrayed me … again." Kaylee tugged Dylan to her.

The boy coughed and buried his head against her. "Uncle Chris. Please don't let them hurt Uncle Chris."

Kaylee feared her mother had extinguished the last ounce of trust she had for her, and if that was so, nothing would ever get her back to Baltimore again.

Herb slipped his arm around her, and she trembled as she changed the channel to cable news.

Christian may not have been under arrest, but even with the cooler temperatures that hit the harbor, the sun beat down upon his back as he worked to Herb's specifications to prepare the park for the snow that would be produced later. On the perimeter of his vision, Agent Foul-Mouth Jenkins stood, his gun visible in its holster. Christian might as well have been a convict doing hard labor.

But that was okay. The work kept his mind off of Cassie, whom Marielle had reported had awakened during the night for a brief moment before slipping to sleep again. *Lord,* Christian looked heavenward, *I'm not going to pretend that I'm guiltless here or that I don't need You to keep Dylan safe. If I dare, I'm going to ask You to make sure that Kaylee is unharmed and that my sister comes back from this with a renewed purpose to protect her son and herself. I'll gladly pay for my wrong, even if it means that the truth comes with prison time. All I want is for those that I love to be safe and whole.*

"Chris!" Abigail ran toward him. "You need to come with me."

Agent Jenkins came to attention.

"I need to get this done," Christian balked. "I still have to help build the ice slide and put up the booths."

Abigail tugged on his arms. "You!" she shouted at Jenkins. "You need to come, too, sir."

Christian dropped his rake and allowed Abigail to drag him with her. He nearly laughed aloud when she grasped Jenkins and pulled them both with her to the community center.

Abigail opened the door and people who lined the inside gave away grudgingly, but when they turned and caught sight of him, a wide berth was given as Abigail tugged them to the front of the room and to a large screen on the stage. A commercial blared on the television.

Remy and Ephraim joined him as they stood in the front.

"You aren't going to believe this." Ephraim slapped Christian's shoulder.

The station returned to programming. The reporters discussed some topic that had no interest to Christian, but in a small area of the screen was a live scene. Christian recognized the early-American architecture of Philadelphia's Pennsylvania Hospital. Crowds of reporters stood around an unmanned podium. A screen banner announced that America was waiting word of a Christmas miracle and news of the little boy that had captured America's heart over the last few days.

"Is that …?" Remy leaned forward as if he could get a closer look into the crowd behind the television. He leaned back, his hands at the back of his head. He turned to Christian and puffed his cheeks, blowing out air. "Buddy, you might be served as cooked goose this Christmas."

"Well-done and with the rest of us as part of the main course." Ephraim whistled. "How did the old guy let this happen?"

A man in a white coat stepped to the podium in the small square, and the cable news reporter announced that a press conference was about to begin. The square was enlarged, but they left room for another picture—of Christian, his headshot taken as part of his professorship at Penn State. That one was replaced by another taken of him by a reporter in the station in Mullet Harbor.

His images were taken away, and a picture of Cassie was shown. Cassie. In her hospital gown. Lying in bed. Her eyes open.

Christian searched for something to brace himself. His sister was alive and awake.

Remy brought a chair and motioned for Christian to sit. Instead, Christian turned the chair and leaned against it. "Thank You, Lord. Thank You, Lord."

The man at the podium was a doctor. He explained that his patient, Cassie Abrams, had signed a HIPAA agreement and asked that he share her story. Cassie had presented in the hospital E.R. with a critical head injury and other internal injuries caused by a severe beating she'd received by a paramour. "Dylan Abrams," he said, "had some brain swelling and facial injuries as a result of a throw against a wall." The doctor paused. "Dylan was alone in the E.R. since his mother remained unconscious. When asked about his next of kin, the child, though only eight years old, had not hesitated to name his uncle, Christian Abrams, a man we later learned was a distinguished professor at Penn State. As the neurologist for both mother and child, I was present when Mr. Abrams arrived in the hospital. Had I been asked by the court to testify as to where I thought the boy should be placed, I would not have hesitated to say that his uncle should have been the only individual to have care of that child, especially since I did not believe that his mother would come out of the coma. Mr. Abrams was attentive to both mother and son until Dylan was released from the hospital and taken into state custody. Mr. Abrams had been denied the right to care for his nephew." The man smiled. "I am happy to report today that Dylan's mother, Cassie Abrams, has defied all medical expectation. She recently began to show signs of improvement. And last night, she regained full consciousness. She immediately asked for her son and when told that he was not present, said that he had been in her room, that he was calling to her."

The man shook his head. "Perhaps it's just that time of the year, but we at Pennsylvania Hospital believe that we have experienced a Christmas miracle, especially since we have become aware that Mr. Christian Abrams was detained for the kidnapping of his own nephew. We have learned this morning that while Dylan is not in Pennsylvania, he is in good hands. For more on that, we'd like to introduce FBI Special Agent Pierce."

A no-nonsense man approached the podium.

"After I was told about the plans to arrest you, I contacted Pierce," Ephraim said. "If you ever meet him, you need to thank him for keeping me in the loop."

Christian nodded and listened as the special agent indicated that after a brief interview with Cassie Abrams, she had indicated that her brother, Christian, was the individual that she'd asked to care for her son if anything happened to her. She further indicated that she would trust anyone with whom her brother entrusted with the care of her son." The man lifted a paper. "Ms. Abrams has released a statement, and she has asked me to read it to you today." He cleared his throat. "First of all, for Dylan, I love you, baby. I would not have come back for anyone but you, and though Mommy has to get better so that she can be the mom you deserve, I will be with you soon. For my brother, Christian, I understand why you weren't there when this happened to us. You were not responsible. I love you so much for loving Dylan the way that you do and for doing what I've learned you've done. Pastor Cooper, whom I've been told came here because of his friendship with you, has been a great spiritual comfort to me, and I'm sure that his prayers are another reason I am here today. And no matter what comes, your prayers have been heard, brother—if you know what I mean." The agent looked up for a second. "I've also spoken with the authorities," the agent continued reading. "I've assured them that you were the only one that should have had Dylan, and I've informed them that they will not have my cooperation in any charges they wish to file against you. Instead, I will stand beside you as you have stood beside me and beside your beloved nephew.

"And to the medical staff at Pennsylvania Hospital, I will forever be thankful to you for your care of my son and for your lengthy care of me. I was told that today is Christmas Eve, and I will not forget that I have been the recipient of a miracle. I intend to fully recover from the injuries I received and from the self-inflicted wounds I committed upon myself. With the assistance of Mrs. LeAnn McFarland, the widow of Senator Robert McFarland of Maryland and investigative reporter, Marielle Arneaux, angels sent to me in my time of need, I have filed a formal Petition for the Appointment of Christian Abrams as the guardian of my son, Dylan. It is my hope that the judge will, in the spirit of this season, hear this cause and allow my son to be cared for by his uncle, whom I know to be the best of guardians. Thank you and Merry Christmas." The man placed the paper on the podium.

"I think it's a safe bet that LeAnn McFarland and Marielle helped her with that statement," Remy said.

Christian pursed his lips for a moment. Then he shook his head. "My sister is at or above genius, part of the trouble I think she has with addiction. She's too easily bored."

On-screen, an officer approached and handed a note to the agent.

He read the note and shook hands with the man who delivered it before looking into the cameras and smiling big. "I've just been informed that in light of the reporting of Marielle Arneaux and the resulting arrests made at the foster home in which Dylan Abrams had been placed, along with the testimony of Mrs. McFarland, that Dylan Abrams is safe in the hands of a party to whom Dylan's care was entrusted by his uncle. The judge has signed a temporary order of custody with a formal hearing set in February, when Cassie Abrams, Christian Abrams, and Dylan Abrams can be present before the court. No charges have been formally filed against Christian Abrams, and none are expected to be filed."

A little girl ran in front of the podium. "Hi, Dylan. See you soon!" Sophie Cooper waved with enthusiasm.

Isaac, face red but looking somewhat amused, reached for his daughter. He turned and waved. "Merry Christmas, Mullet Harbor."

"And there you have it, folks." The news station moved back to studio coverage. "A Christmas miracle to remember."

The community center crowd erupted in cheers.

Christian moved around the chair and sat, head in hands, doing his best to keep emotions at bay. This town had been heroic in their efforts toward him, and he needed to be strong in the midst of their celebration.

"Chris." Abigail stooped in front of him. She practically had to yell for him to hear through the elation. She stood. Holding her phone in one hand, she put her thumb and index finger in her mouth and let forth a whistle that would have sent a banshee running for cover.

Christian stared at her wide-eyed. Was this the woman who didn't want to walk on stage only a few days ago?

The crowd quietened, and Abigail bent in front of him again. "You have a call."

Christian took the phone from her. At the sound of Kaylee's voice, he sobbed, "He's with you?" He nodded, unable to speak for some time. "Kaylee, I love you."

Whistles and shouts accompanied his revelation. He gave up trying to hear her and handed the phone to Abigail. He stood and stared into the dark eyes of Remy Arneaux.

The sheriff stepped forward and gave him a brotherly hug. "Not a bad bunch of rapscallions to entrust with your life, huh?"

"The best." Christian laughed against the sheriff who had truly become his friend.

Chapter Thirty-three

Kaylee allowed Dylan to tug her down the familiar hospital corridor and into the room where Cassie was sitting up, a lunch tray of bland food in front of her.

"Mom!" Dylan ran into the room.

Cassie nearly dumped the food off the tray and onto the bed trying to turn, her IVs still connected. "Dylan, baby. Oh, Dylan." She wrapped him in a hug then pulled back, grasping his cheeks between her palms. "Look how big you've gotten. Oh, baby, I'm so glad to see you."

Isaac stood carefully, lifting a sleeping Sophie and laying her on the chair he vacated before coming to stand beside Kaylee.

"How is she, really?" Kaylee asked.

"The doctors continue to say they can't explain the rapid recovery since she's been out of the coma, but they're looking to medicine for all the answers, aren't they?"

"Thank you for being here."

"I'm where I'm supposed to be."

"Where's Marielle?" Kaylee asked.

"Her return trip was this afternoon. She's probably checked out of her hotel and waiting at the airport. I tasked her with making sure the gifts are around the tree and with a few other things that Sidalee did to make Sophie's Christmas special. We'll celebrate whenever Sophie and I get home." He scuffed his shoe against the square tile on the floor. "The first Christmas without Sidalee. I've been wondering if the Lord didn't bring Sophie and me here for a reprieve, to keep us busy doing what He's called me to do rather than wallowing in memories back home."

"I think that your being here was a blessing to many."

"Mom, this is Ms. Kaylee. She's Uncle Chris's friend. She brought me here to see you when you weren't awake, but we had to leave."

Cassie held out her too-thin arm. "You're LeAnn's daughter. I've heard a lot about you."

"Don't believe a word Christian says," Kaylee teased.

Cassie frowned. "I haven't spoken with him yet. I don't know if he's even gotten word of what's happening. Do you know how he is?"

"He was celebrating with the folks who helped him keep Dylan safe. I'm sure that he's having a little trouble getting away. My grandfather has arranged for a plane back to Mullet Harbor. In fact, we need to get back to Baltimore. I hope that it's okay for Dylan to fly back with them. Christian is there." She looked to the pastor. "Herb said there's room on the plane for you if you're ready to return."

"Your mother told us about your relationship to Herb. Are you going back to Mullet Harbor?" Isaac asked.

Kaylee hadn't wanted to talk about it here, afraid she might cry. "I need to spend some time with my mother."

Isaac moved closer to Cassie. "Will you be okay? If not, I'll be happy to stay with you so that you'll have someone here when you're ready to leave for rehabilitation. Sophie could fly back now. My family will watch her."

The preacher's kindnesses never ceased to amaze Kaylee. He was offering to leave his daughter this first Christmas without her mother. The sacrifice would be great for both father and daughter.

Cassie turned frightened eyes to Kaylee. "The doctors said that it will be a week or more before I'm released. Pastor Cooper thinks that he can arrange a rehabilitation stay for me wherever Chris will be. Do you think that it would be possible for him to return before I'm released so that he could take me wherever that is?"

So many questions ran through Kaylee's mind. Was Christian prepared to stay in Mullet Harbor and work as a day laborer, or would he want to return to Pennsylvania and his professorship? Would Cassie make him choose between her sobriety and his career? Was Kaylee selfish for wanting Christian to give up everything and stay in Mullet Harbor—the place she intended to make her home? And if he decided to leave, would she make it back before his departure?

Lying to the woman wasn't a good way to start a friendship or a trusting relationship, but from what she knew of Christian, he was awaiting Dylan's return and wouldn't leave Mullet Harbor before he saw that his nephew was okay. "I'm sure that he'd be here now, except he's been kept in the dark about a few things." She nodded toward Dylan. "We couldn't talk much on the phone, and no one knew where I took Dylan. Once Dylan's back with him, he'll return here for you."

Cassie smiled. "Pastor, I appreciate your willingness to spend Christmas without that cute little girl. The old me might have begged you to stay, but I'll be okay until Chris returns."

"I'll be back, too," Dylan assured.

Cassie touched her son's face. "Honey, I'd rather you not. Uncle Chris and I have a lot to talk about. Whenever I get settled wherever I'm going, I'll want to see you as soon as possible, but Chris—and Pastor Cooper—are going to do what's best for me and for you."

Dylan hugged his mother again. "Merry Christmas, Mom. I love you. I'm glad you're awake. I can't wait for you to meet our new friends."

Cassie lifted her gaze to Kaylee as if she could read Kaylee's mind. "I hope I get the chance, but remember, Uncle Chris has some decisions to make. He left his job here. He might want to try to get it back."

Dylan's shoulders slumped.

Kaylee hated to separate him from Cassie, but Herb had given them a short window to drive to Philadelphia and return. As it was, the drive back to Baltimore needed to go smoothly for them to take the plane and make it to Mullet Harbor for the big event—the one she wished more than anything she could attend.

"Go." Cassie hugged Dylan again. "And I'll see you after Christmas. Have a good one."

Dylan beamed. "You know what, Mom?"

"What, baby?" She widened her eyes in mock surprise.

"Uncle Chris asked me to make a wish before we got to Mullet Harbor. I made a wish ..." He stopped and turned to Isaac. "I made a wish and God heard me." He kissed his mother again. "You're gonna love Mullet Harbor."

Isaac held out his hand to Kaylee and to Dylan. Kaylee grasped his and reached for Cassie, who also held to Dylan.

"Lord, thank You for making wishes come true. Protect Cassie from prior temptations, comfort her when not in the arms of her family, and we pray for your protection for all of us as we travel over the coming days and months. In Your Son's precious and holy name, we ask these things that we might bring glory and honor to You."

Cassie's amen was the loudest.

Christian returned to Herb's house and called Cassie. They talked about all that had happened since she'd been in the coma. Cassie talked with Isaac about miracles and, sensing very keenly that the Lord had been at work while she lay in the hospital, she'd accepted Christ's love for her. Still, acceptance was easy for his sister. She wanted to be loved. Believing she was loved and returning that love were her downfalls. But he'd have faith this time and do all that he could for her. Christian assured his sister that he'd have Dylan call her the next morning to wish her a Merry Christmas from wherever the boy happened to be.

"I know where he'll be," Cassie said in a sing-song voice. "Love you, Christian."

Not until he hung up from the call did he realize that Cassie hadn't asked about Dylan. They hadn't talked about him much at all. Christian had been Cassie's main concern. If only he had some of that faith. As it was, spending Christmas without Dylan was going to be rough. After all, that's why they agreed to stay in Mullet Harbor.

He hung up from the call with Cassie, took a deep breath, and dialed another number. That call wasn't an easy one to make.

When he ended the conversation with the head of his department at Penn State, he was jobless, and not by choice. Yet, the weight on his shoulders had considerably lessened. Only a sense of duty to the university would have returned him to Pennsylvania for anything except to be with Cassie, take care of the sale of his home, and to clean out his office. One of those tasks had been done for him by the professor hired to take his place. The school even agreed to ship his books and other things to him.

He'd given them Herb's address, but hopefully, he'd have a place soon.

He could access the money in his bank accounts now, and hey, he had two jobs. The thought made him smile as he readied to head out to the festivities, though his heart wasn't really in it. He couldn't skip the party, though. Not after everything the town had done.

And Isaac Cooper had given up such an important Christmas when his daughter should be surrounded by the love of her family. Today was Herb's birthday, and he'd given up the party.

The one Dylan had wanted so badly to attend.

The one that Christian would have loved to attend with

Kaylee.

Christian sat on Herb's sofa and tied his shoes.

The front door of the house banged open. "Chris! Uncle Chris! Where are you?" Dylan ran past him and got halfway up the stairs before halting. He stopped and launched off the steps and into Christian's arms. Dylan covered his mouth and coughed.

"Well, I'm glad to see you, too." Christian hugged Dylan to him and peered over the kid's head at Herb. "And you, too."

"We drove by the park. Mighty fine work everyone did. This is actually the first birthday party since I came to Mullet Harbor that I didn't have to do most of the work."

"Where have you been?" Christian put Dylan down.

"Ms. Kaylee's house in Baltimore. Man, it's huge."

Christian stared at Herb but spoke to the boy. "Go upstairs and get ready. You'll want to wear a sweater, and if you cough too much, we're coming back home."

"I'm good. Kaylee's mom made me better. She put this smelly gunk on my chest. It sure stunk, but it made me cough up all that stuff." Dylan talked as he climbed the stairs.

When Dylan closed his door, Christian turned to Herb. "You found him in Baltimore. Right under Mrs. McFarland's nose." He laughed. "There's no denying that Kaylee is your granddaughter."

Herb nodded and walked past him. "That she is, Christian. And because of it, I want to know what your plans are toward my granddaughter."

"Don't you think that's for Kaylee and me to decide? Where is she?"

"I left her with her mother. You'll see her soon enough."

Christian's heart fell. He'd had a glimmer of hope that she'd be at her grandfather's party, but he guessed that she had a lot to clear up with her mother in Baltimore.

"Son, I think I've earned the right to know your intentions ... now," Herb pressed.

"Penn State let me go," Christian said. "That presents a world of possibilities, but I need to teach."

"There's a good university or two around here if money's important, and if it's not, I know a member of the school board who'd hire you in a second to teach at our high school. But I'm not talking about your employment ..."

"That surprises me." Christian eyed him. "I thought that a man who wanted to be her suitor would have to prove he could provide for her."

Herb smiled and clasped his hands together. He headed upstairs. "Give me fifteen minutes, and we'll get in the golf cart and head to town. Best birthday ever."

It would be ... if only Kaylee had returned.

Fay Lamb

Chapter Thirty-four

Christian and Dylan meandered through the booths of food and arts and crafts set up around the town center. Sidalee Cooper's mermaid fountain was the center of this part of the event. A large pole had been placed on the backside of the fountain and twinkling white lights spread from the pole toward each of the businesses, creating a starry skyscape. A small group of musicians played Christmas music in the park's gazebo where an unattended microphone stood before them. A makeshift parquet dance floor had been erected two feet in front of the gazebo.

"Where's the snow?" Dylan coughed.

Christian pointed to a large black canvas on the other side of the orchestra that shut off the view of the area he'd cleared. "I think it will be unveiled soon. Remember what I told you. If I think you're getting too sweaty in this cold,

I'll have to pull the cord on the fun. Herb said you were pretty sick last night. Ms. Kaylee must be some nurse."

"Ms. Kaylee did okay, but she didn't get me better. Her mother did." Dylan stopped in front of the fountain.

"Then I'll have to thank Mrs. McFarland when I see her again. You can go play with your friends. Just make sure I can see you. I'm sorry Sophie couldn't be here."

"Sophie's here. She came back with all of us. Her dad, Mayor Herb, Mrs. McFarland, and Ms. Kaylee."

"That's not what …" Christian trailed off. Dylan had already run into a crowd of friends. Christian searched the crowd. Kaylee was home? That's not what Herb said … or had the old man played him once again?

Rose stopped in front of him. She hugged him hard. "I know I said it, but I'm sure glad things worked out. Not that I doubted it would. And Herb's told me you're looking for a job. I have options, and I have connections if those options don't work for you."

"I can't thank you enough."

"I gotta go. Abigail's got herself into something, and I have to take over her baked goods stand. You have fun." She scooted away.

Christian, again, looked around him. He had to find Kaylee.

"Your nephew is a very intelligent, very likable child," a woman said.

Christian turned.

Mrs. McFarland stood beside him. He searched the crowd for blond curls and blue eyes on the prettiest ... most beautiful ... most stunning woman he'd ever known. When he couldn't find her, he turned his attention back to Kaylee's mother. "Thank you for nursing Dylan back to health."

"Nonsense." She waved him off. "I love children, and when one is sick, the nurturer in me kicks in. I came over to apologize to you, Mr. Abrams."

"No." Christian couldn't focus on Kaylee's mother. He wanted so badly to confirm that Kaylee had also returned to Mullet Harbor. "You were concerned for Kaylee. I wish I could have allayed your fears, but when you made the accusations, I had no idea what had occurred. To keep my own sanity, I had to cling to my trust in those who promised to keep us safe. Ultimately, I realized I had to trust that God had all of this in hand."

Mrs. McFarland grimaced. "I'm sure I sounded like a lunatic."

"You love your daughter. I understood that. And you are a very big part of the reason that I'm not in prison and Dylan isn't being taken away from me." Christian gave Kaylee's mother his full attention. "I would say we're even, but I can never repay you except to give you some advice, Mrs. McFarland."

"I'm listening."

"Give your father a chance. I think he knows that he's made mistakes, and he has some hurts where you're concerned. He loves you, though."

"I'm not so sure—"

"I've seen how he looks at you." Christian touched her shoulder.

She blinked and turned to look through the gathering crowd of people. "And how is that?"

"The same way that I noticed he looks at Kaylee whenever she's around him. Those blue eyes you both inherited from him sparkle even when he's angry with you. He's an enigma of a man, and on the outside, he appears to be serenely happy. Someone who hasn't gotten to know him as well as I have may not notice that he hides sorrow behind his good deeds and his smiles. He does a lot of good here in this small town, and I think it's his way of making up for what he may not have done for you. Mrs. McFarland, I know how hard it is to forgive someone you feel has let you down most of your life."

She widened her eyes. "Oh, you do, do you?"

"Cassie. We were in the child welfare system for a long time. The only good thing that came out of those years was that we were together. But when we were teenagers, Cassie pulled away from me. I understood why."

"And why was that, Mr. Abrams."

"Self-preservation. Running with the wild ones kept her from being bullied by them." He rubbed his eyes. "And she kept them from bullying me. I struggled with her giving more trust to them then she had in me. When we left the system, I tried to help her, but she pushed back at every turn. I married, and my wife was the only reason that we stayed in touch with my sister. When Dylan was born, I saw some good in her. She stayed sober for a long time during her pregnancy and months afterward. Every time she came to our door, I helped her because my wife insisted. Then when Amy died, I shut the door on Cassie. Problem was, my grief made me forget about Dylan. That is, until the night I got the call from the hospital." He blinked back emotion. "I know you're grieving. I'm sorry for the loss of your husband. We all grieve differently."

LeAnn wiped tears from her eyes. Was she crying for him or for herself?

"I didn't come to my mother's funeral," she said, her lips trembling. "I didn't allow myself to feel anything when I learned of her passing. When Robert died in that plane crash, I told myself that I didn't deserve to mourn him since I didn't mourn her." She dug in her purse and pulled out a tissue. "I didn't come to her funeral because I was angry at her—at him. But to let myself show the utter devastation I had at the loss of my husband ... it meant I hadn't loved my mother at all. Crazy, isn't it?"

"Again, we all handle grief in different ways. Your daughter is still grieving her father. Herb, I can see, has helped her, but maybe if you told her what you'd just told me."

"We had a long talk." Mrs. McFarland tucked her tissue back into her purse and straightened, seeming to gain her composure. "We have some issues to work through, but I promised her some things. The first was to work on getting to know my father again."

"That will be a great start."

"And she made a promise to me ..." Mrs. McFarland held out her hand for him. "Call me, LeAnn."

Christian shook her hand loosely, uncertain of the woman's sincerity.

"Well, that was heartfelt." She smirked.

"I'm sorry, but I don't understand why you're talking to me."

"Kaylee thought that since I tried to not only have you arrested for one murder, but two, that we might want to reset our relationship. I think she's right. And I've been told by my daughter that ..." She leaned in and looked around her, "My daughter will kill me if she knows I'm telling you this, but she said you might be the one."

Christian couldn't help it, but his attention had strayed to the crowd once again. He wanted to see Kaylee in the worst way.

"And Kaylee has assured me that she is not returning to Baltimore. She's staying here in Mullet Harbor. I don't know your intentions toward her, but after seeing that kiss, they better be honorable ones. So ..."

He peered beyond her then gave her his full attention. "Tenure didn't mean anything to the university when I was accused of a federal crime. The mayor and Rose have suggested I'll have work, but that doesn't guarantee I'll be gainfully employed any time soon."

"You know, I can assure you of gainful employment in the Baltimore area." LeAnn hedged.

Christian eyed her carefully. "Still trying to have control over your daughter's life, are you?"

She smiled. "Don't tell her I tried because another promise I made to her was to butt out of the decisions in her life. You can't blame me for trying."

"Your secret's safe with me if you'll tell me where I can find your daughter."

"Kaylee's Grandpa Herb called a powwow with her, Abigail, Pastor Cooper, and what is it that Dylan calls the little girl? Oh, yes ... the pest."

"I'm going to have to talk with that boy." Christian smiled.

Mrs. McFarland laughed and the sound enchanted Christian. He never would have imagined that sound coming from her. "Sophie really does like it, and he's such a fine young man." She sobered. "I really am sorry for the mess I made, but I did it for the best of intentions: I wanted to keep Kaylee safe."

"I understand, but all the same …"

"Is she safe?" LeAnn asked.

Christian blinked at the question. "With me? Yes, she is. I'd never do anything to hurt her."

"I told her I'd try to stop being so overprotective, but my little girl had her heart broken once. I realize now that she thought I was made of ice, that I didn't love her father as much as she did. I loved him very much. He was a good man. A solid man. One who would have done anything for his daughter and his wife."

Christian listened to the woman's heart more than her words.

"I want my daughter to fall in love with a man just like her father."

Christian couldn't find the right words for this grieving woman.

"I think that you could fill his shoes."

"No, ma'am," Christian told her.

She stepped back. "I—Maybe I was wrong. I thought you cared about her."

"I do. Very much. Over the last few days, I've seen her strength and her goodness. I'd love to pursue her, for us to make sure that it's a forever kind of love."

LeAnn smiled.

"But I can't fill her father's shoes. I wouldn't try. What I will promise you is that I will be as good to her as your husband and you would expect me to be. I will cherish her and do all I can to protect her. If she decides that she loves me, I will do everything to show my love in return." Christian touched her arm. "And I'll honor her mother, so long as her mother realizes that her daughter is an adult. She might fail sometimes, but we'll be there to help her up."

"It's a deal."

Christian hugged LeAnn. "So, again, thank you for all you've done, and thank you most of all for …" Emotions welled within him, and he fought to keep them back. "Most of all. Thank you for her. If not for Kaylee, I don't know where my nephew and I would be right now."

"And I suppose that if not for you, I wouldn't be sharing Christmas with my daughter this year."

Christian slipped his arm over LeAnn's shoulder. "And with Herb, or with me, and with my own cute little pest, and with all these—"

"As Kaylee said, rapscallions." LeAnn's laughter rang like bells of joy through the crisp night air.

Kaylee stood at the back of the gazebo with Abigail, Herb, Isaac, and Sophie. Her nerves rippled with fear.

Abigail didn't look any more at ease than she did as she clutched her Bible to her chest.

Little Sophie, holding a tiara in her hands, cried against her daddy as she clutched the crown with tight fingers. Isaac tried to assure his daughter that everything was okay, and she had to do what was expected of her.

A hard lesson for a grieving child.

Even above the crowd, Kaylee recognized her mother's laughter. She was drawn to look for her. Stepping out from behind the gazebo, she zeroed in on the sound.

Mother ... with Christian ... and laughing.

She took a deep breath. God continued to rain down miracles upon her.

She stepped back beside Abigail. She could do this.

"You ready?" Herb asked.

Everyone but Sophie nodded.

Herb climbed the gazebo steps, and applause rang out. "Gather round, folks," Herb announced. "I know that I make a big deal about it being my birthday and all ..."

The crowd that had been spread out, congregated on the other side of the makeshift dance floor in front of the gazebo.

Choruses of birthday wishes rang out, and someone began to sing "Happy Birthday." The crowd joined in.

"Thank you. Thank you!" Herb laughed. "But we know the real reason we're gathered here tonight." Herb lifted his hands toward heaven. "Tonight in Mullet Harbor, we come together with family and friends, new and old, and we celebrate the day of our dear Savior's birth. Tonight, I'm turning over the annual reading in the Book of Luke to our own lovely Abigail Brewster."

The crowd remained silent.

Abigail grasped Kaylee's hand then released it. Then, on tiptoes, Abigail made her way to the stage.

The crowd broke out in cheers as Abigail opened the Bible and found her place. "And … it … it … came to pass." Her voice remained low and unsteady.

"Louder, Abigail," someone in the crowd called out. "You can do it."

Kaylee moved around to stand in Abigail's sight.

She felt a presence at her side. "You can do it," Remy called.

Abigail turned. She smiled at Kaylee and lifted her gaze to Remy. "Let me start over," she said, her voice loud and clear. "And it came to pass in those days, that there went out a decree …" As she read, her voice strengthened, and she added inflection to her tone.

When she finished, she stepped back from the microphone and moved to a small keyboard.

Isaac touched Kaylee's shoulder and motioned to a

crying Sophie as he climbed the stairs. "Let's pray," he said into the microphone. The crowd bowed their heads and not a sound was heard as Isaac prayed over the event, asking God to forgive his faults and the faults of others, and thanked the Lord for all that He had done in Mullet Harbor. "May we trust in You, our Almighty God, whose Son we honor not only at Christmas but every day of the year." He stood back and someone handed him his guitar.

That was Kaylee's cue. She had to keep to her part of the bargain she'd made with Abigail on the dock of the community center when they watched Dylan fish.

Mother might not laugh so loudly now.

Entrusting Sophie to Remy, she stepped with wobbly legs onto the stage and stood beside the preacher.

Isaac turned to the small orchestra behind them on the gazebo and then to Abigail. He strummed and the musicians joined in for the chorus of "Silent Night."

Kaylee waited, her heart beating. Then she lifted her voice in song. "Silent night. Holy night. All is calm. All is bright." The crowd joined in with her in praise. In the crisp air, minus the humidity, she imagined the music reaching Heaven. She turned her gaze there, singing strongly as if her father and her grandmother, in the presence of God, might be listening in.

The song ended, and Kaylee stepped back from the microphone where Herb had asked her to remain.

She swept her gaze to where Mother still stood with Christian.

Mother raised her hands, held together. "Wonderful," she mouthed.

Kaylee smiled and looked to Christian who smiled up at her.

Herb took the microphone again. "When my dear wife, Lacey, threw the first such shindig, she declared her unsuspecting husband, King and herself Queen of Mullet Harbor's Christmas festival. Over the years, we continued her tradition of surprising certain individuals with the title. Sadly, we lost last year's festival queen to a tragic incident, but her daughter is here tonight to do the honors with her father, last year's King. So, by the powers invested in me as the original King of Mullet Harbor's Christmas Eve Festival, I announce this year's King and Queen, and yes, as mayor I declare that I was not impartial in this decision. This year's Mullet Harbor Christmas Eve Festival King and Queen are Christian Abrams and my granddaughter, Kaylee McFarland."

Kaylee gasped and shook her head. She'd only been in town a few months, and Christian might not remain in Mullet Harbor.

In the audience, Christian hesitated until Mother and then others pushed him forward. He climbed the steps to join her on the stage.

Sophie stepped beside her father. Her little breaths came in gasps, and tears trailed down her cheeks. Her little eyes were red as she held fast to the glittering tiara.

Kaylee stopped balking at the award and bent down to tend to the child. She held her close and whispered in Sophie's ear.

Sophie nodded, sniffled, and reached the tiara to Kaylee.

Kaylee took the crown and stood. She stared out at the crowd trying to gain control of her own emotions. This town had poured out so much love to her … to Dylan … to Christian. Her mother, who should have been a pariah, stood among them, welcomed by the citizens.

Christian put his arm around her. She offered him a smile.

Then she turned and placed the tiara on Sophie's head. Taking Christian by one hand and Sophie by the other, she moved to the microphone. "As this year's Queen of the Mullet Harbor Christmas Eve Festival, I declare Sophie Cooper town princess and, as such, I bestow upon her the crown that belonged to her beloved mother, Sidalee. I also decree that a new crown be found for next year's festival and that as the first-ever festival princess, Sophie always maintain her mother's crown."

The crowd cheered.

Isaac Cooper slipped a banner over Christian's head.

Then he moved to Kaylee and kissed her cheek. "You are a prize," he said, emotion filling his words. "Thank you."

Kaylee held tight to Christian's hand, and they stood together on the stage while Herb, who'd stepped down clicked picture after picture. He climbed back onto the stage and took the microphone. "And now, our King and Queen will have the first dance to open up our party."

The orchestra, without Abigail and Isaac, played a romantic song. Christian led Kaylee from the stage and onto the dance floor.

With Christian in her arms, the world faded away. She peered up at him. His green-eyed gaze captivated her. "This is …"

"Beyond anything I could have hoped for," Christian said. "To think that meeting you would lead me to this."

Kaylee pulled back just a bit. "What is this?"

He tightened his hold on her and stepped with her to the music. "I don't know, but whatever it is, I don't want it to end."

"Neither do I, but …"

"Then it doesn't have to. Say you want me to stay, and I'll stay."

Kaylee bit her lip. She could be the bigger person here and let him go, or she could say that she would follow him anywhere.

He moved with her to the music. "Please, stay,

Christian, is all I want to hear."

She wrapped her arms tightly around his neck as they danced. "Stay, Christian," she whispered in his ear. "Stay in Mullet Harbor."

"Whatever the Mullet Harbor Christmas Eve Festival Queen commands. That is what the King desires." He gazed into her eyes then pressed his lips against hers.

She drew him deeper into the kiss.

Cold drops fell onto her face, and she pulled away. Flakes of snow covered Christian's hair and his clothes.

She shivered and stared up into the sky. Snow? In Mullet Harbor on Christmas Eve?

Kaylee twirled in a white wonderland.

A loud whirl sounded and above them a burst of light broke into a swirl of colors.

Christian turned with Kaylee in his arms.

Remy, Ephraim, Marielle, and Abigail held to a hose that shot the falling snow into the air.

Abigail released it, and the two men and Marielle floundered. Snow shot onto the partition, knocking it over. They tried to gain control, but the hose swirled, peppering the crowd with the cold mixture.

Children and adults hurried to the bed of snow once hidden by the partition.

Abigail tiptoed her way through the mess she'd help make. "How's that for romance." She crossed her arms and stared at Christian. "Snow on Christmas Eve and a shooting star to boot. Looks like a romance movie to me."

Christian leaned back and laughed.

"I don't get it." Kaylee laughed without knowing why.

"A conversation Abigail and I had about silly romance movies," he said. "But there's one difference here." He pulled her close to him. "The snow may be manufactured, but this romance is real."

Kaylee turned back to Christian. She reached and placed her palms on each side of his face. "I think I love you, Mr. Abrams." She kissed him, passion flowing through her like she'd never known before. "No. I do love you. Very much." She pulled away. "But my mother might ruin this moment if she spies us."

"Oh, your mother knows," he whispered against her ear.

"What?" She closed her eyes as his breath warmed what the ice had chilled.

"That I love you, too. And your mother isn't watching, so come on, gorgeous. Give me a kiss."

Gorgeous. If he called her that every day for the rest of her life, she was sure she'd never get used to the emotions it evoked.

"What do you say?" he whispered. "I don't think anyone's watching." He leaned his head against hers and they turned to take in the field of snow and the mass of people throwing snowballs.

Her mother, the all-too-proper wife of the late Senator Robert McFarland, was in the middle of a crowd of children, Dylan and Sophie beside her. She gathered snow in her hands and took aim at the primary target of all of the kids: Mayor Herb.

"Mom!" Kaylee squealed.

"Leave her alone," Christian tucked her against him. "I think she's working out her feelings for him while discovering what she's missed."

Kaylee laughed and leaned into him, pressing her lips to his. Then she turned in his arms to watch the craziness. "Best Christmas ever!" she shouted with joy to the heavens.

"Until next year." Christian tucked her to him as if he never meant to let her go.

"Until next year," she agreed.

Acknowledgments

Critique groups are the unsung heroes in fellow authors' lives. When writing this story, Abercrombie was a character firmly affixed in my mind. He simply floated in the waters outside Kaylee McFarland's home on the dock. He gave her someone who would listen when her heart was hurting. Abercrombie wouldn't talk back. He'd just blink his all-too-knowing eyes.

Enter critique partners Gail Golden and Peggy Insula who met Abercrombie early on. Both said, "Oh, now I'm nervous. Something's going to happen with that gator."

I stayed silent. I mulled on it, and I discovered Abercrombie's full potential as a Mullet Harbor character. And I refused to allow him to be overshadowed by the quirky mayor and the other town citizens.

Abercrombie and his antics add a little hilarity and possibly some tense moments, and I have Gail and Peggy to thank for that.

As always, I want to think Marji Laine Clubine for her guidance in all things publishing and for her faith in me that allows me to show my stories. Also, to my editor, Karen Harrison, though it may seem like it at times, I never take a keen eye for granted. You are greatly appreciated.

About the Author

Fay Lamb is the only daughter of a rebel genius father and a hard-working, tow-the-line mom. She is not only a fifth-generation Floridian, she has lived her life in Titusville, where her grandmother was born in 1899.

Since an early age, storytelling has been Fay's greatest desire. She seeks to create memorable characters that touch her readers' hearts. She says of her writing, "If I can't laugh or cry at the words written on the pages of my manuscript, the story is not ready for the reader."

Fay writes in various genres, including romance, romantic suspense, and contemporary fiction. She has contracted three series with her publisher, Write Integrity Press, in addition to the Mullet Harbor one. Amazing Grace is a completed, four-novel suspense series all set in Western North Carolina. Make sure you keep the lights on for this series. Her Ties that Bind romantic series is set in Fay's own backyard of Central Florida and is also complete. You should probably have a tissue for this one. Also set in her beloved state of Florida is her new Serenity Key saga with deep characters and twisted plots. Keep the lights on and keep tissues on hand. Fay has an adventurous spirit, which has also taken her into the arena of non-fiction with The Art of Characterization: How to Use the Elements of Storytelling to Connect Readers to an Unforgettable Cast.

Fay Lamb is also a successful freelance editor and she loves to teach workshops for fiction writers. She enjoys meeting readers, and you can find her on her personal Facebook page, her Facebook Author page, and at The Tactical Editor on Facebook and on Goodreads. She's also active on Twitter. Then there are her blogs: On the Ledge, Inner Source, and the Tactical Editor.

Other Books by Fay

Ties that Bind Romance

Amazing Grace Suspense

Other Favored Books

With warmth and the homespun humor of a bygone year, Betty Thomason Owens spins a retelling of the book of *Ruth* set in the southern hospitality of 1957 Tennessee.

Set in the backdrop of Africa's stunning landscape, these award-winning books of *The Redeemed Side of Broken* series will encourage you and grip your heart

445

Thank you
for reading our books!

If you enjoyed this story,
please consider returning to its
purchase page and leaving a review!

Look for other books
published by

Favored Books
an Imprint of
Write Integrity Press

www.WriteIntegrity.com